RAVES FOR HUNTER SHEA

W9-CBD-061

Forest

"A frightening, gripping story that left me too frightened to sleep with the lights off. This novel scared the hell out of me and it is definitely a creepy ghost story I won't soon forget."
—Night Owl Reviews

"Hunter Shea combines ancient evil, old-school horror and modern style. Highly recommended!"
—Jonathan Maberry,
***New York Times* bestselling author**

Sinister Entity

"This is the real deal. The fear is palpable. Horror novels don't get much better than this."
—Literal Remains

"Culminates in a climactic showdown between human and spirit that keeps you glued to the pages!"
—Horror Novel Reviews

Evil Eternal

"Hunter Shea has crafted another knockout. At turns epic and intimate, both savage and elegant . . . a harrowing, blood-soaked nightmare."
—Jonathan Janz, author of *The Sorrows*

Swamp Monster Massacre

"If you're craving an old-school creature-feature that has excessive gore . . . B-horror movie fans rejoice, Hunter Shea is here to bring you the ultimate tale of terror!"
—Horror Novel Reviews

4 M - CHARTER 2014
347 - PAGES
S.10-10-20
F.11-3-20

THE MONTAUK MONSTER

HUNTER SHEA

PINNACLE BOOKS
Kensington Publishing Corp.
www.kensingtonbooks.com

PINNACLE BOOKS are published by

Kensington Publishing Corp.
119 West 40th Street
New York, NY 10018

Copyright © 2014 Hunter Shea

All rights reserved. No part of this book may be reproduced in any form or by any means without the prior written consent of the publisher, excepting brief quotes used in reviews.

If you purchased this book without a cover, you should be aware that this book is stolen property. It was reported as "unsold and destroyed" to the publisher, and neither the author nor the publisher has received any payment for this "stripped book."

All Kensington titles, imprints, and distributed lines are available at special quantity discounts for bulk purchases for sales promotions, premiums, fund-raising, educational, or institutional use. Special book excerpts or customized printings can also be created to fit specific needs. For details, write or phone the office of the Kensington special sales manager: Kensington Publishing Corp., 119 West 40th Street, New York, NY 10018, attn: Special Sales Department; phone 1-800-221-2647.

This book is a work of fiction. Names, characters, businesses, organizations, places, events, and incidents either are the product of the author's imagination or are used fictitiously. Any resemblance to actual persons, living or dead, events, or locales is entirely coincidental.

PINNACLE BOOKS and the Pinnacle logo are Reg. U.S. Pat. & TM Off.

ISBN-13: 978-0-7860-3475-8
ISBN-10: 0-7860-3475-0

First printing: June 2014

10 9 8 7 6 5 4 3

Printed in the United States of America

First electronic edition: June 2014

ISBN-13: 978-0-7860-3476-5
ISBN-10: 0-7860-3476-9

For Amy—my love, best friend,
and greatest supporter.

From: Ganders@Darpa.mil
To: BioScie@Darpa.mil
Subject: PI Containment

Phillip,
Solid intel points at a level 5 break in PI oversight. Deploying agents to Long Island, NY, ASAP. POTUS has been notified and in agreement that all emergency protocols are to be considered after ground threat level assessment. He requests a full debriefing on File B-2020 at 0600 hours.

How bad is this? What are we looking at? I got a lot of people breathing down my neck and no damn answers. What's your person on the inside saying? Or has that line gone dark, too? If it has, we're in it deeper than we ever imagined.

Gary Anders
Defense Advanced Research Projects Agency
Senior Director of Communications

CHAPTER 1

Hal lowered his glasses so he could see through the yellowed face of the Islanders Stanley Cup Champs clock. It rested at an angle against the behemoth of a cash register that had been there since the bar opened in the '50s. Punching the keys required brute force but it was still functional and thicker than the walls in most bank vaults. He wiped his brow with the same rag he used to clean the bar top and with a tight grin turned to face the regulars.

"Last call for alcohol. Drink your beer and kindly get the hell outta here."

He was met with the usual groans, followed by the flicking of fivers his way for one last draft or shot of cheap whiskey. No one bought top-shelf at last call. Randy Jenks laid out a twenty-spot and asked for four Buds.

"I don't have all night to watch you drink yourself stupid," Hal barked while he poured a PBR for Richie Burnes.

"They're not all for me," Randy said. "Two for me, and two for Rosie. I promise, we'll be quick."

Rosie had been a staple at the Beach Comber since Reagan demanded that Gorbachev tear down that wall. She told everyone she was in her early forties, but her math was as fuzzy as her memory. If she was a day under sixty, Randy would eat Hal's tighty-whities. Tonight she wore a very revealing white blouse with wide pockets on each breast, neon hoop earrings and tight acid-washed jeans, trying to look twenty and forever stuck in 1986. She cocked an eyebrow at Randy, unable to hide her surprise at his generosity.

"Thank you, Randy baby," she slurred. Her lipstick had smeared onto her left cheek and her eyes were as glassy as a pair of fishbowls.

They clinked glasses and took long gulps.

I can't believe I'm doing this, Randy thought, fighting to keep the beer from fizzing back up his throat. *I'm really about to hook up with Rosie. Jesus, she's older than Mom!* He took a long look at her ample, though gravitationally challenged cleavage, and shook his mind clear of thoughts of his mother.

His ex-girlfriend Sherry had left him so long ago, he wasn't even sure if he would remember how to do it. Might as well take little Randy out of storage with Rosie in case the real thing came along. Practice makes perfect.

She leaned into him, hungrily sipping on her second beer. "You should come around more often. This place needs more handsome young men like you," she said, smiling and flicking a dyed-black lock of hair from her face.

"All that matters is that I'm here now. We should make the best of it."

She tottered on her stool. Randy slipped his hand around her waist to keep her from falling.

"And strong, too," she laughed.

"You have anything planned for the rest of the night?"

Rosie shook her head. "I was just gonna go home, watch a little TV Land and have a nightcap. You have something better in mind?"

Old Richie Burnes saw what was about to go down and

winked at Randy. In a loud, drunken whisper he said, "You sure you're up for a Rosie-Go-Ride? You sleep with her, you've slept with half the guys in here."

Randy winced, waving him off.

Stay focused. You need to get laid—bad. Rosie is the patron saint of horny drunks. Maybe after this, the stick will magically disappear from up your ass.

He moved his hand up Rosie's back and asked, "You wanna go for a drive?"

He was more wrecked than he'd thought. Randy actually had to close an eye as he barreled down the Montauk Highway. At least it felt like he was barreling. He couldn't make out the numbers on the speedometer to tell. He'd always thought the one-eyed drunk-drive trick was a myth, but it somehow kept him on the road.

The stars were out in force and the heat of the July day had cooled into a perfect summer night. Salty air poured through the open windows.

"Where're we going?" Rosie said. She'd undone another button on her shirt and he could see the black lace of her bra.

"How about the beach?"

She ran a long, thin finger between her breasts. "A long walk, skinny dip, or—"

"*Or* works for me," he said, struggling to keep the car on the road.

He spotted the brown sign for Shadmoor State Park. It said NO ENTRANCE AFTER DARK. As an employee of the parks system, albeit as a groundskeeper and not one of the park rangers, Randy felt the warning need not apply to him. He turned down the gravel road, clipping the edge of his front tire on a large rock marker. *Please don't be flat when we're done.* The last thing he wanted to do was change a tire in his condition.

He drove up to a pair of grass-topped dunes, killed the engine and helped Rosie out of the car. She giggled when he accidentally brushed his hand along the side of her breast.

They could hear the crashing of the waves as they crested the small sand dune. The moon reflected off the Atlantic in a long, white skunk's stripe. Rosie let go of his hand and nimbly made her way down the dune, casting off clothes with each step.

"What were you, a ballerina?" he asked, catching his sneaker on her discarded shirt.

"Follow the leader," she sang.

In the moonlight, she looked half her age. He had to admit, she had a better body than most college girls. Had to be 100 percent genetics. Clean living was not Rosie's game.

You've gone this far.

Randy fell trying to extricate himself from his pants, but Rosie, still giggling, helped get them off. Her mouth enveloped little Randy like it was an air bag in a crippled plane.

Christ, she was good. He wove his fingers through her hair, pushing her down as far as she could go. He moaned, hungry for release. She pulled away and said, "You're ready."

Before he could ask what for, she straddled his hips and lowered herself onto him.

"I like it slow—at first," she said, dangling her breasts in his face.

"Rosie, you're incredible."

"I know."

His hands grabbed the soft flesh of her hips. She ground her hips into him, leaning close, biting his neck.

Randy thought he heard soft footsteps. Rosie groaned huskily as she gyrated. If someone wanted to watch, let them. After a year of celibacy, he wasn't about to stop.

Rosie paused, sitting up straight.

"Did you hear that?"

Randy smiled. "I don't mind giving some late-night strollers a show if you don't."

"Not that, the other thing."

"What other thing?"

Something grumbled in the dark—low, long and threatening.

Randy's erection collapsed. He gently rolled Rosie off and looked for a stick or rock. If there was a dog nearby, it sounded royally pissed.

"Stay behind me," he whispered. She pressed herself into his bare back.

"Is it a wolf?" she asked.

"There aren't any wolves in Long Island. Probably a stray dog. Just be still, maybe it'll pass."

Huff!

It was to their right, somewhere behind the clump of chest-high reeds. They swayed back and forth. Something skulked within them, moving closer.

Rosie whimpered. All Randy could find was a palm-sized rock. He hefted it in his left hand, cocking his arm back.

"Please don't be a pit bull," he said under his breath.

Just aim for the nose. Give Rosie time to get to the car. You can do this.

The reeds parted as it turned the corner, a large, menacing shadow against the bright moonlight.

"What the fuck?"

The shadow edged closer, snarling.

Randy's mind reeled. *What the hell is it?*

The muscles in Randy's arm twitched. He tensed, holding the rock like he'd grip a fastball back in high school, two fingers over the top, the pad of his thumb underneath.

He'd had a damn good arm then. Only one pitch allowed in this game.

Except this was no game.

"Rosie, run," he hissed through his teeth,

He started his forward motion, his arm uncoiling.

The shadow pounced with such dizzying speed, his arm was torn free from the elbow before he could complete the throw. The rock remained in his hand, fingertips white with pressure, as the limb dropped to the sand. Another slash, and Randy's throat disappeared in a flash of gore. He flopped back, his severed arteries showering a paralyzed Rosie until she was crimson.

Rosie's scream was swallowed by the tumbling surf.

Officer Gray Dalton sat in his patrol car catching up on paperwork. He kept one earbud in his ear, listening to an audiobook. It was Hemingway's *Garden of Eden*, about a newlywed couple and the woman who came between them during their honeymoon. He wished this was the required reading back in high school. Threesomes were more interesting than fishing to a teen boy.

He'd never been much of a student, something he was trying to make right, one audiobook at a time.

It was a nice, quiet night and the car's AC was on high enough to give him goose bumps. He poured a cup of coffee from his thermos while fingering the long scar along his jawline. It was an odd yet comforting habit of his, touching the raised, damaged flesh, courtesy of his attempt to climb into the sea lion pit at the Bronx Zoo when he was seven. It reminded him of being young and dumb and invincible, all the things he had to put aside to become a man. He could never grow a proper beard because of that scar. Girls liked it, especially if he embellished the story of how it came to be.

When he'd first joined the Suffolk County Police, he thought he'd never get used to the midnight shift. Now, two years later, he couldn't imagine working a day shift. He loved his territory, covering Montauk, Amagansett and East Hampton. Small towns, small problems. He may have grown up in a war zone in the Bronx, but he had no desire to police one.

He rolled the window down a bit. He'd parked in a lot behind one of the old motels on the Atlantic Ocean side so he could breathe in some ocean air. It was the smell of trips to Jones Beach when he was a kid. On the small stretch of road, five motels sat side by side, jockeying for tourists to come for the view. Cuts in the six-foot sand barrier allowed easy access to the beach.

Opening the window farther, he lit up a cigarette, savoring the marriage of the smoke with his coffee. He watched the foggy tendrils as they were pulled by the breeze like cotton candy.

No sooner had he put his clipboard down and closed his eyes when his radio squawked to life.

"One-eleven, respond to two possible 14-A's at Shadmoor State Park beach."

His eyes snapped open and he threw his clipboard onto the empty passenger seat.

"One-eleven, I'm close by and en route. 10-4."

He flicked his lights on and hit the gas, the back end of the car swerving in the sand as he sped out of the lot.

Two 14-A's was not good. It meant there were bodies on the beach. No other information was forthcoming. God knew what he was racing into.

He floored it through Montauk's deserted Main Street, spying the gazebo in the plaza to his left. Just eight hours ago, he'd sat there finishing off an ice cream cone, killing time before his shift started. Now he could feel that cone sitting in his gut like a lead ball.

As he veered into Shadmoor State Park, he turned on the driver's-side spotlight, easing up as he wound down to the beach. An empty beater sat at the edge of the beach. He shined his light into the Chevy's interior and the surrounding area. It was clear, at least as far as he could see for the moment. He radioed in that he was on scene and about to go on foot.

Stepping cautiously to the dune, he was overcome by the smell of ammonia and blood and something so foul, so alien, he had no words to give it justice. He clicked his flashlight on, keeping his other hand on the butt of his gun.

The stench made him gag. Could have been a couple of floaters that exploded as they dried out. He'd heard it was a smell that would haunt a man until his dying day. Sooner or later, being a cop surrounded by the ocean and the Long Island Sound, he was bound to come across one. Tonight looked like the night.

"Okay, Gray, just follow your nose."

He thought of that bird on the cereal box and how its nose always led it to a bowl of something that was more colored sugar than actual food.

Not going to find anything like that this time, he thought.

Sand shifted under his feet as if it were trying to prevent him from seeing something that could never be unseen. He stumbled but managed to stay upright. He saw the white-caps of the incoming waves as he crested the dune.

He swept his flashlight's beam to the left, then the right, scanning the immediate area.

It settled on the bottom of a pale foot poking out from behind a smaller dune.

The wind blew from that direction, making his eyes water.

Might as well get this over with.

He scrabbled down the dune. He was still on high alert,

but he moved quicker. As he stepped around the dune, he looked down and saw that the foot wasn't attached to a leg.

In fact, the leg, or parts of what could have been several legs, were scattered around the recessed part of the beach like a trail of chum.

"Jesus frigging Christ."

The ammonia smell was so bad, he had to turn away. It was as if two people—he could see two blood-soaked heads—had swallowed a grenade. Snaking coils of steam rose from the more substantial parts.

An acid-tinged burp clawed up his throat and he backpedaled. No way was he going to lose it all over a crime scene.

He grabbed his walkie and called in to dispatch. "Dispatch, this is one-eleven. Be advised, both 14-A's are confirmed. I need a boss and a bus, ASAP."

This was definitely worth getting his sergeant out of bed. He hoped the ambulance came equipped with plenty of jars.

CHAPTER 2

When the call was made to Sergeant Dennis Campos's house, his wife, Adelle, had to shake him hard several times to wake him. It had been a perfect, deep, dreamless sleep, a true rarity. He fumbled with the CPAP mask, yanking it over his face. The dull, droning machine continued to hiss, pumping out air into the comforter.

"What's the problem?" he huffed, the phone to his ear, his throat raw. Calls in the dead of night were few and far between. It had to be bad if one of his officers had dispatch put a call in to him.

Adelle leaned close, trying to hear through the phone's receiver.

He listened to the code and the few bare details that were available at the moment. Nodding, he said, "I'll be there in ten."

Tripping on the CPAP hose, he kicked the apparatus to the side and slipped on his uniform pants that he'd slung over the back of a chair.

"Is everything all right?" Adelle asked, putting on her robe. She knew the drill. Coffee would be on and in a thermos by the time he hit the front door.

Dennis sighed. "One of my officers responded to a report of a couple of bodies on the beach. I hate floaters and bloaters." He went into the bathroom and pocketed a small jar of vapor rub. He'd smear a little on his upper lip when he got there. It worked wonders for keeping the stench at bay. In the old days, when he'd started out in uniform in Brooklyn, they would light up cigars to mask any strong odors. There were plenty of two-cigar days back then.

Now, thanks to the sleep apnea and the weight problem that defied diets and workouts, Adelle would have his head if he came home smelling like cigars. Plus, he was pretty sure it was illegal to smoke anywhere now except five miles offshore.

As always, Adelle met him at the door with his thermos and a kiss. "Be careful, Dennis. I love you."

"Love you, too. If I'm home for breakfast, I'll pick up some bagels."

"Whole grain for both of us."

Dennis got into his car asking himself how life had turned to the point where he had to choke down that whole-grain crap as a reward for serving, protecting, and standing around dead bodies. His mood darkened the closer he got to the crime scene.

By the time Sergeant Campos pulled into the beach's lot, he had to stop in back of several squad cars, both Montauk and Suffolk County PD, two ambulances and a fire truck. He weaved through the cars, his belly smudging the squad-car doors. More lights and vehicles pulled up behind him. He spotted Officer Gray Dalton standing between a pair of dunes.

"This your call?" he asked.

Dalton nodded. "Sorry, Sarge, but I thought this is something you should see for yourself."

They stepped under the yellow crime scene tape.

Dalton stopped him before they turned the corner. "It's real bad."

"Floaters always are," Campos said, taking out his vapor rub.

"These aren't floaters, at least not as far as I can tell. There's a chance they washed up and someone got at them after, but"—he paused—"well, you'll see."

Officials moved about the beach, setting up a pair of portable lights. They clicked on, throwing harsh light on the scene around the bend.

Campos rounded the dune and felt his muscles lock. "Jesus, Mary and Joseph."

It looked like something out of a war movie. His first thought was that whoever was scattered about the sand and reeds had stepped on a land mine, like the IEDs those terrorist assholes used in Afghanistan and Iraq. He could make out some of the large parts—a leg here, blown off at the knee, the lower part of an arm, the heads—though there wasn't much to identify them. And to the left, was that a breast? "What the hell happened here?"

"Someone walking along the beach called it in. It was like this when I got here," Dalton said.

"Where's the person who reported it?"

"We don't know. It was an anonymous call."

Anonymous calls could mean anything. Could be the person was too scared to stick around—probably ran home to throw up the last week's worth of dinners. There was a possibility it was the very same person who committed the crime. If it was called in on a cell phone, he wouldn't be anonymous for long.

Campos said, "See if there's any way to trace the call. Everyone uses cell phones nowadays. If they get an address, they are not to send a soul until I tell them to."

"On it," Dalton said, radioing in. He pulled his walkie away to shout at one of the EMS guys. "Watch where you're stepping. Just keep back for now."

Campos liked Dalton. He was young, but he wasn't a pissant who felt entitled to the world. He played things straight and knew he had dues to pay. Adelle had liked him when they met at a picnic for the force, but that was mostly because of his looks. He was six foot, lean but solid, with full, jet-black hair and eyes so blue they reminded Dennis of the peepers on those husky dogs. He took great joy in reminding Adelle that Dalton was young enough to be their son.

While Dalton moved away, Campos got down on his haunches to take a closer look at one of the piles of shredded humanity. The smell of ammonia and other foreign chemicals made his eyes water as they retreated up into his head. He flinched, putting a handkerchief over his nose. That didn't smell like a floater or even a recently eviscerated body.

Is it toxic?

Studying it, he could only assume it was part of a torso. A couple of fingers stood up in the meat like they were flashing him a peace sign.

Then he noticed the smoke. An almost transparent steam wavered over the miasma.

Stepping back, watching, his eyes bulged.

"Where's the ME?" he shouted.

Dalton called over, "He just pulled up, Sarge."

"Get him over here now and tell him to bring a hazmat suit. Everything is fucking melting!"

The clanging of the metal lids of his garbage cans jarred Brian Ventura from his sleep.

Maybe it's just the wind.

Two heavy, tinny thumps followed.

"Dammit."

Sam, his neighbor and occasional Jets game tailgater, had been begging him for years to swap out the antique silver cans for plastic, especially the ones that locked the lid on tight. Wind and raccoons liked to play horrible music with his garbage, usually waking Sam up as well.

Something was rustling in the cans. He heard bottles clink against the patio and the crinkle of paper and plastic bags.

Brian got up slowly, scratching under his black T-shirt, giving his eyes a minute to clear.

He used to put bricks on the lids, then cinder blocks, but nothing could stop the raccoons out here. Some were the size of dogs. If they wanted in, they would find a way. That was fine, all part of living in the suburbs, except when it came to the noise level at his house. But dammit, those cans were still good, although dented from the garbagemen tossing them around like tennis balls. When they rusted away or got too misshapen to stand upright, he'd cave and get the plastic ones.

Frugality wasn't a crime yet.

Flicking on the hall light, he went downstairs, through the living room and into the kitchen. He grabbed the bat he kept by the sliding doors, the ebony one he'd gotten at Bat Day at Yankee Stadium, signed by Derek Jeter, and hit the switch for the patio light.

Nothing.

Great. *Now I have to get a bulb tomorrow.*

Pulling the blinds away from the latch, he turned it and pushed the door open just enough to poke his head out. He could see one of the cans lying on its side. Garbage was scattered all over the yard.

The other one must have rolled onto the side of the house.

Something shuffled in the dark. The raccoons were still there, making an enormous mess. There was no way he'd fall back to sleep after cleaning this debris up. He wondered if it was illegal to kill a raccoon. That's all he'd need is for Mrs. Arthurs across the way to see him bludgeoning one of the Dumpster divers. She'd have the police here before he could sing the first few bars of "Rocky Raccoon."

Brian looked up at Sam's bedroom window and saw it was still dark. Maybe he slept through it. Hopefully he did.

Stepping out into the cooler night air, Brian tightened his grip on the bat. The plan was to scare them off, maybe hit the bat on the ground for extra effect. He'd been around long enough to know they worked in pairs. The bat was really there in case one of them was sick or rabid and decided to turn on him. Otherwise, they'd just waddle away, slipping under the row of Sam's azalea bushes.

Fully awake and in need of some small form of revenge, Brian decided to quietly creep to the edge of the house and jump out at the raccoons. Maybe he'd give one a heart attack. It seemed a fair payback.

Inching along the rear of the house, he had to pause a moment to stifle a chuckle. Here he was, a grown man, getting his kicks from frightening a dumb, hungry animal. Another reason to add to his "Why I'm Single" list.

He stepped as lightly as possible, any sounds he made covered by the snuffing and rummaging in the alley.

Feastus interruptus, he thought.

Coming to the edge of the alley, he stopped, raised the bat over his head, bunching the muscles in his legs.

Now!

He leapt into the alley, landing hard on his sandaled feet, letting out a quick grunt to show he meant business.

He was right, there were two of them. Two massive heads pulled out of the refuse, whipping in his direction. One of them growled a deep, guttural warning.

These were no raccoons.

The bat suddenly felt like a lead weight in his hands. Brian took a step back. He couldn't make out any details in the dark, but he could see that they had to be dogs, big-ass ones to boot. His plan had worked, in that his little surprise had gotten them to stop rooting through the garbage. The one drawback, and it was a big one, was that they weren't the least bit afraid. Not of him. Not of the bat in his hands.

They took a step forward. The one on the right flicked a paw, crashing the can into the side of the house.

Brian tried to shout. All that came out was a soft, stammering hiss of nonsense.

The dogs came closer.

What the hell was wrong with them? Brian could feel the heat of their savage intention coming off them in waves.

He tripped as his heel came in contact with the raised brick of the patio. Daring a quick glance to his right, he wondered if he could make it in the door and slam it shut before they got to him. It would be close.

They'd gone disconcertingly silent.

Drawing in a deep breath, he pivoted and started to run.

He didn't go far.

The other garbage can took the brunt of his flight. His shin cracked into it and he somersaulted over the can, landing on his side. The pain in his leg was excruciating.

The ticking of nails on concrete made the hairs at the back of his neck stand on end as the dogs rounded the corner with confident strides.

Brian scrabbled to get back on his feet. The open door was just six feet away. In there was safety. In there was light and a first aid kit to take care of his leg.

In there was a place where pissed-off giant dogs could not go.

His yard was swiftly flooded with light.

"Brian, what the hell are you doing out there?"

The light and Sam's angry voice put a good scare into the menacing dogs. They dashed back down the alley as fast as greyhounds. One of them brushed against the can on its way out, giving it one last ear-splitting clatter against the house.

Hands clasped over his battered shin, Brian couldn't find the words to answer his neighbor.

CHAPTER 3

With three hours to go until dawn, the beach at Shadmoor State Park was buzzing with more activity than it ever would during a midsummer's day. It looked like every first responder in eastern Long Island had gathered in the sand. For the moment, the area was clear of news crews, but that wouldn't last long. Dalton studied the logjam of cars, vans and trucks, wondering how he'd ever get out.

First one in, last one out.

"Gray, is that you?"

He turned to see Norman Henderson, a middle-aged cop with a long, sad face, walk over carrying a couple of cups of coffee. Norm was local PD in Montauk, a man whose voice never matched his size. He was a good guy with a big heart and a porcine belly that obscured his belt. His warnings outnumbered the tickets he wrote, fifty to one.

"Please tell me one of those is for me," Dalton said.

Henderson eyed the cup in his left hand and shrugged. "I was saving it for Jake, but what the hell. Heard you were the one that found the bodies. You need it more than him."

Jake was Jake Winn, another member of the minuscule Montauk PD. Back in the day when cars rode two men at a time, Henderson and Winn had been partners. Winn was rough around the edges but good intentioned. He and Henderson had been a hell of a team. Norm scared them with his imposing size while Jake spit flames from a mouth honed by time spent in the marines. Last time Dalton spoke to him, Jake Winn had been working days. An event like this had a way of getting everyone out of bed.

"Pretty gruesome," Henderson said, blowing on his coffee.

"That's putting it mildly. You get a close look?"

"I went as close as I needed."

"You catch the smell?"

Henderson's brow wrinkled. "Yeah. What is that?"

"I don't have a clue. I'm not too thrilled that I was breathing it in before, and now the only people near the bodies are wearing hazmat suits and masks."

Dalton's stomach had been feeling queasy since Sergeant Campos had ordered everyone upwind and away from the bodies. He tried not to dwell on it. Mind over matter.

Henderson said, "Maybe the killer threw some chemicals around, hoping to dissolve the parts. You're too young to remember, but that was a specialty of the Irish Westies back in the day. No one could whack a guy and melt his body any better. They got so good at it, the Italians used to outsource their bodywork to them. You'd think those Westies were all chemists for DuPont, they were so good."

Sipping his coffee, Dalton shook his head. "But why hack them up like that and scatter them around the beach? If you had a contract on someone and a way of dissolving the evidence, wouldn't you do it somewhere no one could see or smell while the process worked? This makes no sense."

Henderson sucked on his teeth. "Well, it couldn't be the Westies anyway. None of them are left to do the deed." He looked over at Dalton's squad car. "You're not getting out of here until lunch."

"Don't remind me."

Henderson stumbled into Dalton and turned to give holy hell to whoever knocked into him.

Jake Winn, his uniform wrinkled and hat pushed as far forward as it could go, stared at the coffee in Henderson's hand.

"I thought you were gonna get me one. I only got two hours' sleep before the call came in."

Henderson pointed at Dalton. "He found them. He wins."

Winn was about the same age as Henderson but looked a few years younger. He was leaner, with no trace of gray in his hair or mustache. He had sharp, dark eyes framed by the start of crow's-feet. The man was a consummate gym rat who took crap from no one.

"At least let me get some of yours, dipshit," Winn said, grabbing Henderson's cup and tipping it back. He swallowed hard and said, "You know whose fucking car that is, right?"

"I do," Dalton said. "I ran the plates after I found the bodies."

Winn held up a hand. "Don't say it. Norm can figure it out on his own."

Walking over to the abandoned car, Henderson clicked on his flashlight, scanning the outside, then the interior. The beam settled on a hula girl bobblehead glued to the front dash.

"That's Randy Jenks's piece of crap," he said, his voice troubled.

"You think that's Randy over there?" Winn said.

Dalton said, "I saw the heads before the skin and hair started dissolving. There's no way to tell. If there are teeth left, we might be able to get a positive ID."

Winn grumbled, "I'm not waiting for a dentist. I'm going to head on over to Randy's, see if he's home. Maybe someone stole his car, ended up here, came across the wrong angry bastard. At least I hope that's what happened."

Dalton finished his coffee and threw the cup in a nearby trash bin. "That's a good idea. Hey, did Randy have a wife or girlfriend?"

Winn removed his hat and ran his hands through his close-cropped hair. "Norm, was he still with that girl, what's her name?"

"Sherry. Nah, they broke up months ago. I heard about it from his mother during the PAL basketball camp. He was real broke up about it. I'd be upset if I lost a girl like that, too."

"How come you want to know if Randy had a girl?" Winn asked.

"Because I thought I saw a breast."

"A tit? Over there?" Winn said.

Dalton nodded. "It was hard to tell, but I'm pretty sure that's what it was. I'm not used to seeing them unattached to a torso."

Dalton could see the muscles in Henderson's jaws clench. "Come on, Jake, I'll go with you. We'll let you know if we find him."

"Thanks. I'll be here, watching the sun come up," Dalton said.

"There are worse ways to pull a double," Winn said.

Dalton thought about what lay over the dune and wondered what exactly that would be.

Kelly James pulled her dad's pilfered Prius over to the side of the road, keeping her foot on the brake. If her parents found out she'd snuck out, *borrowed* the car and came home at three thirty in the morning, she'd be grounded until the first day of senior year. She rested her head against the steering wheel, getting her courage up.

They'd never understand.

When June had told her that Joey was going to be at Wendy's party—with that slut Adriana—there was no way she could sit home without going crazy. Joey had just broken up with her a week ago with the typical "Look, you'll always be in my heart, babe, but I'm going to college five states away in a couple of months. It's not fair to both of us. You know those long-distance relationships never work. This way, you're free to be yourself and not worry about me. Senior year is supposed to be fun. I wouldn't want to take that away from you."

What a load of crap. He just wanted to get in Adriana's pants before he was too far away to try.

Or had he meant what he said and the rumor about him and Adriana was a lie?

The wondering had Kelly in a slow burn all day. Finally, when her parents went to bed at eleven, she had to find out. She'd never snuck out before and her heart was in her throat from the moment she crept out of her room all the way until the Prius was several blocks from the house.

When she got to the party, things were in full swing. Kids from three different schools packed into Wendy's house in East Hampton. Her living room was a haze of hookah smoke. Red Solo cups littered every surface in the house. There must have been over two hundred people there. Wendy's parents had flown out to L.A. the day before. Her father was a movie producer and her mother was an actress, at least until the latest face-lift hadn't gone so well and the casting calls dried up. Parental jaunts to Hollywood were always cause for celebration. And the celebrations were always slamming, each one more memorable than the last. Wendy would make one hell of an event planner when she graduated.

After searching both floors of the house, interrupting several make-out sessions and one blow job in the master bathroom, she found Joey, alone, sitting in a lounge chair outside the pool house. His eyes lit up when he saw her. She couldn't get into his arms fast enough.

They talked for hours, with a lot of apologizing from his side. He'd had a change of mind the day after he broke things off, but he didn't want to come crawling back and make her think he was just messing with her head.

When she left, he promised to take her out for dinner the next day.

In just a few hours, she'd gone from miserable, to scared, to angry, to blissful and back to scared. God, she was exhausted. All she wanted to do was slip into her pj's and sleep until noon. But first, she had to get back in the house without making a noise.

"You can do this," she said, easing off the brake.

It's not like she snuck out to drink or get high or have sex. She hadn't even taken a sip of beer. That wouldn't matter if her parents caught her, if they even believed her.

She drove to the edge of her long, down-sloping driveway, put the car in neutral and turned the engine off. Gravity pulled the car to the closed garage door. Without power, it was hard to turn the steering wheel but she managed to slip the Prius quietly into its proper place. The garage is where they kept her mother's Navigator. The nicer car got the better space.

Slowly closing the car door until it clicked shut, she bent to the side-view mirror to give herself a once-over, in case her mom and dad were waiting for her inside. The last thing she needed was to look like a wreck. They'd think she was trashed.

Kelly pushed her blond hair behind her ears and straightened her blouse. She was worried that she was so tired her eyes would be bloodshot, but luckily, that wasn't the case.

"Okay, in the door, up the stairs and back to my room. Just three easy steps," she said to her reflection.

Retrieving her house keys from her purse, she walked on tiptoes to the front door. Kelly looked up. All of the windows were dark. That was a good sign.

A deep, foreboding growl emanated from behind the bushes to her right.

Startled, Kelly dropped the keys on the porch. She drew in a sharp breath, worried about what animal was an arm's length from her and if the keys made enough noise to wake her parents.

"Grrrrrrrrlllllll."

What the heck is that? Kelly thought. *Sounds like a drowning dog.*

Keeping her eyes peeled to the bushes, she knelt down, scooping up the keys.

The branches twittered as something moved.

Rabies! Didn't animals foam at the mouth when they had rabies? Maybe that's why it sounds like that.

Kelly's heart trip-hammered.

She had to get inside, fast, but how could she do that without making a ton of noise?

Her hand shook so hard, it took her three tries to slip her key into the lock. She gave it a half turn, slow enough so the tumblers didn't ring out as the door unlocked. She couldn't keep her eyes from the dark swath by the bushes.

The dog, or whatever it was, continued to rumble, almost purr, with its waterlogged warning.

Kelly opened the door.

The ticking of the grandfather clock echoed in the foyer.

She took one step across the threshold.

Something darted out of the bushes, knocking into her leg. She stifled a cry when she felt a sharp stab of pain in her ankle. Off-balance, she tottered on one leg, her wounded ankle hovering off the ground. The welcome mat inside the door slid and she flopped to the ground.

Tears burned her eyes.

It bit me!

There was nothing outside. Whatever it was had taken off.

Doing her best to hold her breath and keep her tears from completely blurring her vision, she got up and closed the door with a fluid *clack*.

The lancing pain in her ankle was unreal. It felt like she'd been stabbed with a hot knife.

Kelly limped up the stairs, one at a time, pausing to listen for sounds of anyone moving about upstairs.

By the grace of God, she made it to her room. She grabbed the pj's she'd left on her dresser and went into her bathroom. Flicking on the light, she almost laughed at herself.

It was only a scratch. In fact, what felt like a seeping wound was a three-inch welt that had barely broken the skin. One tiny drop of blood sat poised at the corner of the scratch like an expectant tear. She sat on the edge of the tub, doused it with stinging alcohol, patted it dry and put a bandage on, just in case.

Slipping into her bed, she couldn't believe how lucky she was, despite her brush with whatever dumb animal had been outside. She'd made it.

And she had a date with Joey tomorrow.

By dawn, she wasn't sure what was keeping her up more, her happiness at reconnecting with her boyfriend, or the growing pain in her ankle.

CHAPTER 4

By four a.m., there wasn't much left for Dalton to do. It was too early to play crowd control. Local PD had created a barrier the two news crews couldn't cross. More would be on the way. A couple of vans with heavy, white satellite dishes on the roof were parked in the Sand Stone Motel's lot. The ME was with the bodies. All emergency responders were ordered to steer clear of the remains until they could determine if the weird smell coming from the bodies was toxic or not.

He sat in his car with the door open, listening to a succession of animal disturbance calls from dispatch. After the fourth call, he went to look for Sergeant Campos. He found him talking to the fire chief.

"Do we have anyone from Animal Control here?" he asked Campos.

The sergeant narrowed his eyes and thought for a moment. "Someone should be here. I asked them to send Anita over about an hour ago. I'd rather this be some kind of animal attack than the work of a psychopath. I haven't seen her, though."

Anita Banks had worked for Animal Control on this end of the island for over twenty years. She was so good at her job that other counties, even neighboring states, brought her in for difficult situations. She'd helped remove several bears from New Jersey suburbs, put down a crazed chimp in upstate New York and handled more cases of rabid animals than anyone could count.

"Why do you ask?" Campos said.

"We've got four complaints about animals going through garbage and knocking things down in the past hour. The last one was at Shorey Road. If we have a rabid animal on the loose, I want to follow up. I was hoping to grab someone from Animal Control for the ride."

Dalton looked over the row of parked vehicles, hoping to spot another county car toward the rear. He was relieved to find not one, but two. Now all he had to do was locate Anita.

The ME shouted from behind the dune for the sergeant. Campos turned to Dalton and said, "Do it, but be careful. If you find something, take your cues from Anita."

"Got it."

Now, if I were Anita, where would I be?

He walked through the crowd of cops, EMS and firemen. Gallows humor was in full effect. People on the outside would be appalled if they could hear the laughter, see the smiles while two people were laid out in pieces just yards away. They'd never understand. If you let the horror creep under your skin, it could destroy you.

Anita wasn't among the throng.

Of course not. Knowing her, she couldn't stay away from the crime scene. She'd be as close as she could, determining whether or not an animal could have caused such destruction, her mind formulating a case to either protect innocent creatures from being pulled into a dragnet or to humanely put down an animal that had crossed a very hard line.

Dalton circled back around the dune, away from the flashing lights and out of reach of the blinding brightness of the temporary crime scene lights. He found her sitting behind a stand of waist-high reeds. She'd parted them with a hand and observed the hazmat team as they took pictures.

"Busted," Dalton said.

Anita fell backward, covering her mouth to suffocate a startled shout.

When she saw Dalton, she shook her head and smiled.

"You nearly gave me a heart attack, Gray."

"Better than leaving you here breathing in God-knows-what. You up to taking a ride?"

"I was planning to wait until I got the all clear to get closer to the scene, though it seems gruesome enough from here."

Dalton looked over at the guys in white suits, taking great care not to step their booted feet into any remains.

"Trust me, you've gotten a good enough view. Your next best bet will probably be in the ME's office where you can check the bodies for bite marks." He left out the part about the flesh dissolving from the bones.

He offered a hand to help Anita to her feet. She tied her long chestnut hair in a ponytail and wiped the sand from the seat of her pants. She was in her late forties, dressed in her everyday uniform of tan slacks with a forest green polo shirt. Her soft, gray eyes could get hard as steel if the moment called for it.

Anita said, "One thing I can tell you is that no single animal did that, unless we have a starved, half-mad lion on the loose. The closest would be at the Central Park Zoo, and I can't see an escaped lion making it all the way out here without being spotted—or reported missing." She took out a pack of gum and offered him a piece.

"I want to follow up on some other animal disturbance calls that have come in since I found the bodies. I thought you might want to tag along. Maybe we can stop this thing, or things, before someone else gets hurt."

Anita took one last look at the crime scene and shook her head. "Lead the way, Officer. I'm all yours. I just need to stop at my van to pick up my tranquilizer gun."

When Dalton got to the county squad car closest to the road out of the state park, he talked to Jerry, an EMS driver, who had been driving the car.

"I think I saw Mickey get out. He was just here talking to Jack a minute ago."

Dalton spied Mickey Conrad, a vet on the force, jawing with Jack Brand, a longtime EMS attendant. Dalton couldn't wait until he was no longer the new kid. It seemed every first responder on this end of the island had been on the job forever.

"Hey Mick, I need to use your car. Mine's trapped."

Mickey rolled and cracked his neck. His normally salt-and-pepper hair flashed blue and red under the strobing lights. Strong-jawed with an aquiline nose, Conrad looked every bit the hard-line cop, even though he could goof off with the best of them. "What for?"

"Sergeant Campos wants me to check out some animal disturbance calls, see if they're what's behind this."

Mickey shot him a long, hard look. His regular shift ended at midnight. He didn't want to be stuck out there any longer than need be, especially since there was little to do at the moment.

"Bring it back in an hour or you owe me a steak."

Mickey was a notorious carnivore. When he said *steak*, he meant a twenty-ounce porterhouse at a good restaurant. No Sizzler or Outback Steakhouse for him.

"I will. I don't make Mickey-steak kind of money."

Dalton opened the door for Anita, who commented on his being a gentleman, and made a U-turn out of the park.

* * *

Officers Winn and Henderson pulled up to Randy Jenks's small cottage. It had powder blue shutters in need of a paint job. Postage-stamp yards with healthy, well-tended lawns were in the front and back of the house. The windows were dark, but that was normal for this time of night. Randy's curbside mailbox was full.

"Maybe he's out of town," Norman suggested as they walked to the front door. The neighborhood was silent as a tomb. Even the feral cats were tucked away.

"Let's hope," Jake said and pushed the bell.

The chimes echoed inside the house, but nothing stirred. He tried again and waited ten seconds.

Norman gave the door a few hard raps. He wanted to roust Randy if he was in a deep sleep, but he didn't want to knock so hard he woke up everyone on the block.

"I'll check the back," Jake said, using his flashlight to lead the way around the side of the house.

A cooling breeze made the tops of the trees sway, carrying the scent of salt and pine. Henderson tried the bell again. He shined his flashlight through the front window into the living room. There was an empty couch, easy chair, a stack of magazines scattered across a glass coffee table, wrestling a pizza box for space. He pressed his face to the glass and pointed the light into the kitchen, sweeping it to the doorway of what must be the bedroom.

Another light pierced the dark from a different angle. Winn had gone to the bedroom window and must have been trying to peer through the gaps in the blinds.

He came back shaking his head. "He's not in there."

Henderson felt a knot tighten in his stomach, staring down the road leading to the Montauk Highway and ultimately, the beach. "For his mother's sake, I hope he's not back there."

* * *

Dalton's first stop didn't yield much intel. An older woman had called in saying her cat had been chased up onto the garage roof by a wild dog with no collar. By the time he got there, the cat was still on the roof, mewling.

"Priscilla won't come down, even when I opened a can of food," the woman said. She wore a white housecoat and a hairnet. She stood by the garage in her bare feet, trying to coax the cat down.

"Do you have a ladder?" he asked.

"In the garage. Let me open it so you can get it."

Dalton looked back at Anita, who was still in the passenger seat of the squad car. "You want to take this one?"

She smiled. "It's just a scared cat. I'll let you be the hero."

He chuckled. Saving cats from trees and rooftops. He couldn't remember what chapter that had been at the academy.

The woman came out with the key and pulled the door open. The segmented wooden door made enough noise to wake the dead. "It's right there," she said, pointing to the back of the garage. He maneuvered his way around the old Buick that took up most of the space and carried the ladder over his head.

"What did you say the cat's name was, ma'am?"

"Priscilla."

He leaned the ladder against the garage and climbed several rungs.

"Hey, Priscilla. Come on, let me help you get down. *Psss, psss, psss.* Come on."

The cat, a gray-and-black-striped tabby, looked at him with wide, emerald eyes, and hissed. When he reached out to get her, she swatted his hand, raking his fingers with her claws and backing up. Dalton drew his hand back sharply.

Damn, that hurt! He'd heard that cat scratches burned so

much because of the urine under their nails. Another reason to be a dog lover.

He wanted to say, *I don't like you as much as you don't like me, Simba. Now get off the damn roof before I have Anita hit you with a tranq.*

Instead, he climbed another rung, calling her name softly. The cat wasn't going for it. No matter. As soon as he got close enough, Dalton snagged the cat with both hands. She struggled mightily, hissing and trying to get at his arms with her hind claws. Midway down the ladder, she broke free from his grasp, hit the ground running and didn't stop until she had dashed into the woman's open back door.

"Why did you drop her?" the woman cried. She looked as upset as the cat.

"She wasn't easy to hold on to," he replied, putting the ladder back in the garage.

"You could have hurt her. Who's your supervisor?"

He couldn't believe it. Here he was, climbing up on a roof to get a vicious cat and the woman was threatening to complain to his supervisor. No good deed . . .

After giving her Sergeant Campos's information, realizing the laugh this would give him when and if she did call, he asked if she could describe the dog that had run Priscilla up the roof.

"I just happened to look out the window because I heard Priscilla crying. She does that when she's scared. I didn't see much, but I could tell it was big. Like a pony."

"A pony is considerably larger than a dog. Are you sure about the size?"

"I *know* it wasn't a pony, but you could put a saddle on it if you wanted."

"Could you see the type of dog it was, the color of its fur?"

"It was too dark."

"But you could see it had no collar?"

"People around here think there are no laws. They walk

their dogs without collars or leashes and let them poop on my front lawn without picking it up."

She droned on for a couple of minutes while Dalton looked for a way out of the conversation. It took another ten, fruitless minutes before he got back in the car. Anita couldn't stop tittering.

"I take it you're not a cat person," she said as he keyed the ignition.

"Or a cat *lady* person. Next stop is someone who said he was attacked by a couple of dogs in his yard. I hope he's quick. I don't want to have to buy Mickey a steak."

CHAPTER 5

Benny Franks shivered under a sheet, two blankets and a comforter. Even though the night was humid, he'd turned off the air-conditioning in his room. His stomach had been queasy all night, but it looked like whatever illness had crept into him was taking things to a whole new level. Bubbling noises percolated from his abdomen. His nose had started to run an hour ago and he burned through a box of tissues at NASCAR speed. A pair of sodden hand towels lay draped across his blanketed chest.

Maybe it's food poisoning, he thought. The pulled pork sandwich he'd had at Summer's barbecue had tasted a little off. Leave it to his girlfriend to make him sick. She was always experimenting with different food. Just because she watched the Food Network, she thought she was a chef. He remembered the time she'd fed him homemade sushi—though she left out the *homemade* part at the time—that had landed them both in the ER the next day. He'd shit himself three times before adding a fourth in the car ride to the hospital. They laughed about it now, but it wasn't funny at all at the time.

Or maybe his stomach was just repulsed by what he saw at the beach. Holy God, that was awful.

Summer had asked him to stay the night, but the way his stomach had been cramping, he'd rather be home alone. Sitting on his couch, watching *Gladiator* for the twentieth time, he'd started feeling woozy and desperately needed some fresh air. Sitting on the porch only made things worse, so he went for a walk. That seemed to settle things down, so he kept on walking. It was a nice night and the moon gave him plenty of light to see by.

Tired of looking at the same weather-battered homes on his block, he'd jumped in his car and headed for the beach. The state park was closed after dark, but no one really cared if you dipped inside for a bit. He'd pulled in at the western edge of the beach. The ocean air made things even better.

He was just getting back to normal when he spotted what looked like heaps of garbage past a stand of reeds.

Fucking slobs.

It wasn't like he was about to clean the beach himself, even though there was a trash bin nearby. Let the parks people do it. It's what they got paid to do.

Only, the closer he got, the more he realized it wasn't someone's picnic refuse.

It was *someone*!

Then he saw the heads. It was *two* someones.

Stepping onto a matted-down section of reeds, he knelt down to get a closer look at a gelatinous stack of human ruin. Did they blow themselves up? No way. People would have heard it and the beach would be clogged with morbid onlookers.

Whatever comfort he'd restored to his stomach was turned on its head. He gagged. The pulled pork lodged in his throat.

The last thing he wanted was to be connected to this scene. He'd had enough trouble with the law and despite what most people thought, he'd put those days behind him.

He ran to the water and let his dinner fly. The Atlantic could have his DNA, not the Montauk PD.

Head reeling, he stumbled back to his car.

Just go home and forget you saw it. Someone will find it soon enough and call the cops.

He started the car, putting his hand on the gearshift.

What if some little kid looking for shells finds them in the morning? That kid would be scarred for life.

He punched the steering wheel, silently debating with himself. He opened his cell phone, then snapped it shut. If he called it in, the cops would have his cell number and easily trace it back to him. He remembered the old phone box beside Hanson's thrift shop on Main. It was like a tiny monument to another time, before even five-year-olds had their own iPhones.

Would it still work?

When he pulled in front of Hanson's, he grabbed some quarters out of the console. The phone was nicked with scratches and deep gouges. Some kids must have taken a knife to it for shits and giggles. To his complete surprise, a dial tone sang in his ear when he lifted the phone off the hook.

At least something went his way tonight.

He put his shirt over the mouthpiece and did his best to alter his voice when he connected with the police. He kept it brief and urgent and hung up before they could ask any questions. Then he went back home and crawled into bed, where his stomach decided to pick up right where it had left off.

Revulsion at the bloody mess wouldn't explain the chills, sweats and runny nose. Of course, every time he thought about the moment he reached down and touched the mass of flesh and red meat, bile would hit the back of his teeth and the chills would deepen.

Why the hell did I do that? Seeing it wasn't enough?

He always had to take things a step further. It's what landed him in jail when he was nineteen.

Sure, he'd done some good by calling the cops, but what on earth possessed him to even go near that?

Benny sneezed, filling the hand towel. He'd call Summer in the morning and see how she felt. It was probably the pork. His nighttime discovery just added fuel to the fire.

Dalton and Anita pulled up to a tidy Cape house on Herkimer Street. All of the downstairs lights were on.

Dalton looked at his notepad. "This house belongs to Brian Ventura. He said two really big dogs were going through his garbage. When he went to scare them away, they turned on him and chased him into the house."

Anita got out of the car. "Let's hope he got a good look at them."

Ventura opened the door before Dalton could ring the bell. He looked to be in his midthirties with dark, curly hair and tired eyes. His Mets robe was worn, the ends of the sash tattered. He was slightly stooped over and holding an ice pack to the small of his back.

"Please, come in and have a seat," he said. "Thanks for coming. I wasn't sure if I should even call and make a big deal of it at first, but there was something way off about the way those strays acted."

Dalton eyed the ice pack. "Are you all right?"

He shook his head. "I tripped over one of my garbage pails. Took a nice spill. Nothing some ice and Motrin can't handle."

Dalton introduced Anita, who shook his hand.

"If you came to get them," he said to her, "they're long gone. As soon as my neighbor turned on his floodlights, they took off like a shot. They were like mini-Thoroughbreds."

Or very fast ponies, Dalton thought. He asked Ventura

to take them through what had happened, which he happily did, complete with plenty of hand gesticulations. Whatever he saw, it had put a damn good scare into him.

"When the lights came on, were you able to see the dogs?" Anita asked. With anxious fingertips, she worried at the end of her ponytail.

"Not really. I'm telling you, they zipped back down my alley way faster than I thought a dog could run."

"You didn't catch anything, like an approximate size, color, if they had long or short hair?" Dalton prodded.

Ventura winced when he settled back into his chair and paused to think. "Look, I know they were big, kinda like that dog from the comics."

"Snoopy?" Dalton said. He wasn't much of a comics-page guy and Charlie Brown's beagle was one of the few dog comic characters he knew.

"No, the huge one that gets in all the trouble."

Anita said, "You mean Marmaduke?"

Brian snapped his fingers. "That's it."

"That would be a Great Dane," Anita said. "They can get pretty big, scarily so for people who've never seen one up close before."

Dalton took down notes. Ventura added, "I think they were short-hair dogs because I would have seen a lot of hair, you know? It happened so fast, I couldn't tell much. I just know this."

He stopped to adjust the ice pack. Dalton glanced at Anita, who looked concerned.

"These dogs, they weren't afraid of me one bit. I didn't surprise them. I *pissed them off.* If you find them, you better be real careful."

Dalton thanked him for calling it in and left a card to reach him if they returned to the yard. He advised Ventura to stay in the house should they come back. He didn't need to be told twice.

Back in the car, Dalton looked at his watch and said, "I better get back to the beach. What's your take?"

Anita tugged on her hair. "I can see one dog, a stray Dane or mastiff, with a bad temper. But two working in tandem? I don't like it."

Neither do I, Dalton thought as he turned the car back toward Shadmoor State Park.

CHAPTER 6

By the time Dalton returned to the beach, the sun was cresting on the horizon, hot and amber with promises of a hazy, humid day. Many of the first-responder vehicles were gone. The sun glinted off the sand as if it were a sea of gold. The beaches in Montauk were some of the prettiest in the state—until they were the setting for a grisly double homicide.

He tossed the keys to Mickey, who grabbed them in midair and checked his watch.

"I'm five minutes early, Mick," Dalton said.

"Lucky for you," he said, smiling. "The ME's almost done collecting all the parts. Whatever gas was coming from the bodies is gone, too. All we have to do is keep the early joggers away for a little while."

A dozen seagulls squawked overhead, circling the area where the bodies lay. Mickey followed Dalton's gaze and gave a short laugh. "You missed it. One of those sea buzzards swooped down and gobbled up some of the parts. I thought Campos was going to shoot the damn thing out of the sky."

"As far as they know, it's just entrails thrown from the

back of one of those party fishing boats. A meal's a meal to them," Dalton said.

Anita placed a hand over her stomach. "And on that note, I'm heading home. Gray, you call me if anything else comes up, okay?"

"I will. Go home and get some sleep. You earned it."

She adjusted the strap of the case for her tranquilizer gun over her shoulder and headed for her van, waving back at them.

"Any luck?" Mickey asked. He took a sip of the dregs of coffee in his cup, grimaced and dumped it on the beach. A slight breeze blew the foam cup from his hand and they watched it tumble under Dalton's car.

"Followed up on a few reports, but no one got a good look at whatever woke them up. They all agreed that whatever they saw, it was huge, like a Great Dane. One guy was chased by a pair of them back into his house."

"Two dogs together? That's strange. I wonder if we have one of those fight-dog places around. You know, those Michael Vick jackwads who abuse dogs so they'll kill anything in sight? You think it could have anything to do with this?"

Dalton massaged some of the tension from his neck. "I haven't a clue. If it's dogs, what kind of dogs could do that? Anita said it looks like a lion tore those people apart. But there's no way a lion, or a tiger or bear, could make it all the way out here without riling half the people on the island. I think some lunatic lost his mind. Hopefully the ME can pull some prints, give us some answers."

Mickey clapped him on the back. "Bet you didn't think you'd be dealing with psycho crap like this out here, did you?"

"No. It is kind of out of place."

"You have no idea. I've been working Suffolk County a

long time and I've never seen anything like it. Is it weird that I'm starving?"

"For you, no."

The first jogger of the day, a woman in her forties in a black tracksuit, her hair tied up and earbuds firmly in her ears, approached the crime scene, oblivious. "I got this," Dalton said. He intercepted her before she could get too close. Jogging in place, she asked him a few questions, which he declined to answer, then turned and went back the way she'd come.

It went like that for the next couple of hours. Dalton kept checking in on the progress of the ME. Almost everything had been collected, bagged and tagged. Sergeant Campos left along with Mickey not long after. Dalton stayed around with a couple of guys from the Montauk PD. One of them was Officer Norman Henderson.

"Randy Jenks wasn't home," he told Dalton.

"Any chance he may have crashed at a friend's house?"

Henderson stared at Randy's car, scratching his beer belly. "I doubt it. If I had money to bet, I'd put it all on Randy being one of those bodies. Now we have to find out who the woman was." He considered the news crews. A pretty young brunette talked to the camera, the wind blowing her hair across her face. "If that is Randy, I don't want to be the one to tell his mother. This will kill her. And I really hope she doesn't find out by watching the news. If she sees Randy's car on TV, she'll assume the worst."

"Should we tell them to keep their cameras away from that area?" Dalton was more than happy to relocate them to another part of the beach.

"If you do, they'll get more curious than ever, and you can guarantee that they'll focus on the car. Better to let them yammer where they are."

By eight o'clock, a new shift of county cops came to relieve him. Dalton stuck around to fill them in, telling them they should appreciate the fact that the bodies had been taken away. Everyone was stunned by the severity of the murders. A typical crime out here was a celebrity getting drunk and making a scene in a fancy restaurant. He left the beach at nine.

He was glad he'd moved to his tiny apartment in Montauk. When he'd first joined the force, he lived near Queens, which was another world and hours away. Now that the adrenaline had worn off, he barely made the ten-minute drive home without falling asleep at the wheel.

After a long, hot shower and before crashing in his darkened bedroom, he rooted around his drawers for a road map of Montauk and some Post-it notes. He dropped them on his living room table, yawned so hard and long his jaw cracked, and stumbled into bed. Maybe things would make more sense after a few hours of sleep.

Kelly first mistook her alarm for the chiming of the ice cream truck. In her dream, she ran down her driveway dressed in a one-piece bathing suit, her wet hair loose and wild, shouting for the ice cream man to stop. If she didn't get a Creamsicle, the rest of the day would be ruined.

The dream shattered and she bolted up in bed long enough to slam a hand down on the snooze button. She settled back into her pillow and moaned.

It was Saturday morning. She wasn't going to spend the day swimming in the pool and she sure as hell wasn't going to wait around for the ice cream man. No, she had to get up for work at the Montauk information center. All she wanted to do was fall back into her dream, to a time before she had real responsibilities and summers meant total and absolute freedom.

Her head pounded. When she tried to move onto her side to get comfortable, a barbed pain rocketed up her leg.

Cringing, she looked at the clock. If she was lucky, she'd slept two hours. She just couldn't shut down. Joey invaded every thought.

Well, Joey and the dull throb in her ankle.

While she pondered calling in sick, she kicked the covers off so she could go to the bathroom. Kelly looked down at her ankle, wondering if she'd somehow twisted it when she tried to get away from that dog last night. The way it felt, she had to have a nice bruise.

She had to grab a pillow and bite down to hold back her scream.

"Oh my God, oh my God, oh my God," she stammered, flicking her hands to work out her mounting anxiety.

Her entire foot, from the ankle down, looked like it'd been driven over by a garbage truck. Her normally pale skin was mottled black and red and varying shades of purple. She felt a sick heat building under her tainted flesh.

Clear pus seeped from under the wet bandage.

Kelly had to drag her leg behind her as she dashed to the bathroom to throw up. Her stomach heaved until her ribs ached. Trembling on her knees, she voided everything until she was left convulsing with dry, painful hiccups.

She pulled herself up, holding on to the edge of the sink.

Her face was pale and beaded with sweat. Gray smudges underlined her eyes.

"How can I get so sick so fast?" she asked her ghostly reflection.

Now that the vomiting was over, the chills settled in.

The information center would have to live without her today. Kelly limped back to bed and called her boss. For once, she didn't have to fake sounding sick.

And what the hell was up with her foot? Did she break something? It hurt like hell when she put pressure on it.

This is going to ruin everything!

If she didn't get herself together by tonight, she might lose Joey—again. That couldn't happen.

She had to practically shout at her body to get off the bed and go back to the bathroom. While she searched for some aspirin, her mother knocked on her door.

"Time to get up, honey. I'll drive you to work today. Your father's playing the Lawn Ranger."

Kelly fumbled with the childproof top. It popped off and landed in the toilet with a plop.

"I'm not feeling so good, Mom," she said. "I already called in. I'm just going to go back to sleep."

"Is there anything I can get you? You want something to drink or some toast?"

"No, I don't need anything. I just want to sleep." She dropped four aspirin on her tongue, chasing them down with a glass of water. She gagged, but forced herself to keep the pills down.

Somehow, she stumbled back into bed and pulled the covers up to her chin. Her foot felt like it was on fire. Hopefully the aspirin would take the swelling down, as well as the pain. She *had* to see Joey later.

Her mother came in, breaking the rule Kelly had set when she'd turned sixteen. Normally, an infraction like this would lead to a mini-war. She didn't have it in her at the moment to fight.

"Oh, you don't look good at all." She pressed her lips to Kelly's head. "You have a nice fever going."

"I just took some pills. I'm going back to sleep." Kelly rolled over, wincing when her good foot brushed against her bruised foot.

"How about I get you some burnt toast? It's good for your stomach."

"I hate burnt toast, *Mother*. Can you please just let me sleep?"

Her mother sat on the edge of the bed, stroking her hair.

"Don't get mad. It's part of being a mother. You'll know all about it some day." She kissed the side of Kelly's head. "You get some sleep. I'll check on you later. You let me know if you need anything."

A ball of fire worked its way into Kelly's stomach. She held her breath for a moment, waiting for it to pass, which it did after a few seconds. On the one hand, she wanted to be a little kid again and throw herself into her mother's arms. On the other, she knew she was well past that and would have to go through it herself, especially if she wanted to see Joey later.

"Thanks, Mom," she said.

"I love you, honey."

"Love you, too."

Her mother quietly closed the door. Kelly shut her eyes, praying she'd wake up feeling like a human being again.

Benny Franks woke up to the worst smell of his life. At first, he'd hoped it was a phantom odor from a bad dream. He'd had plenty of them through the night, thanks to the fever and stomach cramps.

As he shifted in bed, he realized it was no dream.

He pulled up the sheet and peered down, lifting his hip to the right.

"You did not crap yourself in your sleep," he sighed.

His head throbbed and his tongue felt like cardboard. He was so tired, so weak, he was actually contemplating staying in his own waste and trying to get a few more hours' sleep. The chills he'd had were gone, replaced by hot flashes. He closed his eyes. *Just put it out of your mind. You've been lying in it for who knows how long. A couple more hours couldn't hurt.*

Try as he might, the stench refused to let him sleep. Grimacing, he rolled over, plopping one leg over the side of the bed and onto the floor. Standing on shaky legs, he inspected the damage.

There was no saving the sheets. Or the mattress, for that matter.

"Thanks, Summer. Your pork turned me back into a damn baby."

He grabbed a pillow and shuffled into the living room, shutting the bedroom door behind him. Maybe Summer would clean it up if he sounded pathetic enough when he called her later. Pathetic wouldn't be a stretch.

Man, it was hot.

He staggered to the bathroom, chucked off his clothes and cleaned himself up as best he could with a soapy washcloth. Grabbing a bottle of Gatorade, he fell onto the couch stark naked. The remote for the air conditioner was on the coffee table, within arm's reach.

The cool air felt amazing on his skin. His stomach was on fire, but at least the cramps were gone.

Benny turned on the TV and caught a live feed from the beach. He watched the news for a few minutes, which only conjured up images of the bodies. Black tarps had been placed over the parts as the reporter droned on about the viciousness of the attack. The victims had yet to be identified but sources speculated it was a man and a woman. You knew it was bad when the cops had to *speculate* on the sex of the bodies.

He thought back to the feel of the blob of flesh he'd been compelled to touch.

Disgusted, he changed the channel to an infomercial about bras without underwire and passed out.

CHAPTER 7

Gray Dalton woke up at four p.m. as hungry as he'd ever been. He hadn't eaten anything in over sixteen hours and had passed starvation some time in his sleep. Normally, he went to the gym before eating breakfast, but after last night, normal had been thrown out the window.

He made a five-egg omelet, sprinkling in some green onion and cheese, wolfing it down with several slices of wheat toast while standing over the sink. His mother called as he was loading the dishes in the dishwasher.

"Did you see it?" she asked without preamble. Muriel Dalton was high-strung and nervous on the calmest of days. When he'd told her he wanted to be a cop, she'd actually fainted, visions of his demise overwhelming her senses.

At the time, joining law enforcement had been a no-brainer. Three weeks after graduating Saint Francis Academy, his best friend Sal Mottola, "Wiggy" to everyone who knew him because his hair was too perfect to be real, was gunned down in a botched robbery at a convenience store. Poor Wiggy had gone to pick up some milk and bread for his mother. It was a heartbreaking case of being in the wrong place at the wrong time. His mother had told Gray at the funeral that she'd asked him to go to the store so she could make him French toast the next morning. As far as she was concerned, no one was to blame more than her and there wasn't a soul who could convince her otherwise. They cried in each other's arms until his chest ached.

The shooter was never caught. Wiggy's mother overdosed on sleeping pills a month later.

Gray's passing interest in criminology, an elective he took in his senior year, kicked into overdrive and he submitted his application a week after her funeral. A typical high school kid previously with little direction, he knew then exactly what he wanted to do for the rest of his life—catch bastards like that gunman and save lives, not just potential victims, but the ones they left behind in tatters.

His mother didn't see his vision, though his father was proud as hell of his decision. She slept little during his time at the academy, waiting to get the news that he would be sent to one of the many war zones in the five boroughs.

Getting the gig out by the hoity-toity Hamptons helped to ease her fears, but like the great mother she was, she still worried every day.

"Hi, Ma, nice to talk to you," he said, smiling, absent-mindedly brushing his fingers over his scar.

"I saw what happened on the news. Please tell me you weren't involved."

"You're talking to the first man on the scene. Well, aside from the anonymous tipster who called it in." He heard her partially cover the phone, then her muffled voice called out, "John, he said he was there. I told you."

"I'm fine. There's nothing to worry about. It was just a couple of bodies. I didn't stumble into Hannibal Lecter. Whoever or whatever did it was long gone."

"You sure you're all right, Gray? Seeing a couple of dead people must have been awful."

There was no way he was going to tell her just how awful.

"It's part of the job. Remember last year when I told you I had to break into that house where the owner had died a week earlier?"

She gasped. "That's right, you did."

"So this wasn't my first rodeo. And the smell was much better, seeing as it was out in the open on the beach. There's nothing to worry about." Truth be told, the smell wasn't better but it was much different than the fruiting old man who had melded with his couch.

"Does anyone have an idea who did it?"

"No, not yet." More like *what* did it, he thought.

"I want you to call me when your shift is over."

"I will, Ma."

"Promise?"

"I swear on Dad's Civil War collection."

They both laughed.

"You be careful. Knowing you, you'll throw yourself right in the middle of things. You're not invincible, kiddo."

"I'm not?"

"Don't be cute."

"I'm always careful. I'll call you tomorrow when I get off my shift."

Dalton placed his cell phone on the kitchen counter and spied the map he'd left on the table. He fumbled through his junk drawer, extracting a pair of scissors. Sitting down, he cut the Post-it notes in half so the strips resembled little flags.

He turned his iPod on with a remote. It sat charging in its docking station on the living room side table. He had to scroll through several dozen playlists until he found some music to concentrate by. A live club performance by Sam Cooke played softly in the background. No one his age even knew who Sam Cooke was. Dalton was a sucker for soul music. He got that from his father.

Studying the map, he thought about the time he'd taken his niece out to lunch when his sister was visiting. She was eight and grabbed every brochure and map that was on display in the front of the diner. When she opened the map, she pointed at the drawing of the eastern end of Long Island and said, giggling, "It looks like a chicken finger!"

He'd thought of Long Island as a chicken finger ever since. Montauk itself was the last stop before the Atlantic Ocean. It boasted everyone from the rich and famous to the poor and nameless. Sprawling mansions could be found less than a mile from fishermen's shacks. There were a good number of artists out this way, and more mom-and-pop motels than you could count.

When he first patrolled Montauk, he was shocked by how relatively small it was. He'd thought of it as this sprawling vacation mecca. It was actually pretty narrow, surrounded on one side by the ocean and the other by the Long Island Sound. The waves crashed and convulsed on the ocean side, where they lapped feebly along the beaches of the sound. It was like living between two worlds separated by a slender spit of land. Whatever was out there didn't have many places to hide.

Flipping open his pocket notebook, he checked the time that the murder scene was called in, wrote it down on the half Post-it and stuck it to the beach at Shadmoor State Park.

12:37 A.M.: 2 bodies on beach

Aside from the two animal disturbance calls he'd followed up on, there were two other reports that no one had the time to get to. He'd written them down as they came in, just in case.

He scribbled the time and incident for each and tacked them on to each street.

1:25 A.M.: *Wild dog chased cat on roof*
1:48 A.M.: *Animals knocked over 5 garbage pails*
2:31 A.M.: *Garbage knocked over, man approached by 2 large dogs*
3:18 A.M.: *Animal tried to paw through screen window, ran away*

Dalton looked at the pastel flags and exhaled. "I'll be damned."

All of the calls last night had happened on the southeast end of the island. It looked like everyone in the area was either a light sleeper, or something (or things) was on the prowl with no concern about keeping a low profile.

The timeline followed a very specific path. Whatever had torn into that couple on the beach had then made its way slightly north and west from the beach while keeping to a relatively tight cluster of houses.

The last two calls bothered him the most. Animals went through garbage, chased cats and fought all the time. Whatever was out there wasn't afraid of people and wanted in. Even more disconcerting was the possibility that there was more than one.

Were they working together? How would that even be possible?

He folded the map and put on some sweats and a PAL T-shirt. Maybe a jog would help him think. He grabbed his iPod, headphones and keys. The moment he closed the door, he turned around and went back inside. He found the small can of pepper spray he'd stuffed in his dresser drawer.

If some fearless, man-eating animal was lurking around, he wasn't about to run around defenseless.

* * *

Can Man rooted through the garbage outside Nicky's Cafe. A family of tourists passed by, crinkling their noses at him. He paused to smile, show there was nothing to be afraid of. He was dressed in his trademark Bermuda shorts and hideous Hawaiian shirt with a fresh pair of sandals that had been given to him by Annie, the owner of the thrift shop. His hair was long but he kept it clean. It was more gray than brown, as was his beard, which ended in the center of his chest. If he hadn't been rooting through the garbage, they would have most likely thought he was just another old hippie.

The wife looked at him with a flash of pity before taking her husband's hand and disappearing around the block.

Probably going back to get in their bathing suits to spend what was left of the day at the beach. This time of year, Montauk's endless motels, both large and small, were packed to the gills with summer folk. The town was happy to take their money, offering beautiful beaches, whale-watching tours, fishing and golfing. For Can Man, whose real name was Paul Landon in a time and place too far removed to recall, Montauk in the summer meant sleeping under the stars with the rolling of the surf to lull him into dreamland. During the cold months, he spent his time on the streets in Queens.

But every year, when summer came around, he cleaned himself up at a shelter, scrounged up enough money to take the Hampton Jitney bus out to the end of the island and became a kind of tourist himself. He couldn't think of a better place to be homeless in the summer. At least not somewhere that was a short and cheap bus ride away.

Collecting cans was his game. It kept him fed. Most locals and even some of the businesses intentionally left empty cans and bottles within reach when they saw him. He wasn't crazy or an alcoholic or drug addict. He'd simply fallen on hard times many moons ago and decided he preferred living free to going back to an office and a family, complete with stress, deadlines, bills to pay and expectations that could never be met.

A pair of teenage boys rode by on their bikes. "Hey, Can Man!" one of them shouted, waving. He waved back, smiling. The boy who hadn't greeted him made a half turn, putting on the brakes just in front of him.

He reached into the big pocket of his shorts and pulled out an empty cola can. "Here you go," the boy said.

"Thank you," Can Man said. "You boys do anything fun today?"

Both had crew cut hair and white sleeveless shirts. They could have been twins. It was the official summer look of most boys their age.

"Nah, just rode around a lot. My game system broke and my father said I had to get some sun and air."

"Your father's a smart man. You play those video games too much and you'll get cross-eyed and fat. It'll get dark soon, so don't ride too far from home." Can Man didn't want to tell them about the bodies that had been found at the beach the night before. It was the hushed talk of all the adults today. The locals were on edge, the tourists were intrigued. He hoped the boys were still young enough to avoid the news and live in their own special and fleeting world.

The boys turned around, pointing toward the eastern end of Main Street. "We won't."

He watched them go, envying their youth. Hefting the plastic bag with its dozen or so cans, he whistled an intricate tune as he walked toward the beach.

Dalton started his shift at exactly midnight. He'd arrived at the station earlier than usual to see if there had been any progress made with yesterday's grisly discovery.

"Nada," Meredith Hernandez said from her desk. In her early thirties, Meredith had become a permanent desk jockey the night her squad car had been steamrolled by a stolen garbage truck. A couple of out-of-towners had gotten stinking drunk and thought it would be fun to nick a truck and take it out for a boisterous joyride. They never even hit the brakes when they rammed her patrol car. Three back surgeries later, she still found it hard to walk. She used a cane with a forearm cuff to get around.

"How about animal disturbance calls. Any come in yet?"

She wrinkled her nose. "What the heck does one have to do with the other?"

He pursed his lips. "Probably nothing. I spent last night looking at body parts and following up on stray-dog crap. I'm hoping for a little more variety tonight."

"How about no variety and no problems?" She stapled a stack of papers with a hard smack.

"That I wouldn't mind, either. What are you even doing here this late?"

She sat back against the large cushion strapped to her chair. "It's either this or stare at the walls in my house."

"You need to get out more," he joked.

Meredith narrowed her eyes and grinned. "Oh yeah, and do what?"

Dalton shrugged his shoulders. "I don't know. Go out to a nice dinner, maybe catch a movie."

"Women just love eating and going to movies alone. No, thank you."

"Did I say 'alone'?" He sat on the edge of her desk and leaned in to her. "I'd be more than happy to share a nice steak and see some chick flick."

Meredith blushed. She was so pretty—medium height, olive skin and long dark hair, with gray-green eyes that had the ability to hypnotize him if she so desired. Guys couldn't get past the cane or the way she walked, as if they were models of perfection. Dalton could care less. If he had to be honest, there was something about her slight disability that made him like her even more. Maybe it was the compulsion to protect everyone he met that made him want to wrap her in his arms.

"That's very sweet of you, but you're young enough to be my little brother. In fact, even he's older than you."

"Shouldn't charm make up for any difference in age?"

She locked gazes with him and sighed. "You're just going to keep on trying until I crack, aren't you?"

He got up and squared his hat on his head. "That's for me to know, and you to find out." She tapped him in the back of his leg with her cane.

"Be careful tonight, all right?" she called out.

He left the station with a growing tension in his stomach. Why was everyone telling him that? It was like a football game where the announcer says so-and-so has never missed a field goal under thirty yards. A nanosecond after the words are spoken, the ball will inevitably clang off the post, caroming to the sideline. Dalton walked over to the wood picnic table out back by the squad cars and gave it a hard knock, just in case.

Doc 452-1002
NATIONAL SECURITY AGENCY—Listening Station Omega 19/47
RE: Call Intercepts—Montauk, NY

In light of your request to focus efforts on eastern Long Island re: PI, following transcripts provided that may be of concern. Suspicious level of activity in tandem with communication loss with PI and unidentifiable double homicide. Will continue close monitoring and provide up-to-minute details as they arrive.

CHAPTER 8

Insomnia was nothing new for Margie Salvatore. She hadn't slept a whole night through since she'd given birth to Michael, and that was over thirty-five years ago. She'd fallen asleep on the love seat around nine, woke up at eleven and now wasn't the least bit tired.

"You want me to watch something with you?" her husband, Les, asked.

"You go to bed. You've got work tomorrow. I'll watch Letterman for a little bit. There's a Claudette Colbert movie on TCM at midnight. I'll come to bed when it's over."

"Why don't you take one of those pills the doctor gave you?"

"Because they make me feel groggy the next day."

"Aren't they the ones that aren't supposed to do that?" He gathered their empty glasses from the coffee table and put them in the sink.

"You know me and meds. I'm fine. Don't be jealous that I get to watch more movies than you. I have a little viewing party every night."

Les bent down to kiss the top of her head. "I married a nut job."

Margie laughed. "I was fine until I said 'I do.'"

He wagged a finger at her. "They do say old people need less sleep."

She whacked him with a pillow. "Then you should only need a catnap, old-timer. I'll see you in the morning."

Les trundled up the creaky stairs. Margie clicked between Letterman and Jimmy Kimmel. Both monologues were terrible tonight. At midnight, she flipped ahead to catch the start of *The Egg and I.* Claudette Colbert's husband decides to move his new bride to a run-down chicken farm with neighbors Ma and Pa Kettle. "*Green Acres* before Eva Gabor," Margie muttered, laughing as Colbert, a big-city woman, struggled with country life.

Midway through the movie, she was more awake than ever.

"Time for a smoke," she said to Irene, her white, orange, and black calico cat. Irene liked to lie along the top of the love seat and sleep twenty-two hours a day. It was an enviable life.

Margie plucked a pack of Kools and a lighter from the kitchen table and went out the kitchen door. Their house had central cooling, and it felt good to get some fresh air, even if it was slightly warmer and about to be laced with cigarette smoke.

The first cigarette disappeared like it was a prop in a magic act. She lit another with the dying stub of the first and took a long drag. Insomnia and chain-smoking weren't ingredients for a long, healthy life, but they were her crosses to bear. On nights like this, three or four coffin nails put her in the frame of mind to get a few more hours' sleep.

A blazing white moon hung large and heavy in the sky. The soft, steady night wind carried the smell of mint from the patch she'd planted in the back of the yard.

"I have to make mojitos tomorrow when Les comes home," she said, tapping her ashes into the dented tray they got from a long-ago trip to the Catskills. It was sad knowing the ashtray outlived the resort.

She walked around the yard, enjoying the quiet of the night, eventually finding herself in the front yard. Every house along both sides of the street was dark. More than one of her neighbors had told her they slept better knowing she had an eye on the block. Her inability to sleep made her the unofficial neighborhood watch. In no small way, it made her embrace her condition. Everything happened for a reason.

Margie jumped when something crashed in the backyard. Flicking her cigarette into the street, she dashed along the side of the house. She pulled up short when she entered the yard.

"What the—"

Her patio table was turned over on its side. The folded umbrella had snapped in half from the fall.

It would have taken a hell of a breeze to knock that over. She sighed with relief when she got close enough to see that the glass top hadn't cracked. Les would have a fit when she told him they needed to buy a new umbrella.

She thought about waking him up to help her right the table. It was lighter than she thought and she was able to do it on her own.

"Unbelievable," she said, inspecting the break in the umbrella stand.

Snap!

Margie whipped her head around to see what had made the noise. It had come from the impenetrably dark strip under their dogwood tree.

Stupid kids, she thought. Late-night pool hopping was common in July, and her yard was part of the route between the aboveground pools to the left and right of her house.

"You're going to pay for a new umbrella," she called out. "I know you're there. Swimming's over for tonight."

Something moved in the dark. There was no muffled teen laughter. She felt whoever was under the dogwood tree was watching her, waiting to see what she would do next.

Margie's chest turned to ice.

She stood motionless, her hands atop the table. Try as she might, she couldn't see a thing back there.

Scritch!

It was the sound of something sharp dragging across the bark of the tree.

There was more movement than ever now; the sound of shuffling feet amidst her rhododendrons.

She slowly reached into her pocket. Running her thumb over the wheel of her lighter, Margie hoped the flame would discourage any strange, stray animals from getting any closer.

Whatever was in her yard brought a palpable weight of menace.

The night breeze shifted, blowing from the dogwood's direction. A sharp, terrible odor bit into her. She recoiled, and the light went out.

A large paw emerged from the shadows, followed by another.

Margie's heart thudded into overdrive when its hideous face emerged.

And it was not happy.

Dalton pulled his car around the plaza in Montauk, the grassy roundabout that was home to the town gazebo. The wooden structure, with its peeling chestnut paint and an interior roof that was a favorite nesting spot for every bird in the county, was a meeting point for families, lovers young and old, and tourists. He'd been told to spend the entire night patrolling the streets there, rather than dividing his time with Amagansett and East Hampton. Another county car was parked in line with the gazebo. Mickey Conrad rolled down his window and waved him over. Their cars idled side by side.

"Pulling a double?" Dalton asked.

"My wife wants a new deck. I have to pay for it somehow."

Main Street was empty. The rope used to hoist the enormous American flag atop the forty-foot flagpole tapped hollowly against the pole. The bank, Irish tavern and small shops that circled the plaza were dark and quiet.

Mickey said, "Hey, did you hear what happened to the bodies?"

Dalton shook his head.

"The ME nearly had a stroke," Mickey said, rolling his eyes. "All of those parts he and his team collected had turned to liquid by the afternoon. They don't even have frigging teeth to help identify them. He sent out what was left to see what kind of acid was used on them. You're either smart or lucky for not getting too close last night."

"Lucky is more like it." Dalton offered up a silent prayer that the weird odor he'd breathed in wasn't going to haunt him later on. "Everything been quiet so far?"

Mickey waved a hand around the plaza. "What you see here is what you've got. Last night was enough excitement for ten years, at least. You plan on rescuing any more cats?"

Obviously word had gotten around the station. He wondered if the old lady had called Campos. Now that Mickey knew, he would milk it for every drop. Mickey had razzed Dalton from the moment he'd joined the force. It wasn't hazing. He knew Dalton could take it, and dish it right back.

"If you start showing your face around during my shift, there'll be more than cats running onto rooftops," Dalton said.

"We can't all be pretty boys. Since you're here to stay, I'm going to take a quick ride into Amagansett and circle back in an hour. Try not to stir things up while I'm gone."

Dalton gave him a half salute and watched him pull away.

One of the things he had to do was check in at the beach and make sure no wackos had entered the park to see where the top-trending murder had taken place. He could count on one hand the number of locals that would do such a thing, but with so many tourists in town, you never knew who was skulking about. What the hell was people's obsession with death and dismemberment?

Turning into Shadmoor State Park and entering under the canopy of trees that lined the gravel drive, he rolled down his window and cut the engine. Before he cruised all the way down to the beach, he listened for voices or movement. Since the car was at the top of an incline, his plan was to glide down in neutral and hit the lights and siren the second he pulled up behind any nocturnal sightseers. That momentary look of shock and unabashed terror, especially if they were teens out for an illegal party, was one of the perks of the job.

The only sound that came into the window was the chittering of cattails swaying in the breeze and the relentless crash of the surf below.

"No fun for you," he said, turning the ignition and pulling behind the dunes. The abandoned Chevy had been towed to impound some time in the afternoon.

He got out and saw the yellow crime scene tape that had been wrapped around upturned metal trash bins, forming a ring around last night's horror. The ME had even shoveled all of the sand that had been stained with blood into big, black bags. If it weren't for the tape, anyone walking by wouldn't even know two people had been brutally torn apart just twenty-four hours ago.

Standing with his hands on his hips, he took a deep breath. It was a humid night. Looking up, he saw a scattering of tattered dark clouds obliterating swaths of star fields, swirling together like silver glitter on his niece's little art table.

Might as well take a walk around while I'm here.

He grabbed his Maglite from his belt and swept the beam from left to right, giving the area the once-over. This whole section of the beach had been closed off all day, but you'd never know it by the mass of footprints in the sand that hadn't been washed clean by the rising tide. Every official and their second kissing cousin had been here. It was going to take a long while for things to settle down. Sure, the news would move on to the next disaster du jour, but for the folks who lived here, there would be little rest until they confirmed who the victims were and who or what killed them.

If that car belonged to Randy Jenks, who had been his unlucky passenger and where had they come from? So far, they'd kept Randy's name out of the press, quietly following up to locate him for questioning. It was looking more and more like he was the male victim.

The sound of movement in the reeds to his left startled him. He spun the flashlight's beam into the five-foot-high crop of beach grass. Their tops wavered back and forth. Was it the wind, or was there something behind them?

Squinting, he peered within the gaps of the beach overgrowth, the arcing light giving life to sweeping shadows. His arm jerked to the right when something shifted, then stopped.

I'm not fucking around. Not here.

With his free hand, he unclipped his holster and lifted his gun.

"This is the police. I need you to come out of there right now with your hands up as high as they'll go."

A soft gurgling sound gave a solemn reply.

Dalton felt the first trembling jolt of adrenaline push through his system. He took a deep breath and steadied his gun hand. Part of his training was learning to work with your body's responses to potential danger. The fight-or-flight instinct was a nasty SOB of a primal urge to wrangle. The good cops learned to master it, make it their bitch.

He may not have been on the force long, but he knew he was a good cop.

"I don't like to repeat myself. I said to get the hell out of there now, where I can see you, hands high. Now!"

The reeds trembled.

"Ggggnnnnccchhhh."

Looks like I'm going in.

Dalton took a step. The sand shifted and his right ankle nearly rolled from under him.

"Last chance to come out before I start taking this personal. You're not going to like the way I drag you out."

Two more steps.

The reeds became still. The strange yet familiar noise had stopped.

Someone was there.

Or was it some*thing*?

The tip of his freshly shined shoe touched the edge of the reed patch. Using the barrel of his gun, he pushed the tall stalks aside.

CHAPTER 9

Margie's lungs felt like they'd been crushed between two trucks. The thrumming of her pulse was so deafening, she could hear nothing but her own frantic heartbeat.

One, two, three animals, creatures so foreign to her it appeared as if they'd been dropped from an unseen, hovering alien craft, slinked from the shadows. They stepped in tandem, their heavily muscled backs undulating with each movement of their massive paws.

The more they emerged from the shadows under the tree, the more Margie knew for certain they were not stray dogs or wandering deer. Mottled fur and heavy, impossible faces were brought into crisp detail under the incandescence of the moon.

Her stomach tightened. She opened her mouth to scream but nothing, not even a stuttering exhalation, would come.

Noiselessly, the creatures continued their wary advance.

An acrid redolence, so strong her eyes began to tear, bullied the fresh air like a canister of tear gas set free.

Les, help me! She pleaded mutely, praying her husband would wake to go to the bathroom and give a curious look to see if she was taking her nightly smoke break.

Margie felt a patch of liquid warmth blossom on her crotch, snaking down her legs.

What the hell are they?

All three were roughly the same size—huge. When she was a kid, Margie had a Dalmatian. It was the biggest dog in the neighborhood. Her father was a tall man, and Dizzy, their amiable, gentle and exceedingly patient dog, stood about waist-high next to him. But where Dizzy was a wonderfully built pure breed, these things were a confusing mix of not only other dogs, but other *species*.

The fur on each was a different color. One a mix of black and gray, the other brown and the last one on the right a patchwork of colors. Clumps of hair were missing on each, revealing scraps of raw flesh that, to her dread, appeared to be varying shades of blue, as if they were oxygen deprived. Other than birds and fish, she couldn't think of any mammal that had blue skin.

Maybe something was wrong with them, like whatever made their hair fall out also damaged their skin underneath.

But it was their faces that froze her to the spot.

They weren't long like a dog's, but blunt, with oversized, black eyes and snouts that tapered down to a sharp point. She could have sworn they had beaks underneath the coarse fur that covered their heads. Their lower jaws were markedly smaller than their upper, each possessing an overbite that looked like it would make it very difficult for them to chew.

And yet there was something disturbingly piglike about them, or maybe more like a wild boar. In fact, one of them had the makings of a tusk protruding from the side of its mouth.

In all, they were a nightmare made real, the monster lurking under your bed or the beast waiting in your closet for you to fall asleep.

As they came closer, she heard their labored breathing, rattling with phlegm-filled lungs.

Margie's own lungs unlocked, and were now pulsating as she began to hyperventilate.

Run, dammit, run!

The one with the brown hair opened its mouth wide. The sound of its jaw popping echoed in the yard. A sharp-tipped tongue slithered over rows of small, jagged teeth.

The stench that wafted from its open maw, a vile gas originating from what could only be a diseased digestive system, slammed her like smelling salts, even from ten feet away.

Her husband's name erupted from her lips. "Les!"

The creatures reacted not by pulling back, but coiling their hind legs to sprint toward her, their eyes wet with hunger.

Margie gripped the edge of the patio table and pushed it over, attempting to create a barrier between her and the embodiments of her worst nightmares.

The moment the table left her fingertips, she spun, running for the back door. She flinched at the sound of breaking glass. As she gripped the latch to her screen door, she turned to gauge her chances of making it inside before they got to her.

The black and gray beast had barreled straight through the tabletop. Shards of glass poked out of its hide and razor-like muzzle. The other two had either gone around or leapt over the upturned table.

At best, they were two steps away.

She yanked the outer door wide, giving the knob of the inner door a hard twist.

As it opened, fire erupted on her calf. Margie looked down in shock. The brown one had clamped down on her lower leg. One of them hit into the side of the screen door, warping the metal pane on the bottom. The other fought to get past the one biting her so it, too, could have a piece of her.

Margie's cry shattered the silence in the house. She heard Les's footsteps running down the stairs. Half in and half out, she shook her leg to free it from the monster's bite. Something tore. Her stomach lurched as she watched her blood paint the door.

Fumbling along the kitchen counter, her quivering fingers happened upon the handle of her metal meat tenderizer. She'd left it on a dish towel to dry after doing the dishes. Six hours ago, she'd used it to pound out her chicken cutlets.

Now, she brought it down as hard as she could on the side of the creature's head, catching part of its eye in the process. It struck with a loud crack as well as a sickening squish as the tip of the tenderizer plowed through its black eye.

It released her, backing into the other one that was eager to get at her leg.

Margie fell backward as Les turned into the kitchen. Sobbing, shouting and mumbling incoherently, she had the presence of mind to use her good leg to kick the door shut. One of the beasts thumped heavily into the door.

Les's bare feet skidded along the smear of her blood. He put his hand on the door handle.

"No, don't open it!" Margie screamed. "Lock it! Lock it!"

Les saw her leg and the look of unadulterated terror on her face, dropped to his knees and pulled her into his arms. She dug her nails into his back and buried her face in his chest, the fear and pain reducing her to uncontrolled, heaving sobs.

A lone seagull buzzed overhead. Its undulating cry masked the crunching sound of the dry reeds as Dalton stepped farther in. The beam of his flashlight bobbed up and down, side to side in a controlled attempt to avoid any surprises.

"Guuuunnngghh."

There it was again!

It was just off to his right. If his ears weren't playing tricks on him, it sounded like it was coming from somewhere low to the ground.

He took a deep breath, pointed the flashlight down and swept the reeds aside with one quick motion.

Something skittered in the dark, rolling away from the light and deeper into the reeds.

"Stop!" Dalton barked.

A pair of eyes peered at him. Dalton couldn't make out the face.

"Please don't shoot," a shaky voice said.

Dalton exhaled. He knew that voice.

"Can Man, get the hell up," he said, slipping his gun back in his holster.

"Is that you, Officer Dalton?" the older man said, pushing himself to his feet.

Can Man emerged from what he thought was the safety of the reeds, his hands held high. Dalton knew that their annual summer eccentric often slept on the beach. Normally, he'd assume it was Can Man snoring up a storm, but after last night, his instincts were off-kilter.

"You can put your hands down," Dalton said. "You're not in any trouble. It's my fault for coming in all commando." Can Man held a hand over his chest and smiled. Dalton asked, "You all right?"

"Just a galloping heart. It's good for the blood flow."

Dalton put a hand on his elbow and helped him out of the reeds. A particularly large wave slammed into the beach. Flecks of the distant spray carried on the wind pelted their faces.

"I'm sorry for waking you up, Can Man. But maybe you

should reconsider sleeping on the beach for a while. You heard about what happened?"

"No way not to know."

Of course he did. For an itinerant homeless man, he was plugged right into the heart of Montauk. The locals had a soft spot for him. He'd seen plenty take the time to shoot the breeze while he went about his daily routine.

"Any chance you were camping around here last night?"

Can Man shook his head. "I was out at the other end, by Fort Bay Pond. There was a wedding over at Garbo's and they had a big party at the beach. I stuck around to watch them from a distance. It was nice. I only came out here because I figured lightning wouldn't strike twice in the same spot. Plus I knew folks like you would be on patrol."

Dalton clapped him a couple of times on the back. "You got somewhere else you can go tonight; somewhere away from the beach?"

"I always have alternates." He dusted sand from his baggy Bermuda shorts and shirt. "You have any leads?"

"Not yet, but we will. Until then, I want to make sure you stay safe. I have four shopping bags of beer cans in my house and I'm too lazy to redeem them. I need to keep you around." They chuckled, staring out at the ocean.

Something caught Can Man's attention in the rolling surf. He tapped Dalton on the upper arm and pointed. "You see that?"

Dalton squinted but saw nothing. "Tell me what you see. Maybe I'll be able to pick it out of the dark better."

"It could be some Styrofoam or a bag. It's round and light in color, hanging out before the waves break."

Dalton stepped closer to the incoming tide. He finally saw what Can Man was pointing at. He was right. It looked like one of those foam floats used all around the island—they were used to mark where nets had been cast, as lines of demarcation, you name it. Those things broke free all the time.

"I see it. Just garbage."

"Then why isn't it coming in with the waves? It looks like it's fighting the surf."

Dalton was about to tell him he was crazy when the blob darted away from them with a speed that was anything but natural. Before Dalton could react, it was gone.

"That's some pretty fast-moving garbage," Can Man said, his mouth hanging open.

Dalton was about to run along the beach to track it when his radio crackled to life. It made them both jump.

He stepped away from Can Man to take the call from dispatch.

"Are you sure it's an animal attack?" he asked.

"That's what the woman's husband said. An ambulance is en route."

"I'll be there in three minutes." He waved Can Man over. "Listen, do me a favor and hole up somewhere safe tonight, okay? If you see any stray dogs sniffing around, don't approach them."

Can Man looked worried. For all Dalton knew, he should be. But he wanted him to be aware. It could save his life.

"I will."

Dalton jumped in his car and sped away from the beach. He watched Can Man double-time it as he power walked the path away from the beach.

Kelly James wiped heavy beads of sweat from her forehead and chest. Her pajamas were soaked to her skin. She felt disgusting, but didn't have the strength to get up and put on something new and dry. Hell, she couldn't even call out for her mother at the moment.

When she realized earlier that day that there was no way

she would make her reunion date with Joey, she cried. No matter how hard she tried, she couldn't get ready. She kept throwing up into her small, pink garbage can every time she lifted her head from the pillow. She tried calling Joey but he didn't answer his cell. Same with the texts she sent.

He had a bad habit of leaving his phone in his car's console. But sooner or later, he always realized it and would check his messages. Not today. That's how she knew he was pissed. It was over.

By late afternoon, her tears over Joey had turned to sobbing for the state she was in. She was terrified to look at her foot. The pain in her ankle was excruciating. There were a couple of times she swore someone had poured acid on her. At one point, she actually passed out from the pain. That must have been when her mother checked on her, thought she was in normal sleep and left dinner on a tray as well as a note telling her that she and her father were going to the Newmans' to play cards. They'd be home late.

Somehow, when she woke up, she managed to turn on her AC and directed the cold air right at her bed. She did so without looking down at her legs. If she didn't see anything, nothing could be as wrong as it felt.

The AC was unable to quell the fire that had been building up inside her.

All thoughts of Joey were distant and inconsequential. Her tongue felt like shaved wood. Her eyes itched and burned like there was harsh soap in them.

The only thing she wanted was for the blaze to stop. Kelly was on fire. She just couldn't see the flames.

CHAPTER 10

Dalton arrived at the same time as the ambulance. It was from Southampton Hospital. He'd never met the two female EMTs before. They were met at the door by Les Salvatore. "Come in, quick! My wife is hurt real bad."

"After you," Dalton said to the serious-looking EMT. She nodded and was followed by her partner. Dalton looked over his shoulder to see quite a few lights flickering on in the surrounding houses. This would be the talk of the neighborhood tomorrow.

He wasn't prepared for the sight that greeted him when he walked into the living room. The man's wife was stretched out on the couch. One leg rested on the coffee table, the bottom half wrapped in a bloody towel. She was crying, great heaving sobs. He could hear the pain in her voice.

One of the EMTs bent close to her and asked, "What's your name?"

The woman winced and replied, "Ma-Margie."

While the one talked, the other unwrapped her leg. The wound was horrendous. Dalton could see the fallow of bone beneath the glistening maroon of torn muscle. He had to clamp down on his back molars to keep himself in check.

Turning to Les Salvatore, he said, "Tell me what happened."

Les's eyes darted between Dalton and his wife. He desperately wanted to be by her side, not talking to a cop.

"We need to let them do their job right now," Dalton assured him. "When you called 911, you said your wife was bitten by a wild animal."

Les swallowed hard, his shaking hands rubbing the back of his neck. "Yes, she said one bit her. But there were three in the yard."

"Did you see them?"

"No. I was asleep when it happened. I only came down when I heard her screaming. They—they smashed against our back door, trying to get in. The whole thing is destroyed."

The EMTs wrapped Margie's leg in gauze and took her temperature.

"I'll go take a look. Stay with your wife while they get her settled down. I'll be back."

Les hurried to the couch and grabbed his wife's hand. She looked up at him with pleading eyes.

What the hell happened? Three dogs this time. And they tried to bust down the door? He had to see it for himself.

Neighbors were gathering outside, trying to peer into the Salvatores' windows and open front door. He motioned to them to step back. "Everyone, please go back to your houses. It's a minor emergency. Give your neighbors their privacy, please." He knew his words would have no effect, but it was worth a try.

He trotted to the back of the house. A pair of lights lit up the yard.

The screen door, or what was left of it, had been torn off the top hinge. The bottom looked like an aluminum foil ball. The wood door was splintered in a dozen or more places. A sizable hole had been punched into its center.

"Fuck me sideways," Dalton muttered. Dogs couldn't do this. *Rams or bulls, maybe.* It was a miracle the door held.

A long smear of blood stained the bottom panel of the door, with more spatters on the patio itself. The table was also destroyed. Pebbled glass crunched under his shoes. If Anita thought two animals working in tandem was next to impossible, wait until she heard about this.

When Dalton returned to the living room, the EMTs had Margie Salvatore on a stretcher.

"Her fever is spiking. We may need to put some ice packs around her," one of them said to the other. Les stood close by, scared and confused.

Margie's head swiveled on the small pillow they'd placed under her. Sweat ran down her face. Her eyes were closed and starting to swell, as if she was having an allergic reaction. There was no way he was going to get a description of the animals from her right now. It would have to wait. As they left the house, a couple of Montauk PD cars arrived.

"I'll stop by the hospital later, see how you're both doing and if your wife can go through what happened," Dalton said to Les Salvatore. The man nodded nervously and followed his wife into the back of the ambulance.

Officer Norman Henderson ambled up the walkway while another cop—it was too dark to tell who it was—tried to convince everyone to go home.

"What the hell happened?" Norm asked. He chewed a great wad of gum that made his cheek bulge.

"Another animal attack. This time, it was three. You have to go in the yard and see what the hell they did to the doors. Something weird's going on here."

"None of us need to be Sherlock to come to that conclusion," he said without sarcasm.

Henderson stared at the entrance to the yard as if he was gearing himself up to look at the carnage.

He said, "Speaking of which, I think we just ID'd the couple. Winn and I talked to Hal, you know, the bartender over at the Beach Comber? He said Randy Jenks was there the other night and he left after last call with Rosie Wilson. We verified it with Richie Burnes. He said they left to get to know each other better."

"Rosie, the old barfly? Randy's like, what, thirty years younger than her?"

Henderson shrugged his large, round shoulders. "Hey, you drink enough and everyone's fair game. Randy'd had a bad breakup with his girlfriend of about five years. And you know Rosie."

Dalton stared at the Salvatore house. "Yeah, I *knew* Rosie."

"One-eleven, please respond to a 211 at 14 Marty Drive."

Dalton answered quickly, "In progress?"

"Negative."

"Looks like another busy night," Henderson said. "I'll follow you."

What now, Dalton thought as he ran to his car. It felt like the whole town was coming apart at the seams.

He couldn't shake the feeling that something far, far worse was yet to come.

When Mandy Sullivan first heard the glass break, she'd been in the bathroom patting a cold, wet washcloth to her head for the second time that night. Menopause was once again having its fun with her, refusing to let her sleep, scorching her with hot flashes and making her feel like crap. She needed sleep desperately and was contemplating calling in sick to work in the morning.

She'd just wrung the washcloth out when something crashed into the kitchen downstairs. She heard a lot of frantic movement and her chairs being scattered about. Holding in a scream, she ran into her bedroom and locked the door. Her husband, Chris, was up and rooting around the closet for his old rifle.

"What are you going to do with that thing? It's just an air rifle."

His graying hair was as wild as his eyes. The rifle was pointed at the floor. "It'll put a hurt into whoever's down there."

Somehow, she'd convinced him to stay in their room and call the police.

Whoever had been crashing about either left or hid when the two cop cars pulled up. Chris opened the bedroom window and called down, "Someone's in the kitchen. It sounded like they were trashing the place. They must have heard you coming because they're not making any noise right now."

The young county cop nodded and cautiously moved toward the house and out of his sight line. The older local cop said, "Stay right where you are. We'll call you down when everything is clear."

Chris and Mandy had been meaning to have an alarm installed. Their house, a three-story Victorian, sat in a lot all its own with no neighbors in clear sight. It was a beautiful place. They'd gotten it for a song when the housing market tanked. Mandy was always paranoid about it standing out too much and being an easy target for burglars. Chris assured her constantly that burglars were not a concern, not out here in Montauk. They left New Jersey in the rearview mirror specifically so they didn't have to worry about things like that.

And now this. Chris groaned in silence, knowing that Mandy would put the full-court press on him to move.

"You can come down now," one of the cops said from downstairs.

As they walked out of the bedroom, Mandy looked back and slapped his arm. "Would you please put that air rifle away? What do you want, to be shot by the cops by accident?"

When she saw the state of her kitchen, she had to bite her tongue to keep from screaming.

"What kind of animals would do this?" she said through gritted teeth. Chris held on to her shoulders.

The kitchen was demolished. The thieves, or better yet, vandals, had reduced her table and chairs to splinters. The refrigerator had been tipped onto its side and the entire contents were strewn about the floor. A thick sludge of liquids oozed from the tiled kitchen and onto the dining room carpet. The double window over the sink had been smashed to pieces, filling the sink with shards of glass.

"I know it's hard," the younger cop said after introducing himself, "but do you see anything that might be missing?"

Chris looked around. "How the hell can we tell? I do know what's broken."

Even the oven door had been ripped off. These vandals were thorough, if anything.

"Why us?" Mandy asked.

The cop brought a dining room chair over for Mandy to sit on. "I know it's hard to make sense of this right now. All we can do is get all the facts in order so we can catch the people who did this."

Mandy smiled, appreciating the sincerity in his face and voice. She began telling him about everything before dialing 911, when there was a knock at the back door. "Dalton, it's me."

The cop excused himself and carefully walked through the mess to open the door. The older cop stood on the top step, using his flashlight to scan the yard.

"Sir, do you have a light for the yard?" he asked.

Chris exhaled heavily. "It has a short. I actually meant to have it fixed next week." Mandy shot him an angry look, as if this were all his fault. Of course, vandals would never break in if he had a working backyard light, especially one that would be on this time of night.

"Well, whoever was here left by the same way they came in, the window. There's bits of glass out here, and I think I can see depressions in the grass." He finally looked into the kitchen and whistled. "Holy crap, they did a number on this place. You see any footprints? It's a little muddy out here."

The good-looking young cop, Gray something, looked around. "There's so much food and spilled condiments and juice, it's just one big mess." He gingerly stepped to a dry spot. "Wait, see over there? What's that?"

The cop in the doorway leaned in, holding on to the doorframe to keep from falling. "That can't be right."

Chris approached the kitchen but stopped shy of going in. "What do you see?"

"It looks like—paw prints," the young cop said. He exchanged a look of alarm with the other one.

"There's no way a dog could knock a refrigerator over," Mandy said, joining Chris at the kitchen entrance. "And look at my table. That's solid oak."

The older cop reached for his walkie-talkie. "I'm calling in for backup."

"Good idea," the younger one said. "Ask for Anita Banks if she's on call."

Mandy looked at Chris with utter bewilderment. What was happening? Why were the cops suddenly so worried?

"Mr. and Mrs. Sullivan, I just need you to go back to the dining room. I'll be with you in a minute," the young one said.

Chris was about to protest but Mandy pulled him back. "Just let them do their job," she whispered. Her head was spinning. Whether it was from the menopause or the madness that was her kitchen was up for grabs.

She held her husband's hand tight when he pulled a chair

next to hers and sat down. They watched the police as they talked to each other in hushed voices.

No one saw what was about to happen coming, least of all the cop standing on the back step.

And even if they had, there was nothing they could do to stop it.

CHAPTER 11

Henderson leaned in close to Dalton and said softly, "Kid, you may be right. I didn't want to say it in front of them, but from what I see out here, this was done by animals. Just how many I can't tell. There are too many tracks and they go all over the place. I've done enough hunting in my life to know the difference between human and animal prints. The part that worries me is that only a bear could wreck a room like that. I'll swear on my mother's grave that when we get some light back here, we won't find a single bear track. These prints are big, but they're not bear."

Dalton unconsciously balled his fists, clenching them. He hoped to hell that Anita could make it out here now, before things cooled off. Maybe she could tell them what they were dealing with and where the animals were headed. Judging by their strength, he wasn't sure her tranquilizer gun would be the way to go. This might be the night he used the shotgun in his car.

"I don't like the idea of a bunch of animals not being afraid of breaking into houses," Dalton said. "I mean, who the hell ever heard of such a thing?"

Henderson shook his head. "I'll be damned if I know. It's like one of those stories where the circus train crashes in the night and the animals descend on the town. Except there's no circus, no train and we have no idea what's out there."

They turned to look into the dark, empty yard. A bat chirped overhead, disappearing behind the stand of pine trees that lined the back of the lot.

When Dalton turned to talk to the Sullivans, a soft, galloping sound caught his attention.

Something was coming.

"Henderson, I think you should—"

It happened too fast for his eyes and brain to register. One second, Henderson was standing in the doorway, his feet planted on the top step. The next, a gray blur darted from Henderson's left, barreling into the man. He let out a heavy grunt.

And then he was gone.

Dalton paused for a moment, a temporary paralysis that turned his muscles and joints to hardened cement. Shaking it off, he ran into the yard, heedless of his training and the mantra to always use caution.

The yard was empty.

An L-shaped depressed trail in the grass, about the width of a man, snaked away from the house, leading into the pine trees.

He turned to Mandy and Chris Sullivan, who stood holding each other. "Lock this door! Other units are on their way. Tell them I'm in pursuit of whatever took Officer Henderson."

Both nodded rapidly, neither able to verbalize a coherent reply.

Dalton slammed the door shut and turned his flashlight on. He spoke into the walkie clipped to his shoulder.

"Dispatch, this is one-eleven. I have a downed Montauk PD officer, Norman Henderson. In pursuit."

He started running.

"One-eleven, are you requesting an ambulance?"

"Yes. I don't know! Something took him! Send everyone you have out here, now!"

He pumped his legs as fast as they could go, his shoulder slamming into the bark of a tree as he slipped under the thick awning of full, lush limbs. The darkness here was absolute, swallowing the meager illumination from his flashlight. Scanning the ground, he saw the wide track continue through browned pine needles. It weaved around trees while maintaining a direct course deeper into the woods. If he remembered right, the trees would soon peter out, leading to Ditch Plains Beach.

Which was adjacent to the beach at Shadmoor State Park.

"Henderson! Norm!"

His lungs burned as he ran, calling out for the man who had always been his favorite on the Montauk PD. It was Henderson who took the time to show him every nook and cranny of the town when he first arrived, a cherry red recruit who had never gone farther than Jones Beach and thought Montauk was in another world, which, in a way, it was. He and his wife had had him at their house for a couple of barbecues, where there had been as much laughter as food.

He'd be damned if he gave up on him.

He broke through the trees, coming upon an open field of tall grass and ragweed. Again, following the trail was made simple by the indentation in the vegetation. And there was something else: a strange odor that burned his nose. Back under the trees, the strong scent of pine must have kept the heady stink at bay. Now, it smelled like he was running behind an open garbage truck in August.

"I'm coming, Norm!"

Dashing into the sometimes chest-high ragweed, he lost the trail a couple of times but was able to quickly regain his bearings. He stopped for a moment to listen between his ragged breaths. He had to be close behind. Any sound would at least confirm that.

All he heard was a series of waves breaking on the nearby beach.

"Shit."

He resumed his pursuit, using his hands to block the brittle stalks of ragweed from his face.

The trail and ragweed ended at a small rise overlooking the beach.

Looking down, his stomach clenched.

A wide swath ran in an almost straight line through the sand. It stopped at the surf line.

Dalton leapt down the hill, the soft sand suctioning his feet, trying to hold him back. He ran into the ocean up to his thighs, calling Henderson's name until his throat hurt. He looked up and down the beach, but could find no reentry point back onto the beach.

The big man, and whatever had taken him, was gone.

Jason Kwap took another hit from his favorite bong, the one shaped like a naked Jenna Jameson. He'd found it in a head/porn shop down in Florida. He'd just finished his second year at the Art Institute of Jacksonville and was enjoying his reunion with his best pal since grade school, Tom Morton. They had big plans. While Jason honed his art skills, Tom stayed closer to home, getting a degree in English at NYU with heavy doses of every writing program they had.

When they graduated, they planned to collaborate on graphic novels and children's books. Diversity was a good thing. The key was that they worked together and got rich and famous together. Somehow, they were going to be the next Stan Lee and Jack Kirby, or Shel Silverstein and, well, Shel Silverstein.

"Pass me the remote, Jay," Tom said, leaning as far into the couch as he could.

"No. You're not changing the channel."

"Dude, I am not going to get baked to a cooking show."

Jay passed him the bong. "Are you kidding me? Look at the tits on Giada. And you know she wants the world to see them. Why else would she wear shirts cut down like that?" Then he said in an awful Italian accent, "Now those are-a nice cannolis!"

Tom coughed out a thick lungful of weed smoke. They both laughed, staring at the wide-screen TV. After a minute or so, Tom said, "You're right, man. Her rack is crazy."

Jason backhanded him on the upper arm. "I told you. People think I don't appreciate the classics." On the screen, Giada rolled out some phyllo dough to make little spinach pastries. The camera panned down to the flour board, giving them a glance at her cleavage as she worked the dough.

"Speaking of racks," Tom said, taking a long pull from his beer, "you talk to Trish about the party?"

Jason sat in a haze of smoke. He frowned. "I don't think she's gonna come."

"Why not?"

"I think she's still pissed about my breaking up with her on the limo ride to the prom." He ran his fingers through the tight curls of his hair.

"It's been two years."

"I know. Then again, that's what I do. I break hearts. The city of Jacksonville has been filled with tears ever since I left."

Tom grunted. "The town of Montauk has been crying ever since you came back. So, no Trish. Well, I asked Annie and she's good to go, *and* she's bringing her three hot cousins visiting from North or South Carolina, like there's any difference. Counting everyone else, I think we'll have like twenty people."

They gave each other a hard fist bump. Jason said, "Sweet. It'll be nice to get everyone together again. I'm picking up the keg tomorrow afternoon. You need to get like a dozen bags of ice."

"Got it covered."

Giada went to commercial and they were about to see if anything good was on Skinemax when something thumped against the sliding glass doors.

"What the hell was that?" Tom asked, staring at the darkness past the glass with wide, watery eyes.

Jason made a motion to get off the couch, then eased back down. "If that was Tim playing around, I'm going to run out there and kick his ass."

They jumped when the glass rattled again. This time, Jason did get up, clutching the Jenna Jameson bong. "How much will you give me if I make Tim drink the bong water?"

Tom waved him off. "Tim will make you clean up what he pukes with your tongue. He's a fucking gorilla."

Jason looked at the door, then at the bong, hefting it.

"Just tell him to cut the crap and come in."

"You're such a pacifist," Jason said.

"I'm a rationalist. Now open the door and tell him to get his fat ass in here."

Jason walked with bare feet across the cold tile. It was so dark outside. Tim could be hiding anywhere. *So help me, if he tries to jump me, I'm introducing Jenna to his head*, Jason thought as he slid the door open.

Cool, fresh air washed over him.

"All right, asshole, you can come inside. We'll share. Hurry up. Giada's coming back on."

Tim didn't reply. It was as quiet as an empty funeral

parlor, which was weird. Normally, this time of night in the summer, the chirping of crickets was deafening.

"Tim! Come on, man. I haven't got all night."

He heard the bumper music for Giada's show. "All right, funny guy, enjoy sitting in the yard."

As he went to grab the door's latch, something leapt out from the bushes. The shrill scritch of nails scraping against the new brick patio beat a frantic pace. He saw a large shadow loping toward him.

Jason tensed.

That isn't Tim.

Before it could get too close, Jason did the first thing his instincts told him to do. He swept his arm back and threw the bong as hard as he could at the approaching shadow. He flinched when he heard a wet smack as the bong hit home.

Something yelped, high and agitated.

Jason jumped back into the house, slamming the door shut. He watched the shadow retreat, hopping over the seven-foot wooden fence into his neighbor's yard.

Tom was still on the couch, mesmerized. "What just happened?" he asked, never taking his eyes from the TV.

Jason pressed his thumbs into his eyes and shook his head. "I have no frigging idea. All I do know is that I just busted Jenna."

CHAPTER 12

Anita Banks had driven to the Sullivans' house in a daze. She'd had a hard time falling asleep after a night of too much coffee and catching up on bills. The moment she felt herself drifting off, her phone rang, asking her to come to the scene of a break-in.

It hadn't made sense at the time.

Now, standing in the ransacked kitchen, she understood why Gray Dalton had requested her. And she was wide awake.

This definitely was not the work of vandals of the bipedal sort. Just looking at the scratches and bite marks in the wood, the smeared prints on the floor, and tufts of fur told her that. Between here and the yard, there was a mélange of paw prints and something else that made everything even more bizarre. In some places, there were cloven hoofprints, like a large, wild boar.

It was impossible. Well, one of many impossibilities.

The paw prints looked too big to belong to any domesticated dog she knew of, and there were slight deformities to the overall structure. Judging by the nicks and gouges in the floor and appliances, these animals had immense and powerful claws. The destruction was on a scale akin to a much larger creature.

The stink of milk mixing with soy sauce and pickle brine made Anita cringe. She looked over at Dalton, who was being questioned by his sergeant as well as most of the Montauk PD, all of them having been rousted from their sleep, just like her. There wasn't a soul in the house without heavy bags under their eyes.

When she'd heard that Officer Henderson had been dragged off by a large animal, taken right into the ocean only to disappear completely, her stomach dropped.

She stepped gingerly out of the kitchen, glancing at the nervous couple on the couch. Neither had uttered a word since she'd arrived. She'd ask one of the paramedics to check them for shock.

Anita closed her eyes, trying to picture the type of animal that could have done this. She mumbled to herself while she flipped through an assortment of images. "No, not a bear or big cat. Paw structure is way off for that. Dogs? Maybe, but what breed? Some unknown mix, like a wolf-dog? They can get pretty big. But they can't tear off oven doors or snap thick furniture in half. Those hoofprints just can't be. Bovines and canines wouldn't work together. Think, Anita, think."

Dalton's light touch on her shoulder made her jump.

"Sorry," he said. He looked terrible. His hair was a mess and he'd sweat through his uniform. His eyes, they told the entire story. Whatever had happened would stay with him for a very long time. "Do you think I'm right? I mean, this has to be the work of an animal."

"It is, but I honestly can't tell you what kind. Nothing makes sense. There are things that look normal, familiar, and others that defy logic. I'm going to take plenty of hair samples as well as the broken glass from the window. There's blood on some of it. That should tell me more."

He angled her out of earshot of the Sullivans. He looked desperate, angry. No cop wanted to lose one of their own, especially before their very eyes. Dalton needed a flesh-and-blood bad guy, someone he could pursue, capture and make sure they paid. She wasn't so sure he was going to get what his every instinct desperately needed.

"Best guess, Anita. What are we dealing with?"

She reached for her ponytail and twiddled the end between her fingers. "Off the record?"

"Completely."

"Everything I see, it looks like some kind of hybrid. They may give the base appearance of dogs, but in essence, they're not. It's like someone raised generations of different breeds, selecting the largest, strongest and most violent to create the next-gen until they ended up with a monster. Think of a pit bull dosed with gamma rays."

Dalton's eyebrows went up so high, they were lost in the tangle of hair that had flopped onto his forehead. "Did you just say these are *Hulk pit bulls*?"

Anita sighed. "I said it's *like* that. Now you know why I asked if this would be off the record. If you tell this to anyone, they'll think I've lost it."

Dalton stared off into the kitchen. She knew his mind was still at the beach, still searching for Henderson. A team of police and firefighters had been sent down to look for him. It must have been hard for Dalton to not be there. "You wouldn't be the first," he said.

Man, it was a perfect night for fishing. The sound was calm, the air had cooled from the heat of the day and the moon was all he needed to see by. Dan Hudson was in fisherman's heaven.

If Jamie wanted to ride his ass about his staying out late with his pals at the Rotary Club a few nights in a row, he damn well wasn't going to sleep on the couch and beg her forgiveness in the morning. It was better to catch a bucketful of fluke and flounder and enjoy the peace and calm of the evening.

He'd explained they were all putting in extra time for the CF fund-raiser, which was mostly true. But put a room full of guys together with access to liquor long enough and things were bound to get—happy. Since he had the day off tomorrow, he hadn't felt the need to stop at three beers. By the time he'd realized he needed some time to sober up for the drive home, he was already two hours late.

Dan checked his watch. Almost three in the morning. The salty air did wonders for the early onset of his hangover, keeping his headache from splintering his skull. His Suncruiser rocked lightly. He could see the lights of the boatyard on the shore. When it came to night fishing on his relatively small bay boat, he'd learned the hard way to stick to the sound rather than the ocean. Especially when he'd had a few drinks in him.

Reaching into the Coleman cooler by his feet, he pulled out a Bud and popped the top. Hair of the dog never failed.

He was tempted to turn on the radio and try to catch that *Coast to Coast* show, the one that talked about aliens and ghosts and government conspiracies. He always got a kick out of that. It was so much more entertaining than the news or sports or another gasbag spouting his political vitriol. But, he didn't want to spook any fish, so he sat in silence, or at least the degree of silence you could get on the water as it lapped against the hull of the boat.

Dan looked in the white bucket, saw the one flat-bellied fluke he'd snagged minutes after dropping his line. It had stopped flopping.

"Did you warn your buddies after I hooked you?" he said to the still fish.

It had been over an hour without so much as a nibble.

This time of night was usually prime. It would be a couple of hours before the party fishing boats hit the water. As far as Dan could tell, it was just him and whatever swam under the dark waters of the sound.

He nearly dropped his rod when the cell phone in his vest pocket rang. A picture of a smiling Jamie popped up on the display. It didn't take a rocket scientist to know she wasn't smiling now. Dan ran his thumb over the screen, deciding whether to slide it over the *answer* or *ignore* icon.

Before he could do either, his rod jerked in his hands. He dropped the phone to prevent the rod from being dragged overboard.

"Dan, where the hell are you?"

Slowly turning the reel, he glanced at the phone on the seat next to him. He must have hit *answer*. He hadn't selected *speakerphone*, so Jamie's voice was muffled and hard to hear.

"Hold on," he said, giving the rod an upward tug.

He had a good one. As the fish fought back, he thought, *This might feed us for three days.*

"Are you on the boat? Jesus, Dan, do you know how dangerous it is to go out when you've been drinking? Have you lost your mind?"

There were many things he wanted to say. Instead, he ground his teeth and pulled in a couple more feet of line. Jamie would have to wait. He came out here to get away from her. Why the hell did she have to nag him from ship to shore?

His forearms strained against the tug of the fish. This couldn't be a flounder. They didn't put up a fight like this. Had to be a bluefish. Some of those bastards were strong and ornery.

"Dan. Answer me, Dan."

The reel clicked, slow and steady. Dan planted his foot against the side of the boat. He dipped the rod, gave the line some slack, which the fish greedily took up. He pulled, feeling the full weight of it.

"Oh, I've got you now," he hissed.

Jamie continued with her diatribe. Dan didn't pay her any mind. He just kept turning the reel, *tic-tic-tic*, despite the considerable weight at the other end. He shifted in his seat, nudging the phone off its perch and flipping it into the bucket on top of the fluke. Now *that* made him smile.

"Come on, you know you're beat," he grunted.

The line jerked, zigging and zagging from left to right.

Must be close to the surface now.

The water rippled. Dan brought in another foot of line. Sweat trickled down the sides of his face. Adrenaline flooded the hangover from his system. This could be one of the biggest catches he ever made in the sound.

"Dan, are you listening to me?" Jamie's voice echoed in the bucket.

"That's right, you bitch!" Dan shouted, to the fish, not his wife, though he knew she'd never believe that.

With one last tug, the fish, a bluefish, its cold flesh sparkling in the moonlight, broke the surface in a spray of boiling foam. Dan stood, maneuvering so he could bring it over the side. It hung in midair, its mouth impaled by the hook, struggling to break free.

"You gotta be at least twenty pounds. Wait'll I show Gus and Ernie."

The fish was going to wreak havoc on his boat. He might have to give it a whack with the lead-filled baton he kept on board. Keeping the dangling fish within the confines of the boat, he bent his knees and reached down for the baton. He'd bought it at a garage sale of a cop's widow. It had seen its share of fish heads ever since. He often wondered what other kinds of heads it had bludgeoned in its history.

"Sorry to have to do this," he said.

As he went to deliver a stunning, if not killing, blow, the boat rocked to the side. Dan stumbled, trying to retain his balance.

The water exploded as if something launched from a canon below. It sailed onto the boat, a dark, writhing shape, snarling like a rabid animal. Dan screamed, falling back into the hard plastic seat.

When he looked at its face, he felt an immediate pain in his chest, radiating down his left arm.

The animal sank its large, pointed teeth into the bluefish, popping it like a water balloon filled with entrails.

It hunched on all fours. Its massive head jerked from side to side, spraying fish guts everywhere. Dan stared in horror, each breath a struggle through the heaviness in his chest. It had the body of a dog or a wolf, even, but its head looked like something out of the mythology class he took in college. That face, that horrid, physically impossible face, was a cross between a large bird, like an eagle, and a pig. Its snout was long but ended in a rounded wet nose dark as charcoal. Tiny feathers intermingled with fur around the collar of its neck. Its body was as round and solid as a wine barrel. Its small, round eyes glowed a hazy blue, like a husky.

Those eyes fixed on Dan's.

"Dan, what's all that noise? What's going on?"

He desperately wanted to answer her, but his arms had locked up. The grotesque animal peered down at the phone. It sniffed the air. Its lips curled back, revealing purple gums. It thrust its elongated muzzle into the bucket, clamping down on the plastic phone. It shattered into small shards under the weight of the creature's jaws.

Dan's eyes went wide as a jolt of fire ripped through his chest. His heart fluttered out of rhythm, a deaf drummer in a black parade. The pain was excruciating. When it subsided, he looked on with mute horror as the animal bit into his knee, tearing the cap free with a twitch of its demonic head.

For some reason, he couldn't feel his legs at all. Not even when it went for his other knee, hobbling him in seconds. Was it shock? Or had his nervous system already shut down, part of a domino drop of total system failure?

Dan prayed his heart would stop before the beast came at him again.

CHAPTER 13

Dalton and Anita's conversation was interrupted by a red-eyed Sergeant Campos. The Sullivan house was a crawling, buzzing hive of activity. When an officer was down, everyone was on duty.

"Anita, we just got a call that's close by. Something about a dogfight," Campos said. "I'll send you over with one of my officers."

Dalton volunteered to go. He needed to do something to take his mind off Henderson's face just before he was dragged away. That and his dire need to find out what the hell was going on in his adopted town.

"You've already given your statement?" Campos asked.

"Many times over."

Campos ran a beefy hand over his face and grunted. "It's only four blocks away. Come right back when you're done. You're not finished here."

He nodded, motioning with his head for Anita to follow him out to his car. He got the address from dispatch. Apparently, someone's German shepherd was going at it viciously with a stray.

As they drove to the house, Dalton asked, "You think there's any chance it's the same animal that took Henderson?"

She stared out the window, her hands gripping her tranquilizer rifle. "I honestly don't know."

They both heard the desperate growls, yelps and yips as he pulled into the driveway of the gold-and-black-trimmed Tudor house. An anxious woman, her hair in rollers, poked her head out of the front window. "They're in the yard!" she shouted, pointing. "Please, save my Bruce!"

Like every neighborhood he'd been in so far, the lights were on in every house. No one was getting any sleep tonight. Whatever had invaded Montauk brought an ugly tide of fear that was steadily sweeping from one end of the town to the other.

"Just stay inside and close the window," Dalton said, drawing his gun and taking the lead. "Do you have a back light?"

"I do."

"If you can do it from inside, please turn it on."

She ducked back into the house and pulled the windows down.

Bruce sounded like he was in the fight of his life. Deep, guttural growls, high-pitched shrieks and what could only be described as a canine battle cry rang across the neighborhood. Everything he heard screamed that it was going to be an ugly sight.

"Anita, if they charge us, I want you to run back to my car and get inside fast."

A dull, yellow glow trickled into the alley between the two houses. It wasn't the best light, but it was better than trying to get a handle on things with a flashlight.

"Gray, if there's a chance I can sedate it—"

"Forget that. If it's not a dog, you can look at it all you want when it's dead. I just watched one drag a two-hundred-fifty-pound man like he was a doll."

Anita pulled in a deep breath, then nodded. "Okay, you're right." Looking down, she crouched, found a water valve, gave it a twist and handed a hose to him. "Best way to break up a dogfight without getting yourself bitten. That should separate them. Once you've done that, we might have a chance of saving the shepherd."

Dalton gripped his Glock 17 with one hand and hose nozzle with the other. The image would be comical if the escalating events weren't so grave.

The cacophony in the yard had been reduced to strangled grunts. It sounded like the animals were gnawing on each other.

"Stay behind me," he said, charging the last few feet, his fingers clamped down on the hose trigger.

A steady stream of water rocketed at a pair of twisting bodies. The German shepherd had turned crimson. The creature that had the dog's neck in its mouth loosened its jaws to glare at the intruder.

Dalton met the beast's malevolent gaze and felt his insides flush cold.

Without turning, he said as forcefully as he could, "Anita, run like fucking hell now!"

Officer Jake Winn pulled up to the split-level ranch house on Exton Street seconds before the paramedics. It was another "all hands on deck" night but he couldn't get his head around the news of Henderson's abduction and disappearance. He'd known the man for years, had thrown up alongside him in the middle of his wedding reception. They'd shared more beers and bullshit stories about hunting, both game and girls, in their younger years than he could count.

And now Norm was gone. Taken in the night by who-the-hell-knew-what.

He'd been on his way to the house where it happened when the emergency call came in about a girl suffering some sort of seizure. Normally, it wouldn't be a matter for the PD, but the girl had told her parents earlier that she'd been attacked by a dog.

All animal attacks and sightings were being treated as top priorities.

So, as much as he wanted to be with everyone else looking for Norm, he knew his place was here, helping out an innocent girl.

"Glad to see they brought the A-team," he said to the paramedics, Jack Brand and Jerry Santana. They'd worked this beat as long as he and Norman had.

"You hear about Norm?" Jerry said, casting his eyes heavenward as if he was offering a silent prayer for his safe return.

Winn rang the bell and gave the door a couple of hard knocks for good measure. "Yeah. I'm heading over after this call."

"Do you think he was really attacked by an animal?" Jack asked. "I mean, Norm's a pretty big guy."

Jake narrowed his eyes. "If he was, I wouldn't put odds on it seeing another dawn. Norm's one strong son of a bitch."

The door swung open. A harried, terrified Mary James led them inside and upstairs without so much as a word. They ran after her. Winn felt the severity of the situation in his chest before he even made it to the girl's room. It was too quiet. *We're too late*, he thought as they jogged down the carpeted hallway.

As soon as he saw the girl on the bed, her father kneeling alongside it, pressing a wet washcloth to her forehead, he stepped aside so Jack and Jerry could do their thing.

"What in holy hell?" he whispered.

The girl lay on the bed dressed only in a thin nightshirt. The covers were pulled back and lay in a crumpled ball on the floor. She wasn't seizing, which was a good thing. But her leg. It didn't even look like it belonged on a human being.

Her right leg was swollen to the point of bursting. In fact, her skin had split in more places than he could count, each wound weeping a foul, green pus. The entire leg had turned a ghastly shade of purple. Dark blue lines etched across her skin like twisting winter tree branches. The blue spider veins ran all the way to her throat. A yellow froth bubbled from the corners of her mouth. Heavy drops of perspiration ran down her body. The smell boiling out of the room made him step back.

She was still breathing, but by the look in her glazed eyes, she had checked out. When the pain was too much, the brain had a foolproof way of escaping the worst of it.

"Mr. and Mrs. James, I need you to come outside with me. The paramedics are the best we have. They'll take good care of her."

Jerry flashed him a look that told him all he needed to know. This was not going to end well.

Richard James reluctantly staggered away from the bed as Jack cut the girl's nightshirt open with a pair of scissors. Winn had met Richard at a couple of fund-raisers over the years. He was an average man with an above-average propensity for charity. The kind of guy you could take half your classes with in high school and never know his name or be able to pick him out of a lineup of two. Winn felt bad for recalling his checks better than his face.

He needed to get some basic information out of them fast. By the looks of things, Jerry and Jack would have her loaded in the ambulance in minutes, racing to the hospital.

"I know this is very hard right now, but I need to ask you a few important questions."

Mary James gripped her husband's hand. "Yes, we understand." She turned to look at her daughter. Winn spoke to keep her eyes from lingering too long. Some things were best left unseen. The girl's body looked like it had been infected by gangrene. Jack checked her blood pressure. His lips pulled back in a tight grimace.

"What's your daughter's name?" Winn asked.

Mary turned at the sound of his voice. He didn't think she'd blinked since the moment she'd opened the door. "Kelly."

"Kelly," Richard added. The man looked as if his wife was the only thing keeping him upright.

"You said she told you she was attacked by a dog. Did she say when and where?"

"She—she'd snuck out to a party to see her boyfriend two nights ago. When she came home, it was late. We were asleep upstairs. Kelly said a dog came after her but only managed to scratch her ankle. It hardly even bled. I thought she had come down with a stomach virus. She ran a temp the next day. She didn't mention her ankle. Not until earlier tonight. She was so afraid. She kept hoping it would get better on its own."

Fat tears sprang from her eyes, rolling down her cheeks.

"It wasn't this bad even an hour ago," Richard said, picking up the narrative so she didn't have to. "Her ankle was a little bruised, but we were more concerned about her temperature. We gave her some Tylenol and put some ice packs around her. When she started her seizure, everything changed in an instant."

Winn heard Jack say, "She's at one-oh-four point three. We have to get her out now."

"Did she describe the dog to you?" he asked, feeling time slip through his fingers.

They both shook their heads. "She said it was too dark to see, but it looked big. The scratch hurt more than it should have, and only got worse."

Winn flinched when Kelly James suddenly screamed bloody murder. Jerry and Jack had lifted her onto the stretcher. Their touch seemed to set her off. Mary and Richard ran to her, each grasping a hand, shoving the paramedics aside.

Kelly continued to wail, her back arching. Winn stared at her leg. The rotten flesh undulated in rhythm with the pulse at her neck. Jerry and Jack tried to maneuver the stretcher so they could get her out of the room.

"No-no-no-no-nooooooooooo!" Kelly shouted. "Oh God, I'm on fire!"

"Mr. and Mrs. James, please step aside so the paramedics can get her in the ambulance."

Either they didn't hear him through their daughter's cries or had resolved not to let her go. He was about to go into the bedroom and ease them away when the unthinkable happened.

CHAPTER 14

The synapses to Dalton's brain snapped and misfired. His eyes took in the carnage with the cold precision of a camera lens. What he saw and how he comprehended the unfathomable image had become as difficult as advanced calculus.

Anita, in blatant disregard of his command to get back to the car, sidled next to him. She seemed equally perplexed.

The creature, seeing it had something new to toy with, took a fatal bite from the German shepherd's throat. It was a merciful end.

"Gray, I don't know what the hell that thing is," Anita croaked.

If she didn't know, Dalton had no chance of figuring it out himself. It looked like a lot of things, yet like nothing at all. Had it been bathed in direct light, its shadow would have suggested a dog, though one on a very large scale. It stood on four thick legs, each leg sprouting a paw the size of a wrestler's hand. Each paw had considerable claws, some retracted, like a cat's. Their savage effectiveness was etched all over the poor dog. It was covered in fur, but the coat looked diseased, frayed, coarse and wiry. The fur was a mix of colors, but the flesh that was exposed between the crumbling patches of fur was an otherworldly turquoise. It had no tail. The face was unmistakably that of a goat, with a long tuft of blood-soaked hair under its chin. Yet the muzzle was distended like a dog's, ending in a slight, downward curve, like an eagle's beak.

"It's a whole damn petting zoo wrapped into one animal," Dalton said, pointing his Glock at the unidentifiable beast.

It growled at them, its shoulders tensing, hind legs coiling.

A woman's voice split the tension. "Oh my God! Bruce!"

Dalton turned to his left, taking his eyes off the monstrosity for a split second. The dog's owner had opened the back door. She stood frozen in her nightgown, her shivering hands covering her mouth.

"Ma'am, I need you to get back in the house and lock the door."

The creature slowly turned its deformed head toward the woman. A long, blue-tinted tongue lolled from its mouth, dripping saliva onto the dog's carcass.

She sobbed and shook, but couldn't move her legs. Her grief and horror rooted her to the spot. Even when the creature took a step in her direction, lifting its blood-soaked front paw over her mangled Bruce, she remained locked in place.

"Shoot it, Gray," Anita said.

The gun felt as if its weight had quadrupled. Dalton flexed his fingers around the hard, plastic-encased steel. He'd never fired his gun outside the firing range before. Just the presence of a drawn firearm was an effective deterrent. Many cops went their whole careers without ever discharging their weapon. People knew the power and deadly consequences of a gun.

This animal did not.

"Please get back in your house now!" Dalton shouted, trying to get the creature's attention back on him. It worked. The woman blinked her eyes rapidly, as if emerging from an interrupted sleepwalk. Out of his periphery, he watched her take an unsteady step backward, slipping into the doorway. He heard the door latch close.

He felt something brush past his shoulder and turned to see Anita had brought her rifle up. She squeezed off a quick shot, sending a tranquilizing dart into the animal's hindquarter.

It didn't even flinch. Dalton held his breath as it turned to look at the feathered dart protruding from its mottled hide. It then swiveled back to them with eyes that flashed red.

"I think that only pissed it off," Anita said.

"Yeah, it's not happy."

Dalton steadied his gun hand. The barrel shook imperceptibly, but he could feel his nerves twitch.

Just shoot the damn thing! his mind screamed. He couldn't pull the trigger. *What are you waiting for*? Everything he'd learned and trained for was failing him. Suddenly he was a child again, waiting for his dad to go downstairs and check on the strange noise coming from the front door in the dead of night.

"Anita, please, get in the car. I'll take care of this," he hissed. A bead of salty sweat curled into his eye, stinging him. She touched his shoulder. "I'll go slowly, so it doesn't overreact. Just take it down. You're all clear now."

Her hand slipped away as she took a step back.

The creature snapped its jaws, barking like an asthmatic tiger. It sprang forward with alarming speed.

Dalton was pushed aside by the leaping beast before he could react. He slammed into the side of the house and tumbled onto the ground. His gun fell from his hand.

Anita screamed.

The creature bit into her arm and dragged her down the alley. There was a sickening pop as her shoulder was pulled from its socket. Still on the ground, Dalton reached for his Taser. He unclipped it from his belt, firing into the rear of the retreating monster. The two electrodes hit the mark, causing the animal to jump. It let go of Anita's arm. What it didn't do was stop moving. Instead, it continued to the front of the house, pulling the Taser gun from his hands. It clattered along the pavement as the beast escaped into the street.

Dalton ran to Anita. She was pushing herself up so she could lean against the house. Her arm was a bloody mess.

"I'll be fine," she said, though her eyes told him different. "Go after it."

There was no way he'd be able to catch it on foot, even with a tranquilizer and being tased. Right now, Anita was his primary concern.

"I'm getting you to the hospital. Come on."

He lifted her up, careful not to touch her wounded arm and cause her more pain. As they emerged into the front yard, the dog's owner burst from the front door. "You didn't get it," she accused him.

When she saw Anita, she pulled up short.

"I'm going to call for another officer to come here. Right now I have to get to a hospital. Did you see which way the animal went?"

She pointed north, down the intersecting street. His biggest hope was that everything would hit the beast at once and drop it somewhere they could find the body and cart it away before it did any more harm.

Something like that couldn't be allowed to run free.

He'd had his chance to stop it, and failed.

Anita took off her button-down shirt and wrapped it around her arm. "Christ, it burns," she said.

He helped her into the car and called the situation in.

First Henderson, now this.

Dalton pushed his troubled thoughts away, concentrating on getting Anita to the hospital as quickly as possible.

His siren blared as he sped down the Montauk Highway, just one of many screaming police cars in the night.

Kelly James convulsed so hard, the stretcher's rubber wheels lifted off the carpet. Jack tightened the strap around her waist while Jerry did his best to hold her head in place. She slammed it onto the padded gurney over and over again. A crimson lather bubbled from her mouth. Her mother screamed, throwing her body over her daughter.

Richard James gripped Kelly's hand, his expression one of mute, frozen fear.

"She's so hot, Rich," Mary said, her voice trembling, tears pouring into the side of her mouth.

Jerry attempted to move Mary James to the side. Winn may have imagined it, but he was pretty sure she snarled at the paramedic.

Everyone paused at the sound of a wet pop.

"What was that?" Jack asked.

The girl's seizure subsided.

"Mrs. James, I really need you to let the paramedics get your daughter to the hospital. They can't move with you like that. I promise, you can ride in the ambulance with her. You won't leave her side."

Mary James turned to him and her eyes, glazed over with grief, cleared. She shook her head and eased herself off her daughter's chest.

When she pulled herself away from her daughter's body, they all saw where the popping sound had come from.

Kelly's stomach had literally exploded. Her mother's shirt was covered in blood and bits of entrails. Somehow, the girl was still breathing. Even Jerry and Jack took a step back, trying to figure out what the hell had just happened and what needed to be done next.

"Mary," Richard James croaked, pointing at her shirt. When she looked down, all hell broke loose.

She wailed, staring down at her shirt, then the inside of her daughter's stomach. Winn had never heard a sound like that come out of a human being. It was punctuated with "Oh my God, it's burning me!" Mary frantically pulled her shirt over her head, tossing it away. The pale, soft flesh of her torso was stained red.

Richard ran into the bathroom and came back with a wet towel.

Kelly moaned, catching everyone's attention. Her eyelids fluttered. As her head lolled to the side, her gaze landed on Winn.

She was already gone. He'd been around his share of dying people, and he knew that look. Whatever spirit her body possessed had taken flight from the pain and despair. The whites of her eyes had begun to yellow beneath a thick sheen of mucous. Her mouth opened and her teal-tinted tongue distended. Kelly's chest heaved, drawing her last breath.

No one was prepared for what happened when she exhaled.

The open wound in her abdomen exploded, sending up a two-foot-high fountain of blood and gore. No one in the room was spared. Everyone shouted as if they had been set upon with a flamethrower.

Jerry was quick to regain his senses. He saw Winn make a move to help them and blocked the doorway with his heavily built body.

"Don't come in here! There must be some kind of contagion. Do you have any on you?"

Winn's pulse hammered. *Contagion?*

He looked down at his uniform and saw it was unblemished.

"I have to find a mirror," he said and darted down the

hall. The sound of Mary's and Richard's crying, both in sadness and agony, trailed after him. He found a bathroom, decorated in pink, every surface covered in lotions and liquid soaps. Staring at his haunted face in the medicine cabinet mirror, he looked over every pore to make sure it was clear.

Whatever had come out of Kelly James had, *thank you, God*, missed him.

Winn ran back to the bedroom. "I'm fine, I think."

"Call the hospital, tell them what happened and to send a hazmat team over as fast as fucking possible," Jerry said, wincing.

"It hurts that bad?"

"More than you can imagine. If I didn't know better, I'd swear we'd had some kind of acid thrown on us."

Winn unclipped the walkie from his shoulder and put the call in. He was told units would be on their way ASAP.

Jack stood away from the body on the stretcher, silent. If he was in any pain, it didn't show for now. Richard held Mary up, both of them in obvious agony, weeping over their daughter's cooling body.

Jerry said, "Jake, I don't think you should be around this. No telling if it's airborne. Wait downstairs and make sure no one comes up here without protective gear."

He slammed the door in Winn's face, muffling the Jameses' cries.

Winn went down the stairs with leaden legs.

What had he just witnessed? What did it mean for Jack and Jerry and Mary and Richard?

What did it mean for him?

Worst of all, what did it mean for the entire town?

CHAPTER 15

The moment Dalton entered the ER he could sense something was wrong. At this time of the morning, it should have been quiet as a church. In bigger cities and towns, the emergency room got more hectic as the night bled into early morning. Alcohol and drugs led people to do damn stupid things, especially after two a.m. But here in East Hampton, the ER was typically a place to get a good night's rest, undisturbed by knife wounds or drunk driving accidents.

This morning, there was a buzzing undercurrent that could be felt more than heard. The triage nurse looked harried and a good number of doctors and other personnel flashed back and forth with a sense of urgency.

The overhead speaker blurted, "Dr. Wallace to telemetry, Dr. Wallace to telemetry."

He'd grabbed a wheelchair for Anita before getting her out of the car. Her wound was hidden beneath her bloody shirt, but the pain was written all over her face. On the way to the hospital, she moaned about a creeping heat that swallowed her arm whole. He got to the hospital in record time, damning himself every inch of the way for not shooting the monstrosity when he had the chance.

"She's in good hands," the triage nurse said with a faltering smile. A pressure cuff was around Anita's good arm and a digital thermometer was under her tongue. When it was removed, the nurse said, "Just a little over a hundred. I'll get you in to see a doctor in just a minute." The nurse left the little triage room and walked down the hall.

"I'm so sorry," Dalton said.

Gritting her teeth through the pain, Anita reached out to hold his hand. "You have nothing to apologize for. I shouldn't have shot it. Maybe it would have eventually run off."

He knew there was no way that thing would have left without taking its pound of flesh. He'd never seen something so menacing, so fixed on annihilation.

"You have to find it," she said. "Mother Nature didn't create that thing. There's no need to stay with me. I'll be fine. Just need to get my shoulder put back in and I'm sure I'll be flooded with antibiotics. Rabies shots, too. Needles don't bother me."

"Is there anyone you want me to call, have them come down to the hospital?"

Anita shook her head. "I have a brother in Massachusetts. No sense getting him out of bed for this. I'll call him later." She pulled Dalton down to eye level. "Gray, you're a good kid. I need you to get that animal. When I get out of here, I hope I can get my hands on it. This may sound funny, but I want to know what it is and where it came from more than getting my arm fixed up."

Dalton smiled. "It doesn't sound funny. A little crazy, maybe. You just relax. I'll get it. I promise." As he turned to leave triage, he said, "Hey, maybe it'll make you famous. You could be the woman who uncovers the secret behind a monster."

"I hadn't even thought of that." She gave him a smile that looked more like a wince.

"You take care of yourself. I'll be back later to check on you."

It hurt like hell to leave her, but she had a point. While that creature was out roaming around, no one was safe. He'd go back to the house where Anita had been bitten and try to track it down.

Before he left the hospital, he went over to admitting and asked the woman behind the Plexiglas if she knew how Margie Salvatore was doing.

"Are you a relative, Officer?" she asked. The woman was young, not much older than him, though she had considerable bags under her eyes. She must not be used to the graveyard shift yet, Dalton thought. He remembered the luggage he carried on his face for the first few months while he adjusted to living like a vampire.

"No. I responded to the call. She was bitten by a stray dog. It got her pretty bad. I just want to make sure she's all right."

"Let me check." She typed away on her computer. Dalton heard a door slam down the hall and the squeak of rubber soles. The woman stopped typing, narrowing her eyes at the screen. Her lips pressed tight. "I'm sorry to say this, but she passed away a few hours ago."

Dalton rocked back on his heels. "She died? But it was only a bite on her leg. Do you know why she died?"

"I can't say. You'd have to ask the attending physician, and he'd only be able to tell you if her next of kin gave him permission or if it was part of an investigation."

He took a deep breath and looked over at the now empty triage room.

Margie Salvatore was bitten, in all high probability, by one of those things. Now she was dead.

What would happen to Anita?

He thanked the admitting clerk and ran to his car. More than ever, he had to find that animal. By doing so, he might find out what it was and in the end, save Anita's life.

As the sun came up a searing tangerine in the western sky, Summer Olchak took a shower, got dressed for work and grabbed a bottle of iced coffee from her refrigerator. She wasn't due in the office until eight thirty, but she wanted to stop at Benny's house to check up on him. The last time they'd spoken, he'd told her he had some kind of stomach flu or food poisoning. It wasn't lost on her that he blamed her if he had the latter.

Unlike every other man she'd dated, Benny wasn't a big baby in search of a younger mommy. He took care of himself. When he was sick, he was more like a bear than a toddler, going off to his cave to will himself better. It was one of the many qualities that made her overlook his checkered past. He'd done those things when he was young and stupid. He'd assured her those days were over and he'd been nothing but a good man ever since they'd met at a *Rocky Horror Picture Show* marathon at the Kent Theater three years ago.

She'd tried calling and texting him all day yesterday but he wasn't replying. It was agony not to go to his house last night but she had a full plate of work to do and she had to take her grandmother to the senior center. By the time she got back, it was too late. If he was sick, the last thing he needed was her waking him up in the middle of the night.

When she turned her car on, the radio blared, *"in a series of animal—"* She turned the radio off and plugged her iPod in, searching for her Pink playlist.

She was tempted to stop at the pancake house and pick him up something for breakfast, but odds are, he wouldn't be in the mood. Best to get some water and plain toast in his system until he fully recovered.

As she walked up to his front door, she could hear the TV on inside. It sounded like he was watching some kind of action movie. There were lots of explosions and yelling. Summer knelt by the small garden to the right of the door and found the hide-a-key that looked like a rock. She'd once asked him why he didn't give her a key to his place. His answer was typical Benny. "Honey, you know where I keep my spare. It's one less thing to keep on your keychain."

The moment she opened the door she was hit by a stench so foul, she had to back out into the fresh air.

"Benny?" she called into the house, her stomach refusing to let her go back inside. What the hell was that smell? It reeked. When was the last time he'd taken out the garbage? She'd once visited a landfill in Staten Island during a school trip when she was in eighth grade—some lesson about pollution and man's propensity to make waste. This smelled kind of like that, but worse.

"Benny, are you all right?"

The hard staccato of heavy gunfire blared from the TV speakers. Looking in her purse, Summer found a packet of tissues. She pulled them out and covered her nose and mouth with the entire pack.

Stepping over the threshold, her stomach heaved. Nothing could dampen the foul odor.

As she turned to look into the living room, the tissues fell from her mouth.

Summer shrieked.

Benny's purpled corpse lay on the couch, the remote still in his hand. Dark rivers of dried blood streaked from his eyes, nose and mouth. His body was half its normal size, as if he were a beach ball that had been partially deflated. A grayish fluid pooled around his feet and the couch cushions.

Summer ran from the house screaming at the top of her lungs for someone to call 911. As neighboring doors opened, she fell to her knees in the street, painting the blacktop with bile.

On the way back to the house where Anita had been bitten, Dalton spotted the first dead animal. It was a raccoon, fat from summer pickings. It wasn't on the side of the road, a victim of poor street-crossing judgment.

He knew he was supposed to go back to the Sullivans' house but he couldn't ignore this.

The raccoon, its body torn to shreds like a gruesome piñata, lay under an elm tree in the front yard of a tidy Cape home. A tire swing dangled over the raccoon's remains.

One of the creatures had been here.

Dalton pulled over and rang the doorbell. A tired-looking man with two days' worth of stubble answered.

"Sir, did you hear or see anything out of the ordinary last night, like animals fighting?"

The man rubbed the back of his neck. "What?"

Dalton pointed at the dead raccoon. "That raccoon was attacked last night. I need you and everyone in your family to keep away from it. We'll have someone come by and pick up its remains."

"So now they have you on dead-raccoon duty?" he said, grinning. "How did they get that past the union?"

Dalton fixed him with a "don't mess with me" glare. "Do you have kids?"

The man nodded, no longer so flippant.

"Keep them inside the house. If I find out they were anywhere near that raccoon, you and I will meet again under much different circumstances. Am I clear?"

"Y-yes."

"Good. It's probably best you keep them away from the swing entirely for a few days."

Before the man could question him further, Dalton

turned back to his car. When he got in touch with dispatch, he was told his was not the first call for carcass removal, preferably with a hazmat team.

Had the entire town been thrown into the *Twilight Zone*? Dalton leaned back into his seat, the leather creaking. He suddenly felt very tired. The adrenaline that had pumped through him the entire night began to ebb, leaving him exhausted and worried.

"Have there been any more instances of animal disturbances or attacks?"

There was a pause, then, "No, not since around five this morning."

He checked his watch. It was a little after seven. It looked like it was going to be another hot, humid, sunny day. There wasn't a cloud in the sky.

Throwing his cruiser in drive, he didn't go far before finding a maimed cat hanging from the low branches of a tree. The gray and black tabby dripped blood onto the sidewalk. Again, he parked his car, warned the residents of the house by the tree not to go near it, and called it in.

The entire process was repeated five more times as he made the ten-block journey to the house where he'd watched the strange animal kill a German shepherd with almost humanlike precision and attempt to drag Anita away. All told, he found two cats, two squirrels, a muskrat and a small mutt he'd seen often around Main Street. He'd even fed it some french fries once.

The woman who owned the shepherd was beside herself. Her eyes were swollen and rimmed red. Dalton drew a sharp breath when he saw her robe.

It was covered in blood.

"Were you with your dog?" he asked.

"Of course I was," she said, her breath hitching. "He was all I had left. My son got him for me when my husband died ten years ago. And then he passed away a year later."

Maintaining a calm yet firm tone, Dalton said, "I'm very sorry to hear about your losses, but I need you to do exactly what I say. I want you to go back inside your house and change out of your bloody clothes. Remain inside. Don't go back to be with Bruce, okay? I'm going to call some paramedics to come and make sure you're all right."

Confusion washed over her face. "I don't think I need paramedics. I'm just upset. Anyone would be."

Dalton put on a tiny smile, faking it as best he could, careful not to get too close. "I understand. You have every right to be upset. It would just make me feel better if I knew you were going to be fine. Standard protocol for something like this."

"You have protocols for strange animals killing dogs?"

He wanted to say, *We will after last night.* Instead, he said, "The eggheads who draw up police manuals have a lot of time on their hands. They think of everything."

"Oh, okay." She looked down at her gore-soaked robe. "I better clean myself up."

"That's probably best."

As soon as she closed the door he was back on line with dispatch. "I have a woman covered in what might be infected blood. We need an ambulance but they need to proceed with extreme caution. Treat it like it's contagious."

Treat it like it's contagious.

He drove back to the station, passing by the first hazmat team as they dropped the raccoon under the tire swing into a black bag.

CHAPTER 16

Can Man emerged, old bones popping, from his secret hiding spot—the cold case in the old butcher's shop that had closed a year ago. He'd kept the heavy door open a crack all night to let some air into the stifling, derelict shop, but he felt safer knowing he could shut it at a moment's notice and no animal, no matter how big or mean, could get inside.

Shuffling through the plaza, his mouth open in a wide O as he yawned, he felt something different in the air. Normally this time of day, even though it was still early, the plaza and Main Street were packed with hungry vacationers lining up for pancakes and hot coffee.

Today looked more like a normal day after the summer season. There were no lines outside the dueling pancake houses, very few kids anxious to get to the beach.

"What happened last night?" he asked the sky, tilting his head back to feel the sun on his face.

Fumbling through his shorts pockets, he felt the three crumbled dollar bills he had left. It was enough to get a coffee and a Danish. Everything felt wrong. He needed to stick to his breakfast routine, even though he didn't feel much like eating. Routine was good. Routine could restore order. Routine always made him feel better. Even living in the streets had its own cadence, an order to the day. It may have sounded irrational, but he felt that if he could stick to his morning ritual, everyone else would follow and normalcy would return.

He walked between a pair of parked cars to get to the coffee shop. His foot lodged under something heavy and he catapulted forward, landing on his chest in the middle of the street.

He was lucky. There were no cars on the road.

"Thank you, Jesus," he said as he pushed himself up.

When he turned to see what had tripped him, all thoughts of munching on a Danish vanished.

The routine had been thrown to hell today.

A pile of fur and bone and blood lay wedged between the cars. A swarm of flies flitted on and off the body. It had to be a dog. And a big one, too. A cool breeze came off the sound, carrying the sweet yet rotted smell of the destroyed animal to his nose. He quickly turned away, burying his face in the crook of his elbow.

That dog hadn't been hit. It was as if someone had taken it apart, limb by limb, and attempted to put it back together. But whoever had done it had no concept of anatomy or form.

As much as Can Man wanted to put distance between himself and the corpse, he felt a duty to stay close in case any children came by. He'd wait for one of the cops to drive past and flag them down. They'd know who to call to cart it away.

Dalton ended his shift the same time as Meredith Hernandez. Sergeant Campos left word for him to knock off for a few hours. He needed him fresh to start earlier than usual. Since the morning, everything had gone quiet.

Everyone in the field was on cleanup duty. Parts of the town looked like the killing floor of an animal shelter.

When Meredith saw him walk into the station, she eyed him warily. "Hey, what happened out there last night?"

He undid the top button of his shirt and rubbed his eyes. "It was a complete nightmare. There weren't enough of us to keep track of everything."

Using her crutch, she got up from behind her desk, following him. "Is it true that Anita Banks was bitten by some wild dog?"

He sucked in a sharp breath, felt the start of a headache at his temples. "Yeah. It was bad. And it wasn't a dog."

"Then what was it?"

He looked around, making sure no one was listening. The precinct was just shy of a madhouse. Phones rang off the hook with residents concerned both about the dead animals and the hazmat teams sent to clear them out. It looked like everyone on the day shift had been called in. Leaning in close, he said, "I don't have a frigging clue. I saw it with my own eyes and I don't believe it."

Meredith's eyes grew wide. "You actually saw it?"

"One of them. There's more out there." He stopped and stared into the distance, lost in his thoughts. "Any word on Henderson? Did they find him?"

She shook her head. "I heard you were there, too. I can't imagine what you've been through. Are you okay?"

If he put some time into thinking about it, he would have to be honest and say he was as far from okay as heaven was from hell. With each passing hour, each interlocking incident, he'd felt a pressure building inside him. Right now, he felt ready to erupt. Things were happening so fast, he didn't have time to process, much less breathe. Something was going to give. He hoped the pain in his head wasn't a prelude to an aneurysm.

Instead, he said, "I'll be fine. Once I hear Norm is all right and Anita is released from the hospital, I'll be perfect."

Meredith touched his arm. "Well, until then, you're taking me out for breakfast. I need you to tell me everything. It'll do you good to talk it out."

"Are you the department shrink now?" It came out harsher than he'd meant. She took it in stride.

"Just a smart woman who knows what's best. And I'm your elder. Don't worry, I'm a cheap date."

As much as he desperately wanted to go to his apartment and crash, he knew his brain would never shut down. Not the way he was feeling now. "Is this an actual date?" he asked with a tired smile.

"After what you've been through, you can call it anything you want. Come on, I'll drive."

CHAPTER 17

Meredith took them to a little café off Main. It had opened the previous summer and was the local answer to Starbucks, with the added attraction of fresh-baked pastries, rolls, and on weekdays, omelets. The coffee was a little pricey, like most things in town, but it was damn good.

Dalton ordered a black coffee for himself and hazelnut for Meredith, along with two croissants. Dalton told her about what happened to Henderson as he peeled the layers of his croissant apart. Meredith didn't even touch hers, too wrapped up in his recounting of the absolute horror of the worst shift in his life.

"You really think it dragged him into the ocean?" she asked, gingerly sipping her coffee.

"It did at one point. If it reentered the beach with Norm, I didn't see the track. The fucker was fast. And strong. I couldn't have pulled Norm behind me like that. No way. And I'm a pretty strong guy."

"The one you saw at the animal disturbance call with the dog. What did it look like?"

Despite himself, Dalton sat back and yawned. The night was catching up to him fast. "You'll think I'm crazy. Shit,

I think I'm crazy. I don't know how I'm going to write everything up. They'll definitely send me for a psych evaluation when they see my report."

Meredith reached across the small table and placed her hand over his. "Don't worry about the report. You can write whatever you want when it comes time. You can tell me what you saw. It stays between us."

He looked into her dark eyes, her eyeliner wearing thin, wondering if he could trust her. She'd never given him a reason not to. Then again, he'd never had something so bizarre to tell that it could get him put on mental leave.

But he needed to tell someone. If it didn't all come out, it would fester, rotting him from the inside out.

"Promise you won't tell anyone?" he asked.

"Promise."

Dalton took a deep breath and let it all spill out. He described the dog-goat-bird creature as best he could. The words sounded unreal as they poured from his mouth. To her credit, Meredith didn't interrupt or flinch when he told her how Anita was attacked or the state of all the animals in the surrounding neighborhood.

When he was done, she finished off her coffee, stared up at the ceiling for a moment and finally met his gaze, whispering, "Holy crap. It's real."

"What do you mean, 'it's real'? I know it's real. I was there."

She waved her hand. "I'm not questioning you at all. What I mean is, I've heard about this before."

"Are you kidding me? There's nothing outside of a horror movie even remotely like this."

"That's what I thought, too. But now I'm beginning to doubt it." She leaned her elbows on the table and said softly, "Have you ever heard of the Montauk monster?"

Dalton shook his head. "I don't watch those kinds of movies."

"I'm not talking about a movie. I'm talking about the bodies of real flesh-and-blood animals that have been washing up all around this part of Long Island for the past ten years."

He chuckled. "I think you need as much sleep as I do."

"Hey, I didn't doubt you. I need you to extend me the same courtesy." She folded her arms across her chest and leaned back in her chair. "See, you're not from here. I've lived on the island all my life. There's a lot of weird history out here, and I'm not talking ancient history. Over the last thirty years, there's been enough strange crap going on in Long Island to fill a season of *The X-Files*." She checked her watch. "You have a few minutes to spare? I want to show you something."

All he wanted was a bed and his pillow, but he said, "I can spare a few. Where are you taking me?"

"My house."

The words startled him, pushing a good portion of his weariness aside. She must have seen it in his expression, because she quickly added, "Don't get any ideas. I came across one of those things about six years ago over at Sag Harbor Bay. I took some pictures and saved a few for home, along with a copy of my report. I want you to see it and tell me what you think."

Twenty-four hours ago, if anyone had told him with any degree of seriousness that there were such things as Montauk monsters, he would have burst out laughing. It sounded as ridiculous as *Sharknado*.

That was before Henderson and Anita and the dead animals strewn about the town.

"Show me."

* * *

Officer Jake Winn heard the call about Benny Franks and headed over before going to the beach to look for Norm. He was wasted beyond measure. Every bone felt like jelly. *Plenty of time to sleep when you're dead*, he thought, pulling into Benny's driveway. *Didn't Jon Bon Jovi use that in a song? Christ, I must be tired, quoting Bon Jovi tunes.*

He and Benny had a history. When Benny was a cocksure, dumb-shit teen, Jake had busted him multiple times for vandalism, public nudity, disturbing the peace, you name it. They were minor infractions, but he could see them leading to bigger and worse things. Benny didn't disappoint. Winn was the first one on the scene when a neighbor reported someone breaking into the Mathesons' house. When he pulled up, gun drawn, there was Benny with two Hefty bags of stolen jewelry, appliances and every scrap of loose change and bills he could find.

Benny was nineteen when he did it, and he paid a grown man's price. Since getting out four years ago, he was a different person. He'd finally grown up, one of the few who was rehabilitated and not made into a more accomplished criminal. Winn watched him from a distance and in a strange way, he was proud of him.

Looks like he'd never get the chance to tell him.

He recognized Summer Olchack as she spoke to one of the officers, George Ryker, in the front yard. Her legs couldn't stay still and her makeup had run down her face. Pretty girl, under different circumstances.

"What do we have here?" Winn asked, stepping into the house. The smell hit him first. It made him wince.

"You might need this," Mickey Conrad said, offering a small jar of vapor rub. Winn dipped his finger and rubbed it across his upper lip. Mickey stopped him from getting too close to the couch.

Winn looked at Benny's body, or the semi-soup that was left of it, and asked, "It looks like he's been dead for a frigging year in a locked house. What the hell happened to him?"

Mickey shrugged. "That's for the ME to find out. I was told to make sure no one got near the body or touched it. They said I should wear a mask but I don't have one and I don't have the time to find one."

"This is like those bodies on the beach."

"I thought that the moment I saw him. If it's toxic, it's too late for me. That's three bodies in two days, and I've breathed whatever's coming off them both times."

Winn thumped his fist against the doorframe. "It's a fucking shame. He finally got his life straightened out."

"You know him?"

"Yeah. We had quite a few run-ins over the years. He was a good kid at heart. His dad left when he was five and his mother kinda fell apart. He was left on his own a lot. I used to call him 'that feral kid.' Always dirty, always on his own, never up to any good."

They both turned toward the yard. Ryker was having a hard time keeping Benny's girlfriend calm. Winn's brain was a whirlwind of thoughts, none of them pleasant.

"The ME's gonna be a while," he said. "I left him with a handful over at another place. A teenage girl got sick and—" He wasn't sure how to say the rest. He could still hear the pop of her guts as they exploded.

"And what?" Mickey asked.

Winn wiped the sweat from his forehead with his sleeve. "It was bad. Like nothing I'd ever seen before. But when it was over, she looked a lot like Benny."

"Jesus."

"He ain't got nothing to do with it. Did you see those Animal Control guys out there with their protective suits?"

Mickey nodded. "I saw a couple on the way here. You have any idea what all this means?"

Winn took one last look at Benny and squared his hat on his head. "It means I can smell the feds on the wind. I'm a proud man, but I'm not too proud to admit this has gotten out of our control. And if they come, things are gonna get worse before they get better."

Meredith's house was a modest, detached single-family home with bright yellow shingles, a white picket fence enclosing an ample yard and a one-car garage. The grass looked like it was in need of a good mowing. There was a stone birdbath by the side of the house, placed alongside a window. He wondered how much time she spent watching the birds cool off in her little public pool.

"Very cute," Dalton said. "I've passed by your house a thousand times. I always wondered who lived in the house so yellow, it could be seen from space."

She backhanded him in the chest. "You must be an apartment dweller."

"Yep."

"Then I won't begrudge your house envy. Come on, what I have inside will blow your mind."

He followed behind her as she limped up the gravel walkway and three steps onto the porch. For a woman who was permanently handicapped, he couldn't help but notice how in shape she was. *How can you even think of that after last night?* he scolded himself. He'd always been attracted to her. Why should the descent of chaos make things any different? Seeing everything go to hell brought a raw edge to all his emotions, even desire. He felt like the man in the plane about to take a thirty-thousand-foot nosedive sitting next to the beautiful woman, neither of them wanting to die a virgin.

Get a grip, Gray.

The interior was cluttered yet cozy. Despite the disarray, he could tell that everything was exactly where it should be. The colors inside were as intense as the exterior. There was no mistaking that a single woman lived here: shades of pink, gold and purple adorned walls and fabrics.

"Don't mind the mess," she said, bending down to pick up her cat. She gave it a kiss on its nose and set it onto the couch. "Ruffles and I weren't expecting any visitors today."

"Your place is neater than mine seconds after I'm done cleaning. Hey, Ruffles." He held out his hand so the cat could sniff it. It nudged him with the top of its head and he scratched between its ears. That was all it took to get it purring. "He likes me."

"He likes everybody," Meredith said, going up the stairs. "Come on up here. I have a little office where I keep everything."

He passed by her bedroom on the way to the office. An unmade, king-sized, four-poster bed dominated the room. He noticed there wasn't a television. It seemed odd. He didn't know many single people who didn't have a TV in their bedroom. On most nights, it was all one had for company.

Her office was a cramped, converted closet. It had enough room for a small computer table, chair and rows of shelves mounted on every wall. The shelves were overloaded with books, files and magazines.

"You ever watch *Hoarders*?" he asked.

"No. What's it about?"

"Never mind."

She grabbed a red box off a shelf, threw the lid aside and shuffled through a mound of manila folders.

"You mind turning on my PC?" she asked. He had to squeeze past her to get at the power button, grazing her hip. He apologized but she didn't seem to notice.

"I was partnered with Frank Russo at the time," she said, extracting one of the folders. It was stuffed with pictures and dog-eared papers. She dropped it on the desk. "A family went to the beach early to get a good spot. The father spotted a dead animal near the shoreline. When he went over to take a look, he immediately called 911. He said some unknown creature had washed up on the beach and someone needed to look at it. Our shift had just begun, it was a nice day and Frank figured spending some time on the beach, even in uniform, wasn't a bad way to start the day."

When Dalton went to open the file, Meredith lifted her crutch, slapping it down on the cover.

"Not yet. As we drove there, I figured we'd either see a waterlogged dog or maybe even a seal. They've been known to come around every now and then. Seals die just like everything else. People around here look at seals when they're alive, in zoos or on TV shows. They're not familiar with dead ones, especially if they've been rotting in the water awhile."

Dalton touched the scar on his jaw, recalling his youthful fascination with seals and sea lions.

"By the time we got to the beach, there was a small crowd gathered around. People were taking pictures and I see a guy poking at something with a long stick. Frank cleared them out fast. He was a big guy with an even bigger voice. Real old school. He'd cracked a lot of heads in his day. I don't think he was too crazy about having me as a partner, but he was a year away from retirement so he didn't bitch, too much. As everyone peeled back, I walked past them and nearly lost my breakfast."

"Superfloater?" Dalton asked.

She shook her head. "Couldn't be further from it. No, this thing hadn't been dead or in the water for very long. I just didn't know what the hell it was. It was like a pet that dropped from some kind of alien spaceship. I took a bunch of pictures with my phone. I mean, this thing was wild. See for yourself."

Meredith flipped the file open. Dalton picked up the first picture and felt his heart race.

He'd seen this thing last night. And it was very much alive.

CHAPTER 18

Tom and Jason never went to sleep that night. They'd gotten so engrossed in a wicked game of *Mob of the Dead* that they'd simply forgotten to go to bed. The beers were eighty-sixed by three in the morning and the weed held out until around six. Now it was nine and they were wired from drinking several cans of Monster to keep any hangover from creeping into their dry skulls.

"Jay, you wanna go to IGA and pick up some of the shit we need for tonight?"

Both were slumped on the couch watching a rerun of *Charmed* with the sound off. "I'd rather watch *Halloween* and go to sleep. Where'd you put the Blu-ray?"

"It's all the way upstairs." Tom pried himself off the couch. "Seriously, we might as well get it done now so we can sleep the rest of the day and be ready to party. I promise we'll watch *Halloween* tomorrow. Hell, we can watch all of them if you want then. Just as long as we take a break to watch *The Shining* at some point."

Jason broke out in a big smile. "Now you're talking, swizzle stick. Who says youth is wasted on the young?"

Tom went to the bathroom to make himself look less

like a meth head. He didn't want the oldsters working at IGA calling the cops because he made them skittish. Through the bathroom door, he said, "You still never told me what made you break the Jenna bong. That was irreplaceable."

Jason bumped into the couch as he tried to slip into his Vans.

"Must have been someone's dog. I kinda freaked when I heard it coming at me. My ninja skills went into high gear."

Tom splashed water on his face. "Dude, we could make an awesome comic about a ninja that uses bongs instead of throwing stars."

"We could serialize it in *High Times*," Jason laughed.

They clambered into Tom's car, a twelve-year-old Chrysler that was a year past being taken out behind the woodshed, and headed into town. The IGA was the first store before the little shops took over on Main Street. As he pulled into the lot, Tom looked in his rearview mirror and frowned.

"What the hell kind of circus is that?"

"Where?" Jason asked.

Tom pointed over Jason's shoulder.

He parked the car and they got out to watch a dozen unmarked, white vans tear down the Montauk Highway. The windows were tinted so dark, they couldn't make out anyone inside. Even when the light turned red, they all kept right on going. Cross traffic came to a standstill as those who were out and about stopped to stare at the strange procession. They drove past the plaza and beyond, never slowing down.

"Dude, that was crazy," Jason said.

"Maybe they're an undercover team looking for the puppy that spooked you like a little girl."

"I swear, I will find another Jenna. I'll even go to the city and hit every head shop if I have to."

Tom slapped him on the shoulder. "I might hold you to that. Now let's get everything we'll need for tonight's munchies."

They were approached by Can Man, looking the worse for wear. The older man stopped in front of them but peered somewhere past them.

"Hey, Can Man," Jason said, offering his hand. He didn't respond.

"Can Man, you all right?" Tom asked.

His eyes flittered about, then came into focus, settling on their faces. "Sorry. I've got a lot on my mind today. I found a dead dog this morning. It was torn up really bad."

"I wonder if that's your dog, man," Tom said to Jason. "That's freaky."

Can Man shook his head. "The cops said it was a golden retriever. But someone tore it apart."

Jason gave a short laugh. "You been hitting the hard stuff? I didn't know you drank."

His demeanor changed swiftly. He was not in the mood for jokes. "You fellas better watch yourselves. I know what you and your friends do at the beach. And I know all about that party of yours tonight. If you're smart, you'll cancel it. If you're lucky, the cops won't even let you get to the beach. Stay home."

Tom didn't question how he knew about the party. Can Man was plugged into the town like no one else. He heard everything. The whole shtick of the old man warning the kids was a little too much out of *Friday the 13th* for him, though.

Instead of questioning him or blowing him off—which could only make things worse, judging by the shroud of anxiety surrounding the man—Tom said, "Thanks, Can

Man. You're always looking out for us. You take care of yourself, too."

They left him before he could say anything else. Once inside the air-conditioned mini-market, Jason said, "I wonder if what he said about the cops closing off the beaches is true. That would suck balls."

Tom grabbed a cart and headed for the junk food aisle. "Can Man's just having a bad day. We'll be fine."

Meredith saw the shock on Dalton's face and knew she was right. He leaned against the wall, his icy blue eyes darting all over the photo. The muscles in his jaw clenched and unclenched.

"You took this?" he asked.

"Yep. I took about a dozen and made copies. One for my report, the others for myself. It was just too strange to watch it get lost in the paperwork shuffle."

The photo showed a slightly bloated, blue-skinned animal lying on its side. Tufts of dark fur sprouted here and there, but most of the flesh was exposed. The face looked something similar to the mythical Minotaur, though the nose had been broken off. It had a massive lower jaw with serrated rows of teeth. The skin of its jaw had been flayed away, revealing stark white bone. Its front paws were cloven hooves, while the back were more like a dog's, with four-toed padded paws.

"What the hell is it?" Dalton said, mostly to himself.

"No one knows," Meredith said, handing him another picture taken from a different angle. Dalton's eyes grew wider. "After Frank and I moved everyone away, we called Anita Banks over to claim the body. A call came in and we had to bail before she got there. When I caught up with her later, I was psyched to hear what she thought of it. The only problem was, she never saw the body. By the time she got there, which was about twenty minutes after we called her, it was gone."

"Maybe it washed back out with the tide."

Meredith firmly shook her head. "Nope. It was low tide at the time. The only way that thing made it off the beach was by someone taking it away. But that's not all of it."

Dalton shuffled through the pictures, stroking his chin, deep in thought. "This thing looks a little smaller than what I saw, but the rest of it looks pretty close. I should have shot the damn thing." He tossed the file onto her desk. "Tell me the rest."

She pointed a finger at him. "I will, but if you tell me I'm nuts, I'll introduce my crutch to your head. Understand?"

For the first time that morning, he smiled. "I do. I want to figure out what these things are and I don't think anyone else is going to tell me much. For now, you're the expert."

Meredith sat in her computer chair and typed *Montauk Monsters* in her search engine. Up came dozens of images of dead, ghastly beasts, all of them rotting in the sand. "The first few were found right here, which is how they got their name from a guy named Loren Coleman on the cryptid circuit."

Dalton leaned over her shoulder, staring at the thumbnail pictures. "What the hell is a cryptid circuit?"

"You ever heard of cryptozoology?"

He shook his head, leaning over to use her mouse to click on an image and make it larger.

Meredith said, "It's the study of strange, unknown animals like lake monsters, Bigfoot, giant squids, chupacabra, you name it. It's not a recognized science, but plenty of people all over the world are really into it. They call these animals *cryptids*. Our local beasties are on the top-ten lists for anyone interested in cryptozoology. But since it's a kind of underground thing, no one in authority really takes it seriously."

"So you're telling me these things are like Bigfoot?"

"No, they have no relation to Bigfoot, other than the fact that people have seen them and can't explain what they are, and there's no solid evidence for their existence."

Dalton scrolled down the screen. The pictures seemed to go on forever. "And all of these things have been washing up here and no one talks about it?"

"Again, no. The majority have been found here on the eastern end of Long Island as well as coastal Connecticut, but creatures like these have been seen as far south as Chile and as far north as Halifax."

"So how isn't this news?" Dalton stared at her like she was a teacher and he was the new kid in a new country who couldn't comprehend how his adopted society worked.

"Because it looks and sounds crazy. Every now and then one of these things will appear and get a little press, but it's always done tongue-in-cheek, like when the news reports on strange lights in the sky and they play over-the-top creepy music in the background and the reporter can barely keep the shit-eating grin off her face."

He walked out of the little room and halfway down the hall. "But there are so many pictures. That's evidence."

Meredith had to suppress a sigh. "In this day and age, photographs are hardly evidence. My ten-year-old niece can cook up an image of one of these things on her computer and you'd never know that it wasn't real. The other side of the problem is that the bodies disappear in every single case. Sometimes they'll make it as far as an animal hospital, but not for long. The official word is that they're raccoon carcasses disfigured by time spent in the water. Does that look like a raccoon to you?" She tapped one of the pictures. "Someone knows what they are and they've been collecting the hard evidence so the whole thing is trapped within the world of cryptozoology, which people think is best left for kids who don't know better and adults who've gone fruit loops."

Dalton pinched the corners of his eyes. He looked like seven shades of hell. She needed him to believe. Ever since the one she'd seen with Frank, she'd carried her secret obsession around with her, not even telling her mother about it. Gray was one of the only people who had ever seen one of these things alive.

"So, are you ready to report me to Campos? Tell him I'm not mentally fit for the job?" She held her crutch across her chest as if it were a talisman that would ward off any reply she truly didn't want to hear.

He came back into the room and reopened the file, tossing the pictures around the desk and over her keyboard. His head swiveled from the pictures on the desk to the ones on the monitor. "They all look alike, but different. If they're the same things I saw last night, they're strong. Stronger than any man. And vicious."

Meredith leaned close to him. "Is that your way of saying you believe me?"

He paused. "I don't know. I believe what I saw. And I believe that these things resemble it. My questions are why are they here now, alive, where did they come from and where are they hiding?"

When he straightened up, he staggered and Meredith had to grab his shirtsleeve to keep him from tripping over her leg. "Okay, you've officially crashed," she said. "That's what happens when you mainline endorphins for hours and suddenly stop. You're going down there." She pointed at a doorway down the hall.

"What's down there?"

"My guest bedroom. You need some sleep and you're not driving. You'll feel better when you wake up. When your head is a little clearer, I can answer at least one of your questions."

One of his eyebrows cocked up. "Oh yeah, which one is that?"

"I'm pretty sure I know where they came from."

CHAPTER 19

Anita Banks awoke in her hospital room to a geyser of fire racing through every cell in her body. Her sheets were soaked with sweat. She could feel a haze of heat hovering over her skin. It hurt too much to breathe, much less ring for the nurse or even cry out for help.

What's happening to me?

Against her will, her bowels let loose. It felt like lava. Her eyes rolled to the top of her head from the unbearable agony and shame that came with it. Her tongue was an immobile emery board. It even hurt to blink.

Oh God, I'm going to die.

What was that thing that had bitten her? What poison was roiling inside it that could do this to her?

Somehow, she managed to turn her head, each stolen centimeter bringing ripples of agony as her burning skin brushed against the pillow. The bandage around her arm, covering the bite wound, was solid red. A thick, yellow substance oozed within the filaments.

This was the source of her pain, the ground zero for the wildfire infection that was incinerating her alive. The IVs of antibiotics hooked to her arms might as well have been flowing with water. She realized with sickening clarity that nothing could save her.

I won't be the only one. If they don't kill it, other people will end up just like this. I'll never know what they really are.

She stiffened as what felt like a river of boiling oil poured down her spine. Every organ along the way flinched, twitched and spasmed, fanning the flames of torment.

There's still so much to do. I never made a will. I never told anyone how and where I wanted to be buried. Please don't cremate me. I don't want to burn like this anymore.

Hot tears rolled down her face as she felt herself come to a boil. Her heart stuttered, racing to keep her systems going, but failing.

Something popped, but she couldn't see what it was. The room grew darker. An awful smell washed over her.

Is that me?

The uneven rhythm of her heart constricted her chest. She prayed it would stop before the fire finished having its way with her. She struggled to remember how to say the Our Father, the first verse circling through her head, *Our Father, who art in heaven*, until all thought, and mercifully, all pain, ceased.

Sergeant Dennis Campos led the pair in their discount suits out of Captain Hammerlich's office and through the station. Every line on Hammerlich's phone was lit. He was irritated and had little time to play usher. Campos was impressed by how stoic his boss had been through it all. But he knew him better than that. Hammerlich was not happy with their visitors or their news.

Campos felt like he hadn't slept in weeks. The harsh glare of the sun stabbed his eyes and hammered the inside of his skull.

One of the pair turned to him. His name was Dr. Greene but he didn't look like a doctor. He had a Cary Grant air about him, tall with dark hair and a vibe of always being the calm within the storm. "And you haven't had any calls or sightings since daybreak?"

"No, nothing. I have my guys out patrolling every street, looking in every crevice they can find."

He was going to have to call the night and graveyard shifts in a few hours. They'd been dead on their feet and in need of a few hours' rest. He hoped they got enough to get them through the night. These fucking things were like vampires, descending on the town at night and fleeing from the sun to some secret hiding place.

"It's best if you closed all of the beaches. We'll be happy to write up the warning. We could say the bacteria levels in the water are too high for safe swimming." This from the younger of the two, a redhead who made a pantsuit look pretty damn sexy. Campos struggled to remember her name.

He rubbed at his temple and said, "That'll work for the sound waters, Dr. . . . Ling, but not the Atlantic side."

"We could use the hypodermic-needle scare," Dr. Greene suggested.

"Wouldn't it seem suspicious to have two warnings at the same time?"

Dr. Greene gazed into the distance. "We're not concerned about suspicion, Sergeant. For now, we need to keep people away from the beaches. We have a team at the East Hampton hospital now, quarantining the victims. Suspicion will be high and rumors will fly, especially in a close-knit community like this. We can deal with that later. Have everyone debriefed before they go out so they take the proper precautions. I'm sure we'll be seeing a lot of each other."

Greene held out his hand and Campos reluctantly shook

it. The two doctors walked to their sedan and pulled out of the lot.

He pulled his cell phone out of his pocket and called Adelle. She answered on the first ring.

"Adelle, I need you to pack a couple of bags, get in the car and drive to your sister's house."

She laughed, thinking he was joking. "I don't think I'm going to drive all the way to Cape May today. I just put a load of laundry in and we have dinner with Linda and George tonight."

Campos breathed heavily into the phone, wanting to yell but knowing that wouldn't make things any easier. "I'm not asking you, I'm telling you. Honey, I love you, and I need you to do exactly what I said."

There was a long, uncomfortable silence. "Dennis, what's wrong?"

"I'm not sure. But I can't do anything effectively if I don't know you're safe. You need to be off the island before it gets dark."

Dalton had been asleep for only a couple of hours when Meredith knocked on the door. "Are you decent?"

He had to lift the covers and look to be sure. When she had offered a bed to crash in, he had been too exhausted to protest. He didn't even remember how he had gotten in the room.

"It depends on how you define *decent*," he replied. His throat felt as dry as the sand at Coopers Beach.

She came in wearing a formfitting, black jogging suit and carrying a glass of orange juice. "I would have brought you breakfast in bed but that costs extra. Plus, it's a pain in the ass to balance a tray with this damn crutch." She smiled and sat on the edge of the bed. Her smile snuck right inside him, planting the seed of an ache to take her in his arms.

He'd thought about getting this close to her many times, but never in the manner in which it actually happened. Reconciling his fantasy with their reality was difficult first thing in the morning when dreams and desires were just seconds from feeling as real as the warmth of the sun.

He took the glass and downed the juice like it was a shot at the bar.

"Jesus, I was thirsty. Did you sleep?" he said, pushing himself up. His uniform was draped over a rocking chair by the window. *Did I do that?* he thought. No, he wasn't that neat. He wondered what Meredith saw while he snored.

"I got my catnap in. I've told you, I don't sleep much. Besides, some very interesting things have been happening while you dreamt about bikini babes at car washes."

He was about to defend his dreaming honor when she slapped his leg and snorted. It was a very unladylike laugh, which made it all the more endearing.

Dalton heard the low murmur of a television coming from downstairs. "I bet the news is buzzing right now."

"That's the interesting part," she said. "There isn't a thing on the tube or the radio about last night. Not even the local news is covering it."

"How is that even possible? Those guys are up our asses when we pull someone over for speeding."

"If you ask me, someone's come in and put the lid on everything. But there is one little tidbit of news every station is hooked on. All of the beaches on eastern Long Island are closed because of, get this, high levels of bacteria in the water."

Dalton shifted and said, "I'll feel more comfortable if I have some clothes on. Do you mind closing your eyes for a second?"

"And here I thought all this time you wanted me to see you in your birthday suit." She closed her eyes and put her hand over them.

He jumped out of the bed and slipped into his pants and shirt. "Not before we've at least had dinner. You can open your eyes now." She pulled her hand away, fishing in her pocket for her phone. "Closing the beaches isn't abnormal. Happens all the time. This is New York, the sludge capital of the United States. Well, other than Philly. I guess that's why it's a perfect excuse."

Meredith said, "Exactly. And no one is questioning why they're closing the sound and the ocean at the same time. I don't remember that ever happening. Check this out."

He took her phone. It was open to her Twitter account. She'd pulled up everything under the Montauk hashtag. The screen was loaded with short bursts of people talking about the odd events of last night. They covered everything from the animal attacks to Officer Henderson's disappearance, people in protective suits collecting dead animals and some kind of lockdown at the hospital.

"It's the same with Facebook," she said.

Dalton scrolled through the sometimes-frightening messages. "You can't stop social media. Just ask Egypt." He opened some photo links to see pictures of mauled cats and dogs. "You said you think you know where these animals are coming from."

"I'm not the one who originally came up with the idea, but I've looked into it a lot and it makes sense," she said.

She pulled herself up with the aid of her crutch and started to make the bed. Dalton grabbed the sheets on the other side and helped. As she tucked everything in, she said, "You ever hear of Plum Island?"

He did his best to mimic her bed-making skills, knowing he was failing miserably. "No. Sounds like a place you land on in Candy Land. I play that game all the time with my niece."

"I'll forgive you that. You're not from around here, so there's no reason you'd know. Hell, I bet a good number of island lifers don't even know it's there. Read this." She typed onto her phone's screen and gave it back to him, this time with the Wikipedia entry on the island. It was pretty sparse and only took a minute to read through.

"Okay, it's an island where the government studies animal diseases. You think these things live on Plum Island? That wouldn't make a hell of a lot of sense. Anyone working there would have seen and reported them a long time ago."

Meredith plumped up the pillows and placed them on the bed.

"They don't live there," she said. "They're *made* there."

Meredith stared at him expectantly. His thumb swiped over the screen. He took a long time to read through the several web pages he'd searched. "Well, this place definitely has the conspiracy guys jumping. It says they think that Lyme disease and the West Nile virus both escaped from there on the back of bugs or workers who weren't decontaminated properly. I admit, that's some pretty serious shit if it's true and it's crazy to think they got away with it without even a slap on the wrist. But it seems a little far-fetched that no one's caught on to them. This is major stuff, Meredith."

She took a deep, calming breath. He'd come this far. She didn't want to lose him now. But things weren't going to get easier to digest. The little three-mile-long island wasn't even listed on most maps. Since it had been purchased by the government in the '50s to house their animal disease research labs, it was as if they had wished it away—the great and powerful Oz hidden behind a curtain of secrecy. "I know. Look, I don't believe everything I read on both sides of the issue, but there's enough smoke there to know there's a fire burning."

Dalton paced around the room, handing her phone back. The doubt in his face suddenly changed and he sat down in the rocker, resting his elbows on his knees. "Those people on the beach, Margie Salvatore," he mumbled. He sat straight. His eyes looked panicked. "Dammit, Anita. I have to call the hospital."

Meredith thought of Anita. She was one of the sweetest women she'd ever met. When Meredith had gotten in her accident, Anita was one of the first people to come see her in the hospital. Over the next grueling fourteen months, she had baked Meredith more brownies and cookies than she could eat in two lifetimes.

She had forgotten that Anita had been bitten, right in front of Dalton. Her heart sank as Dalton dialed his own phone, his jaw tightening as he listened to the hospital rep deliver what appeared to be very grim news.

CHAPTER 20

It was surreal seeing the beach devoid of sunbathers and swimming kids on a hot summer day. Instead, the sand was dotted with dark-clothed men and women, all of them searching the last known location of Officer Norm Henderson.

Jake Winn went back to the spot where whatever had dragged his friend had broken through the brush and first entered the beach. The trail was as deep and fresh as if it had just happened moments ago. What looked like hoofprints from some kind of large pig tapered along the edges of the heavily indented drag mark.

I know some pig didn't take him. Not even the biggest son of a bitch wild boar from Africa. So what the hell are these prints doing here?

Bits of semi-dried plaster sprinkled a few of the more defined prints. Casts had been made hours earlier. Winn wondered who on God's green earth they would call in to look at them. Last he heard, Anita Banks was in the hospital. What they needed was someone with more brains than hair follicles to tell them how it was possible that some giant pig snatched a full-grown man, outrunning the most fit kid on the force in the process. That was a mystery for Stephen Fucking King.

He wasn't close to giving up on Norm. But the more he looked at what was left behind, the less sense his brain could make of it all. And that only made him angrier.

You need to rest, gain some perspective, the rational part of his mind cried out amidst the jumble of scenarios and frantic questions.

That wasn't going to happen.

He spied a pile of white and gray feathers rippling in the wind. A seagull lay in a bloody heap, its lower half missing. In its place was a pool of congealed, black goo. *What the hell happened to you?*

The back of his neck felt like someone had taken a hot poker to it. He rubbed it with his hand, feeling the heat of a whopper of a sunburn. Walking back toward the shoreline, his face was pelted with cold, salty spray. It felt good. If no one else had been around, he'd have considered walking right into the ocean, clothes and all. The frigid jolt might spark something in his mind. At the least, it would chase any exhaustion off.

A gaggle of indiscernible voices was carried to him on the Atlantic breeze. He turned to his right and saw a group of searchers running to someone standing by a dune, waving his arms. Winn bolted.

He pushed through the crowd of a dozen or so people to see what the commotion was about. A volunteer fireman, Mark something, pointed at a spot by his feet. "It has to be his," he said to no one and everyone.

Winn knelt down, careful not to obliterate any nearby prints.

A shredded section of a blue shirt lay against the hot sand. A badge was still pinned to the scrap. Small indentations pockmarked the badge, as if someone had hammered a chisel into it—or something with powerful jaws had gnawed on it. The bottom edge of the badge was crusted with blood, already dried from the unimpeded sun.

Jake read the badge and felt his chest tighten.

"It's Henderson's," he said. "Everyone back the hell up. I want to preserve whatever I can. If anyone contaminates the scene, you'll answer to me."

Everyone cautiously took several steps back. Winn knew his eyes were on fire. The heat from his sunburned skin couldn't compare to the inferno that had been stoked in his belly.

He spotted a smudged hoofprint going up and away from the cloth and badge. Looking back at one of the county cops, he said, "You watch over this. I'm going to see where this leads."

His hand strayed to the butt of his gun. As he tracked his prey, he hoped to Jesus it was dumb enough to stick around and cross his path.

Dalton paled as someone at the hospital talked. He muttered a quick thank-you and shoved the phone in his pocket.

"She's dead."

"That's not possible," Meredith said. "You said she was bitten on the arm. Even if it had rabies, she'd be okay."

"They said not to come to the hospital. Her body was put in quarantine. They asked me not to tell anyone else for now. What the hell does that mean?"

Meredith limped down the hall. She grabbed her keys off her dresser and rummaged through her night table drawer for her battered little address book. Dalton stood in the doorway with a distant look in his eyes.

Flipping through the red book's pages, she said, "You want to get to the bottom of this before we're locked out?"

"Locked out? By who?"

Meredith rolled her eyes. "I keep forgetting you're a rookie. If they've quarantined the hospital and closed the beaches, the higher-ups are aware of what's going on. This town is going to be crawling with feds by tonight. We'll be reduced to traffic control. This is where I grew up. I joined the force to protect my town, my friends and family. I'm not going to let someone sweep this under the rug."

Dalton breathed heavily, as if he were working himself up to her challenge.

He shocked her by saying, "I killed her." His lips were pulled back hard against his teeth and his eyes closed to tiny slits.

"No, you didn't. Whatever that thing is out there killed her."

Punching the wall, he hissed, "I had the damn thing dead to rights. I couldn't pull the trigger. If I'd shot it, she would never have been bitten. It's completely my fault."

Meredith didn't know him well enough to judge how he'd react to any words of reassurance. Guilt could swallow a person whole, especially a guy like Dalton. It was pointless to try and convince him that he wasn't the reason Anita had died. That would have to come over time, if ever. For now, the best thing she could do was give him a purpose to funnel his emotions.

"You want to find the fuckers that started this?" she asked.

He stopped clenching his fists, staring at her with a glimmer of hope. "Right now, that's all I want."

"Good." She tapped a number into her phone. "I have an ex who works for Homeland Security. They run Plum Island now. He also captains the ferry from Orient Point to the island. I'm calling in every favor he owes me to get us out there."

* * *

Dominic Nathan and Bobby Gilligan had been thick as thieves since preschool. Both towheaded boys of short stature but larger-than-life dispositions, they were throwbacks to another era. Now at the ripe old age of ten, they avoided staying indoors to play video games. Why waste time shooting things when adventure was just outside your door every day? Together, they'd explored every swamp, creek, rocky bluff, empty lot and abandoned house in the three-mile area around their neighborhood.

Bobby had left his parents arguing in the kitchen, walking into Dom's house, where his friend's mother laid out a plate of pancakes and bacon for him. The two boys made quick work of breakfast, anxious to be outside. There wasn't a cloud in the sky. Bobby wore only his swim trunks and a sleeveless Captain America T-shirt. Dom was just as ready for the water, only his shirt sported Batman. The differences in opinion over comic book greatness—Bobby was a Marvel man, Dom DC to his core—was their only point of contention, one they'd stopped arguing about a long time ago. Neither was going to convince the other to come to the dark side.

Dom's mother dutifully took them to the comic book shop every two weeks, a weatherworn storefront lit by forty-watt bulbs and smelling of decades of mildew, but bursting with the colorful pages of comics spanning over five decades. They were the only patrons under the age of thirty-five, more proof that they were born too late.

"Can we go to the comic book store today?" Dom asked his mom as she rinsed the dishes before placing them in the dishwasher.

"I was just going to ask you if you wanted me to take you two this morning. Your dad left twenty dollars so you can stock up."

Bobby looked over at Dom, puzzled. On a good day, they might have ten bucks between them, and that was money socked away from allowance. Dom's father never laid out so much cash for them. Something had to be up.

"Is it your birthday or something?" Bobby asked, dreaming of the Avengers, Fantastic Four and Deadpool.

Dom shrugged his shoulders, equally bewildered.

His mother solved the mystery. "The beaches have been closed off today. We thought it would be a good idea if you stayed inside. If you want, you can even rent a movie on demand."

The boys felt the wind go out of their sails. Getting a bunch of comics was great, but not at the expense of being trapped in the house. The only place to properly read a new comic book was either out by the big rock behind the Kelleher house or backed up against a sand dune at the beach. Anyplace else lessened the magic.

"Do we have to stay inside all day?" Dom said, not bothering to take one iota of the whine from his voice. Bobby raised his little eyebrows, pleading.

She looked at them both and Bobby could see she was starting to break. "Can we go out for just a little while?" he asked.

Dom's mother flipped a dish towel over her shoulder and leaned against the counter. She looked up at the pig clock on the wall. "You boys have one hour to get everything out of your system, but you have to promise me you won't go near the water."

"We won't," Dom said, pushing his chair back with a loud scrape.

"We promise," Bobby added.

She shook her head, smiling. "One hour. Any longer, and it's no comics or movies."

They ran out of the house before she could dictate any

more restrictions. The already humid air felt like an elixir to their young lungs. "You wanna check the bird?" Dom asked.

The day before, they'd come across a dead bird lying in the grass with its stiff claws pointing skyward. They'd found a thick stick, used it to dig a deep hole and given it a proper burial, complete with a Hail Mary. Bobby had found a speckled, polished rock and sunk it into the soft earth as a miniature headstone.

"It's only been a day," Bobby replied.

"So? You waiting for it to turn into a zombie?"

"That's stupid."

"Right. Come on."

Dom sprinted through the backyard, scaling the five-foot picket fence like a seasoned marine. Bobby was just as fast and nimble and at his side in no time. They ran to the vacant lots behind Mrs. Losapio's house. Maple trees filled the lots and were a favorite shady spot for the boys to escape the heat of the day. They also made good climbing.

The tiny headstone was where they had left it but had been knocked on its side. Dom searched the ground for the stick they'd used the day before.

"It's probably gonna smell," Bobby said.

"So does your butt," Dom said, laughing. He walked over, holding the stick. "We can check it every day to see how it decompotes."

"I think it's *decomposes*," Bobby corrected.

Dom started digging. "Whatever. They say worms eat dead things from the inside out. You think it'll be full of worms?"

"It's in the ground where worms live, so, yeah. If it stinks, I might puke." Bobby pulled his shirt up over his nose just in case. Dom shook his head at him.

As he pulled the dirt away from the grave, Dom said, "This is going to be cool. Gross, but cool."

A strong wind huffed from between the maples, chattering the leaves. Bobby fanned his hand in front of his face. "Crap, it's worse than I thought. Put the dirt back on."

Dom's nose crinkled. He dropped to his hands and knees and plunged his head into the hole. "It's not coming from here."

"Then what's making that smell?"

They turned to face the secretive darkness between the trees.

Dom pointed. "I think it's coming from somewhere back there. You think it's another dead animal?"

Bobby did his best to breathe out of his mouth, but it only made it feel like he could taste the stench as well. "It's gotta be big to smell like that. Maybe a deer or something. And I'm not burying a deer."

"Me neither. But I want to at least see it before my mom locks us up. Let's check it out."

Before Bobby could protest, Dom was creeping through the trees. There was no questioning whether he would follow or not. He was just as curious as his best friend, just a little more cautious.

A reedy whistling called to them like a mythical Siren. It was like the sound of a tiny, boiling teakettle.

They followed their noses, several times gagging as they got closer to the source.

When they stepped past the last row of maples, they found it.

Dom felt like he'd been hit with some kind of paralyzing ray. He didn't hear Bobby whimper with pained, sucking breaths. He couldn't move. He couldn't speak.

The flesh began to expand, the surface bubbling like a

peach balloon hooked to a helium canister. The boys watched, mouths hanging open.

Dom thought about his mother and wished like he'd never wished before that he'd listened to her. They would have been at the comic book store right now, far away from here. That's all he wanted to be. Far away from here.

Then it erupted.

CHAPTER 21

Meredith drove them out to the North Fork in her Chevy Suburban. What she lacked in speed on her feet now, she more than made up for behind the wheel of the SUV. Dalton actually loved the reckless way she drove. Punching the accelerator in his squad car when he chased down speeders was always the highlight of any shift. He wondered if all cops were secretly speed junkies.

The Cross Sound Ferry that shuttled folks between Long Island and New London, Connecticut, mostly so they could gamble at the big Indian casinos, hulked in the dock. The huge ferry bobbed empty and silent.

"Looks like we missed takeoff," he said.

"Takeoff is for planes," Meredith said, grinning. "We're not taking that ferry, unless you want to visit the submarine museum."

"Some other time."

She pointed at another, smaller ferry to their right. "That's our ride to Plum Island."

There was a small car lot surrounding the slip for employee cars. At the moment, several dozen cars filled the white-painted slots. The ferry itself was a two-level structure.

It was designed to transport people, not their vehicles. Dalton looked at the name imprinted on its side.

"Fort Terry Ferry. Cute," he said.

"It's anything but. Fort Terry was built on Plum Island during the Spanish-American War as a first line of defense for New York. It's ironic that what they think they're doing out there is still in the vein of defending the country. I hear you can still see remnants of the fort out there."

He nudged her with an elbow. "You know a hell of a lot about this place."

"Like I said, seeing that thing on the beach and the way it disappeared opened my eyes. I've had a lot of time to do research."

A massive-shouldered, square-jawed man emerged from a small hut and waved. When he saw Meredith, he broke into a blinding smile. He walked with a military stride, his close-cropped hair slicing the air.

Dalton nudged Meredith. "Was dating this guy part of your research?"

She gave him a look that could melt an iceberg in seconds. He'd hit a raw nerve, and he realized just how deep she'd gotten into her quest for the truth. While everyone else on the island was running around chasing their tails and afraid of the dark, she saw this as a sort of personal vindication and a chance to uncover a disturbing mystery. If he hadn't seen the beast with his own eyes and what it did to Anita, he would have turned right around.

All of this was crazy, right? What Meredith had said couldn't possibly be the truth. It had to be far more mundane. Sure, he saw something that he couldn't explain, but he was no vet or zoologist. Dogs were born deformed and diseased just as much as people.

But Anita couldn't even tell what that thing was.

"Robert Nicolo, this is Gray Dalton."

He'd been so lost in thought, he hadn't even noticed their

quick reunion. The big man rested a hand over Meredith's shoulders. He held out the other to him. His grip was surprisingly soft.

"Hey, Robert," Dalton said, meeting the man's steel gaze. "I'm kind of tagging along on this. Meredith is the one in charge."

Robert smiled. "She always is." There was a hint of regret in his voice.

The midday heat baked off the lot's blacktop. Dalton felt sweat trickling down his sides. "Meredith tells me you're with Homeland Security."

"Five years in," he said. "Before that, I worked homicide in Queens. This place has been a vacation compared to that. Though they do ask me to do stuff I'd never dreamed of."

"Like piloting the ferry?" Dalton asked.

Robert shook his head. "Budget cuts. Almost everyone who draws a paycheck from Plum Island has more than one job. When they heard I used to pilot fishing charter boats out of Red Bank, I became the de facto ferryman. Come on aboard."

As they stepped onto the ferry, Meredith turned to her former boyfriend and said, "Look, I don't want you to lose your job over this. You can tell us to hit the road and I won't take it personally."

He ran a hand over the short spikes of his hair. "To tell you the truth, I'm a little concerned about things out there."

"How come?" Dalton asked, leaning against a rail, listening to the chop of the water as it sloshed against the big boat.

"Things have been getting stranger the past few months, and that's saying a lot for this place. And after everything Meredith told me about what's been going on in Montauk, I get the feeling something's gone wrong. There was talk of shutting everything down and moving all of the labs to a place in Kansas. They had already closed and sealed Lab 257 and moved everything over to Lab 101 a while ago. The writing was on the wall. Head count had been cut by over thirty percent. I was waiting for them to tell me I'd been reassigned, but it never came about." He went to the narrow staircase that led to the upper deck. "Let me get this tug started and I'll tell you the rest on the way over."

The ferry started up with a dull thrum and Robert came down to untie it from its mooring. They followed him back up to the pilot's cabin. Inside was mercifully air-conditioned. Tinting on the windows kept the broiling sun at bay.

I'm all in now, Dalton thought as they pulled away from the dock. *And so are Meredith and Robert. Either they're both insane or there's some validity to this.* They were either on the path to career suicide, exposing a colossal black-op-type situation—which would make them heroes or snitches, depending on each person's perception—or waltzing right into the heart of something so savage, there was no getting off the island alive. At best, they'd be taking a leisurely jaunt to a prohibited island, find out that Meredith's theories were unfounded, and somehow make it back undetected.

He didn't hold out much hope for that last one.

"Fuck it," Dalton said under his breath.

Meredith snapped her face in his direction. "What did you say?"

"Just thinking out loud. Robert, just so I'm a little more comfortable with this whole thing, tell me why someone who works for Homeland Security is willing to break his oath and risk his job by taking us to Plum Island. I know Meredith is awesome, but it can't all be for her."

Again, she tried to liquefy him with her gaze. The way Robert looked at her, he could tell the man still had strong feelings for her. She had to have been the one to break it off.

Robert turned the wheel, scanning the horizon. A tiny smile curled the corners of his lips. "Not to deny Meredith's allure, I haven't been comfortable with the way things have been run lately. Over the past thirty years, Plum Island has been a disaster waiting to happen. I'm sure she told you about the different diseases people believe escaped from the labs onto the mainland."

Dalton nodded. Meredith settled into the copilot seat, resting an arm over her crutch.

"The place was initially built to study different animal diseases, specifically hoof-and-mouth. Did Meredith tell you that a former Nazi was actually one of the founders of the lab?"

"No, that's one thing she left out." The bizarre was taking a turn to the surreal.

"Sounds nuts, right? Back in the '40s, Operation Paperclip was designed to import all of these Nazi scientists into the country and get them working for us. One of them was Erich Traub. He worked on biological warfare agents during World War II. Someone in our government was willing to forgive his dubious past so they could use his mind against our enemies. They needed someone who could help us come up with offensive and defensive capabilities against the Soviet Union. Traub was only too happy to accept a full pardon and assist. For a Nazi operating under the Third Reich, I'm sure he felt right at home. Did you know they used to experiment on Gypsies and other races to see how each responded to different diseases?"

Dalton shook his head. He'd never been a big history buff. He knew Nazis were the embodiment of evil, but was fuzzy on their specific atrocities outside of the death camps.

"Nazi scientists did anything their sick little minds dreamed up without having to heed to a code of ethics or morals. When they weren't pumping other races with diseases to see how they reacted, they looked for ways to sterilize anyone that wasn't in their plan for a master race."

It didn't take long for the island to come into full view.

"We're going through what's called Plum Gut right now," Robert said. He pointed at an old, brass-colored lighthouse. "Believe it or not, that's a functioning lighthouse. Coast Guard automated it a long time ago. Plum Island isn't a place for lighthouse keepers."

The island was chock-full of trees and high grass. It looked like an untended, wild sanctuary from this end.

"Why is it called Plum Island?" Dalton asked.

Meredith said, "Because of all the plum trees. I wouldn't eat any fruit grown there, though. If you could see Plum Island from above, it looks a little like a musical note. Most people call it the pork chop. Naturally, it was first inhabited by Indians, then ownership passed down to different families until the government took it over to make Fort Terry, then the animal disease labs."

Dalton waved his hands. "Hold up. I'm still stuck on the Nazi part. So this place was made for crazy Nazi scientists to make diseases?"

"Not exactly," Robert said, angling around the eastern side of the island. "Traub, I'm pretty sure, was the only former Nazi involved. Everyone's job was to study existing diseases, find cures, as well as ways to militarize them. Think of it. The best way to bring a country to its knees is to destroy its crops and livestock. Sick, starving people will either overthrow leadership, or be too weak to defend themselves. All it takes is a few well-placed microbes, and you win. The U.S. and the Soviets were both looking for ways to take each other out, as well as defend themselves from the other. Plum Island was at the center of that. Like Wernher von Braun, Traub was milked for his knowledge. We used them as much as they used us."

Meredith chimed in, "Foot-and-mouth disease was their

first area of concentration, but they moved on to things like the Marburg virus, Ebola, Rift Valley fever, you name it. Plum Island is home to almost every deadly disease known to man. And the scary part is, between management and budget issues, the labs are not the most secure facilities. Contaminants get out all the time. Plenty of workers have gotten sick and died, and have even brought lawsuits. So far, no one has been able to beat the island in the courts. Everything associated with Plum Island gets swept under the rug."

Dalton watched a lot of History Channel and saw an immediate correlation. "Sounds a little like Area 51."

Meredith snickered. "Kind of like that, yeah, but without the little green men. The shit here is real and it's serious."

"Gray men," Dalton countered.

Meredith and Robert looked at him. He stood his ground. "The aliens are gray. At least that's what they say."

It broke the tension that had been building as they chugged toward the island. A grouping of white buildings appeared out of the green forest.

"That's Lab 101," Robert said, positioning the ferry so it faced the dock. Turning to Dalton, he said, "I wouldn't blame you if you ask me to turn back."

"Holy crap."

Mickey Conrad removed his hat, hoping the sun would evaporate some of the sweat that beaded his head like he'd stepped into a downpour. He looked over at Jim Kanelos, one of the daytime-shift cops who was more comfortable doing stop-light warnings than body patrol. Jim had his back to him, trying to shield the woman and two boys from the mess of human flesh piled in the crimson depression within the empty field.

The boys' faces and shirts were smeared with blood. So was the mother's. After finding the body and having the misfortune of being there when the corpse's internal gases blew out of the distended stomach, they'd run home like an axe murderer was on their heels. It was obvious she'd held them both tightly, calming them down, forgetting to wash the stains off. Her hands caressed their heads, keeping them from looking. Mickey didn't think the kids would ever want to glance this way again.

"You can get them back to the house, Jim."

Kanelos said, "I'll come back." He was a slight guy, maybe one-fifty on a good day, with olive skin and a perpetual five-o'clock shadow. Mickey liked to joke with him that he was the swarthiest Greek that had ever stolen his way into America. Jim liked to tell him what he could do to himself with a bottle of olive oil and a shish kebab skewer. The guy loved to laugh, even if it was at his own expense.

Mickey had never seen him so serious. Everyone was nervous. Not a single soul knew what they were dealing with. Since morning, things had quieted down. And now there was this. He'd been hearing rumors about something going on at the hospital and sightings of a procession of strange, white vans. He'd yet to come across them, but something was up. He could feel it in the atmosphere as easily as a strong ocean wind.

When Kanelos turned, Mickey saw the moist patch of scarlet on his partner's hand. He called him over.

Keeping his voice low, he tilted his head toward Jim's hand and said, "Wash that off as soon as you get to the house. Try not to get any more on you."

"Shit, you think this is some kind of infection?" Jim Kanelos's sizable Adam's apple bobbed.

"It's better not to take any chances. Pull the paramedics

aside and tell them what happened. Maybe they'll know how to properly disinfect it."

He spat a string of Greek under his breath. By the tone, Mickey assumed it was all foul. Kanelos composed himself and walked the woman and kids back to her house.

That gave Mickey a chance to look around the area and see how the body was brought here. The grass was pretty high. If it was dragged, there would have been a line of depression. There was none. Did someone carry it and drop it here? And why?

The lower half of the body had been mangled so badly, you'd think it had been put through a meat grinder. All of the soft tissue of the face was missing, revealing the yellow-white skull beneath. The bone's surface was scored with long gouges. As far as he could tell, the torso had been left alone. There was an exit hole on the left side of the stomach where the gases had rocketed, dousing the boys in the man's bowels. The high-riding odor made him dizzy the closer he came to the body. Stepping away and covering his nose with a handkerchief, he called it in.

"I'm also going to need some paramedics at 125 Amble Drive," he said.

"That's going to be a while."

Crap, it's starting again, he moaned.

"Why is that?"

"I've been told there aren't any local paramedics available. We're getting some from East Quogue."

He wanted to scream, *Are you fucking kidding me?* That would only earn him an official reprimand and wouldn't get paramedics to see the woman, boys and Jim any quicker.

"I'll remain on scene with the body."

Walking in a wide circle around the roasting corpse to clear out the frustration pounding through his system, he spotted a brown rectangle lying within a patch of fiery dandelions. It was a wallet. Crouching, he removed a pen from his shirt pocket and used the tip to flip it open. A driver's license stared up at him, tucked behind a clear plastic pocket.

Mickey studied the vitals on the license, then looked over at the body. Height and weight looked about the same. Closing the wallet, he noticed a dark stain along the bottom of the leather. Had to be blood.

"Dan Hudson, what the hell did you stumble into?"

The corpse gave no answer.

CHAPTER 22

Dalton had expected they'd be met at the dock by security personnel, possibly with weapons drawn when they saw a couple of faces they didn't recognize.

All he saw was tall saw grass swaying in the breeze, an empty dock and tight clusters of trees so thick, they concealed the labs beyond.

"This is a secure government-run island, right?" he said, looking back at Robert as he tied the ferry to the dock.

"Yes," he answered, crouched over the deck, sweat dripping down his nose.

"So where's the security?"

Robert stood straight, looking up the path leading to the labs. "That's why I was concerned and agreed to take you and Meredith along. You are cops, after all."

Dalton helped Meredith to her feet. She said, "Tell him the rest."

Robert's complexion had paled considerably since they'd arrived. His eyes kept flicking to parts beyond, as if he was waiting for someone to take notice and acknowledge his transgression and their illegal entry.

"You know how I told you they study different animal diseases? That was the original charter for the facility, something they stuck to for five decades. This entire place was run by the USDA all that time, until it was privatized in the early '90s. When things go private, money gets tight. The newer lab, Lab 257, was closed a few years later. It had been the site of a germ meltdown and the building was deemed unsafe. No one was going to pony up the money to fix it. All that's left is Lab 101, a series of labs that were in major need of renovation to get up to safety code."

His mind fixating on poorly built labs and escaping germs, Dalton worried that every breeze carried the seeds of their doom. Something was obviously wrong here. The door to the empty concrete guard shack was open, swaying back and forth with the wind. The island wasn't necessarily quiet. The sounds of the surf and cawing gulls filled any moments of silence.

It just *felt* deserted.

Robert still hadn't put down the gangplank so they could get off the ferry. He continued.

"Everything changed after 9/11. If people thought this place was secretive before, they were really in the dark after those fucks took down the towers. It became more than staying ahead of our enemies and protecting ourselves against all forms of agroterrorism. We altered the entire course of R and D in 2003. Scientists were recruited from bioengineering and genetics companies to come here. So we had an island full of geneticists, DNA and disease specialists. It was all for one reason. Finding ways to create organic weapons. We have a volunteer military now and no one likes to see kids die. It's very bad PR. One of their goals was to create an expendable weapon and spare human lives."

Dalton interrupted him. "How the hell would you know all of this? I doubt that they would release classified information like this to the guy who drives the ferry."

He saw the concern drop over Meredith's face like a cut

curtain. Robert's chest expanded, bristling. He was a big man, but Dalton was no ninety-pound weakling. If he wanted to throw, let him. Dalton could use the chance to vent his own frustration.

Meredith stepped between them. "Because people talk. Robert was around all of these people while they talked shop on their ride to and from the island. The history, we learned together by doing a little research. I doubt anyone else was in a better position to know what was going on than Robert."

Closing his eyes, Robert took a calming breath. "She's right. I also brought a ton of test animals onto the island. Dogs, sheep, cattle, pigs, mice, you name it. They came by the hundreds. There's another boat they use for the livestock. The only way the animals get off the island is through the incinerator. Over the past year, the number of large dogs, pigs and goats increased exponentially. Six months ago, I overheard a doctor mention a party to celebrate their breakthrough. One month ago, all personnel were taken to the island to complete a major, top secret project. No one spoke about it. I was told they would remain on the island until further notice. Well, I still haven't gotten any notice and all communication with the island has gone silent. When I called my superiors in Washington, I was told to stand down and wait for their call. That was a week ago. I still haven't heard a thing, from anyone. I knew something was wrong."

"And then the shit hit the fan in Montauk," Meredith said. "You see, scientists have been playing around with genetic manipulation and crossbreeding longer than you'd think. It didn't just start twenty years ago or with the decoding of human DNA. Even back in the 1920s, a Russian scientist named Ilya Ivanov actually got funding from the government to crossbreed humans with chimpanzees."

"You get that from some conspiracy website?" Dalton asked.

Meredith poked him in the chest. "It's a heavily documented and noted fact. What Ivanov did was implant human sperm into chimpanzees to create a human-ape hybrid. The why has been speculated about for decades. I tend to think that like most scientists, he tried to do it because he could. If he succeeded, which he didn't, I'm positive the Russian government would have found a way to militarize his creations. It's the way of any large governmental entity. Just like we have here, now. Plum Island is a perfect place to do all kinds of things on the wrong side of ethics without prying eyes gumming up the works."

Robert released the gangplank. It hit the dock with a dull thud.

Meredith continued, "If we had the time, I'd run down all of the crazy things the Nazis tried to do before and during the war, from eugenics to create a master race, to crossbreeding of animals that should never have been thrown together. Unlike back then, we have the technology now to make these nightmares come true."

"And here we are back to Nazis," Dalton said. He hadn't realized until now that he was grinding his back teeth. His gums were sore.

Meredith nodded sagely. "Life is all about going in circles. You still want to come with us?"

Robert's face was clouded with concern. There was no denying something had happened here. Dalton would never forgive himself if he bailed out now. The more he heard, the angrier he felt. If the things that happened to Anita and Norm Henderson were the result of the government playing God, he wouldn't stop until everyone involved was exposed and burned.

"Do you at least have any masks?" Dalton asked. Meredith was visibly relieved. He was anxious to see what the hell was going on, but felt the need for at least the bare minimum of protection.

Pointing up the paved path, Robert said, "There are safety garments in the decontamination section before we hit the labs. I think we're safe out in the open."

"Your positivity is very reassuring," Dalton said, taking the lead. He turned back to offer Meredith a hand. She waved him off. "I have a feeling no matter what we find, we're not going to be happy."

It wasn't long after finding Henderson's pitted badge when the search was called to an end. And it wasn't for the reason Jake Winn had been hoping for all along.

About seventy yards from the badge, a volunteer fireman stumbled upon a well-used fire pit in the yard of one of the houses along the beach. Within the pit lay the foaming remains of Norman Henderson.

There was no way to tell it was Henderson from the body itself. They had to go by the uniform, or at least what was left of it. Whatever had attacked the man did so with the savagery of a pride of lions. Winn lost track of the number of searchers who had to run off to vomit after catching a glimpse into the fire pit.

When the meat truck pulled up, Winn watched the guys step out and asked, "Hey, where are Dale and Frankie?"

"Called in sick," the younger one said, concentrating on getting the stretcher out of the back of the van.

As tough a guy as he'd known himself to be, he couldn't bear to watch them gather Norman's remains. He stormed off toward the water, his eyes burning, vision blurry. There was still a chance the body wasn't his. The tatters of the uniform were sprinkled around the fire pit, sticking out of the exposed meat.

No, don't give yourself false hope, he thought. *You know damn well that's Norm. What you need to know now is what did that to him, find it and erase it without prejudice. Don't fall apart now, Jake. Be a cop, dammit. Man or animal, something murdered Norm.*

A slight commotion behind him made him turn back. Two white vans had pulled up to the scene, discharging several people dressed in tan hazmat suits with rectangular glass visors sewn into the full hood. Winn ran back to the yard.

"What's going on here?"

The MEs had been pushed against the van, held in place by a pair of towering men in protective gear. Winn couldn't make out any faces behind the tint of the visors. The team that had worked on the search was being urged back by a half-dozen other men.

"Are you in charge of this crime scene?" said one of them, his voice muffled by the hood.

Winn folded his arms across his chest, flexing his forearms. "I am. Who the hell are you?"

"The new man in charge. I need you and everyone else to vacate this area immediately."

Winn stood his ground. "That's my friend over there. You're not doing a goddamn thing with him until you tell me who you are."

The man's shoulders slumped as the hood swiveled over to the fire pit. "Look, we have a job to do here and you're not in a need-to-know status. Trust me when I say this is over your jurisdiction."

"Are you kidding me? This is my frigging town. It's been my jurisdiction for over twenty years. Maybe if you take your little mask off, we can talk like men."

Winn reached for the top of the hood. The man recoiled. Another came up from behind him, wrapping him in a bear hug. Jesus, he was strong. Winn was lifted off his feet and carried to one of the white vans. No matter how hard he struggled, he couldn't break the iron grip. When everyone else saw how easily he'd been dispatched, they left the area without further provocation. Winn watched the MEs go back into their truck and pull away.

The monster holding Winn said, "Now, can I let you go or do you have to make things harder on yourself?"

Winn's options raced through his mind. In almost every scenario, he couldn't see himself coming out on the winning side of any physical confrontation, not with this guy being one among many.

As much as it pained him, he sighed, "You can put me down."

His constricted lungs gathered in as much air as they could hold the moment the pressure was eased from his rib cage. The other hooded mystery man came back to him.

"I'm sorry it has to be this way. Thank you for cooperating. I don't want things to get any uglier than they already are. Rest assured, we'll take the utmost care with the deceased."

A team of men were gingerly lifting Norman's remains into a body bag that looked to be made of thick rubber. Something slipped from one of their gloved hands and landed back in the pit with a heavy plop. Winn's stomach flinched.

"I'm going to find out what this is all about," Winn said, boring a hole into the visor. "Where are you taking him?"

"Some place safe. Any questions that can be answered will have to come through your superior to mine."

"And who the hell are your superiors?"

The man turned his attention to the extraction team. The big man placed a paw on his shoulder. "We need you to leave now."

Jake glared at him. "Get your fucking hand off me."

As he walked past the open double doors of the white van, he stole a quick peek inside. There was a small command center on one side of the van, with a bank of computers, a narrow shelf and several chairs, all of them empty for the moment. Something nudged him in the back, moving him along.

Jake didn't resist. He'd seen what he needed to see.

On one of the screen savers, there'd been a platinum background with three black letters emblazoned across the center of the screen.

Those letters were CDC—the Centers for Disease Control.

A uniform shirt lay draped across a chair that had been welded to the floor. There was an official patch on the upper arm of the dark blue shirt.

"Fuck me sideways," Winn whispered. It was a DARPA patch—the Defense Advanced Research Projects Agency, the military development arm that was synonymous with black ops and other unseemly things that fueled political debates and inspired a multitude of conspiracy theories.

If DARPA and the CDC were staging their coup, they were all in deep shit.

"If you don't mind, Kathryn, I'm going to take a little break," Dr. Harrison Greene said, tapping her shoulder. She was hunched over her laptop in an empty grammar school classroom. It was as good a place as any to set up their temporary command center.

"Do you need some water?" she asked, eyeing the silver pill container he'd extracted from his pocket.

He nodded. She reached for the cooler under her desk and handed him a bottle.

By the faraway look in his eyes, he was overdue. When the panic came, it overtook everything. He wouldn't be able to read a passage in a book when he was like this, much less pore through the information dump that had been coming at them from all sides.

Dr. Greene tilted a couple of pills into his palm, one Klonopin to settle his nerves and stop the anxiety attack before it fully blossomed, and one Donepezil to slow the hands of fate.

She wasn't sure he'd even told his wife about the early-onset Alzheimer's. It had come on so suddenly, so damn fast, but he was just as quick to realize the implication of the symptoms and seek discreet help. That was six months ago. It was only his steadfast belief in full professional disclosure that made him confide in her. Kathryn wasn't to tell a soul, and she'd been true to her word.

With the sure knowledge that his mind—his greatest asset, the foundation upon which he'd built his working and personal life—was failing, in came the tide of panic.

He fought them both with his will and two simple pills.

To say she was concerned about him and his ability to sift through the madness they'd been unceremoniously dumped into was putting things mildly. This was a crisis that had all the earmarks for a pandemic. Worst of all, no one was talking to one another, at least not in a productive manner. The whole thing reeked of official secrets. Human lives, thousands of them, were at risk. It didn't take a genius to see that someone was pulling strings, shifting them like pawns, greedily hoarding information. Vital information. Life-and-death information.

Did someone higher up know about Dr. Greene's condition? She couldn't shake the feeling that they'd been set up to fail.

While Dr. Greene walked out to the bathroom, Kathryn went through the various e-mails that had been sent to her by their teams in the quarantined hospital and in the field. The news was dire.

The infection had a 100 percent mortality rate. Death

came in hours, a day at the most. The physical effects of the contagion were horrendous. It was as if the infected carried within them the materials for a nuclear meltdown. The hospital was such a hot zone, Dr. Greene had requested they evacuate one square mile around the facility.

That request had been denied.

Kathryn assumed the DARPA spook that had attached himself to her rapid response team had put the evac order on ice. He'd intercepted them when they stopped in Westchester to gather needed supplies. No one was even given a name or rank of the DARPA man—just a badge and an order to do whatever was asked of them. Her protest was cut short by Dr. Greene. He'd pulled her aside and warned her not to cross the man. DARPA caused tougher men to lose their lunch.

The man offered no assistance or information in return for their cooperation.

Oh, but he and other DARPA agents on the ground watched. They had the ear of whoever was in charge of this disaster.

The more she thought of the size of the rapid response team they were allotted, with members from Atlanta and the tristate area, the hotter her anger flared. They needed five times the personnel if there was ever a hope to get a handle on things here. They had been hamstrung from the start.

She had to push her frustration aside and concentrate on the things she could control.

How long can we contain this?

Or was that a question too late in the asking.

Maybe containment was no longer an option.

CHAPTER 23

The walk to Lab 101 was quick, but not without its share of surprises. From his vantage point, Dalton felt like he'd entered a wildlife sanctuary, not a government facility. The vegetation had been left to grow lush and dense. The humid air was heavy with the smells of damp earth and greenery. It called to mind days spent on his grandmother's back porch, the acre of tilled land spread before them, snapping green beans and tossing them in a brown paper bag. A pair of feral cats, all dirty fur and tattered ears, skittered to his right, disappearing within the tall, dark grass.

The lab itself was a study in governmental architectural blandness, an unimpressive series of whitewashed connected concrete blocks, fronted by a grassy quadrangle. It had the look and feel of a ghost town. Dalton wouldn't have been surprised to see a tumbleweed blow past. Cold, empty windows stared down at them, indifferent to their presence.

"I can't believe I'm actually here," Meredith said, her voice dripping with awe.

"On an island full of labs?" Dalton asked.

"You don't understand."

Meredith stopped and pointed with her crutch to a grassy area on their left. "What is that?"

Robert shaded his eyes and scanned the foliage off the paved walkway. "Hopefully not what I think it is."

He cautiously stepped over the steel handrail, dropping onto the grass. Dalton touched Meredith's shoulder and said, "I'll go with him. Wait here."

She followed his gaze to her crutch. He immediately felt like a creep, pointing out her disability like that. Yes, he wasn't sure how she'd fare on the uneven terrain, but that was her decision to make, not his. It was too late to take it back and he felt saying he was sorry would only make things worse. He avoided her eyes and ran after Robert.

The man stood over a crumpled pile of stained clothes. There were rents in the fabric of the dark blue shirt and tan Dockers. One brown loafer lay on its side, just a few feet from the pile. A dried, unidentifiable substance flowed from the shoe to the clothes. When Robert bent down to get a closer look, Dalton warned him, "Don't touch it!"

"Thanks for the warning. Trust me, I'm not going to touch anything on this island if I don't have to. I just wanted to see if there were—"

He craned his neck, scanning the bundle. "Glasses. Blue Gucci frames. Only Dr. Stanley wore those."

"I saw something like this a couple of nights ago. A couple on the beach was torn to pieces. They were scattered all around a dune. The chunks of their bodies were smoking, like they were dissolving in acid. I heard that everything completely melted in the morgue. If this is anything like that, Dr. Stanley is right here with his clothes."

Robert straightened and took a few steps back. "What the hell were they messing with?"

Dalton looked up at the stark white structures that made up Lab 101. "Something they shouldn't have. And if we don't find any answers in there, a whole lot more people are going to end up like this guy."

When they rejoined Meredith, she asked, "What was it?"

"One of the doctors," Robert replied, forging ahead.

Meredith drew her Glock from her holster. "I'm not taking any chances."

Dalton did the same. "I think that ship has sailed." He cast a glance back at the ferry.

The vegetation outside the walkway to the lab looked as if it hadn't been tended in years, though this time in the summer it took only a couple of weeks for Mother Nature to take over. "Is it always like this?"

Robert turned to him. "Usually overgrown, but not this bad. They had us take turns with the grounds keeping. We all hated it, so we half-assed it. If any duty here could stand cut corners, this was it."

They stopped in front of a squat building with double steel doors. There were no markings on the building to indicate its function; a square, gray card reader was fastened to the wall.

"This is the decontamination room," Robert said. "Every employee is expected to go through here when they get to the island and repeat the procedure when they leave. It's to make sure nothing gets on or off the island. There are more areas like this throughout the lab. Depending on your job, a person could have to strip and shower up to twenty times a day. We're skipping the shower part because I'm pretty sure safety protocols have been rescinded."

He produced a white card from his pocket and waved it over the reader. A green light came on, followed by a loud buzzing as the door unlocked.

"There goes my chance to shower with you," Dalton whispered to Meredith.

"You always get this goofy when you break into government labs?"

"This being my first one, I guess so."

"Try not to let Robert hear you. He knows these people. This is going to be hard on him."

The decontamination room had lockers and cubbies to hold shoes. A line of shower stalls spread out before them. They walked through, sans water. Stacks of plain white overalls, masks, gloves and shoe booties were piled in cubbies on the other side.

Robert handed masks and gloves to each of them. "Better safe than sorry."

Dalton fastened the elastic bands of the mask around his head and donned the gloves. He was astonished to look up and see spiderweb cracks in the ceiling. Some of the gaps in the cracks were considerable in size. If this was a decontamination room, shouldn't it be sealed tight?

They came to an opaque glass door that slid open when Robert flashed his card. A draft of welcome, cold air enveloped them.

"At least the generators are still working," he said.

But what's flowing in the air? Dalton worried. He tightened his mask, showing Meredith she should do the same.

"Is anybody here?" Robert called out. Anyone in the vicinity had to hear it and know he was serious. "Hello? It's Robert Nicolo. If you can hear me, let me know where you are and if you're okay."

The hallway was lined on either side with numbered doors. Most of them were solid, but a few had small windows constructed in the upper portion. As they walked down the hall, Dalton peered inside. It looked like regular labs with test tubes and glass piping and instruments that must have cost thousands of taxpayer dollars. Behind some of the doors were offices. The general appearance of the interior of Lab 101 was one of neglect. It had the patina of a typical government building, one that wasn't made for the public to see, so why bother with décor?

"How many levels are there?" Meredith asked.

"Three. This is where most of the personnel did their work. If no one is here, I'm not sure where they'd be."

Dalton tried the knob of a solid door. It didn't budge. "Maybe someone's in one of these rooms we can't see into."

Robert flashed his card. The door didn't budge. "It doesn't work on the individual rooms. My clearance didn't take me that far. We just have to hope they hear us and come out."

Meredith and Dalton banged on doors, identifying themselves as police and asking if anyone was inside. Neither received any replies. Coming to the end of the hallway, the three paused, taking in the sounds and overall feeling of the lab. It was eerily quiet in here. Even the soft hum of the air units had been muffled.

"I've never been in here with it so silent," Robert observed. "And I've been here on graveyard shifts."

"As far as I know, diseases don't make noise," Meredith said. "I feel like something is all around us, but that could just be paranoia."

"It's a justified paranoia. All of the deadliest diseases in the world are in here," Robert said. "If we came in and the power was out, I wouldn't have let us go this far. As long as it's cold, the specimens, if they're put away correctly, should be in deep freeze."

They listened for sounds of any movement on the floors above and below. Nothing.

An idea hit Dalton. He may have been new to the whole Plum Island mystery, but there was a pragmatic line of thinking they had all forgotten to follow since they stepped into the building. It was easy to throw practicality out the window when you were immersed in a modern-day Frankenstein's lab.

He said, "If something escaped, like these Montauk monsters Meredith showed me, and made it to the shore, where would they have been kept before?"

Robert's eyes lit up. "Shit. The animal holding pens."

"I'd think if they had a crisis there, everyone would have

been diverted to that area to see what they could do to put a lid on it before it boiled over. Where are the pens?" Dalton asked.

"The next section over. Even on a good day, the place is something out of a horror movie. I'll find us some protective suits and we'll go there." He patted Dalton on the shoulder. "I'm glad Meredith took you along."

They descended the stairs and followed an enclosed breezeway to a door marked ANIMAL TESTING. Robert popped a locker open by the doors and pulled out three suits that would cover them from head to toe.

"Try not to puke in the suit. I hear it's very unpleasant."

Sergeant Campos said he needed to stop home for a minute but he'd be right back. In his squad car, he hit the lights and sirens, tearing ass all the way to his house.

Pulling in to his driveway, he left the car running and door open and jogged to his front door. His lungs wheezed as if they were filling with fluid. Adelle's car was nowhere in sight, but it could be in the garage.

The moment he opened the door, he knew she'd left. His wife had a way of filling their house, making it a pleasant place to be, no matter what his mood. It was as if she was a source of flowing energy, keeping their house standing.

Adelle's energy was absent. He silently thanked God that she took him at his word and left. Her closet door was open and he saw several missing sundresses.

Knowing she was gone was one less thing he had to worry about. He walked over to the liquor cabinet and eyed the bottle of Macallan eighteen-year-old whisky he'd been saving for a special day, his retirement. The doctors had forbid him from drinking the hard stuff anymore and Adelle was quick to squash any temptation.

Opening the glass cabinet door, he grabbed the whisky

by the neck, savoring the feel of the bottle in his hand. The nectar sloshed ever so slightly as he turned it from side to side. He pulled a crystal tumbler from the shelf and poured three fingers' worth. He almost added a splash of water before remembering that this was single malt and in no need of anything but a clean glass. The first sip went down easy with just the slightest burn. Warmth spread throughout his body as the whisky ran down into his belly.

After the second sip, the glass was empty.

"If I knew you were this good, I would have cracked you open a lot sooner," he said to the bottle.

As he poured a second glass, a distant, steady roar broke the silence of the hot afternoon. He slowly walked to the window, sipping the whisky as he went. The floor carried the tiniest vibration. Pulling the curtain aside, he looked down Ash Street to Second House Road. The street was empty save for some parked cars, a yellow Hummer and Vic Tyndale's Kawasaki motorcycle in the driveway next door.

He may not have been able to see anything, but he knew the sound, had felt the same vibrations underfoot during his three-year stay in Fort Bliss.

The military was here.

The moment Dalton, Meredith and Robert opened the doors to the animal holding area, every atom in their bodies screamed to turn away. The smell of blood and offal was so pungent, their nasal tissue swelled on contact in an effort to block the horrid odors from entering. Though they couldn't see a thing out of order at this early juncture, it didn't take a Plum Island expert to realize something terrible had happened here.

Dalton's eyes watered but he couldn't wipe the tears away within the suit.

"Why are we able to smell through these?" he asked. "And is it always this bad?"

"I don't know," Robert said, breathing through his mouth. "And no, it's not supposed to be this bad. I've been here on days when they'd had to put down a dozen sick cows and it was nothing like this. I don't think it's going to get better the farther we go. Just try to put it out of your mind."

Meredith placed a gloved hand over her stomach. "I can never un-smell this. Jesus, Robert, what the hell were they doing here?"

"Whatever it was, it came back to bite them in the ass," he replied.

Dalton pointed at a gooey mass in the far corner, wedged between a pair of waiting-room-style chairs. A bloody white coat, torn skirt and loafers rested atop the remains.

Meredith gasped. "What is that?"

"It *was* a woman," Dalton answered. It was just like what he'd seen at the beach at Shadmoor Park, only in a far more advanced state of putrefaction. "Whatever they created here doesn't just bite you or tear you to pieces. It infects you with something—some kind of chemical or disease that melts you from the inside out. You know of anything that can do that?"

Robert shook his head, studying the gelatinous puddle for clues as to who it was.

"Doesn't the Ebola virus make you bleed out?" Meredith said.

"Bleeding and melting are two different things," Dalton said.

"This is a lab where they create bad shit. Ebola could have been the base. Add some Marburg virus and a few other things and who knows what they came up with," Robert said.

The big man turned to Dalton slowly, as if he was moving underwater. He muttered something but they couldn't make out the words.

"We should be extra careful. Some of those things might still be around," Dalton said, motioning with his head to the gun in Robert's hand. "If we come across one, shoot it. Empty your gun if you have to. They move faster than you think."

"That's not comforting," Meredith hissed, checking to make sure there was a bullet in the chamber.

His elbow crooked and the barrel of his gun pointed at the ceiling, Robert led the way past a pair of swinging doors. There were a few blood spatters along the metallic bottom of the doors. It was far worse on the other side. The doors and the hallway looked as if someone had tossed a can of red paint in every direction. Along the walls was a series of long, Plexiglas windows. Deep, white scratches gouged the surface of each window.

As they cautiously crept down the hall, Dalton looked into one of the viewing panes. It looked down on what appeared to be a kind of barn. A pair of corrals led to filth-smudged doors at the end of each room. Piles of hay and droppings littered the floor. The room was devoid of any livestock.

"What did they keep in there?" Dalton asked.

Without turning to him, Robert answered, "Mostly medium-sized animals like sheep and goats."

"Where are they?"

"They might all have been fed into the incinerator before things went bad."

"Or became food for whatever got loose," Meredith said.

"Could be that, too. On the other side is the cattle area. It's one enormous room. We should check it out."

They crossed the silent hallway, the rubber of their soles squeaking on the blood-smeared tile.

Peering into the Plexiglas, they faced what could best be described as true hell on earth. The cattle had not made it to the incinerator. Instead, they had been put through a meat grinder. The floor was awash with blood and a white, fizzing substance that rode on crimson waves. Shredded bits of hide bobbed along like tiny islands. A torn shirt was draped over a wooden post, a lab coat stuck to the wall with what, no one could guess.

"There might have been a couple hundred cows in there," Robert said. Dalton couldn't see his face, but he was pretty sure it held the same expression of disbelief they all had.

"Look at the shoes," Meredith whispered.

From what they could see, the soft fibers that made up everyday clothes had dissolved in the acidic wash. But the tough leather of shoes, like the cowhides, had resisted. Dozens of shoes swayed in the bilious mire.

"They must have tried to contain things in there," Robert said. He punched the glass.

Meredith placed a hand on his arm. "I'm so sorry, Robert."

Something stirred below. A large plank of wood that had been leaning against a metal bench shifted. They stared as the wood slid to the floor with a splash. From the shadow beneath the bench emerged a paw. It took a tentative step, and was joined by another paw. When the head and shoulders became visible, Dalton was no longer the only one among them who had seen the impossible.

CHAPTER 24

Mickey Conrad volunteered to go to Dan Hudson's wife and ask her to come in to identify the materials that were scattered within his remains. There was no way for her to confirm it was her husband by viewing what was left of his body. Everyone decided it was best she not see that.

She'd started to cry the moment she came to the door and saw him standing there in uniform. To her credit, she didn't collapse or slam the door in his face.

He said he'd drive her to the morgue and back home, even going so far as asking if there was anyone, a friend or family member, that she'd like him to pick up along the way. She chose to go it alone. She talked about their fight the night before and how Dan had gone fishing to blow off steam. In fact, the last time they'd spoken, she'd yelled at him while he was on the boat. Then it sounded like he'd gotten mad and tossed the phone. It wouldn't have been the first phone he demolished in anger.

"I told him, wreck all the phones you want. You pay for them. Some guys hit their wives or kick the dog. Dan broke cell phones. And fished."

Mickey just listened, letting her pour everything out.

She was already beginning to realize that she would have to live with the guilt of her last words with her husband. It was a horrible burden to bear.

After she positively ID'd her husband's clothes, wallet and wedding ring, she became eerily calm. She didn't say a word on the way home. He walked her to her door, handing her his card should she have any questions or need any help. She quietly thanked him and shut the door softly.

By the time he got back in his car, he was hours past being done with his shift. He needed a break. The station was a madhouse. He walked through it all as if he was on another plane, somehow avoiding the chaos, shutting out the voices and bodies and clanging of phones and computers. He was alone in the locker room as he changed into black jeans and a blue pullover.

He thought someone called his name as he left but he didn't bother to linger around and see who wanted him. Flipping the AC on high in his Subaru, he found AC/DC on the radio. Between the throaty wailing of Brian Johnson and rush of air piping through the vents, the outside world couldn't penetrate the car.

The Subaru cruised to an even seventy on the Montauk Highway. All he wanted right now was a couple of beers and the biggest, greasiest cheeseburger money could buy. The Fair Weather Tavern just outside of Montauk proper fit the bill.

Sharp sunlight glinted off the car's hood, so he slipped on a pair of sunglasses he'd bought for ten bucks at a gas station. Looking down to change the station, his eyes flicked back to the road. His body stiffened.

Jerking his right leg, he pushed as hard as he could on the brake. The Subaru fishtailed, crossing over the dividing line. Mickey turned the wheel into the spin, correcting the trajectory. Slamming the car in park, he jumped out, leaning on the doorframe.

Several dozen pairs of eyes stared back at him. Some wore small caps, but most of the closely shorn heads were bare and dappled with sweat. Two olive transport trucks faced each other, blocking off the road.

"What the hell is going on here?" he shouted. "Are we under martial law or something?"

One of the soldiers, a sergeant by the bars on his sleeve, approached the car.

He looked at Mickey with hard, calloused eyes.

"Not yet."

Dalton was sure Meredith wasn't even aware she was squeezing his arm hard enough to cut off his circulation.

"Is that what you saw?" she said, her eyes glued to the monstrosity lazily nosing around the bloody muck.

At first glance, the animal resembled a wolf, though one with some kind of debilitating skin disease. The gray and black of the hunks of fur that still clung to its flesh looked oily, the fibers clinging to one another like spikes. It had a strange, blue corkscrew tail that flicked left and right with agitated twitches. If he judged right, Dalton figured its shoulders would stand level with his hips. So much of it looked like the one he'd encountered with Anita, but the face, the horrid skull swiveling on a bull's neck was completely different.

All of the fur was missing from its head, revealing sickly, mottled skin. Like its neck, the face was very much like that of a bull's, with eyes black as onyx, a wide, flat nose with large, flaring nostrils that rippled the blood and froth when it exhaled close to the lake of death it waded within. But the lower jaw was all wrong. This creature had a massive underbite. Long, sharp teeth jutted along its snout, at times scraping the flesh. When the teeth caught on its nose, the calloused flesh flicked upward for a moment before settling back in place, unscathed.

"Were they out of their goddamn minds?" Robert spat.

Maybe because he had already come across one at much closer quarters, Dalton was able to think clearer and not become swallowed up by the horror in the cattle pen. He started to make connections, loose as they may be, but perhaps a line of logic that could explain how this had happened.

He said, "If the government wanted to create Franken-creatures for military purposes, why not make them as strangely terrifying as possible? The fear of seeing them alone would be enough to cause widespread panic. Add to that whatever twisted disease they seem to carry in their bite and you have all you need to throw a military camp, town, shit, a whole fucking city into chaos. Think of it. You drop these things on a known terrorist village in Afghanistan. All you need to do is sit back, let them do the dirty work, wait until everyone is dead and the virus or whatever they carry dies off and sweep the place clean."

So far, the creature hadn't taken notice of the spectators. It spied a swath of cowhide, opened its jaw so wide it could swallow a man's head whole, and clamped down. When there was no resistance, it dropped the hide and looked for more prey.

"The big problem is, we don't know how many of these things exist, and out of that number, how many made it to Montauk and other parts of the island," Meredith said, mesmerized by the walking nightmare. She had the presence of mind to take out her phone and snap off a dozen pictures of the creature. "I wasn't crazy," she murmured to herself.

Robert took a heavy breath. "That's only half the problem.

If they carry some kind of biochemical agent, there's got to be an antidote somewhere. Nothing was created in the labs without an antidote. The big question is, where do we find it?"

"This is a big place. Where do we even start to look? Maybe we should grab some boxes, load them up with every thumb drive we can find and any files that look remotely related to this," Meredith said, pointing with her crutch the way they'd come, back toward the offices.

Something dropped in the cow pen. The creature crouched into a fighting position, its massive head swerving about, looking for the source. During its scan of the room, it caught sight of them through the Plexiglas. It fixed them with a glare of raw hunger. From what Dalton had seen, these things were smart. There was no way it was going to plunge headlong into a solid wall. Unless it was that mad with bloodlust.

As it neared a metal door at the rear of the pen, it leapt, hitting it with its front paws. The door swung open easily, revealing bright sunlight and the scattered remains of stained clothes left behind by Plum Island workers trapped on an island, fighting to contain their own creation. The creature skidded in their viscera as it rounded the corner, slipping out of sight.

"Shit!" Robert shouted. "I have no idea how many entrances have been breached."

As if in answer to their question, a door slammed somewhere below them.

"I think it's safe to say it's inside," Meredith said.

Robert sprang into action, shouting, "Move it, move it, move it!"

Slinging an arm around Meredith's waist, Robert practically carried her down the hallway. Halfway down, she dropped her crutch. Dalton's shoes skidded on the floor as he stopped, turned and ran back for it.

The moment his fingers touched the cold aluminum, another door down the hall sprang open, banging off the wall.

"Leave it, Dalton!" Meredith screamed. She bobbed up and down in Robert's embrace, helpless as a dog toy.

He made the mistake of looking down the hall. His eyes met the soulless orbs of the bull-headed wolf. It paused long enough to take him in and assess that he'd make a very tasty target. Dalton pulled at the snaps around his hood, throwing it off. He was going to have to make a mad dash and he didn't want the disadvantage of compromised sight lines. If there was some disease floating in the air, so be it. Sometimes you have to pick your poison.

The beast didn't make a single noise, not even a growl, save for the ticking of its claws off the tile floor.

Were they bred for stealth, too? he thought. If that was the case, it was going to be even harder to track them down, and near impossible to hear them coming.

The harsh crack of Robert kicking open the door at his rear let him know Meredith was at least safe for the moment.

"I should have brought a cape and a sword," Dalton said to the creature. It cocked its head to one side as if trying to understand the strange words being spoken to it. These things were monsters in every sense of the word. It was a safe bet that during their creation and subsequent raising into adulthood, no one had spent much time addressing them in any manner other than, at best, harsh commands. Maybe if he kept talking, he could stall it long enough to make his escape.

Tightening his fingers around the crutch, he said, "That's a good boy. Just stand there and look ugly. That's right. I'm just going to take this crutch and give it back to my friend. Nothing to get excited about."

The creature's eyes compressed into tight slits. Its fathomless nostrils flared.

That was not good. All that was missing were a few paws at the ground before the charge.

He heard Meredith cry out to him. She sounded far away. Good. Robert was doing what he should. He'd seen how fast these things were. She wouldn't stand a chance in a footrace. Hell, neither would he.

As soon as he pulled the crutch from the floor, the creature made a beeline toward him. Its mouth opened wide, ready to deliver a killing blow.

This time, there would be no hesitation.

CHAPTER 25

Dalton drew his Glock, firing four shots in rapid succession. Two traveled down the monster's open maw, exiting the back of its head with a bright explosion of blood and bone. The other two hammered into its chest, stopping it in its tracks. It flipped over backward and was still.

"Fool me once," Dalton grunted.

He stared at the crimson and blue body, glad he'd shot it at enough of a distance so it didn't bleed on him. If its bite was that toxic, God knew how diseased its blood was.

Dalton turned to join Robert and Meredith, running down the hall in case any other strange beasts were lurking about. All he wanted to do was jump on that ferry and get back to Montauk. Robert could alert the feds that the entirety of Plum Island had been compromised. Dalton would have to relate everything to his superiors and hope they didn't throw him in a straitjacket. Hopefully, having someone who worked on the island would be an added boost to his credibility.

Hitting the double doors leading out of the Animal Testing sector, he jogged down the breezeway to the main labs. He got there in time to see Meredith arguing with Robert. Both of their hoods were off. Her neck was tilted as high as it could go, her eyes just to his square chin. When they heard him come in, she turned and her face visibly brightened.

"Christ, I thought it got you. I heard the gunshots but I didn't know—"

She threw her arms around his neck, holding him tight.

"Did you kill it?" Robert asked. He looked none too happy about the affection given Dalton's way.

"Shot it four times, all direct hits. It's dead. We need to get the hell out of here now. Let the military come in and clean this place out. This is their mess anyway. We have to get to the mainland and stop these things before they hurt more people."

"He's right, we have to go back," Meredith said. When Dalton offered her her crutch, their hands touched.

Robert's jaw pulsed as he thought their situation over. His eyes were fixed on the other end of the hall, obviously waiting to see if Dalton had been wrong and hadn't killed the creature.

"This is bigger than what the three of us can do," Dalton said. "How many people were on the island when these things got loose?"

Robert rested his chin in his chest and said, "Fifty-seven."

"Any of them armed Homeland Security?"

He nodded.

"If fifty-seven people couldn't stop them, we don't stand a chance. Come on. Like my father always tells me, live to fight another day."

He grabbed the loose arm of Robert's protective suit, leading him out of the building. He followed, but with palpable reluctance.

They had just closed the door to the decontamination room when something heavy hammered into it from the other side. Menacing snarls emanated from the airtight door.

Robert turned on him. "I thought you said you killed it."

"I did. Looks like it has a friend. We've made enough noise to alert any of those things that someone's here."

The door jounced on its hinges. A small dent popped within its center.

"That's a steel door," Meredith said, pulling the suit down around her ankles.

The creature slammed into it again and again, making the dent more pronounced.

"I'm not worried about it bending through the door, but I'm not hopeful about those hinges," Dalton said. They'd started to separate from the doorframe. They quickly doffed the bulky suits, concerned about bringing any contaminants outside the lab with them, and stopped at the exit door.

Robert said, "Meredith, you stay behind us. We'll go out shooting if we have to. No telling what's waiting for us out there."

Dalton counted his bullets in his head. He didn't have a spare clip on him. If there were any more than two of those things, they were in trouble. It was going to take more than one shot to get them down, and they weren't going to sit still and wait for them to take aim.

Bang! Bang! Bang!

The creature stepped up its efforts. The top hinge went with a sharp pop.

"Time to go," Robert spat, swiping his card over the reader. A buzzer sounded, which to the creatures may as well have been a dinner bell. He kicked open the door. Blinding sunlight hit them in the face. For a terrifying moment, they had only their sense of sound to tell them if there was a welcome committee waiting.

"Oh, thank God," Meredith sighed.

The walkway to the dock was clear.

Crash!

Their heads swiveled in unison to the outer door of the

decontamination room. The Franken-animal had made it inside.

"Just in time," Dalton said. "Let's get out of here."

"No!" Meredith shouted, pointing.

The outer door was still in the process of closing. A gap wide enough for an adult to slip through sideways mocked their momentary revelry. Dalton and Robert aimed at the dark gap.

They could hear claws scraping on the ground, ticking madly as the creature sped for the opening.

When the door flew open, both men fired low, estimating where the head and body should be. They miscalculated. The new monstrosity bounded through the door, hitting it high and above the whizzing bullets.

Had it seen what happened to its brethren and learned?

It pounced on the walkway just a few feet from them. This one was mostly canine, except for the pair of tusklike teeth that hung from either side of its lower jaw. Its ears were wide and pointed, like a bat's. Similar to the others, it appeared to have a sort of mange, again exposing ripe patches of bluish skin. Its maw dripped red. They must have interrupted its feeding time.

As the creature craned its deformed head to give them one last withering glance before tearing their throats out, it suddenly recoiled with a loud whimper. Scrabbling on its hind legs, it retreated to the shaded sliver by the closed door.

"You think it knows what the guns can do?" Dalton said, drawing a bead on its head.

"I think it's the sun," Robert said.

They pulled their triggers at the same time. The creature jumped as each bullet found a home in its hide. One took out its lower jaw, another created a blossoming, scarlet hole in its throat. Dalton and Robert walked backward as they fired, careful to avoid any spatter. Blood splashed the side of the decontamination room. It was a mural that would have been right at home at the Guggenheim.

Pointing his gun to the ground, Robert said, "That must be the fail-safe."

"Fail-safe for what?" Meredith said. Again, she took pictures of the ruined animal.

"If you're going to create a weapon like this, you need to program a weakness so you can extract it when the time is right. That thing acted like the sun would kill it."

"In a way, it did," Dalton said.

"Exactly," Robert said. "Come on. Keep an eye out. No telling if the sun rule applies for all of them."

Going down the walkway was difficult for Meredith. Dalton pulled beside her to take the brunt of her weight. "I learned this in Boy Scouts," he said with a wink. Holding her that way was awkward, and at one point the barrel of his smoldering gun scorched the side of his thigh.

As they ran, they continually looked to their sides, wary of anything hiding within the wild vegetation. If the groundskeepers had done their job, there would have been clear sight lines. Either these things broke loose weeks ago or all nonscientific functions on the island were suspended while they completed their deadly masterpieces. Sequestering everyone on the island was like the cram session before a final exam. In this case, they passed with flying colors while failing at the same time.

Robert was a good ten feet ahead of them, his gun at the ready. He paused and raised his left arm when he got to the dock, giving it a quick survey. "All clear!"

Dalton swept Meredith off her feet and carried her the rest of the way. She didn't protest.

Robert was already throwing off the lines that moored the ferry. Dalton sprinted on board, setting Meredith into a plastic chair on the outside lower deck. "Take this." He handed her his gun. He was off before she could say a word.

Robert jumped onto the rear of the ferry, rummaging through a metal chest. Dalton's blood froze.

To Robert's back was a long awning. Under the awning was a storage shed made of corrugated metal. In his haste, Robert hadn't realized that he was completely enveloped in shade.

He also didn't see the mother of all the creatures they'd encountered so far squatting under the awning, preparing to pounce.

"I really don't have time for her highness's crap today," snarled Grace Bavosa, of the Bavosa Land Development Corporation. The megarich contracting company had built half the homes in every affluent suburb in New York over the past fifty years. She was dressed in a red, white and black stained-glass-printed dress by Alexander McQueen, checking her makeup in a jewel-encrusted compact. She looked around to make sure none of the cameramen were lurking about. Food services had opened up the buffet, which usually gave them all a merciful break from the traveling dog and pony show.

"Just think of it this way. If it wasn't for her crap, we wouldn't have enough drama to carry us for a third season." Nancy Primrose had risen into the elite ranks by a series of failed marriages to men with means. It was said her prowess in bed was second to none, but her interpersonal skills left a lot to be desired. Most men were willing to overlook the latter, at least until after they'd had their fill of her carnal delights. She wore a pair of gray jacquard slacks and matching jacket by Red Valentino. The ensemble had been a gift from a new admirer during a short jaunt to Rome.

"I just don't know why I keep doing this to myself," Grace said, snapping her compact shut.

"Because what's the sense of fortune without fame, honey?" Nancy said with her patented sly grin.

"Well, after tonight, I may be famous for being the woman who stabs Princess Van Dayton with a salad fork."

Nancy smirked. "Just think of the ratings that would get. We'd be at the top of the *Wealthy Wives* chain."

Grace nudged her in the ribs. "You would. I'd have to watch the show behind bars somewhere in Wisconsin."

"If O.J. walked, so would you."

Sitting outside Samar Van Dayton's Hamptons estate, enjoying the view of the ocean while sipping on Cristal was almost enough to make them forget this was all a show. It would have been nice, Grace thought, to be at her own Hamptons mansion, maybe with Nancy, definitely not with Samar or Bea Colon. How the producers had managed to mash them into the same social circle was, for the network, a stroke of genius. All four couldn't be any different. The only thing they had in common was money and property out on the end of Long Island. And unlike the others, Grace had to earn her place in the family business. Her father was a tough Sicilian immigrant. For every give, there was a take. She learned the business the hard way. She'd earned her time to relax and enjoy the finer things.

The Wealthy Wives of the Hamptons had been a success right out of the gate because all of them basically hated each other. Fans wrote to Grace often, wondering why a woman with such supposed class and breeding would act like a common thug on a weekly basis.

They didn't understand the scripting that was involved. Sure, none of them really got along, but how interesting was a show where women made sharp asides from time to time? In the words of Derek, the head of production, fur needed to fly.

Grace looked at it as an acting gig. She'd always wanted to be in movies. Now, just shy of fifty, this was her chance, possibly her last. Her agent was already in talks with Paramount about a potential two-movie deal. She wouldn't headline, but she'd get plenty of screen time.

If she had to throw down with these bitches to get it, that was no skin off her surgery-enhanced ass.

Nancy, their resident whore, she could tolerate, at least until the black widow had too much to drink. Then all bets were off.

"Here's to another disaster of a dinner party," Grace said, clinking her champagne flute against Nancy's.

"We can only hope."

As Grace swallowed the last of the Cristal, she thought she saw movement down on the Van Dayton private beach. Probably Lenny, the sound guy, tossing off. The middle-aged letch undressed them with his eyes constantly. Grace almost felt sorry for the balding little man, until she caught him rifling through Nancy's lingerie closet. She'd never told Nancy about it and didn't make a fuss when her eyes locked on his.

Let him make a mess on her slut-wear, she'd thought. *It'll just blend right in with all the other stains.*

CHAPTER 26

"Robert, look out!" Dalton yelled.

The big man turned just in time to wrap his arms around the leaping beast as it barreled into his chest.

This one resembled a wild hog, with short, stocky legs ending in cloven hooves. Its snout was long, like a dog's, but the animal was devoid of ears. The bulk of its body was massive. Robert smashed onto the deck, the massively thick creature plowing into his chest with a jarring crack.

Robert still had the presence of mind to bring his arm up and shoot into the beast's belly. It twitched, then dove for his face. With a clamp of its jaws and quick jerk of its neck, Robert's entire face was removed as easily as pulling off a blood-soaked bandage. The torn flesh flicked from its mouth, landing wetly by Dalton's feet. Robert's body convulsed under the weight of the nightmarish animal.

Gunfire filled the air. Dalton jumped.

Meredith limped forward, both hands on the Glock, firing again and again until it was empty. Each blast opened a dark, meaty chasm in the creature's side. Its dead weight flattened Robert's body, crushing his lungs.

Dalton said, "I have to get him out from under that thing."

Meredith grabbed his arm, hard. "You can't go near them. Look."

White and red foam spilled from the animal's mouth, flowing over Robert's face and neck like lava. His legs and arms twitched, fingers flexing and trembling. They heard the fizzing of acid as it ate away his flesh. The stench coming from the dead animal, carried by a briny breeze, brought a ball of vomit to Dalton's mouth. There was no warning. Only enough time to pitch his head over the side of the ferry and let it all out with a hot rush.

Meredith must have felt the same. She turned quickly, covering her nose and mouth with her hand.

His ribs aching from the sharp convulsions, Dalton looked over to see her make her way up to the pilothouse. Robert's body had gone still, his chest immobile. Still not sure that he was done getting sick, he followed her. It was a mercy to move from being downwind of the dead creature and Robert's dissolving face.

Meredith was already starting the ferry by the time he got inside.

"You know how to drive this thing?" he said.

She sucked her teeth, scanning the various controls. "I'm pretty sure I can figure it out. I grew up on boats. This one's just a little bigger than most."

He noticed the tears building under her eyes. Robert had meant something to her at one time. He still did, beyond being a source of information on her obsession. He put a hand on her shoulder and felt the tension release.

The sky was rippling from a rich, cloudless blue to a beautiful coral. It wouldn't be long until night fell. And with that, a return to bedlam. They had to get back before sunset.

The ferry rumbled as Meredith backed away from the dock. Turning the wheel sharply, she pointed it away from Plum Island.

"I have to warn you about one thing," she said.

"What's that?"

"I'm good at getting boats moving. I really suck at stopping."

"Give me a pack of Marlboro," Jake Winn said, laying a twenty on the scratched counter. He eyed the foil packs and mini-bottles of energy-booster drinks and pills. "You ever take any of these?"

The gas station attendant, an enthusiastic kid named Marcus, who always seemed to have more energy than a golden retriever puppy, plucked a little silver packet from the rack behind him. "I use these when I have a paper due and for big tests. They keep me up without the huge crash."

"You do good on those papers and tests?"

"Three-point-eight GPA so far, Officer." When he grinned, Winn saw black bits of Oreo caught between his teeth.

"You sold me. I'll take three of those."

"They have you guys doing double duty?" Marcus asked, fishing change out of the register drawer. "I guess that makes sense. Something feels weird today."

If you only knew half of it, kid, Winn thought, shoveling the change in his pocket.

He didn't want to freak him out any more than he already was, so he said, "Just getting prepared for my lady friend to visit." Winn shot him a conspiratorial wink. Marcus broke out with another Oreo smile and winked back.

Winn stepped out of the frigid gas mart into the waning humidity of the day. Because the beaches had been closed, Main Street was packed with people, all of them clueless as to what to do with their time. Ever since word had gotten around that the beaches were closed, every tourist in town had nowhere else to go. With the local and tourist populace crammed into one space along the main thoroughfare, there had been plenty of witnesses to the arrival of strange caravans of SUVs, vans and even a military transport truck, filled with soldiers in battle fatigues.

He couldn't remember the last time he'd slept, but he damn well wasn't sacking out until he had a better idea of what was going on. His boss had told him to go home and recharge five hours ago, so basically he was working unpaid overtime. The money didn't matter. He looked all over for the CDC van but couldn't find it. The troops were stationed out near the lighthouse, along with throngs of tourists. He watched the soldiers try to blend in with the day-trippers, some taking the tour, others walking on the beach or navigating the stone walkway that encircled the bluff.

To anyone who wasn't looking for clues, they looked like a group of reservists out for a little R and R.

Nothing was adding up.

Standing on the corner two blocks from the start of Montauk's quaint Main Street, something else caught his attention. At this time of day, there should be tons of cars swarming in for an overpriced seafood dinner at any one of the little restaurants that dotted this end of the island. He hadn't seen one since he'd pulled into the gas station.

Was there an accident on the Montauk Highway clogging up the lanes? He didn't have his squad car, so it was possible he'd missed the call.

Walking to his Ford Explorer, he opened the door and froze at the sound of an approaching vehicle. A tall, white Winnebago came to a screeching stop at the red light.

Don't get many of those, he thought. Montauk was a getaway filled to bursting with little motels harkening back to another era. RVs were not a preferred mode of kicking back for vacation here.

Winn strode to the driver's-side window of the Winnebago and looked up. He was surprised to see a man in a suit, no tie, behind the wheel. He'd expected a middle-aged man in a Tommy Bahama shirt with a zaftig wife at his side, leaning over to hear what the policeman had to say. His iron gray hair was swept back, wet with gel.

The man in the suit saw him, smiled and rolled down the window.

"You're just the man I was looking for," he said. He had a very noticeable lisp and the eyes of a fallen minister.

"How can I help?" Winn said, letting any information come *to* him, rather than peppering the man with questions and arousing suspicion.

"Our GPS died on us about twenty miles back. We're looking for Shadmoor State Park. I assume that's where everyone else is."

Everyone else?

Acting like he was in on things, Winn pointed down the road. "Sure. You just stay straight. You'll see the signs for the park about four miles from here. Take the turn into the park slow. It cuts in at a sharp angle. These tubs aren't good at cornering." He offered a phony laugh.

"Sounds simple. Thanks. I assume we'll be seeing more of each other. My name is Don Sorely." He reached his hand out the window. Jake took it, returning a firm grip.

"Jake Winn, Montauk PD."

"Well, thanks again. I'm sure you're busy as a one-armed wallpaper hanger."

The light turned green and Don Sorely drove away in his Winnebago. The way it hung low to the ground, Winn knew something heavy was inside. He made sure to catch the license plate as it passed.

Above the license numbers it read: OFFICIAL.

Beneath them was something even more intriguing.

FEMA.

So now Montauk was playing host to the CDC, DARPA, the military and FEMA.

He jumped into his Ford, gunning it to the station. He was reporting for duty and he wanted answers.

The ferry's engine struggled mightily as they chugged through the churning waters of Plum Gut. Meredith pinned it as fast as it could go. After what she'd witnessed, she could care less about destroying the government-owned ferry. Her only goal was to get to the mainland as soon as humanly possible, somehow docking it without killing her and Dalton.

Robert's body slipped off the deck, along with the Montauk monster, when she crossed the wake of a passing yacht. Dalton, who had been staring at the body, had informed her of the impromptu burial at sea. Her stomach somersaulted and she had to clamp her teeth to hold down her breakfast. Robert had been a great guy. He'd never caught on to the fact that she'd seduced him at the oyster fest only once she'd found out he ferried Plum Island employees.

He'd turned out to be a pretty good catch, though he could be intense at times. His seven-year stint as a marine had hardened him in ways that she knew would make him difficult to figure into long-term plans. She'd never pushed him for information on the infamous testing facility; just pried little bits here and there.

She'd broken things off as gently as she could when she realized he was falling hard for her and she wasn't on the same wavelength. He'd taken it like a man, and they'd managed to keep in touch over the years.

And now he was gone.

Killed by the very thing that drew her to him.

She wondered if there was a VIP section in hell for people like her.

"The dock should come up in a few minutes," Dalton

informed her, breaking her from her ruminations. "You were kidding that you're not good at stopping, right?"

Keeping her eyes pinned to the way ahead, she said, "I wish I was. Knowing me, we're going to hit the dock hard. Just be prepared."

He looked around the pilothouse. "Well, it's not like there are any seat belts around here."

"Then I suggest you go limp when we get to the dock. That's how drunks survive car accidents."

Dalton wiped a hand over his face. "I could use a drink right now."

"You and me both."

Meredith noticed the setting sun with leaden dread. They'd literally walked out of the frying pan and were heading into the fire. But it was a fire she wanted to face. She'd spent too much time stuck behind a desk. Tonight, she wanted to make a difference. Hopefully all those years trying to dig for answers would come in handy.

It hadn't been enough to save Robert.

"There it is," Dalton said, pointing.

The area around the dock was mercifully empty. The ferry plowed through a succession of waves, heading for an inevitable collision.

"You should probably slow down."

Meredith turned on him. "If I slow down now, we'll drift. I've been fighting a current the last few minutes. Once I know we can slip right in, I'll cut the motor and hope for the best."

"Hope for the best?" Dalton's face turned waxen.

Her face crumpled and her shoulders fell forward. "It's all I've got. Would you rather I say 'pray for the worst'?"

Dalton sat uneasily in the seat next to her. "No, I like hope better. I just realized I left my cell phone in the car. I can only imagine how many messages I have from Campos.

With things this bad, I'm sure he's been trying to reach both of us."

"You maybe, not me. Don't know how much he thinks a cripple can help tonight."

He fixed her with his sincere gaze and said, "You might be the one person that can make sense of all of this. Don't sell yourself short. We need you more than ever tonight."

She smiled, brushing her fingers across his cheek.

Why do you have to be so damn young? she thought.

The ferry dock came into view. She pulled back on the throttle, feeling the large boat break free from the fast-moving current. When she got to within a couple hundred feet of the slip, she cut the engine entirely.

She turned to him and said, "Remember, loose as a drunk." Trying to convey more confidence than she felt, she reached out to hold his hand. He eagerly took it.

The ferry silently but quickly slid into the slip as if she'd been doing it all her life. The only problem was the speed. She never figured out how to reverse the thrust and slow down properly so docking was as soft as bouncing into a pillow.

With a resounding crash, the ferry plowed into the waterworn woodwork of the dock. The hull of the ferry gave way with a rending of metal that could be heard for miles.

Meredith and Dalton were expelled from their seats. She hit the wheel hard, bearing the brunt of the blow with her breasts. The wind exploded from her lungs. She collapsed on the floor, gasping for air.

Dalton didn't fare much better. He catapulted over the console, dinging his head against the window. Somehow, the glass didn't crack. He crumpled into a heap on the floor, his body slamming into the wall as the ferry came to a gut-wrenching stop.

A succession of waves buffeted the ferry. The bow had ripped right through the dock and was wedged within the thick planks of wood. It was as good as dropping anchor. Only a tsunami could free the damaged boat from its final resting place.

Meredith rose to her feet and huffed a weak cheer. She kept a hand across her chest, feeling the dull ache in her breasts. Dalton got up on wobbly legs. He already had the makings of a world-class bump on his forehead.

"I told you I sucked," Meredith said. "But at least we're alive."

"That remains to be seen," he replied, touching his head and wincing.

The accident had drawn the attention of every living soul within shouting distance of the Orient Point ferry landing. They both looked out the window in time to see a stream of humanity come rushing.

She pulled Dalton by the arm. "Come on. We need to get out of here before we're penned in by a horde of Good Samaritans." Grabbing her crutch, she managed to hobble down the narrow stairs while still clinging to Dalton. He jumped over the rail and held his arms out to her.

"I've got you. Just lean over and fall into me."

Tossing her crutch ahead of her, she didn't hesitate to do what he asked. True to his word, he caught her with strong, sure hands.

They turned to face the first wave of worried citizens.

"Are you okay?"

"Is anyone else on board?"

"What happened?"

"Holy Christ, thank God you're alive."

"Was it a terrorist attack?"

They didn't have time for questions. Dalton pointed to the badge on his chest. "If you'll please stand aside, we have official business we have to tend to. Someone will be here shortly about the ferry. No one is to go on the ferry. I repeat, *no one*. Anyone caught on board will be arrested."

The last thing he wanted was a concerned citizen slipping on Robert's and the creature's blood and getting infected. The deck back there had buckled badly, but he had to stress the area was off-limits.

He bullied his way through the crowd, which was actually more interested in the state of the ferry and the dock than the lone couple who had walked off it in one piece.

"Rubberneckers," Dalton said, his voice heavy with disappointment.

"Don't knock it. That works in our favor. Let's get in my car and get out of here."

The inside of Meredith's car was like a furnace. The summer sun had baked it all day while it sat in the blacktop parking lot. Meredith hit the AC as high as it could go. Dalton found his phone on the dashboard. It scorched his hand and he dropped it to the floor.

His head throbbed as they hit the road.

CHAPTER 27

Tom Morton read through over a dozen texts on his phone. The news wasn't good.

"Yo, Jay, I think we're screwed tonight," he said.

Jason had just rolled out of bed, or couch, to be more precise, when *Jeopardy!* came on TV. He'd just shouted out the answer to the Daily Double and fist-pumped when he got it right.

"I do know my Potent Potables," he said, leaning back into the couch as the show faded into commercials.

Tom jabbed his leg with his foot. "Are you listening to me?"

"I'll be honest with you, no. When my head's in the game, the rest of the world is just white noise. What's up?"

"Everyone's been texting me that the beaches are totally closed off."

"We already saw that this morning on the news." He leaned over to grab a warm can of Pabst from the coffee table, downed the dregs and let loose with a heavy belch.

"That was about the water. It's more than that now. Kara, Greg, Skeets and Finn all said that the entrances to every beach have been blocked. There are cops and weird unmarked vans all over the place. I'm thinking we should postpone the party. With so many five-oh around, you know we're going to get busted fast."

Jason closed his eyes, lost in thought. "We could always have it—right here."

"No fucking way. They'll tear this place up so bad, I'll never have enough time to put it back together before my parents get home."

"I'm just putting it out there. I didn't get all this beauty sleep so I could waste it on you tonight. I got a lot of love to share."

"You've got a lot of crabs to share."

Tom opened the mini-fridge and grabbed two cold cans of Schaefer. They believed in spending most of their money on good weed. Bad beer wasn't a problem.

He had to sit through Jason screaming questions at the television for the next ten minutes.

When the show ended, rolling into *Wheel of Fortune*, Jason jumped from the couch. "Don't cancel the party! All is saved. Your little bud Jay knows exactly what to do."

"I told you, it's not happening here."

Tom folded his arms across his chest for good measure.

"You're right, it ain't. I have a better place in mind. You said all of the beaches were blocked, right?"

"That's what everyone says."

"I'll bet the cops only took the time to close down all of the *official* beaches." He pumped his eyebrows up and down like a modern-day Groucho Marx.

Tom's eyes lit up. "You're right. That leaves—"

"Our party central for tonight. No one's going to be able to even get to us there. And that means I'm setting off all the fireworks in my trunk. I want to get drunk, laid and blow shit up. Failure is not an option."

* * *

Stopping at the light at Edgemere Street, Meredith's car was almost creamed from behind by a guy driving a white van. She was about to jump out of her car to let the driver not-so-gently know he'd nearly hit a cop when the van jerked over the divider line and blew through the light.

"Asshole!" she yelled.

Dalton motioned for her to remain in the car and sit tight. "He went too fast for me to get his plate." Seeing her hands tighten on the wheel, he added, "Campos called me to go on duty about three hours ago. You think he'll be too pissed to notice we're late?"

She hadn't spoken a word about Robert, but then again, they hadn't had time to think, much less speak. Something would have to give sooner or later. The question was, when.

"We're not that lucky, especially today," she said.

She hit the gas the second the light turned green.

Dalton said, "I don't know. We made it off Plum Island alive. I'd say that makes us exceedingly lucky. I hope it holds out when I tell the boss about everything."

Driving the next seven blocks to her house, they spotted two more white vans, both bearing official plates. But official what? An army jeep loaded with four soldiers in full gear trundled toward Eden Street.

"Okay, something happened while we were away," Meredith said, stopping to watch the jeep disappear around the corner.

Everything seemed like an understatement to Dalton now. They drove the rest of the way in silence. Dalton's brain whirled with thoughts of what was to come. How many people would die tonight? Who the hell were all these officials and what did they have to do with everything? Someone knew what was going on at Plum Island. Were these people here to prevent things from getting worse, or were they a cleanup crew?

The shadows of the trees painted Meredith's house like a two-story canvas as the sun roiled like a sinking ship into the horizon. Dalton couldn't believe they'd been gone for only a few hours. It felt like days.

Inside was hot and stuffy. Meredith turned on the ceiling fan in the living room. She tossed him an ice-cold bottle of water. He downed it in one long, loud gulp. "You want another?" she asked.

"Yes. I promise I'll take the next one slow."

Handing him a second bottle, she wrinkled her nose. "I hate to tell you, but you stink."

He leaned against the back of her couch. "Since we're being honest here, I'm not the only funky one. Safe to say we're both covered in that smell."

Whatever exuded from those creatures clung to them like an ominous fog. It got into the fibers of their clothes, the pores of their skin. He was tempted to ask Meredith if she had any whisky so he could burn it from his tongue.

"Follow me."

At the top of the stairs, Meredith went into a linen closet, handing him a towel, robe and bar of soap. "I can't do anything about your clothes except run them in the dryer with about a dozen dryer sheets. Just toss them out the bathroom door. You can take a quick shower. Save some hot water for me."

As she turned toward her room, he touched her arm. "Thanks."

"I'm doing this for my nose as much as yours," she said with a wry smile.

"No, I mean for confiding everything in me. I know that took guts, no matter how crazy my own story sounded at the time. And for getting us off that island, crash landing and all. If we can somehow put an end to this tonight, it's all going to be because of you."

She considered his words for a moment. He waited for

a wise remark. She gave a silent, half nod instead and closed her bedroom door behind her.

He stripped down quickly, folding his pants and shirt and laying them in the hall. The shower was ringed by a clear curtain with bright yellow rubber ducks. The shower racks were filled with shampoos, conditioners, body washes and creams. Everything was clean and devoid of mildew. He dreamed of the day his salary permitted a maid to come to his place at least once a month to make it quasi-presentable.

Despite the heat of the day, he stepped under a scorching shower, hoping the hot water would cut through the cloying stench that he imagined taking root in his bones. Lathering up until he looked like a bubbling snowman, he applied two different kinds of shampoo to his hair. The more scents the better.

Eyes closed, he turned to rinse the suds and let the water relax the muscles in his back. He staggered, hitting into the wall, when he heard the curtain pushed aside.

Meredith stepped into the tub, breathtaking in her nudity. Firm but full breasts with large, tan areolae, a belly that was flat but healthy with rounded hips. One of her legs was more toned than the other, an unavoidable result of her accident, as well as the crisscross of scars on her thigh. Her tan lines showed that she sunbathed in a very small, very revealing bikini. She probably wore it only in the privacy of her enclosed backyard.

She didn't speak a word.

They pulled each other into a wet embrace. The crush of her lips against his own, the delicate probing of her tongue, hardened his cock. It pressed into her supple stomach.

There was no time for delicacy. Hands and mouths clutched and sucked and licked. Dalton hadn't even realized he'd slipped inside her until she moaned urgently in his ear.

Oh God, this is even better than I imagined, he thought as he cupped her ass in his hands, driving himself farther into her. Her nails dug moats into his back but he didn't notice, couldn't feel anything but his lust set free.

They fucked as only two people who knew there might not be a tomorrow could.

"Finish me from behind," she commanded, her voice shaky, breath reedy.

He turned her around, gripping the shower rod with one hand, the fold between her hip and thigh with another.

When they were done, the shower rod lay on the floor, bits of shattered tile everywhere. When he apologized, she laughed.

"You can fix it some other time. And if you play your cards right, we'll test it to see how good a job you've done."

When Can Man heard that troops were at the Montauk Point Lighthouse, because he heard everything, he decided that being near armed soldiers was the safest place to be. Everything was off today. Folks talked in hushed tones, at least the locals, wondering what all of the strange activity meant. The tourists complained loudly about being banned from the beaches, their only reason for coming to Montauk in the first place. All of the shops along Main Street did bang-up business, as there wasn't much else to do but shop.

It was a banner day for cans. The garbage bins along the sidewalks were brimming with empties. By late afternoon, he'd plucked so many, he had to stash his haul behind the latticework under an empty house, his secret hiding spot, and start with a fresh lawn bag.

After stowing away what would be cashed in for his return trip to Queens—things here were getting too strange for his taste—he walked several miles to the lighthouse situated at the very end of Long Island. By the time he got there, night was just beginning to draw across the clear sky. Park rangers were in the process of clearing everyone out. Everyone but the couple dozen soldiers in dress fatigues.

Can Man had been in the army back when he was fresh out of high school with grades insufficient for college and zero career ambitions. He was stationed in the 1st Infantry Division out at Fort Riley in Kansas. He'd never liked Kansas. The storms were a little too much for his taste. Plus it got too damn hot.

Come to think of it, he'd never much liked the army, either. But they did provide three hots and a cot and did their best to instill a modicum of discipline in his scattered life. The army did have something that he felt was needed in great abundance now—trained men with high-powered weapons.

He hid in a reed-covered depression off the sand-and-rock-strewn trail to the left of the lighthouse that led to the beach. No one would be able to see him, especially once the sun went down. More than a half-dozen soldiers were stationed below his vantage point, M16s slung over their shoulders.

Through the gossip train, he'd heard that soldiers had been seen all along the coasts on both sides of the island. As far as he knew, nothing bad or strange had happened out by the lighthouse, so it made sense to camp out here under the protection of the military.

The sound of straining engines drew his attention away from the beach. Metal doors slammed shut where he couldn't see. Someone whistled, and a soldier staring across the ocean, a stocky guy with short arms, looked up, nodded and made his way back to the parking lot.

"Marching orders," Can Man whispered, recalling his days in boot camp.

The other men on the beach assembled, turning their backs to the water.

Something emerged from the cold ocean, riding in on a wave of white spray. It leapt onto the rocks, pausing to shake the water from its body.

What is that?

The four-legged creature turned its long, heavy, undefinable head toward the gathering of soldiers.

Is it a wolf? Some exotic zoo animal? He'd never seen anything like it. It was powerfully built. Even on all fours, it would come up well past a man's hip. It exuded menace, from the twitching of thick muscles to the hard, calculating glare in its cold, clear eyes.

Can Man thought it best to rise from his hiding place and call their attention to the strange chimera. Before he could get to his feet, the creature bolted down the uneven rock path around the lighthouse, disappearing from view.

CHAPTER 28

Dalton dressed in the guest room after Meredith brought his clothes up to him. She wore a long towel cinched under her armpits. He was still recovering from his surprise in the shower. He'd never experienced anything like it. They actually had a mutual orgasm, and judging by the sounds she'd made, they also shared the same mind-numbing intensity.

"Now that was some end-of-the-world sex," she'd said, burying her face in his water-slicked chest.

He hoped she was wrong.

As he laced up his shoes, she knocked on the door. It seemed strange that they had changed behind closed doors in separate rooms, but strange was the order of the day.

"I made you a sandwich. You can eat it on the way to the station. Come on, cowboy, we have to get moving."

He opened the door, saw her face and wanted to kiss her. She must have sensed it, because she smiled and turned to the stairs. "No time for distractions. We have a lot to do."

Her Montauk Monster file was tucked under her arm. She'd downloaded the pictures from her phone and printed up so many copies, she'd run out of toner.

Once Meredith turned onto the Montauk Parkway, she gunned the accelerator. The station was over in East

Hampton, just over ten miles away. She drove like she was attempting to set a new land speed record.

"Try not to get us or anyone else killed," he said, reaching for the handgrip mounted by the window.

She rolled her eyes. "Don't worry, I'm using my good leg."

That gave him no comfort.

The heavy stalks of trees passed by in a dizzying blur. The car's headlights made a feeble attempt at alerting them to any onrushing obstacles or pitfalls.

Dalton saw a dim light in the distance. It appeared to be in the middle of the road.

"Do you see that?"

"Probably an accident," she said, decelerating until she was under eighty.

As they got closer, he stiffened, practically pressing his face to the windshield. "That's no accident."

She had to pull to a complete stop. An armed soldier held his arm out straight, palm up and facing them. He didn't so much as flinch at the barreling SUV.

Dalton said, "I think someone may have beaten us to our big scoop."

When Nancy Primrose accused her host, Samar Van Dayton, of cheating on her husband while they'd been filming at Turks and Caicos, the decibel level in the house went up to octaves that only dogs could hear. A relatively quiet dinner went into full Armageddon mode in seconds.

Nancy backed out of the argument, letting Grace take over for a while. She stole a glance at the director and saw his smile. Earlier, he was the one who had leaked the information about the affair, telling her she would be the star of this episode and possibly the next if she was willing to not only throw it out there, but to keep pushing the issue.

She'd been only too happy to oblige.

"Do you know what you are?" Samar shouted at her, sneering, or at least the best she could through her frozen, Botoxed face. "You're a low-class bitch who thought becoming a high-class whore would make you welcome in finer circles."

"Oh, and being a cheat makes you so much classier than me?" Nancy shot back.

"That was a rotten thing to say. You're way out of line," Grace barked, rising from the table and pointing at Samar. She picked up a dinner roll and tossed it over her head.

Samar ducked, then leapt from her chair, kicking it backward in the process.

Nancy looked at Grace. *Oh no, you don't. You will not take the spotlight from me.*

"Take it back!" Nancy demanded.

Samar, her bleached hair covering half her face, her stately demeanor shattered, said, "I never recant the truth."

"What kind of pompous ass says *recant*?" Grace countered. "I mean, for God's sake, you're from Brooklyn, not London in the 1850s."

You calculating bitch, Nancy thought. She turned on Grace and said, "Why don't you stay out of it? This is between the queen and me."

Grace blanched. She hadn't expected that. Nancy knew she had to act fast to push Grace into the background on this one.

"You know what, Samar? Screw you! You think I'm low-class. I'll show you low-class."

Nancy reached under the table, grabbed the linen tablecloth and yanked it as hard as she could. Expensive china, silverware, food and crystal glasses scattered, crashing to the floor.

Fiery rage shot from Samar's eyes. "You crazy bitch! That china is worth more than your house!"

"Send me the bill—bitch."

All of the women backed away from the table. Their designer dresses were stained beyond saving. They turned on Nancy like a pride of hungry lions.

Bring it on, bitches. By the time you're done, this whole season will be mine.

Before they could pounce, the sound of more breaking glass startled even the production crew. Cameras turned, ready to capture the next act in this three-ring circus.

Samar was the first to scream, all color draining from her face.

Jake Winn sat in his patrol car, parked by the entrance to Star Isle. The small inlet was fed by the waters of the Long Island Sound and had a heavy concentration of boat and water sports enthusiasts. It was also surrounded by a bevy of small motels, all filled to capacity.

The U.S. Coast Guard had a base of operations on Star Isle. He'd driven over to see if anything suspicious was going on with the guardsmen. His worst fears were confirmed when he found the place empty. Everyone had hit the waters.

Families strolled past his idling car, bellies full from dinner at one of the restaurants on the isle.

A little girl no older than four, her mouth covered with ice cream, her fingers clutched around a soggy cone, looked at him and waved. He waved back, feeling the pressure on his chest.

He'd been told earlier that everyone in the department was to assist with federal authorities.

"What federal authorities?" he'd asked his sergeant, Fred Paulson, a man he'd worked with for almost two decades. He didn't let on that he'd already come across CDC, DARPA and FEMA vehicles. No one had spoken about

Henderson's body or where it had gone. It was as if he'd never existed.

He'd never seen Fred so worked up. His florid features telegraphed an internal blood pressure that was percolating to dangerous levels.

"What federal authorities?" Fred shouted. Everyone had been called in to the precinct, which meant, minus Norm, they were six strong. All heads turned when Fred spoke up. "Hell, all of them, as far as I can tell." He threw his hands in the air. "I've gotten calls from the military, those jackwads at FEMA, some senator I never heard of on some committee that had more letters than a Greek surname."

Sergeant Paulson looked over at Jim Kanelos, the lone county cop in the bunch, and heaved a deep sigh. "Sorry, Kanelos." Jim had stopped by to talk to Jake. When Paulson called his meeting, he'd asked him to stay, figuring he'd need to know this as much as the locals.

"Nothing to apologize for," Kanelos said. He looked sick to his stomach. He was still fretting over the blood he'd gotten on him when they responded to Hudson's body being found. The paramedics had cleaned and disinfected him good and declared him fit for duty, but Winn could tell by his shifting eyes that he wasn't buying it.

He's going to go AWOL, he thought. *And I'm not sure I can blame him.*

"What's really going on?" asked Officer Jane McGrath. Her green eyes flashed liked emeralds. She'd tried to keep her orange hair under her cap, but the wiry strands poked out as if they had a life of their own. She was as proud of her Irish heritage as she was of being a cop. Like Winn, she didn't like being reduced to a step-and-fetch for the feds—especially when she hadn't a clue why they were here in the first place. "You're telling us the feds are now a response team to wild animal complaints?"

She has no idea. I should fill her in when this is over,

Winn thought. Jane had just returned from an extended weekend in Rhode Island with her husband. She hadn't seen the entire town turned inside out, didn't know about what had happened to the bodies or the strange animal deaths and the need for hazmat suits. She knew that Norm had been attacked and dragged off and that was enough to light her anger.

Paulson leaned against the wall, kicking his heel into it. "Look, I don't know what the hell is going on out there. Whatever it is, it's dangerous as hell. I didn't call the feds in. I checked with the county police and neither did they. Something put us on the feds' radar and they're here to stay no matter how we feel about it." He handed out a sheet of paper to everyone. "Here are your assignments for now."

"Are you kidding me?" Winn asked, waving the sheet. "Are you really sending us out on pet patrol?"

Each had been given a quadrant of the town. They were to look for anyone walking their dogs and advise them to keep their pets in for the night. At dusk, they were to order any pedestrians back to their homes or motels and to stay there until dawn.

Paulson stiffened. "I know it sounds like a waste of time." He chewed on his upper lip, his gaze turned inward. He finally said, "Before you mutiny on me, I will tell you what I was told. We need to do this for two reasons. One, to get pets off the street and away from harm, as well as the pet owners. Two—and this is the part that had me drink a bottle of Pepto—and I quote, '*to choke off a potential food supply.*' "

They looked at one another with total confusion.

Kanelos said, "Come again?" His skin flushed a deathly white.

"You all heard me. Now get out there."

As everyone shuffled out, Winn followed Paulson to his office, a tight, cluttered box that had poor air-conditioning and furniture from the 1960s. "What you said about choking off the food supply. Does that mean the animals"—he paused, not even wanting to finish the thought—"or the people?"

Paulson dropped unceremoniously into his chair. "I haven't a goddamn clue, Jake. Just assume both."

Jake patrolled his quadrant and told over a dozen bewildered dog walkers to stay inside until dawn. He also said it would be helpful if they got in touch with friends and neighbors and advised them to do the same. A man in his late fifties accused him of imposing martial law and he had to hear the man out while he railed against the *system.* If he could only know how much Winn agreed with him.

And now even the Coast Guard had been called into action. Worse still were the hundreds of vacationers milling about. As the sky went from purple to black, he turned on his flashers and went about corralling everyone to safety.

Pulling into the lot of the Golden Cabana Motel, a twenty-room affair that had seen better days, Jake slammed on the brakes. A group of kids, all of them under ten, were playing kickball in the lot. Their parents watched them while sitting in resin chairs outside their rooms, having cocktails and talking with one another.

A dark, looming shadow crouched in stark relief against the moon atop the motel. Its head swiveled from side to side, not following the ball, but the children as they darted back and forth, laughing and shouting.

Oh Jesus, what is that?

He stepped out of the car, revolver in hand. The shadow ignored him.

It was enormous, like one of those sheepdogs, only leaner.

He had to get the kids in their rooms before it attacked.

One of the parents spotted him and asked, "Is something wrong?"

The shadowy beast stepped closer to the roof's edge. The aluminum drain groaned under its weight. A couple sitting under it looked up. The children, seeing a policeman with his gun drawn, stopped playing. They stared at him with tiny, open mouths.

"Kids, when I say 'Go!' I need you to run into your rooms." They stood like cherub statues. He took another approach. "It'll be a race. First one in gets a deputy badge when I come back tomorrow. You all understand?"

Some of them nodded, up for the challenge.

A few of the parents made to walk over to him. "Stay where you are," he said. "I need every one of you to open your doors. Once your kids are inside, follow them and throw the locks." The parents hesitated, looked at the closed motel room doors, and took several steps back.

Winn's eyes wavered between the kids, the motel doors and the creature that hovered over them like an expectant gargoyle.

"Hurry up," he said to the parents, trying to keep his voice as level as possible. He didn't want to spook the kids or cause the creature to spring to action.

Just stay where you are, he implored the shadow. *Stay away from the kids.* He thought about what would become of them if he did, indeed, have to shoot it in front of them. *Better they're alive and in therapy than dead.*

He looked across the lot and saw six wide-open doors. Terrified faces peered back at him.

"Okay, kids, are you ready to race?" Winn said.

"Yes," a few of them answered, voices shaking.

Keeping his eyes on the shadow, he barked, "Go!"

The kids ran in a tight pack, their sneakers and flip-flops kicking up gravel as they dashed for their rooms.

They hadn't made it halfway across the lot before everything went to pieces.

CHAPTER 29

Dalton had his door open before Meredith could come to a complete stop. The soldier who stood in their way was tall and broad with cutting eyes that defied you to question him. His dark skin shone wetly with sweat.

Tapping the badge pinned to his chest, Dalton said, "We're with the Suffolk County PD. You need to let us through so we can report to our station."

The soldier shook his head slowly. "Can't let you through. This road is closed."

"Why? Is there an accident?" Not that the military would be called in for an accident, unless it involved a caravan of their own.

"No," he answered in a deep bass. "We have orders not to let anyone out or in."

"Orders from who?" Meredith demanded, joining Dalton's side.

He looked down at her and simply said, "My boss."

Meredith made it a point to slam her crutch on the ground, nearly missing the man's boot. His eyes flicked to the boot, then her face.

"Look, we need to report for duty. Odds are, we'll be sent right back here anyway. Why don't you call your boss and let him know that you're preventing the police from doing their job? Things are bad enough out here. The place could use one less prick," Dalton said.

Somehow, he stood his ground under the soldier's withering stare. Another soldier sitting in a jeep flicked his cigarette out the window and shook his head, as if to say, *You may want to rethink your strategy here, chief.*

Meredith went back into her car, saying, "If you don't want to move, I'll just drive around you. What are you going to do, shoot us?" The engine revved as she pumped the gas.

Dalton got the distinct impression that they *would* shoot them. Because of that, he remained outside the car. He was about to ask whom he could speak to when a familiar voice called out from the side of the road. "Hold up."

Officer Mickey Conrad zipped up his fly as he emerged from the bushes. He walked over to the soldier and patted him on the back.

"They're with me. I'm supposed to take them to the station."

The Goliath in camouflage pulled his lips back, rolling his neck until it cracked.

"These are your reinforcements?" he said.

Mickey said, "They are. Meredith, you're going to have to leave your car here and jump in mine. I promise it'll be safe."

Before Meredith could protest, Dalton turned to her. "Pick your battles wisely. At least we can pass through."

"Just pull it over there," the soldier said, pointing to the shoulder. Meredith did as she was told—angrily. She spun her wheels, the car starting and stopping with tremendous jerks. The rear swerved as she slid into the shoulder.

"Fiesty," the soldier said with the hint of a smile as she stormed past him. A couple of the soldiers snickered.

They walked through the barricade to Mickey's squad car. "That guy is an asshole," she said, slamming the passenger door. Mickey let Dalton into the back.

"He's not so bad," Mickey said. "He needs to be that way to get his point across. Though calling him a prick was probably not the brightest idea."

Dalton asked, "Why are troops here with roadblocks?"

The government absolutely had to know what was going on at Plum Island. If they had any inkling that something was wrong, why wait until people lost their lives? Jesus, were conspiracy theorists the ones who *weren't* crazy?

"They're not telling me, but it doesn't take a genius to figure out it has something to do with the people who've been murdered the last couple of days. I came across another body today, some guy who went out fishing and was dropped back on land as if he was a sack of spoiled meat. We just found his boat adrift in the sound."

Meredith flashed the folder. "We may know what's going on. Dalton and I did some recon this afternoon. It's not pretty."

"I hope you have something good because Campos is pissed. He's been trying to reach you two all day. When I came across the roadblock and called in, he told me to wait for any sign of you and bring your asses right in. Everyone's on duty now. No excuses."

Dalton leaned forward until his forehead leaned against the safety glass. "Trust me, it's good. But we're going straight to Hammerlich with it."

Mickey gave a short laugh. "Boy, you're really looking to get on Campos's good side."

"He'll have to deal with it. What we saw is bigger than him, hell, bigger than Captain Hammerlich, but we have to start at the top so it gets to the appropriate people, and before it's . . ." Dalton trailed off, feeling in his gut that forces were operating against them. Meredith shifted in her seat, beaming with approval. He was in it all the way now. After what he saw, there was no way to half-ass it. Genetically bred killers had descended on his beat. They had taken the lives of people he liked and respected. When it came time to drop the hammer, he wanted to be holding the handle.

"So I guess you're not going to tell it to me first."

"Trust me," Meredith said, "when we're done, everyone will have to be told."

If we expect to get everyone out alive, Dalton finished quietly to himself.

Don Sorely had originally wanted to set up their disaster field office, which would be composed of seven trailers and just under a hundred personnel, at Sag Harbor. From the scant information he'd been given, he felt it would put them in perfect position.

A check of the current running through Long Island Sound told him different. Sag Harbor would leave them with their asses blowing in the wind. They needed to be in the eye of the storm, not out in the rain bands.

He'd been with FEMA too long. It seemed he'd been running to a string of never-ending weather disasters for the past ten years.

This time, Mother Nature, that fickle bitch who gave and took with the best of them, wasn't the problem. He had to shift his brain and stop thinking in climate terminology.

A change of plans was necessary, so they settled into a string of vacant plots of land by the Montauk Airport, a lone airstrip that catered mostly to small, single-engine planes. Earlier, he'd watched several Pipers take off, banking north toward Connecticut. Shortly after, he'd placed a call to the FAA and had them shut the entire operation down. He hoped the passengers in those Pipers packed a change of clothes, because no one was coming home until they got a handle on things. Now the airport sat dark and silent.

He wasn't thrilled with the level of secrecy that had been part of the operation from the start. Directives to local law enforcement had been handed to him from his superiors. For now, he was a middleman and he had no answers to their questions. When he questioned the CDC's involvement, he knew he wasn't given the whole story. Being half in the dark made it a bitch to handle things from the ground, but it wasn't as if he had a choice.

When he saw the military and DARPA prowling around, his stomach dropped. This was big. Too big to not have the heads of each agency fully debriefed. DARPA gave him nightmares.

What the hell have I gotten myself into?

He was used to having information withheld from him. But this was life-and-death business. DARPA were the symbolic men in black. Their presence alone meant something supremely bad was in the works. They weren't here just to watch the show and they sure as hell had nothing to add in the way of help. He felt their eyes everywhere, carefully evaluating events as they unfolded. They were here because they had a vested interest in the place. The trick was finding what that interest was.

Don was beginning to feel like a minnow on a very big hook, cast into a sea of piranha.

A knock on the Winnebago's door had him bounding from his seat. A tall, older man in a suit and a younger woman stood outside.

"Are you Mr. Sorely?" the man asked with a mild, Midwest accent.

"That would be me." He leaned against the doorway. A blast of humid air made him grateful the big bus, as he liked to call it, was air-conditioned.

"I'm Dr. Harrison Greene. This is my assistant, Dr. Kathryn Ling. We're with the CDC. We were told by your director to come see you."

Dr. Greene offered his hand, then Dr. Ling. She was a real looker, with shoulder-length hair so red she'd stand out in any crowd, and lips to match. *If my doctor looked like that, I'd fake being sick once a week*, he thought. He hadn't met many redheaded Asian women. Ling looked too young to be a doctor, but he was happy she was here.

Sam Bunker, FEMA director and his direct boss, had e-mailed him an hour ago letting him know to expect their company. *We're three blind mice*, Don thought. *Maybe they have some puzzle pieces I don't.*

"May we come in?" Dr. Greene asked awkwardly, seeing that Don had lost himself looking at the lovely Dr. Ling.

Don shook his head to clear the cobwebs in his brain. "Sorry, where are my manners? Yes, please, come in and have a seat."

The big bus was divided into two parts. The front half of the oversized Winnebago was like any normal, though well-appointed RV, with swiveling captain's chairs, a plush couch, marble table and even a full galley kitchen. The rear was more of a command center. Dan had four men back there locked on to their computers, communicating with the EPA, Department of Health and Human Services and, most important at the moment, National Communications System. The nagging problem of public Internet access on this end of the island was about to be solved. Social media only worked if people could get online. He wondered how they planned to scrub the tweets and posts that had gone out all day.

Not my problem.

The doctors walked and sat in perfect synchronicity, right down to crossing their right legs over their left. Dr. Greene unbuttoned his suit jacket. Dr. Ling worked at the crease in her dress pants.

"Care for a drink? We have everything from water to the hard stuff." Dan opened the fridge, ready to grab a couple of waters.

"It's been a long day. You have any beer?" Dr. Ling asked to Don's utter shock.

"Do you have any coffee?" Dr. Greene said, unfazed by his partner's choice in beverage.

"We have one of those one-cup coffeemakers. I'll whip one up for you."

He got a beer for Dr. Ling and one for himself. The coffee was ready a couple of minutes later. Don sat in a captain's chair opposite them and leaned back, taking a sip from the sweat-beaded bottle.

"So, what did you hear from Director Bunker?"

Dr. Greene said, "He called us in the early morning and said there was a potential viral outbreak at a hospital in the Hamptons. We flew up immediately and met our local response team. The hospital has been in lockdown since this afternoon. There were some very unfortunate events that, from every earmark, indicate a deadly contagion has been introduced to this area. Some of our best doctors are on the scene." He put his coffee down and sat forward, leaning his elbows on his thighs, hands clasped together. "Now here's my concern. I have a strong suspicion someone knows exactly what this is and hasn't been totally honest with us. One of my response teams was met by a representative from DARPA. He's been with them ever since, even causing a bit of a scene at the recovery of a body, a local policeman, I've been told. When I inquired why we had to integrate with DARPA, I was instructed to speak to you."

Don took a long, slow sip of his beer. He could tell Dr. Greene was a man who always got his way. He pegged him for a God complex multiplied by ten. And judging by the look in his eyes and body language, God was ready to smite any puny human who got in his way.

"Our colleagues and friends are running a quarantine, exposed to a potentially fatal infection at this very moment," Dr. Ling added. "There are thousands of people packed in a very tight space. The military and their weapons and technology development team aren't talking. Someone is coordinating everything and knows more than they've let on. So you can see why we're concerned."

"I'm just as concerned," Don said. "No one could take this job without public safety being their number one priority." If he sounded defensive, he wasn't concerned. He didn't like what they were implying. "I can assure you, if someone knows more about what's been going on here, that someone isn't me."

"Then what, exactly, do you know?" Dr. Greene asked. "FEMA isn't exactly in the practice of deploying itself for infectious diseases."

There was a long, uncomfortable silence. Don shifted in his chair, the leather making a racket.

"I didn't know there was going to be a contagion," he finally said. "The NSA contacted us last night. The cat's already out of the bag on them, so I'm sure you're well aware of their extensive monitoring program, from news wires to phones calls, e-mails and web searches. It's a ton of white noise to try to filter information out, but it's made easier when they're given a target."

Dr. Ling put her beer down, uncrossed and crossed her legs, studying him like he was some kind of bacteria on a slide under a microscope. For all her unexpected hotness, she could be damn unsettling.

He continued. "The Department of Homeland Security, our current boss, also runs the Plum Island research facility."

"The CDC has consulted with succeeding directors at Plum Island over the years," Dr. Greene interrupted. A prescient awareness dawned in his eyes. "That explains the contagion. Why on earth wouldn't you put us directly in touch with the doctors at Plum Island when we arrived? If they've been working on a particular disease, their assistance will be invaluable."

Don raised a hand to cut him off. "I agree. But it's not so cut-and-dry. About a week ago, Plum Island went dark. The entire facility had been dedicated to a high-level, classified project for the military. They were close to a breakthrough. Every single person who worked on the island was ferried in a month ago. No one was to leave until their mission was complete. Not hearing from them for a few days wasn't unusual. With this particular project, they were required to give briefings twice a week with the director of Homeland Security and members of the committee driving their research. Sometimes, even the President would be present. When they missed the first briefing last week, it was assumed they were engrossed in their work, maybe holding back until they had a larger picture to paint. When they missed the second briefing, people in high places got concerned. They asked the NSA to focus on the lab, this area and the families of Plum Island personnel."

He finished his beer and tossed the empty into the sink. It clattered and popped out, rolling across the floor.

"What did they find?" Dr. Ling asked.

Don shrugged his shoulders. "Nothing. Like I said, the place went dark. No communications going in or out. The powers that be thought that maybe there'd been a power outage. The backup generators on the island were supposed to have been replaced twenty years ago, after a hurricane slammed the island. No one could count on those."

Dr. Greene looked alarmed and highly irritated. "You mean to tell me they have a facility only a mile from a densely populated coast that is filled with deadly viruses and no reliable power backup? That's gross incompetence bordering on homicidal."

"You work for the government, doctor. This shouldn't surprise you."

"It doesn't so much surprise as it sickens me."

Rising from the couch, Dr. Ling paced between them. She said, "So if the power went out, all of the cooling systems would have gone off-line. Any airborne virus could easily escape containment once a certain temperature is reached. From there, it's easy enough to slip through ventilation systems and be carried on the winds, or in the water current." She chewed on the tip of her thumbnail. "It could also easily be another Lyme disease screwup. Flying insects could bring any one of those viruses to Long Island and Connecticut."

"We don't think bugs are doing it," Don said.

Dr. Ling stopped pacing, turned and stood over him. "Then what is?"

Don cleared his throat. "It's an animal. Or, I should say, *animals*."

"Deer and dogs are good swimmers. They could easily make the trip," Dr. Ling surmised.

"I wish it was that easy. We didn't realize we were dealing with two major issues until we got here. These animals, they're not exactly something you'll find in nature." He looked at his watch. It was after nine. "And as for DARPA, your guess is as good as mine. I don't like them being here any more than you do. I know how they work. No one would even know them if they stood nose to nose. They're goddamn ghosts, bad omens, a government-sanctioned secret society. Even my boss is keeping his mouth shut when I bring them up. If I knew why they were here, I'd use my psychic powers to win the lottery." Looking out the port window in the door to Dr. Greene's right, he saw nothing but darkness. "From here on in, you'll need a military escort."

"What?" the doctors said in unison.

"It's for your safety. That's everything I know. I have my own people working their keisters off trying to ferret out more intel. I don't like this any more than you." He suddenly wished he'd never given up smoking. He'd kill for a cigarette right about now. "We need you to work on whatever ultimately killed those people. It appears that everyone who would know what we're dealing with is dead. A team of SEALS is out at Plum Island gathering all of the information they can. The place holds fifty years of research and notes, so it'll be like diving for needles in haystacks." All of the air and energy left him like he was a slashed tire tube. "If this gets out any further, I don't even want to think about what will come next."

CHAPTER 30

Jason's first great idea was to move the party from the beach to Money Pond. It was a bit of a hike through the state park to get there, but he was positive it would be police free. He'd always been fascinated by the small lake when he was younger. Money Pond was supposedly one of the places where the infamous Captain Kidd deposited his treasure. Gardiner's Island just off the coast was a definitive location for some of Kidd's booty. The Gardiner family, who had been threatened by Kidd to conceal his cache under penalty of death, was said to have delivered all of it to the court during the captain's ill-fated trial. Rumors had been circulating for centuries that not all of it had been turned in. Plenty of people went there every year in search of any that may have been left behind.

Jason still thought about taking scuba lessons so he could plumb the murky Money Pond and waters around Gardiner's Island himself one day. Even finding a handful of treasure would be enough for him and Tom to start their own publishing company, and they wouldn't have to fight the uphill battle to get their comics and books in readers' hands.

Tom, who had been staring at the keg sitting on the

porch like it was a girlfriend about to board a plane to Zambia, said, "We can't go there."

"Why not?"

"We'd have to wear jeans and long-sleeve shirts. It's frigging hot and humid. I'm not going to sweat my balls off, and neither are the girls."

Pounding the arm of the couch with his first, Jason let out a string of expletives. "I swear to Christ, I hate fucking ticks."

Montauk was tick—and therefore, Lyme Disease—central. They'd known plenty of people who had gotten it over the years and it wasn't pretty. Everyone lived in fear of ticks. That's why late-night parties were best done at the beach, where there were fewer ticks.

"Dude, it was a good idea. We could have gone crazy out there and no one would have even heard us." He patted his friend on the shoulder and handed him a smoldering joint.

Jason took a hit, leaned back and closed his eyes, deep in thought.

"Look," Tom said, "we could scale the whole thing down. I'll ask Annie to bring her cousins over here and we'll have some fun."

"And leave out Skeets?"

"Okay, we can have Skeets over, too."

"If Skeets comes, you know we also have to let Greg and Tim over, too."

Tom rolled his eyes. "And before you know it, everyone will be here trashing my house. Forget it. Just us and the girls. I'm sure everyone will understand. This whole town is in, like, lockdown."

Jason smiled and grabbed his cell phone. "Start texting everyone. We're going to Highland Beach."

"Are you crazy?"

"Yes, but that's beside the point. We'll have a beach, privacy and it'll be tick free."

"No shit, Jay. And we'll all be drunk and dead within an hour."

Jason's fingers flew across his phone's screen. "We'll be fine. There'll be a bunch of us. If someone gets stuck in quicksand, we'll have plenty of people to pull them out."

Tom sighed, staring at his own phone. Highland Beach had been closed to the public for as long as he could remember. It was way too dangerous. He and Jason had done some exploring there when they were in high school. Using a very long stick as a guide, they'd managed to steer clear of the quicksand, but it was everywhere. One wrong move and you were in serious shit. It was the only beach the police wouldn't have bothered to patrol. No one went there, especially at night.

Tonight, they were about to be the exception to the rule.

As Mickey Conrad turned into the station's lot, Dalton said, "Thanks, Mick. I owe you a steak for this one."

"It's gonna cost you Morton's," he replied, smiling. "Unless Campos suspends you. Then you won't be able to afford it."

Inside, the station house was empty. Everyone was on duty and on the streets. Even Sergeant Campos's office was dark.

"This is just eerie," Meredith said, taking in row upon row of empty desks. Phones rang with no one to answer them. They would be diverted to an emergency phone center after four rings.

"You're in luck," Mickey said. "No one's around to drill you a new asshole."

"I have to see if Captain Hammerlich is here," she said. Mickey shot Dalton a look, warning him to disavow Meredith of her intention.

Dalton gave a slight shake of his head. He was with

Meredith on this one. They knew what was out there and it would be a crime *not* to tell the captain.

"Suit yourselves," Mickey said. "I'm going back out. I'm sure I'll see you at some point."

When he left, Meredith started walking to Hammerlich's office with Dalton in tow. It was in the rear of the building, some distance from the normal madness. His door was closed, the opaque glass revealing little. They could tell the light was on, but he often left without shutting out his light.

"You don't have to do this with me," she said, her closed fist pausing at the wooden frame. "With my current status, they'll just push me into early retirement. But you have a whole lot of good years ahead of you."

There was no way he was going to let her go this alone. In reply, he knocked urgently on the captain's door.

They heard the casters on his chair squeak, then heavy footsteps. The door flew open. Captain Darren Hammerlich was a tall, wiry man with hard eyes and a cleft chin that looked like it'd been cleaved with a hatchet. He looked ten years younger than his fifty-five years and could outbox any man on the force who dared to step into the ring with him at the gym. He didn't look happy to see them.

Framed, signed pictures of Mike Tyson, Joe Frazier, Evander Holyfield and even one of once-governor Jesse Ventura lined the wall behind the captain's desk.

"Dalton, why aren't you on patrol, and Hernandez, you were supposed to be at your desk hours ago. If I hear those GD phones ring one more time I might throw them all out the window."

Dalton steeled himself. This wasn't going to be easy. Meredith stood her ground, her knuckles white from squeezing the folder. Some of the pictures she'd printed up had started to slide out one end.

"Sir, if you don't mind, we need to speak to you."

He waved her off, turning his back on them. "I don't

have time to listen to excuses. Just get to work. I'll deal with you both later." He sat down and pulled up to his desk, engrossed in whatever was on his computer monitor.

They followed him inside, Dalton shutting the door.

Hammerlich looked up with a withering glare. "Have you both lost your minds?"

Dalton spoke up. "We thought so, at first. But we have to show you something. We think we know what's going on."

He studied them for an interminable length of time, folding his arms across his chest. Dalton met his gaze. If he wasn't so sure of himself, of the evidence, he knew he would have caved and hightailed it out of the captain's office.

Meredith placed the folder gently on his desk and opened it. A picture of the creature in the cattle pen stared up at him. He looked down at it, then raised his eyes to them.

"What the hell is this?"

"One of the things that's on the loose," Dalton said.

Hammerlich riffled through the papers. He motioned for them to take a seat.

"Where did you take these pictures?"

Meredith answered, "Some at Plum Island, in the government lab, and those others at the beach several years ago when I responded to a dead animal call."

Each hand held one of the pictures. His head went back and forth between them like he was watching a tennis match. Finally, he put them down, spreading everything across his desk.

"Tell me what I'm looking at and why I'm not going to give you an official reprimand."

CHAPTER 31

Officer Jake Winn's gut clenched the moment the shadowy creature leapt from the roof.

The children, who had been running as fast as they could, one of them even sprinting right out of her light-up sneakers, pulled to a terrified stop. Now that he could see the thing under the amber lights that circled the parking lot, his hopes for getting all of them to safety withered and died.

It was beyond words or comprehension.

What he'd at first thought was a dog was anything but. It had the basic structure of a large, powerfully built canine, but that's where the resemblance ended. The face was like that of a wild boar, coarse, thick whiskers covering a blunted snout. Canines half a foot long snapped at the air, thick saliva splashing the gravel at the children's feet. It had hooves instead of paws but the tail was long, twitching with agitation. Most of the fur on its body had shed. Blue-tinged skin gave it the appearance of a drowned animal.

The children shrieked as one, scampering back toward Winn.

Shit!

Their sudden movement gave the monster pause.

"Get behind me!" Jake shouted.

He saw husbands throw protective arms across wives, urging them to go inside. None of the women moved. Their babies were out there.

Winn drew his gun on the creature. It stared back at him with yellow eyes that shone with a spectral gleam of intelligence. It saw Jake for what he was—a threat to its next meal. Black and pink lips curled back. A throaty growl gave warning that he should stand down.

All of the children were now gathered at his back, some crying, the rest too petrified to make a sound.

He looked past the creature to the motel rooms. Several parents were making their way to the lot. It was understandable that they would do anything to save their children, but right now, they were destroying his chance to shoot the damn thing. If he went wide or high, there was a frightened parent within range that would take the bullet instead.

"Stop."

They kept coming, now getting the attention of the creature. It took a quick look at them, then returned its attention to Winn and the children.

To make matters worse, it began to shift from side to side, bobbing its head as if to latch on to their scent, looking for the fastest way to get at them. Winn's gun followed its movements.

It knows, he thought with blossoming dread. *It made itself a moving target so I can't shoot. What kind of hell did this thing come from?*

Tiny hands touched his waist and legs, as he if were a totem of protection. In a sense, wearing his uniform, wielding a gun, that's exactly what he was supposed to be.

"Folks, if you don't stop, I can't take this thing down," he said evenly through gritted teeth. "If I can't shoot it, someone is going to get very, very hurt."

A boy bawled for his mother. One of the women walking toward them stopped, her face a mask of worry, pain and confusion. She must have been the mother of the boy. Her hands were clutched against her breast. Tears rolled down her cheeks.

All of the parents had stopped. The creature, sensing the change, flicked its terrible head to them and gave a hoarse bark. As fully formed and muscular as its body was, something was very wrong, almost unfinished, with its ability to vocalize.

Two men and one woman who had been to the left of the creature stepped carefully away, giving Winn a comfortable buffer should he miss.

"Kids, cover your ears," he said, never taking his eyes off the prowling beast.

He pulled the trigger.

Incredibly, it seemed to anticipate the shot, bursting to its right in a full gallop. The bullet buried itself into the wall of one of the hotel rooms with a sharp crack. A man standing by the room leapt away from the splintering wood.

Winn watched the creature run in a half circle, its cloven feet pounding the gravel, never losing stride.

It was angling around them so it could get to the children from the rear, where no adults stood in its way.

Children and parents shouted, piercing wails that echoed into the night. The parents sprang into action, running for their kids. Most of the children dashed toward them. It was pure chaos. Two girls, neither older than seven, stood rooted to the spot beside Winn, following the creature's line of attack with wide, wet eyes. They held hands, shoulders bobbing with sobs, too scared to break free.

Winn fired three rounds at the swift-moving monster. All missed, kicking up gravel, thudding into a car door and the last sailing off into the darkness.

It made a tight turn, now facing them, hurtling like a missile.

Winn fired again, this time grazing its hind flank. Blood

misted the air, but didn't slow it down. Before he could squeeze off another shot, it barreled into the girls, breaking their grasp on each other. Their bodies spun, hitting hard into the sharp gravel.

It dove into Winn. He heard, rather than felt, his ribs crack when its snout crashed into his chest. As he collapsed on his back, all the breath expelled from his lungs. His head turned in time to see the creature continue on as if he'd never been an obstacle. It pounced and took a chunk out of the back of a man's neck. The light of the moon briefly caught the white of his spinal cord. The man collapsed. The little boy whose hand he'd been holding also went down. Adults and children scattered.

The pain in Winn's lungs was excruciating. His diaphragm hitched, desperate to pull in air, but too shocked to do so.

When the beast made it past the fleeing children and adults, it skidded to a stop and rounded back to Winn. Its face was smeared with gore. Jaundiced eyes bored into the little boy shaking his mortally wounded father, trying to get him to stand up. From what Winn could see, the man was probably already dead.

It charged at the boy.

Despite the white spots dancing in Winn's periphery, he rolled onto his stomach, raised his arm and fired. The boy screamed, his body leaping away as if he'd stepped on a hornet's nest. He rolled on the lot, holding his arm.

Winn fired again. And again. His finger twitched against the trigger as fast as it could, sending round after round into the approaching creature.

This time, they all hit their mark.

It wasn't until the hammer had fallen down on an empty magazine a half-dozen times that he realized the creature was down. Its shredded body had collapsed just five feet from him. The face was in ruins. Blood and scarlet tissue and shattered bone stared back at him. The stench coming out of it was unreal. His lungs, finally able to draw air, threatened to clamp shut again.

Turning his face away, he pulled himself up to his knees. He felt hands touch his arms. The girls were at his side, trying to help him up. One of them smiled at him, bits of gravel clinging to the side of her red face.

"Thank you for making the monster go away," she whispered to him.

On his feet now, he patted her head. A woman brushed against him, nearly sending him back to the ground. She scooped up both girls, pulling them to her chest, kissing the tops of their heads.

Everyone staying in the motel was outside, gathering around the lot.

Winn remembered the boy. He was crying, hard, his armed pulled tight to his side.

He knew he'd shot him the moment the boy jerked away from his fallen father. Stumbling to him, he prayed he'd only grazed the boy. Anything worse was unthinkable.

West of the carnage at the motel, in a $3.8 million summer home on the Hamptons coast, the cast of *The Wealthy Wives of the Hamptons* was getting their first dose of reality.

A brilliant explosion of glass pebbles spilled from the raised deck overlooking the beach into the living room. Pam, a fresh-out-of-college production assistant, was lashed from head to bare calves by the shrapnel. She ran from the room, hands raised and trembling, screaming both with fright and the burning pain of dozens of tiny wounds.

Samar Van Dayton's shrill shriek brought their epic battle to a halt. From her vantage point at the head of the mahogany table, she could see straight into the living room.

Her chin quivered as she pointed toward the production crew, their backs to the scene.

"What the hell is going on?" Nancy Primrose shouted, upset that her grand moment was being usurped.

She followed Samar's finger, head swiveling in slow motion, or at least that's how it felt to her.

"Holy shit."

The director tapped the squatting cameraman but he ignored everything around him, the view through his lens the only thing that mattered. Right now, he filmed the color draining from Nancy's face and the rapid rise and fall of her chest.

Grace Bavosa and two of Samar's friends had to tilt their bodies across the table to see. Grace's wail topped all the others. She backed up against the dining room wall, scooting as far as she could, trembling behind Samar as if she were a human shield.

"Guys, get out of there!" Nancy screamed at the production crew.

It seemed as if they had all become statues after meeting Medusa's gaze. Only their eyes moved, rolling back and forth as they took in the approaching trio of monsters.

What were those things?

At first, Nancy thought that a pack of wild, perhaps rabid dogs had come crashing through the doors. The terror of getting rabies had been enough to close her throat.

She would gladly take rabies over anything these creatures would do to them.

All three looked very much the same, like animals born of the same litter. Nancy once dated a man from Wales who bred Irish wolfhounds for British aristocracy. Her favorite, Baldric, was so tall, its back came up to the bottom of her breasts, which were very high at the time thanks to a wonderful enhancement and lift she'd gotten in Beverly Hills several months earlier—a birthday gift from a previous boyfriend. She joked that the dog was big enough to ride. Her boyfriend, an old, rich codger who paid handsomely for a little slap and tickle, told her to go ahead and give Baldric a spin. She had, and the wolfhound pranced about with her bouncing on its back as if she were nothing more substantial than a flea.

These—*things*—were the size of Baldric, but they were certainly not wolfhounds. Their heads were much too small for their bodies, beanlike in comparison, with narrow, rheumy eyes, small, round ears and snouts that curved downward to sharp, tapering points like beaks. They looked diseased, their fur a clotted mess. Deadly-looking rows of sharp, crooked teeth were bared. It seemed odd that they made almost no noise, considering their manic entrance and menacing stance. Their throats could manage only a strange, asthmatic kind of cough.

Samar babbled, repeating, "Why is this happening to me? Why is this happening to me?"

Nancy looked down at the floor for something to defend herself with. She snatched up a handful of forks and knives. If jammed in the right place, they would make a formidable deterrent.

Finally, Ned, the cameraman who had been following their every move the past two seasons, swiveled on his knee to face the intruders.

He was just in time to film their attack.

Without warning, the beasts sprang at the production crew. One of them hit the front of the camera hard, smashing it into Ned's face, shattering his eye socket. Before he could react to the agony, its front paws were on his chest as it lunged at his face, taking his nose, cheeks, lips and chin with one jaw-crunching bite.

Nancy backed up, crouched in a fighting stance, silverware flashing in front of her.

Another monster stood on its hind legs, towering over

the director. It dipped its head down to his neck and shoulder, tearing at flesh, muscle and bone. A heavy arterial spray erupted from his neck, painting the ceiling and walls. The monster continued to work at his neck as he crumpled to the floor.

"Noooo!" Grace's scream even made the creatures pause.

For once, Nancy was grateful for Grace's hysteria.

"Help me lift the table onto its side!" she shouted at her costars. Reaching down for the leg—*Crap, this table is heavy*—she waited for them to take her cue. There was no way out of the dining room. No windows, no doors. They had to create a barrier between them and the bizarre animals that were now feasting on the crew.

Samar was the first to come to her senses. She put her shoulder under the edge of the table. Grace, who was in full-on panic mode, pulled it together enough to wrap her arms around another leg. Samar's friends lifted it by the edge and together they heaved. They struggled to lift it from the floor, but once they had some momentum, it turned onto its side, settling with a thunderous thump.

"How the hell did they manage that?" Nancy exclaimed.

Samar's two friends had somehow positioned themselves so they were on the wrong side of the table barrier. They were now face-to-face with the creatures, and judging by their screams, had gotten their attention.

The table filled half the entryway into the living room. Nancy knew it wasn't going to be enough to keep those things out, but maybe it could slow them down enough so she could bury a fork in their eyes as they struggled over it.

"Samar, Grace, help me!" she shouted.

A pair of pale, well-manicured hands flopped over the lip of the barrier. The women shouted and sobbed. They were too incoherent to understand, but Nancy didn't need words to know they were terrified.

"Grab their hands and let's try to pull them over."

Samar reached for a hand, still muttering "Why me?"

The hand went rigid. It was followed by a glass-shattering scream and what sounded like a water balloon bursting on pavement. Samar put a foot against the underside of the table and pulled. She flew back onto her ass, rapping her head against the floor.

"Samar!" Grace yelled.

Samar looked to her right, saw the alabaster hand in hers. She followed it to the wrist, then elbow, all the way to the torn, bloody shoulder. The rest of her friend was still on the other side.

Nancy struggled to pull the other friend but wasn't strong enough to win a tug-of-war with the creature that yanked the hands out of her grip.

There were no more screams.

Nancy struggled to catch her breath, leaning against the underside of the table. Samar finally let go of the hand and scrabbled on her rump all the way to the far wall.

Grace, having settled down, moved toward Nancy. "Do you think this will keep them out?"

Nancy shot her an incredulous look. "No. Grab a knife and be ready for anything."

When she looked at Samar, she saw a woman who had had a complete break with reality.

Samar rose to her feet, her legs unsteady. "I have to go shopping." A line of blood snaked down her neck. "I have to get fruit at the fresh market. People are coming for the weekend and I have to get things ready." Her eyes were like pinwheels, spinning and seeing something that wasn't there.

"Sit, Samar," Nancy hissed. "And keep your voice down."

She ignored her, walking to the barrier.

"The market only takes cash. I'll have to stop at the bank."

One of the creatures vaulted over the barrier, pinning Samar to the floor. She didn't make a single sound of protest. It bit into her breast, reeling backward when its teeth penetrated the silicone-laden bag underneath. Samar's body trembled, but Nancy thought she heard her say something about looking for her American Express black card.

She spied the knife in Grace's hands. "Go for its eye."

Grace nodded, her hand tightening on the steak knife.

"Now!"

They lunged at the creature, arms held high, knives pointed at the sides of its head. Nancy heard a crunch as Grace drove hers home. Nancy followed suit. The creature's eye popped and a geyser of black and green ichor hit her in the face, filling her mouth. She heaved immediately, vomiting the vile, burning fluid. Her mouth, throat and chest felt as if someone had poured gasoline into her and dropped a match.

The monster thrashed about, knocking into Grace, sending her tumbling into the wall. Samar's breast was still in its mouth. Looking over, Nancy could see one of Samar's exposed lungs.

As the beast struggled, blinded and wounded, the other two scrabbled over the barrier. Both turned to Nancy.

Her mouth had gone numb and it was hard to breathe. *What the hell are they made of?* she thought as she faced her death. It would be a welcome relief from the fire trailing within her.

"Go fuck yourselves," she croaked.

When the first monster bit into her throat, she wanted to cry out in thanks.

CHAPTER 32

It was a miracle that Captain Hammerlich had let them finish telling their story, from Meredith's first run-in with one of the strange, dead creatures on the beach to their narrow escape from the federally protected Plum Island Animal Disease Research Facility. To his credit, he interrupted them only a few times to ask questions. When they were done, Meredith was exhausted. She'd been running on an adrenaline high the entire time. The captain's complexion seemed to have turned a sickly gray. Or was that just her imagination telling her how he *should* look after receiving news both this bizarre and grave.

Staring at the pictures she'd taken, he said, "Wait outside."

She followed Dalton out the door. He closed it slowly, careful not to make a noise. They walked to the break room. Meredith lifted the empty coffeepot from the warming plate.

"Of all the nights for there to be no coffee. I need a cup, bad," Meredith said.

Meredith pulled at her bottom lip as she leaned against the counter. Now that she'd had her chance to lay everything out for the captain, she had a moment to think about what she and Dalton had done in her shower. It was a welcome break from the reality of the creatures that had broken free from Plum Island. *You have to admit, that was pretty amazing. Are we a couple now, or was that just a pre-Rapture roll in the hay? What will my friends say? I can't be a cougar yet. I'm not even thirty-five. And what will his friends and family think, being with a crippled older woman? You stepped in all of it this time, Mer.*

Her thoughts were broken when he wafted a fresh cup of joe under her nose.

"So, you've been here longer than me. How much trouble do you think we're in?" he asked, blowing across the surface of his mug. He didn't look the least bit worried. Just the opposite; there was a hard look in his eyes that said he didn't give a shit what the captain thought. They both knew what they saw. She worried that he might jump in a free squad car and look for a fight.

She shrugged her shoulders. "I have no frigging idea."

Before Dalton could press her, they heard a door bang open. "Hernandez, Dalton, get in here."

Dropping their half-full mugs in the sink, they returned to his office. Meredith saw all four extensions blinking on his phone.

"I made some calls to the directors of the federal agencies that crashed into town while you were playing Hardy Boys."

Oh boy, we're doomed. He looked so angry he could break his desk in two.

"Every time I said the words 'Plum Island,' collegial calls either turned to ice or I was disconnected."

"Sir, we didn't make this shit up. We could get a team together with some heavy-duty firepower and go back to the island."

Dalton touched her shoulder, silencing her.

Captain Hammerlich stood up and pushed his chair away. "What I was going to say is that it seems I touched a nerve. When my call wasn't disconnected, I got the distinct impression I was being fed heaping spoonfuls of bullshit. Did you know we have FEMA and the CDC and the damn military prowling around? And I just got word that the National Guard will be here in the morning. About an hour ago, all Internet service to this end of the island was cut. No one can give me any answers, at least straight ones. Any other night, I'd send you both to be evaluated by a horde of shrinks."

He pulled his hat off the hat rack in the corner of his office and squared it on his head.

"If what you say is true, those goddamn feebs are going to do their best to keep us in the dark."

Opening the door, he motioned for them to leave. To their surprise, he followed them into the hall.

"We just got an animal disturbance call that stray dogs are all over the condo complex over by the plaza in Montauk. Conrad and Leeks are already there. I'm going to assume our communications have been tapped, so the military and feebs will be there soon to make a mess of things."

They exited the station house. Hammerlich grabbed the keys to a squad car on the way out. He said, "I'll drive. You may need some clout to get through that military roadblock getting into Montauk."

Meredith was tempted to reach out for Dalton's hand in the darkened rear seats. *What are we driving into? If it's a pack of those things, we're going to need all the help we can get.*

Dalton stared ahead in silence. She knew that look. She grew up with four brothers, the most rough-and-tumble foursome in their neighborhood, and possibly the county.

He wanted revenge. No roadblock was going to keep him out.

Winn didn't think anything could make him forget the searing pain in his ribs. His call to the station changed his mind.

"What do you mean there aren't any paramedics?" His hip rested against his car, one arm draped over his ribs. Every breath was a struggle. The little boy he'd shot was being tended to by his mother, who was too focused on her son to register the cold fact that her husband had just been killed by some unidentifiable animal.

Fred Paulson sounded ready to explode himself. "From what I've heard, none of them showed up for work tonight."

"Even Jerry?" He recalled the man's face at Kelly James's house when her body went off like someone had dropped an M-80 down her throat. The only way Jerry wouldn't be on duty was if he was dead or dying, which, after everything he'd seen, was probably the case.

He heard Paulson flip through some papers. "It says he went to the hospital with a patient last night"—(*that had to be Kelly James*, Winn thought)—"and since the place is in full quarantine, no one's been allowed in or out."

Winn hoped to hell Jerry was at least getting proper treatment if whatever had killed Kelly had somehow gotten into him.

"Look, Fred, I've got a man down who needs a fucking coroner. I . . . I accidentally shot a four-year-old boy. He'll be all right. It looks like the bullet nicked his arm, but he needs medical attention. And I've gotta have at least a half-dozen broken ribs."

Leaning back to see if that would help lessen the pain of breathing, he stared up at a full canopy of blinking stars. He couldn't tell the difference between real stars and the sparkling bursts of his brain misfiring from oxygen deprivation.

"No one's responding at the medical examiner's, either, Jake. I hate to tell you, but you're just going to have to sit tight until I can find someone."

"Call Dr. Gandhi."

"Dr. Gandhi? He's retired, isn't he?"

"Yes, but he lives nearby. He may not be practicing but he's still a damn doctor. Tell him I asked for him and to get here as fast as he can."

"Right. I'll call him before I head out. I just got a call about a disturbance at the Plaza Condos."

As much as he wanted to lie down in the back of his car and wallow in his own pain and misery, he still had a couple dozen distressed people who needed a level head, even if it was on the shoulders of the man who shot a boy. With each step bringing fresh waves of agony, he made his way to the mother and her son. They were surrounded by several adults, including Ernie, the owner of the motel. The boy's sobs had settled into hitching breaths.

"Is he okay?" Winn asked, staring at the bloody towel wrapped around his arm.

His mother looked up at him. "He will be. The bleeding stopped. Thank you for saving my son."

Winn was too shocked to reply.

She pulled the child close to her chest. He popped a tiny thumb in his mouth. "He's all I have left."

The sound of screaming was carried by the breeze. He couldn't tell from which direction it came. Everyone in the lot stiffened.

"I need you all to get in your rooms and lock your doors and windows. Ernie, Dr. Gandhi will be coming to check on the boy. You still have that .38 you keep under the check-in desk?"

Ernie's bald, liver-spotted head nodded.

"Don't be afraid to use it."

Everyone filed into their rooms, leaving the man's cooling body facedown in the gravel, alone.

Winn struggled to get into his car, turned the ignition, rolled down his window and went in search of the source of the screaming.

CHAPTER 33

As Captain Hammerlich pulled across the entrance to the condo's cramped lot, Dalton saw they were late to the party. It was in full swing and everyone was invited.

"It looks like other people in the know may share your concerns," the captain said, slamming the car into park. The smell of exhaust and gun oil was overpowering.

Aside from county and local police, the three-story condo was surrounded by soldiers wielding assault rifles, grenades clipped to their belts. Dalton lost count at thirty-three men in full combat gear. A FEMA truck sat idling to their right. Looking around the lot, he also spotted a silver sedan with a Centers for Disease Control logo on the driver's-side door. He thought of Margie and Anita and the first two bodies, Randy and Rosie, smoldering in their own juices on the beach. Someone had to know what was going on at Plum Island, and that someone had sounded the national alarm.

Mickey Conrad left his post behind his squad car and came rushing over. "First call came from a woman who said there was a wolf running through the halls."

Dalton looked at Meredith. Her face betrayed no emotion.

"Let me guess; it wasn't a wolf," Captain Hammerlich

said, flexing his shoulders. If Dalton didn't know better, he would swear that his boss was itching to run into the condo and take the monstrosity prowling the halls head-on, Putin style. He wasn't sure he'd hesitate to join him.

"I'll be honest with you, we don't know what they are," Conrad said. The harsh glare of flashing red and white lights made it difficult to see the ground floor of the condo itself.

"They?" Meredith interjected.

"They," Conrad said with a sharp nod. "It looks like there are two of them. Local PD was the first to arrive. She entered the condo and was immediately attacked."

She. There was only one *she* on the Montauk force—Jane McGrath, president of the fighting Irish.

When Mickey showed them the picture he'd taken of her body, the shredded blue of her uniform, stained forever red, her limbs, ten or more feet from each other, tossed about the lobby like the broken bits of a piñata, Dalton had to turn away. What the hell were they going to tell her husband, her kids?

He went on, "Everyone is holed up in their apartments, but every now and then we can hear screaming and something scuffling. The GI Joes are putting together a team to sweep them out."

"Anyone get a look at them?" Dalton asked, ignoring protocol and not letting his captain ask the questions.

"Some of the residents have been on the phone with us. What they're saying doesn't make much sense."

Hammerlich grimaced at Dalton. "Did we leave that folder of yours in my office?"

"We did."

Meredith called up an image of one of the living creatures they encountered on Plum Island and showed it to Conrad. "Does this match the description?"

He took the phone from her hand, his eyes wide and unbelieving. "Are you kidding me? Yeah, this is kinda like it, only the face was a little different. Where the hell did you take this?"

Hammerlich took the phone from him and handed it back to Meredith. "Never mind that now. Point me in the direction of the CO for the military."

Conrad motioned to a tall man with a barrel chest in the center of the parking lot. He looked every inch the grizzled officer.

Hammerlich took several steps and turned to ask, "And where the hell is Sergeant Campos?"

"He left with three men to respond to another call over by Star Isle."

The captain strode off.

When he was out of earshot, Mickey said to Meredith, "What the hell are we dealing with?"

"Your federal government dollars working for the greater good for democracy's proliferation."

He turned to Dalton.

"Those things were made in a lab on Plum Island. They're bred to kill everything in their sight. And they carry some kind of disease that seems to melt you from the inside out, like Ebola on speed."

Conrad hooked his thumbs in his belt. "This is the part where I'd normally ask if you were shitting me, but all these feds wouldn't be here to catch a couple of rabid wolves. I'm not sure how or why, but you two seem to know more than most. What do we do?"

Dalton drew his revolver. "We wait and see what the army can do. Whatever happens, don't get bit and stay the hell away from anyone that does. Even if it's one of us."

He and Meredith left Conrad puzzling over their warning.

* * *

Sergeant Dennis Campos pulled his car to a screeching halt, narrowly missing a man standing in the middle of the street. He was bent at an odd angle, holding his arm up as if it could stop the car.

"What the hell do you think you're doing?" Campos grumbled.

"That's the same question I keep asking myself," wheezed the man in uniform.

Finally seeing who it was, Campos trundled to his side. Officer Winn leaned into him, grateful to have someone take his weight.

"What happened to you?"

"Some kind of animal loose at one of the motels. It must have broken some ribs when it dove into me."

Two other county cars pulled up behind them. "We need to get you to a hospital." Winn was wheezing bad. Blood flecked the corners of his mouth.

The Montauk cop shook his head. "Can't. No paramedics available and the hospital is under quarantine. I'm going to have to tough it out for a bit. Besides, there's this." He motioned with his head to the front yard of the house to their left. The sloping lawn was littered with what looked like garbage.

Campos, still holding on to Winn, walked to the curb to get a better look.

"Don't get too close," Winn warned him.

He pulled up when he spied a dog's leg, pulled from its body like a Thanksgiving drumstick, seeping blood into the grass.

"What the hell?"

Winn pointed to a stake in the ground and two long leashes. "That's what's left of two dogs. The owner saw them ripped to shreds. I spoke to him through the front window. I told him not to come outside, under any circumstances."

Acid reflux burned the back of Campos's throat. "What killed the dogs?"

Winn peered into the darkness, then said, "I think it's hiding on the side of the house. I keep hearing movement."

It was exceedingly dark in this corner of the block. The streetlight across the street was out. The only light they had to go by came from the windows of the house. They couldn't see past the bedlam of the front yard.

"Maybe you should call Animal Control, though I don't think even they'll know what to do with this"—Winn paused, struggling to find the right word—"monster. Whatever's out here isn't a dog or a rabid wolf or fox. I killed one. They're like nothing you've ever seen."

The sound of a plastic garbage can lid thudding onto the pavement had Campos reaching for his gun. He said, "Anita's dead. Animal Control won't send anyone out. We'll have to handle this ourselves."

Winn winced, pulling in a ragged breath. Campos couldn't tell whether it was the pain in his ribs or a reaction to the news about Anita Banks.

"We have to be very careful," Winn said. "These monsters are fast and more vicious than a fucking wolverine."

Campos pulled one of his men over. "Frank, take Austin to Fern Street and come toward us through the backyard. I need you to flush out an animal—"

"A monster," Winn added.

"—I need you both to guide it toward us where we can see it better. If it turns on you, shoot the damn thing."

They jumped into a car, made a tight U-turn and disappeared around the corner.

"Now we wait," Campos said, feeling the burden of his age strangely lifted from his sagging body.

Everything was silent now. He saw the blinds open up in the front window, two heads peeking out between the slats. He hoped they had enough sense to stay inside. He thought of those doctors from the CDC and the military convoys that had thundered into town. Everything was connected, but no one was talking to one another. He'd heard that FEMA was in the mix as well. Weren't they supposed to bring different agencies under one roof, sharing information? Government fuckups, every one of them. The price for their secrecy was going to be the lives of this town.

They heard a sharp "Ho!" from within the darkness. It was followed by the report of a gunshot, then a scream, followed by another shot. Austin Hammel came charging from the side of the house. He tripped and fell face-first onto the grass, the top of his head plowing into a pile of entrails.

More screams came from the back of the house. Campos ran toward the house, Winn lagging behind. He shouted at Pete Kenealy, "Stay back in case it gets past us!"

Before he could get to Hammel, who had flipped onto his back and struggled to get to his feet, something large, fast and feral burst from the darkness. It landed on Hammel's chest. Campos stopped, aimed and shot at the four-legged creature. Blood spattered from its wounded shoulder. Ignoring the pain, it dove for Hammel's throat, ripping everything down to his spine with one bite.

Mouth crammed with Hammel's neck, Hammel's life, it looked to the man who had dared shoot it.

Campos felt his throat close the same way it would when he ate peanuts, triggering his deadly allergy.

It was completely hairless, a topaz wraith from an unseen world of beasts and demons. Its face was at once canine, bovine and something else, something unthinkable. The flesh on its impossibly long snout seemed a paper-thin covering of what he knew was a hard-shelled beak, one with sharp fangs carved into its blackened jawline.

A shot kicked up the turf by the monster. It skidded away. Winn was on the ground, trying to hold his ribs together with one arm. He pulled the trigger again, going wide and right.

Campos shook the inertia from his brain, steadied a hand under his gun hand. He squeezed off a shot. The round buried itself in the spot where the monster had been standing a fraction of a second before.

The sound of crashing glass pulled his attention to the house. The monster had leapt into the front window. The shrieks of a man and woman reverberated down the residential street. For some reason, the crack of gunfire had drawn people *from* their homes instead of sending them farther within.

His heart pounded, out of rhythm, dangerously tripping on its own beat. It was hard to catch a breath.

Somehow he managed to croak, "Kenealy, get everyone inside."

The man seemed eager to move away from the house. Winn looked to be unconscious. The melee inside the house came to a fevered pitch. Furniture was being torn apart, thrown? The monster's snarls were reedy, thin, compared to the bursts of raw terror coming from its newest prey.

Something was very wrong with his heart. He wasn't sure he'd make it even if there were paramedics nearby.

Adelle's safe, he thought. *I wish we could have retired to Vermont like we planned.*

The woman inside the house let loose with a long peel of abject panic.

Taking as deep a breath as he could, Campos ran to the shattered window. What he saw inside froze his blood. A man lay amidst torn cushions, furniture reduced to kindling. His face was gone. Shards of bone, what remained of his skull, looked heavenward.

The open floor plan gave a direct view into the kitchen. The woman had climbed on top of the sink. Her knees were pulled to her chest, one hand holding a carving knife. The monster stood coiled at the entrance to the kitchen. He could tell by the flexing of its blue hindquarters that it was readying itself to charge.

Leaning over the windowsill, he fired four quick shots at its legs. One of them blew apart into tatters. The monster slumped to its side. As it craned its head to cast one last withering stare, he fired once more. Its head jerked back, blood spraying onto the refrigerator and cabinets.

Campos staggered, collapsing onto the windowsill.

Oh God, I can't breathe!

Through the haze that had fallen across his eyes, he saw the woman coming toward him. She seemed a million miles away.

Tears rolled down her face, staining her purple T-shirt. "Are you—"

He felt something stab into his lower back. The pain unlocked his lungs. He was instantly numb. He couldn't feel his legs or arms. Helpless, he slid down the front of the house.

Another of the monsters stood before him. The officer he'd left as a backup lay mauled in the street.

A hunk of his own flesh quivered in its maw.

He couldn't even raise a hand to slow it down as its jaws clamped down on his face.

CHAPTER 34

An unmarked black helicopter hovered above the condo, spotlight skittering over the assembled mass of responders. Dalton listened to soldiers and county cops shouting at the civilians that had gathered to watch the spectacle.

"They'll have to shoot one of them to get them to leave," Meredith said.

They had edged through the crowd so they could stand alongside the soldiers, close to the action.

"If any of those things get out, they'll run fast enough," Dalton said.

Residents of the condo had opened their windows, pleading for someone to get them out. A hook and ladder team was going to each window and helping them down, one by one. They were then loaded onto a military transport truck for safekeeping.

A team of soldiers had gone into the condo ten minutes earlier. Every couple of minutes, he heard someone shout "Clear!" as they made their way up each floor. If he counted the "all clears" correctly, they should be at the top floor now.

Meredith nudged his side and said, "Look, Gray, maybe we should—"

An incredibly loud, harsh gunshot crackled from the

condo. He saw a burst of light illuminate the hall window on the side of the building. There were more shots, along with men screaming, others shouting orders that couldn't be made out amid the cacophony.

Dalton's fingers flexed on the handle of his gun.

The shooting stepped up its pace. Something shattered. It sounded like a wrecking ball swinging into the side of a wood-frame house. A man in one of the upper windows whipped his head around and howled. He leapt onto the windowsill, looking back one more time, and jumped. His arms spread out like featherless wings as he sailed free of the building, landing facedown on the concrete with a gut-churning wet smack.

Everyone was so busy looking at him that they didn't notice the creature as it, too, jumped from the window, followed by another.

They touched down on the roof of a police car, crumpling it so it was level with the interior seats. Both bled copiously from various gaping bullet holes. They were massive, with faces like hairless, wild boars and the lithe bodies of great cats. Their lower tusks were painted scarlet. They sneered at the soldiers, police and firemen.

The nearest troops raised their rifles and fired. The creatures were too fast, springing from the demolished car and into the crowd. Men and women on the other side of the car went down. Bullets meant for the beasts found new, helpless targets.

"Hold your fire!" someone shouted, but no one was listening.

Because everyone in the near perimeter was armed and now in a panic, shots rang out from all directions as the beasts ran among them, taking chunks of flesh as they went.

"We have to move the hell out of here!" Dalton said. He knelt down, got Meredith in a fireman's lift, and ran. "Cover us if you can."

Holding on to her crutch with one hand, she guarded their back with the other.

Looking over the heads of the scrabbling crowd, he saw Captain Hammerlich standing atop an olive military jeep. His elbows were locked and gun drawn, fixing one of the rampaging beasts in his sight. The gun dropped from his hand. He never saw the second one as it high-jumped the hood and windshield, catching one of his arms in its bloody maw. Hammerlich delivered a savage punch to the side of its head but couldn't break its grip.

Throwing a blur of rabbit punches, the captain looked to be getting the better of the creature. He might have gotten free—a temporary reprieve since he'd already received a fatal bite—if a trio of soldiers hadn't opened fire on the jeep. The beast was fast as hell, exiting the jeep before the first bullet struck. Hammerlich wasn't so lucky.

Dalton ran against the tide of humanity.

He had to pull to a stop outside a semicircle of soldiers and cops. They had cornered one of the beasts against the wall of the small bank next to the condo. Everyone opened fire at once. The creature twitched wildly. The shooting ceased. Dalton sidestepped a heavy drop of blood as it sailed over the head of the man in front of him.

They're all infected now! We have to get away from them!

Outside the perimeter, it was a free-for-all. People ran back to their motels, cars and motorcycles until they had bottled up into a writhing mass along Main Street, barring Dalton's way out should he get to an empty squad car.

"Dalton, duck!" Meredith shouted. He dropped to his knees, feeling the full weight of her. The remaining creature sailed over them, knifing into a soldier's back. The soldier's finger pulled back on his rifle's trigger, unleashing a fresh hail of bullets on the crowd. Dalton watched the back of a man's head explode. He wore a county cop uniform. His head disappeared in a spray of bone and crimson mist before Dalton could tell who he was.

The creature drove its sharp-pointed snout into the soldier's skull, piercing it like a chisel. It whipped its head around, spraying anyone near with brain matter.

Its fierce, golden eyes locked on Dalton's. He struggled to get back on his feet, his knees popping in protest.

Several shots zipped from different directions, grazing the savage blue beast.

It pawed at the ground, steadily advancing toward Dalton and Meredith, as if it somehow knew what they had done to its brethren on Plum Island.

Dalton steadied his grip on Meredith, refusing to break its gaze and appear weak.

He could feel Meredith's chest and stomach expand against the back of his neck.

"Get ready," he said.

Her arm tensed atop his shoulder.

With a low, rasping grumble, the creature sprang.

Tom and Jay unloaded the keg from the trunk of the car. They nestled it in a metal tub of ice, twisting it back and forth so the ice rose up along its sides.

"Maybe we should go back home," Annie, Tom's sometime girlfriend, pleaded for the fifth time in the past hour. Except for the car headlights centered on their HQ on Highland Beach, they were blanketed in complete darkness. The deafening roar of waves crashing on the rocks told them how close they were to the shoreline.

Her cousins, three blond hotties from North Carolina, gathered around Jason, who had lit up a blunt, happy to share.

Kara and her brother Woodie leaned against her Mazda, along with Skeets and Finn and a couple of their buddies who Tom knew casually, but not enough to remember their names. Greg had called earlier and said something bad was going down by his house, so there was no way he was going. He lived close to the center of town, the very area they avoided, taking back roads to the off-limits beach for their party.

A few of their other friends texted with similar excuses. That is, until he lost all service. The way Tom figured it, that would be more beer for them. He hadn't been crazy about throwing a shindig on what everyone called Quicksand Beach, but now that they were here, he was happy he'd let Jay talk him into it.

He draped his arm around Annie. "We're fine. Jay and I scouted out the area before we came, so we're perfectly safe. I swear."

A welcome cold wind blew off the Atlantic. Annie shivered against him.

"I'm not talking about the quicksand. I'm just getting a bad vibe. It feels like we're not safe."

Skeets blasted some Muse from his car stereo. He had a red cup of beer in one hand and a fat joint in the other. Tom filled a cup for Annie.

"I admit, there's been some strangeness going around, but have a drink and forget it, at least for a few hours."

She reluctantly took the cup and sipped at the beer. He powered his first cup down and filled it to the brim for another. Jason sauntered over, passing the joint to him. "See, brother, I told you I'd figure it out," he said.

Seeing Annie's troubled frown, Jason offered her a brand-new joint from his shirt pocket. "Just for you, babe. No sharesies."

Annie rolled her eyes. "Oh, so I don't harsh your buzz?"

Jason smirked. "No, to thank you for having such beautiful cousins." He winked at her and rejoined the blond trio.

Tom lit it up for her and several minutes later, felt her

relax in his arms. The stars were out in force tonight. He realized how much he missed the smell of the sea. His dorm back in college smelled like dirty socks and molding cum most of the time.

"Hey, check this out, guys!" Jason announced, fumbling around the trunk.

"Jay, maybe you should hold off. No sense alerting everyone that we're here," Tom said.

"Screw that. Sometimes, a man's gotta play with fire."

He dumped a box of fireworks on the sand. Handing Roman candles to each of Annie's cousins, he lit a punk, then the wicks. The three of them held the candles far from their bodies, shooting colored fireballs into the ocean waters where they were swallowed up by the bubbling surf.

Finn helped him steady a fat rocket launcher in the sand. As soon as it was lit, there was a loud burst. The sky erupted in glittering shades of red, white and blue. The tendrils of flame cascaded back to earth like dozens of flares.

"Holy crap, that was awesome!" Jason whooped. Everyone was clapping, even Annie.

As the dying flames met the shoreline, they illuminated a pack of—were they dogs?—as they emerged from the ocean.

"What?" Jason said, mostly to himself.

"Dude, I think you have a pack of strays that want to hang around for the show," Skeets said, his wool hat pulled down to his eyebrows.

Jason grabbed a Roman candle, lit it and aimed the fireballs in the direction of the approaching animals.

The moment they saw what was coming, everyone roared with dread.

CHAPTER 35

Don Sorely watched the entire fiasco unfold on a row of monitors in the relative safety of the FEMA Winnebago. He and all the men seated at the control panels stared mutely, catching flies. Between the "war machines," as they learned they'd been dubbed, and friendly fire, there must have been two dozen casualties.

War machines.

Those bastards couldn't have picked a more appropriate name.

One of the SEALs had discovered the moniker engraved on a laboratory door. It must have been where the damn things were engineered. Don imagined it like a demonic car assembly line.

What bothered him most was the seemingly paltry response to the release of what could possibly be the most dangerous thing concocted by science for the military since the first atomic bomb. Was it truly an underestimation?

Or was this a live test? It made him sick to his soul to think his own people would use the situation out here as a testing ground. When you got lemons, make lemonade. That couldn't be it.

No one was that twisted. Not in a democratic country. Right?

"Tell Team 6 to be prepared to move in and set up a faux triage unit. I want everyone in protective gear. They are to gather the dead and wounded under one umbrella and seal them in until I tell them what to do next."

He knew the same feed, provided by Team 2 two blocks away from the condo, was being funneled to Director Bunker, as well as a host of higher-ups in the government, not excluding the President.

A lump of sickness that felt more like a nest of writhing, fiery snakes cramped his stomach. This was a clusterfuck of epic proportions.

Before he could hit the narrow bathroom, his phone started playing the theme to the movie *Close Encounters of the Third Kind*.

"Sorely."

"Sir, we think we found some intel." The man on the line, Steven Dodson, had been sent with the Coast Guard and forty infantrymen to Plum Island to scour the labs for all the information they could find. The search for anyone living who might have known what happened turned up empty. Everyone in the know had been on that island when things shit the bed. They also combed over the wreck of the ferry at Orient Point. Someone had been on the island and escaped, but there was no way to find out who. Now all they had to go on were the files they left behind. And the creatures they created.

Dodson sounded out of breath, exhausted. "I was able to log into their mainframe and found a slew of files that had yet to be encrypted."

"What's the situation like there?"

"It's a slaughterhouse. There are more of those things out here. The military lost seven men so far, but they also managed to destroy five of the war machines. They keep coming out of the woodwork."

"Did you send all the files over?" He better have. Don didn't want to have to sacrifice another team.

"Yes, and still downloading more. The war machines are more than just genetically engineered animals designed to kill everything they see. From what I've seen, they're a combination of at least a dozen different species types. Initially, they were designed to test organ viability between species, which would have then led to a greater organ bank for humans. Once the military saw their potential as a way to sweep battlefields and cities without expending manpower, things took a turn."

A muffled report of rapid gunfire sounded in the distance.

"What's happening?" Don asked.

"Must be another war machine. I'm in a sealed room with three guards. I should be okay." *Should be.* "Their breeding protocols changed to engineer animals concentrating on size, speed and intelligence. But that's not the worst part. Each of them carries a disease called Marvola-6."

"What the hell is Marvola-6?"

"A synthetic disease, a combination of several different animal disease strands. It's one hundred percent lethal. Once you contract it, either through a bite or fluid transfer, it turns your inner organs into a furnace that burns you from the inside out."

Another cramp knifed Sorely's stomach, doubling him over. He stumbled onto the couch.

"What about an antidote? I know for a fact that the scientists out there didn't work on anything unless they had one."

There was a long, terrible pause.

Dodson replied in a whisper, "I haven't seen anything. Either it's in a file that I haven't seen yet, or the cure was part of their next stage in development of the war machines. The creatures were conceived before the disease. I'm thinking that they needed to work on the actual creatures themselves to find a cure. Often, synthetic viral strains will change dramatically once they merge with living cells. Maybe they were working with the war machines on that phase when they broke free."

Taking shallow breaths, Sorely asked, "Do we have all the Marvola-6 data?"

"Yes."

"I'll get the CDC on it right away. You have five minutes to finish up there. I'm giving the order to burn the place to the ground."

He disconnected the call before Steven could say anything else. That place was a hot zone, the worst he'd ever come across. It had to be obliterated.

His next call was to Dr. Ling. People were screaming in the background. She must be near the disaster at the condo.

"Can you and Dr. Greene get here fast?"

"We just managed to break free from the crowd," she said, her voice up several octaves. "But we can't get back to our car. It's . . . it's . . ."

"Don't worry about the car. Do you see a tan RV by the shops across the way?"

"Yes, we see it."

"Go over there and tell them to take you to me. I have your disease."

The moment the creature left its feet, Dalton tilted his body to the right, affording Meredith a head-on view. He ripped the Glock from his holster. Both guns erupted, a conjoined firing squad. The creature seemed to hit an invisible wall. It somersaulted backward. Its torso exploded as the rounds ripped it to shreds.

Spirals of foul-smelling smoke poured from the entry and exit wounds, as well as from the open seam that was its stomach. Several soldiers and one woman were covered in its viscera.

"Dammit," Dalton hissed. No matter how hard he tried, someone always got hurt. It was as if these things were designed not only to test a man's courage, but his will to press on despite constant defeat.

Meredith slapped him on the back. "You can put me down now."

"Not yet." The crowd was still in panic mode. For all everyone knew, another one of those things was still lurking about. Jostled left and right, nearly losing his footing several times, he carried Meredith past the town gazebo, across the lawn and to a safe, quiet area behind one of the coffee shops a block away. Once in the darkened alley, he slid her from his shoulders. His heart ran like a wild horse in his chest. He would have killed for a bottle of water and a cigarette.

They peered around the corner of the building, watching the madness unfold. Soldiers were attending to fallen comrades—there were bodies everywhere. People were on top of cars, stumbling over one another. Someone had been shoved through a plate glass window. Even if he could get to a squad car, there was no way of driving it out. The road was littered with the dead and dying. The last thing he wanted to do was get near anyone who was infected.

"It's a damn nightmare," Meredith said, massaging her ribs. "It's like no one knew what the hell to expect. You'd think if the military and CDC and FEMA were called in, they would have a frigging clue."

"I think they have a clue, just not the whole picture. With everything being so clandestine, I'm sure the left hand isn't talking to the right."

"So what do we do now?"

"We have to find everyone we can on the force, tell them what we're dealing with. You saw what the military did back there. When they weren't killing each other and everyone around them, they were getting the rest infected. The least we can do is get everyone local on the same page. If we're lucky, we can take a few more of those things out in the process. The only problem is, how do we do that?"

"We're screwed," Meredith said, steadying herself against her crutch. "I don't have a spare clip. Do you?"

Dalton drew in a great breath. "No."

He ducked back around, looking up and down the street. There was a small, fifteen-room motel to their left. The lot was packed solid with cars. Everyone had retreated inside, watching through their blinds.

"Come with me," he said, taking her hand. Once in the lot, he asked her, "Which one do you think we should use?"

"We are not stealing a car."

"I agree. We just need to borrow one."

"What are you going to do, knock on every door until you find the owner of the car you want?"

He shook his head. "I wasn't always a cop. I did my time as a misspent youth."

He spotted a black SUV that was slightly smaller than a tank. All eyes in the motel rooms followed him. When Meredith caught up with him, he was scouring the garden that buffered the lot from the walkway. When he wrapped his hand around a brick, she protested.

"Dalton, the whole place is watching. What will they think when they see a cop break into a car?"

He held the brick in a high arc, ready to smash the driver's-side window. A door above them flew open and a man came charging out. "Hey, what the hell do you think you're doing?"

"Sir, we need your car. Ours is over there." The man on the balcony looked over at the smoldering catastrophe by the condo and plaza. "If you toss me your keys, I won't have to destroy your window and pull out the wiring to start her up. I promise you'll be compensated."

He looked ready to put up a fight when a tall, pretty woman—his wife?—came alongside him with the keys. She flipped them to Dalton, quietly pulling him back into the room. They could hear his protestations through the closed door.

Dalton and Meredith scrambled inside and the engine roared to life. The SUV hummed with raw power.

"Pretty slick," Meredith said, buckling up.

"I knew whoever owned this wouldn't want to see it damaged."

As he pulled out of the lot, she asked, "Where are we going?"

"To find our own people."

Braking hard outside the plaza, he opened his door and ran across the lawn.

"Dalton, what are you doing?" Meredith shouted. She steadied her gun hand at the open door. It was hard to see in the relative darkness. He sprinted around the battle zone, stooping here and there. As he ran back to the SUV, relief flooded through her. His arms were laden with assault rifles, guns and even several grenades. She opened the back door so he could lay them across the backseat.

"Now we're good to go," he said, peeling down the street.

CHAPTER 36

Jason couldn't believe what he was seeing.

Using the dying Roman candle, he lit two more, directing their blazing multicolored balls of light at the bizarre, wet animals that were still advancing from the water—five monsters straight out of one of his and Tom's coveted horror flicks. They were truly hideous. Each looked similar to the other in body type and size, but their faces, those alien faces, were the stuff of night terrors.

Annie screamed, then her cousins.

Skeets, too far gone to realize these were certainly not dogs, approached them, offering a stick of beef jerky.

"Get the hell back here!" Tom shouted at him.

Once the monsters got within the full range of the Roman candles, they flinched, scampering sideways like crabs to avoid the searing light. Jason turned to Tom. "Dude, get all the Roman candles and come over here."

Skeets shouted, "Careful, Jay, you might burn them."

"Those aren't dogs, Skeets. Just walk back here, slowly."

He turned his back on the lurking monsters, smiling. "What's the matter with all of you? If they were sick or crazy or something they would have tried to bite someone by now."

Kara, stifling her cries by pressing her hand over her mouth, stumbled away from Skeets. Her feet tangled up with her brother's and they dropped onto the sand.

Two of the monster sprang, brushing harmlessly against Skeets's sides and pouncing on the siblings.

"Oh my God!" one of the boys shouted.

"Tom!"

The box of fireworks dropped at Jason's feet. "Light me up," Tom said. His hand shook violently and it was hard to transfer the flame.

"You aim at the three back there, I'll try to get those two off Kara and Woodie," Jason said.

Red, blue, green and white balls of sizzling fire rained down on the monsters. Tom was able to hold the three that stayed back in position. Jason fired shot after shot into the monster's sides. Their beaklike muzzles were buried in Kara's and Woodie's throats. There was no saving them now. All he could hope to do was drive them back into the water.

"Annie, I have some M-80s in there. Grab one for me."

She had been shivering, heaving with tears, her cousins surrounding her, a wall of sisterhood. "I . . . I don't know . . . what it looks like," she sobbed.

Her cousin Tara said, "I do." She picked what looked like a miniature stick of dynamite out of the box, lit it and handed it to Jason.

"Perfect," he said, launching it at the creature atop Kara. It landed by her shoulder. The M-80 went off like a bomb, punishing everyone's eardrums. It turned Kara's shoulder to chopped meat, but also blew the monster back about ten feet. It bled like a water fountain from the side of its head. Its eye rolled out of the socket and plopped on the sand.

Finn and his friends ran to the fireworks box. Lighting up candles and rockets and M-80s, they fired at the monsters with everything they had. The reports were deafening.

The monsters scattered around the beach, which was lit up like it was midday.

"You wanna fuck with us?" Jason screamed.

They had the monsters on the run. A couple had been hit and were clearly wounded. If it weren't for Kara's and Woodie's bodies bleeding into the sand, Jason would have jumped in triumph. They hit them with everything they had in a steady barrage. The girls huddled behind them.

At one point, there were so many explosions, it was impossible to tell what they were shooting at. One last M-80 and cascading rocket went off, blinding everyone, and then it was back to impenetrable darkness.

Pinching his eyes, Jason huffed, "They're probably running halfway to Queens by now."

"We have to get the police out here," Tom said. "What the hell do we tell them, Jay?"

Jason knew none of them would pass a Breathalyzer and they all smelled like weed. Even if they were stone-cold sober, it would be a tough sell. But they couldn't just run away from their friends, even if they were dead.

His ears were ringing something fierce. It was hard to hear his friends, impossible to catch the crash of waves.

"Someone will have to stay with the bodies," Finn said.

Two monsters leapt out from the high beach grass behind them. They crashed into one of Finn's friends, snapping and tearing at his upraised hands and face until his cries turned to wet gurgles.

"Run for the cars!" Tom shouted.

A quick turn, several steps, and they stopped. The remaining three monsters, dripping blood, sporting scorch marks, glaring at them venomously, stood before the cars, barring their escape.

Everyone scattered, the girls shrieking, the boys loosening a string of curses. The monsters went after the fleeing pack. Jason saw one of Annie's cousins get taken down, then Annie. Tom heard her cry and turned around. Trying to come to her aid, he fell forward. His legs were stuck, ankle-deep in quicksand.

Skeets was wailing. Jason saw that he was up to his knees in another pool of quicksand, struggling mightily and sinking faster. In fact, as he pivoted on his heels, everyone was trapped in the stuff, like a captive buffet.

The monsters shifted their attention from Annie and her cousin, whose faces were ruined beyond recognition, to the remaining four imprisoned in the muck.

"Holy shit, Jay, you have to help me!" Tom implored. Everyone was crying for his help. The monsters, realizing there was no longer a need to rush, separated from one another as if deciding which morsel each would take for itself.

Finn, who had screwed himself in quicksand until he was up to his waist in the stuff, was the first to scream. Two monsters attacked him from each side, their sharp muzzles meeting at the center of his throat. His head fell back, rolling away from his body, sinking into the wet sand.

Jason scampered to Tom, careful where he planted his feet. He took off his belt and handed it to him. "Hold on, I'm going to try to pull you out." He'd seen it countless times in jungle movies. Throw a vine to the trapped person and just pull.

The air around them was electrified with the shrieks of the dying.

"Pull, Jay, pull! Don't let go. I can feel myself getting loose."

Tom's body slowly broke from the quicksand, inch by agonizing inch.

Where the hell do we go once I get him out? Jason spotted Kara's car in the distance. Between them and the car were the five feasting monsters. They'd have to be faster than the Flash.

"I'm almost there," Tom said. His elbow popped but he kept his grip on the belt.

Jason struggled, felt the veins throbbing on the sides of his head. The quicksand held firm to Tom's calves.

"Just go slack," Jason said between grunts.

He could see tears in Tom's eyes by the diffused glare of a headlight. Calling up every reserve of strength he had, Jason scrunched his eyes closed and tugged harder.

Somersaulting backward, he saw the stars roll by. The belt, now free, was still in his hands. His fingers cramped shut. He didn't think he'd be able to flex them enough to drop it.

Struggling to his feet, he yelled, "Come on, Tom!"

His heart stopped beating when he saw all five monsters burrowing into Tom's back.

"Tom." His best friend's name slumped from his mouth in a whisper. His chest constricted and his eyes burned.

The blustering roar of a passing motorboat caught his attention. A tiny spotlight bobbed along the waves. He ran to the shore, not really caring if the monsters were in pursuit. His only purpose in getting away was to have another chance to get back at the murderous creatures.

He made it to the water without being followed. Splashing into the surf, he knifed through the incoming tide. Five years as a lifeguard made him an excellent swimmer. It wasn't long before he pulled alongside the two-seater boat. A woman, covered in drying blood, was at the wheel. She startled when he pulled himself into the boat, causing it to tilt dangerously.

She looked like she was in shock.

I'm probably no better, he thought.

Neither said a word. She continued piloting the boat, keeping close to the shoreline. He sat beside her, thinking she looked familiar, at least what he could see through his tears.

CHAPTER 37

Dr. Greene barged into the FEMA command center. He was no longer the embodiment of the dapper man in control. One side of his hair was filled with bits of dirt and grass, as was his suit. His eyes were wild and his hands shook at his sides.

Dr. Ling wasn't faring much better. Both looked like they had been run over by a mob—which they had.

"Christ, don't tell me you were in the middle of that," Don Sorely said.

"We had to be," Dr. Greene said, close to shouting. "People were . . . they exhibited signs of a deadly pathogen just minutes after coming in contact with—"

He paused, at a loss for words. His gaze pulled inward, hands trembling.

"They're called *war machines*," Sorely said. "From everything I've read, close to a hundred of them were engineered and raised to full maturity. We're extracting a team from Plum Island now, but not before we downloaded and grabbed every file we could. It's been dangerous work. There are a dozen or so of those monstrosities still on the island. We lost quite a few men."

Dr. Ling opened the refrigerator and grabbed a bottle of

water, downing half in one long swallow. "War machines? From what I could see, whatever it is they're spreading does so through fluid contact, both with the war machines and from victim to victim. We saw people seizing and bleeding out everywhere. The more exposure to contaminated blood or mucous, the faster it burns through them. People with severe bites died in minutes, in turn becoming transmitters of the pathogen to anyone who touched them. I've never seen anything work that fast, at least on humans."

Sorely lost his balance when Dr. Greene grabbed his shirt collar. "You said you know what this is. Well?"

"We know the *name* right now. I have men working on decoding the makeup of the disease. It's called Marvola-6. We think it's a combination of at least half a dozen diseases, with a dash of something synthetic to increase its efficacy and speed up its gestation period. It's very much like venom, but from an animal that was never meant to be."

Dr. Greene let him go. "This is a goddamn catastrophe! I'm going to have to call for more help. Compared to what we're dealing with, we only have a skeleton crew." He hit speed dial on his cell phone for the CDC switchboard in Atlanta. His phone remained silent. "We must be in a dead zone. Sorely, I need you to link me in to the CDC."

The FEMA man shook his head, wearing a face that was as weary as it was guilty of something that he wasn't permitted to tell anyone about. "I have strict orders that nothing goes out of this area, including phone calls. All of Montauk, and now over to the Hamptons, is on total lockdown. Internet communications have been severed as well. We have to contain this, and that means doing so without causing widespread panic."

"You're too late for that," Dr. Ling said. "After what just happened at that condo, word is going to spread and people are going to run like hell."

"Then we need to keep it *here*. Anyone trying to leave

will be met with military forces under strict orders not to allow a soul to go west of the Hamptons."

"What gives you the right or even the authority to do that?" Dr. Ling demanded.

"Who do you think? This is the mother of all snafus. You don't think the powers that be will let this run on the eleven o'clock news or become a sidebar on the *Drudge Report*, do you? Everything stops here. I'll give you everything we have. I'm just as pissed off as you are. You think anyone's given me the whole picture? We're just the fucking janitors here. I don't want to put too much pressure on you, but if there's going to be a light at the end of the tunnel, you're the ones that are going to have to supply it."

The muscles in Dr. Greene's arm twitched. He wanted nothing more than to punch Sorely square in the face.

What was his first name?

Dammit, he couldn't remember. The not remembering scared him. *How can I find the answers when I can't even recall a man's first name?*

Sorely added, "We're all in the same boat. None of this has been my call. I'm just the schmuck that was picked to relay the call. I'm doing all I can to coordinate things so we can eliminate the initial threat, the war machines. But even when they're dead, we have Marvola-6 to contend with, and for my money, that's where the real problems start. You can hate me all you want, but while you're doing that, I need you to comb through everything to find the antidote."

Dr. Ling slumped into a chair, massaging her temples. "Do you know how long that can take? Weeks! Maybe even months. And that's if we had a proper team working together."

There was a dull explosion followed by a bright orange light shimmering against the night sky.

"*That* was Plum Island," Sorely said, pointing. "You

don't have weeks, or even days. Let's start with hours, and see where that takes us."

Dalton cruised down the darkened Montauk Highway with the windows partially open. Meredith kept her gun in her hand, scanning the road and listening for anything or anyone that might need their attention.

"We should go down there," she said, pointing to Sherman Street on their left. "To get to the condo, those things would most likely have come through there. There's a connection between them and the water."

The calm waters of the sound were a couple of blocks from Sherman. She may have a point.

"After this, I'm going to circle back and see if we can get our squad car back. I'd kill for radio communications right now," he said

"The keys were on the captain."

The image of Captain Hammerlich's body twitching as he was mowed down by friendly fire made him recoil. "At least he wasn't bitten. We won't have to worry about getting infected." They *would* have to be careful about coming in contact with anyone else, living or dead, scattered around the plaza.

All of the streetlights along Sherman were out. It didn't matter, because almost every house on each side of the block glowed. Word of mouth was spreading. People were up and, he assumed, packing to leave. He had a mind to knock on each door and tell them there was no getting out of Montauk, at least for now. That was another reason to get a squad car. At least that had a loudspeaker they could use to warn everyone.

Turning down Circe Street, Meredith reached out to squeeze his arm. "Stop the car. Stop the car!"

They pulled alongside a ranch house perched atop a

gently sloping lawn. Bodies and unidentifiable parts of bodies were strewn everywhere. A county cop lay in the middle of the street, his head connected to his body only by his garishly visible spinal cord.

"I think that's Pete Kenealy," she said, digging her fingernails deeper into his muscle.

Dalton reached around and grabbed an M16. "Stay here and cover me. I'm going to see who else is out there."

He immediately became aware of how deep the silence was—as deep and foreboding as the grave. He saw shadows of people standing in windows of the surrounding houses. They were too scared to be outside. That was good. Fear may save their lives.

Careful to avoid stepping into any of the shredded remains, he walked up the lawn. Bile singed his throat when he looked down and saw Sergeant Campos's ravaged body. One of the creatures had broken through his rib cage, making a sloppy feast of his heart, lungs and stomach. Campos was gruff, but he'd always been good to him, always fair.

He placed Campos's hat over his face. He wanted to get back to the truck, but there was a shattered window in the house that had to be checked out. If someone was still inside, he needed to get them to safety.

Peering inside, he witnessed the end result of another slaughter. Smashed, bloodstained furniture was everywhere. The bodies of a man and a woman lay on the floor of adjoining rooms. He could tell from his vantage point that neither was alive.

They were too late to be of any help here. He really needed a radio. Without it, he was flying blind. They had to get back to the condo, contagious disease or not.

As he turned away from the house, there was an explosion and flash of light on the horizon. It was too big to be fireworks. The light didn't diminish. In fact, it intensified.

While he was running back to the SUV, Meredith shouted out the window, "What was that?"

"I don't know. Something blew up."

He looked inside the squad cars, hoping someone left their keys in the ignition. No dice. He couldn't get close enough to their bodies to search their pockets.

He swung the M16 strap down to his wrist so he could throw it in the backseat. His hand froze on the door handle.

One of the creatures slipped out from behind the SUV, deadly rows of teeth bared. The blue of its flesh was tinted red. Blood wept from its mouth.

Before he could get his finger around the rifle's trigger, it charged.

Can Man scampered deeper into the reeds. Earlier, he'd poured the bottle of water he carried into the dirt. He covered his exposed flesh in mud as a way to camouflage himself, forgetting about his loud Hawaiian shirt. Most of the troops had moved out, but there were still ten men left, all of them up by the old lighthouse. None of them had noticed the steady parade of what he considered demons coming out of the water.

Silently, they padded up the rocky steps to the man-made walkway that circled under the rise that housed the lighthouse.

Another rode a wave onto the pebbled beach, shaking the salt water from the bits of fur still clinging to its muscular body.

"Fourteen," Can Man whispered, keeping count of the demons as they arrived.

He hoped the mud masked his scent. They looked like dogs or wolves or panthers. It was hard to tell in the dark with only the moon to illuminate the horrors on the beach. If they were anything like any of those animals, they would have a keen sense of smell. He hoped they'd catch only a whiff of the earth when the breeze blew over him.

Sooner or later, the terrifying sea creatures were going to notice the men stationed at the lighthouse, or vice versa. When that happened, hell was going to open wide. If there was a God, Can Man would remain unnoticed, no more significant than a large shell rolled into the weeds along the beach.

The surf pounded with increasing intensity. Looking up through the slender gaps in the sea grass, he watched shadowy clouds scud under the luminescent lip of the moon. A storm was coming.

And another had already arrived.

The sound of a shrieking gull, or was it a man, was quickly drowned by the churning waves.

Can Man held his breath, listening. The angry Atlantic masked all other noise.

There was a flash of light by the gift shop, which was to the bottom left of the lighthouse, followed by an echoing report.

Shivering despite the humid warmth of the night, he shut his eyes tight and prayed.

CHAPTER 38

"Where are we going?"

Jason sat a slight distance from the woman piloting the boat. Her jaw chattered with chills. Her eyes never strayed from the bow. The boat clung to the visible, churning coastline. It rocked jerkily along the waves that increased in height and intensity as more dark clouds obscured the stars.

His hands hurt like hell. Looking down, he saw the black powder burns that stretched all the way to his forearms. The salt water only made it worse. Holding his waterlogged cell phone with his fingertips, he tilted it so it could drain. It was completely fried.

"Look, miss, my friends and I were attacked back there. We need to get to the police. My best friend was . . . was . . ." The words couldn't come out. What happened to Tom would haunt him for the rest of his life.

"We have to get away," she said, barely above a whisper.

"No, we have to go to the cops. Are you from around here? I know I've seen you before."

Her long hair was wild and frizzy, and the outfit she wore looked expensive. It was the kind of crazy stuff that only rich people would wear, a runway nightmare. The bloodstains had rendered it useless, even for Goodwill.

He could tell by the haunted look in her eyes that, like him, she wasn't prepared to talk about what had driven her to jumping in a boat to wander along the Atlantic coast. By the way she worked it, she'd obviously had very little boating experience.

The Montauk lighthouse was visible up ahead.

"Look, this little boat isn't made for seas like this, especially at night. You're going to have to land her somewhere. If you turn in there," he said, pointing to a sandy beach on their left with a small dock where a couple of rowboats were tied to one side, "it's just a short walk until we come to a small housing development. We'll knock on some doors until someone lets us in to use their phone."

When she finally turned to face him, everything clicked into place. It was one of the Wealthy Wives of the Hamptons—Grace something. For an older woman, she had a slamming body. He'd actually rubbed one out watching the show one night when he was too lazy to get off the bed and sift through the porn tubes on his laptop.

Whatever had happened had aged her. He almost felt guilty for making her one of his sex fantasies.

"You're one of the Wealthy Wives," he said.

She nodded. A lone tear carved a clear streak through the grime on her face.

"Everyone's dead," she said, her voice quivering. She suddenly collapsed into the pilot's chair, her hands falling from the wheel. Jason jumped up to maintain control of the boat. With the waves as heavy as they were, things could get ugly, fast.

"Where were you when it happened?"

Grace looked far away. "It was supposed to be our last dinner party at Samar Van Dayton's house. Everyone knew their part. Nancy wanted to take the show from us."

The woman was far gone. She had sense enough to move aside so Jason could take over the boat.

"Shit balls."

A large, four-legged animal jumped onto the dock, sniffing the boards. From this distance, it could have been a regular dog, but he couldn't tell for sure. No sense taking chances. There was a spot along the right of the lighthouse where he could land. There were always park rangers on duty out there. It was a national landmark, after all. They said George Washington was the one who ordered it to be built. Jason hit the throttle.

"Just hang tight," he said. Grace mumbled something about the show, wondering if what they filmed would make it to air.

"Sir, we're going to have to move base of operations to a safer zone."

The agent, still a kid with no field experience but good with computers, stood over Don Sorely as he tried to catch a few minutes of sleep. It wasn't easy. With the CDC doctors on board, the Winnebago was packed to the gills. Radio check-ins and the doctors talking between themselves created a steady white noise. He couldn't remember the last time he'd slept. All he wanted was fifteen minutes of peace.

"Safer zone? If I put my head outside, I'd hear crickets," he said irritably.

"It won't last long. We have estimates of at least seventy war machines from the Hamptons to Montauk."

Seventy? Don burped, the acid laying a trail of fire on his tongue. He'd hoped that the tide would have washed more out to sea, leaving them to drown. He'd have to talk to his director, demand he get more boots on the ground. Fucking bureaucracy. Every branch of the government was laden with secrets. Over the past couple of decades, those branches turned against one another. *Communication* was a curse word.

"And here I am, sent to pay for their stupidity," he mumbled.

"Excuse me, sir?"

Don waved him away. "Let me talk to the docs first."

Greene and Ling sat hunched over a pair of laptops. They had dark circles under their eyes but neither looked ready to stop.

"You find anything?"

Dr. Ling looked up at him, her contempt barely contained. "Yes, I've found definitive proof that the people in charge of Plum Island are criminals of the highest order. Anyone who has touched that place should be tried as a war criminal."

Dr. Greene placed a calming hand on her shoulder. "Sorely, this is more serious than you or your bosses understand. Some of the greatest minds in the fields of genetics, microbiology and infectious disease were brought together on Plum Island to create something that nature never intended, from the animals you call war machines to the disease they carry. Doctors and scientists were recruited from China, Russia, Germany and South Africa. They were given free rein and unlimited resources to delve into their most fanciful experiments, ethics be damned. At a time when the Plum Island research lab was publicly revealed to have wrapped up and ceased operations, they went into overdrive."

A crooked grin stretched across Dr. Ling's face. "You had no idea, did you?"

"How and why the hell would I? You think if I knew this I would have even come here?" Sorely huffed.

"I don't know you well enough to answer that. Everyone has a price," Dr. Ling replied coolly.

"What good is money when you're not around to spend it?" He tapped one of the techs so he could sit in his chair.

Dr. Greene cleared his throat. "We need to focus. It appears each success went to the heads of everyone working in the labs as well as those who funded and watched over them. They were able to crossbreed species successfully, to the point where there was zero rejection. It'll take years to decode everything they did. At the same time, using existing diseases and combining them with synthetics, Marvola-6 came into being. The true stroke of genius was genetically modifying the creatures they were creating so they could not only adapt to the disease, but also become organic germ factories. All of this was done under strict orders from the facility's director to reveal less and less information to their benefactors, both Homeland Security and those above."

"He means the President," Dr. Ling added coolly. "There's enough in here to not only have him impeached, but executed. You know what that means, don't you?"

Don bit the inside of his cheek until he tasted copper. He knew the President had some involvement, but having a paper trail was bad. Very bad.

"I don't know the exact reasons for creating these war machines," Dr. Greene said, pacing. "I'm sure if you followed the money you'd have your answer. The problem is, Marvola-6 has no cure."

"None that you've *found yet*," Don said, feeling as if the temperature in the Winnebago had gone up ten degrees in the past few minutes.

"A cure will never be found. It wasn't created to be cured. Wherever they meant to deploy the war machines, the intent was to wipe out entire civilizations. The only way to stop it is to contain the infected and the war machines."

Don jumped from his chair and clapped his hands. "Now we're getting somewhere."

"Sir," a tech interjected.

"Not now!" Don barked. The tech quickly turned away. "What's the containment protocol?"

Dr. Greene coughed, and for a brief moment, looked as if he'd completely left the RV. He rubbed his eyes and continued, "Complete annihilation of every living organism within the infected zone. The war machines were designed to be light sensitive, a manufactured weakness to give a military cleaning unit time to do their work without fear. Within close range, you have to burn the bodies until they are nothing but ash. On a more far-reaching scale, an atomic, or what I feel is the more viable solution, neutron bomb can be dropped. At least with the neutron bomb, you'll still have infrastructure left behind. As long as you can keep it a secret that you delivered the war machines in the first place, you can be seen as a hero nation for eliminating their threat and putting an end to a pandemic, all without laying total waste to a city or even country."

Dr. Ling pushed her fiery hair behind her ears. "We're in a hot zone right now. We also hold all of the evidence of the war machine program implicating some of the highest branches of the government. You know they'll never let us leave here alive."

He'd heard enough. This was as bad as it could get. They were bait. Goddamn bait for some wide-scale beta test. And they had damning proof. His head hurt as he calculated his next ten moves.

"The hell they won't. None of us in here are infected. We're hauling ass out of here now."

Don strode to the front of the Winnebago with heavy footsteps. He keyed the ignition and hit the headlights, illuminating a pair of war machines, each an abortion of the laws of nature. They scattered the second the lights hit them, slipping back into the darkness.

"Our cameras show four war machines outside," the tech called out.

"Yeah, I just saw two of them," Don shouted. "I'll run the bastards over if I have to. They may be big and ugly, but I don't think they'll hold up to several tons rolling over them."

He spun the wheel, making a hard right out of the private lot.

Two heavy thuds sounded behind him. The Winnebago rocked to the right. Dr. Ling screeched as instruments crashed to the floor. Don fought to keep the big rig upright as the war beasts, learning to avoid the lights at the front, assaulted the sides and rear in the safety of the warm, dark night.

CHAPTER 39

Dalton tensed, arms outstretched, hoping to catch the creature by the neck before it could sink its teeth into him.

A loud bang rippled the air around him. The monster skidded and rolled to the tips of Dalton's shoes. The side of its head was missing. He jumped back, frantically feeling his face for any traces of blood.

A shotgun's muzzle rested on the open window of the driver's-side door. Meredith clicked a flashlight and shined it on his face. His heart thumped. She may have saved him from a mauling, but he was still as good as dead if anything got on him.

"Let me see your hands, too," she said. He raised them to chest level, showing her the front and back of each hand and exposed arm.

Her shoulders slumped forward as she sighed. "You're clean. Let's go back and find a squad car."

Despite her reassurance, his nerves still trembled. It took him a few tries to get the SUV started as he fumbled with the keys. He noticed that Meredith had shifted away from him in her seat. For all either of them knew, they were carrying the disease that would melt them from the inside out just because they'd breathed in the charnel house that was the front yard.

They drove in silence, passing a burning house. There were no firefighters to battle the blaze. Other houses would ignite.

One of the creatures dashed away from the roiling house, a black shadow of impending death against the turbid flames.

Anyone trapped in that house could be the lucky one, he thought grimly. He jumped over the curb and onto the grass, getting as close to the front as the tongues of fire would allow. They listened for any cries of help. Mercifully, there were none. He punched the accelerator as hard as he could, racing to the center of town.

The crowd at the plaza had dispersed. All that was left were the bodies, and there were many. All showed early signs of infection. Their skin was waxen, blushed from the inferno that consumed their internal organs. Some convulsed, others arched their backs as if in labor. When Meredith and Dalton opened their doors, the wind carried the nerve-rattling moans and cries of the damned.

"There's one," Meredith said, pointing at Mickey Conrad's car. Mickey was nowhere in sight. "I'll get it."

"Not with that leg."

She gave him a look that said at another time, she would have beaten him over the head with her crutch. But he was right. If one of those things was lying in wait, she wouldn't be able to move fast enough to save herself.

He handed her the M16. "Watch my back. And try not to shoot me," he added to lighten her mood.

It didn't appear to work.

He sprinted across the grassy plaza, eyes flicking downward to avoid infected bodies or worse, parts of bodies. A few soldiers had gathered within the wooden gazebo.

Apparently, they had chosen it as the place to make a tactical stand. By the looks of their shredded uniforms, they'd lost while within the small-scale Alamo.

When he got to Mickey's car, he called out for him in case he was nearby and well. The last thing he wanted to do was pilfer the man's primary means of escape from this unholy nightmare.

"Conrad! Are you here?"

His cries were met by pleading from the dying. It made him sick, knowing there was nothing he could do for them. He thought of Anita Banks and how she must have suffered in her hospital bed.

"I'm taking your car, Mickey! If you can hear me, say something!"

Still only that eerie, zombielike wailing.

Grinding his teeth, he slid into Mickey's car and pulled away from the war zone. It was unavoidable, running over pieces of people as he drove through the roundabout. Holding some kind of huge weapon, Meredith waited for him in front of the SUV.

"No Mickey?" she asked.

"No. Is that what I think it is?"

She stepped aside, revealing two flamethrowers. "I figured it can't hurt to have them."

They moved their cache of weapons from the SUV to the squad car, all while scanning their surroundings for signs of any creatures. Where the hell were they?

"I'll check different frequencies until we find something," Meredith said. She worked the digital display while he drove. He had a sudden change of plans. As much as it pained him to admit, Montauk was lost. His new goal was to get them out of Montauk, seek higher, safer ground. If he had to smash through the military blockade to do it, he hoped their aim wasn't good.

Static blared from the speakers. He slammed on the brakes, the car swerving ninety degrees until they faced the entrance to the IGA. The lights were on inside and he could see a crowd of people peering out the glass doors. They had piled metal shopping carts against the doors inside.

A pair of the creatures pawed at the doors, the glass misting from their disease-ridden breath.

"You want to get their attention so I can toast them?" Meredith said.

"You ever use one of those things before?"

"No, but how hard can it be?"

Now wasn't the time to tell her it could be very hard. He just had to hope she could figure it out—fast.

The moment he pulled into the lot, the creatures' bird/boar/dog faces snapped in their direction. Dalton got out first, aiming the M16 at the nearest one.

"We need to pull them a little farther from the store," Meredith said, strapping the dual tanks on her back.

He knew how fast these things were. With the slightest provocation, they could be on them in a nanosecond, well before Meredith's finger ever touched the flamethrower's trigger.

A little girl, clutching a teddy bear to her chest, stared at them from behind an upturned shopping cart. Her dark eyes swam with tears.

Screw it.

Dalton turned his back on the creatures and started to run. That was all they needed. Both left their feet, lunging at him.

There was a heavy whoosh, and it suddenly felt like the sun had fallen from the sky. Dalton rolled behind a car. Looking up, he watched as Meredith rained fire on the beasts. They skittered and scampered, noiselessly, into the street, collapsing into a smoldering heap.

A loud cheer went up in the IGA.

He rubbed the back of his neck. The ambient heat from the flamethrower had given him one hell of a burn. Dalton went to the doors. "It's best you stay inside and away from the doors. You might want to keep all the lights on, too. It's not safe out here."

Several heads nodded.

Of all the people they'd seen, these were in the best position. The IGA building was sturdy with very few windows. They had enough food and water to last them for a good while, at least until things settled down. It was either that or get stuck in a roadblock and sit in their cars, waiting for those creatures to tear at them like sardines in a can.

There was just one more thing that needed to be done to make things extra-secure.

"Meredith, help me with this."

She was still admiring her handiwork, watching the creatures burn. It smelled like someone had set a garbage barge on fire. He rolled a shopping cart past her, tipping it over at the door and wedging it in place.

Snapping out of it, she worked with him, piling more shopping carts on the outside of the doors. Glass wouldn't hold those things back for long. They needed to mask the most vulnerable part of the small market.

"At least there are a couple more down," she said.

"But who knows how many are left?"

They pushed the last cart in place, the metal scraping against the concrete. Dalton saw Mr. Hempill, the store manager, through a gap in the carts. The burly man gave him a thumbs-up and ushered everyone deeper into the store.

Dalton was so hot, he'd sweat through his pants. "We

do good work," he said, sluicing perspiration from his forehead with his sleeve.

"I almost wish I was in there with them. I could go for a Yoo-hoo and some crumb cake," she said.

Meredith's body was suddenly thrown into the hodgepodge of carts. Her head cracked against one of the thick, black wheels. She slumped to the floor. Something scampered atop the barricade.

Dalton looked up, right into the eyes of a monster that had no place on this earth.

"Fire! Fire! Fire!"

The order was barked from the darkness. Muzzle flashes lit up the lighthouse as round after round bit into the landmark, as well as the beach and surrounding cliff face.

A plume of sand shot up in front of Can Man's hiding space. He recoiled, pulling his legs to his chest, pressing his back into the soft earth as far as he could.

Sweet Jesus, it was an abomination.

What were those things? Were they demons? Was this the end times? He grew up with a Pentecostal aunt who actually prayed for the Rapture, imploring him to do the same. This life was the true hell. Better that God set the devil loose so he could call his children home where there was peace and love, an eternity of no regrets, no worries, just pure light.

Soldiers scrambled, abandoning the beach. Everything seemed to be concentrated on the lighthouse itself. He couldn't make out much from his vantage point. The noise, though, was deafening.

He couldn't believe he'd actually chosen this as the safest place to be. When soldiers fought other soldiers, they stood a chance. Not so when hell spawn were let loose.

There was no way he could stay here. If he ran now, while the creatures were focused on the soldiers, he might be able to slip by. But there was the chance he'd be struck by a stray or ricocheting bullet.

"Get it off me! Get it off me!"

A man screamed for his life. There was a quick burst of gunfire, followed by more peels of terror.

It was madness to stay. He had to go—now!

Can Man jumped from the reeds and ran as fast as he could up the gravel-and-seashell-lined path. Bright spots danced before his eyes as the bursts from dozens of rifles burned into his retinas.

Huffing wildly, he made it to the top of the path. The parking lot, with its row of olive military vehicles, lay ahead of him. He just needed to get past them and follow the road out to the Montauk Highway. He'd find a better place to hide once he put this place behind him.

A heavy clack echoed across the lot. A spotlight sprang to life, beaming onto the lighthouse.

Can Man stopped at the bumper of a jeep and turned.

At least a dozen of the demons were climbing the lighthouse. A band of soldiers stood at the base, firing at them with reckless abandon. Chunks of the mortar poured down on them, as well as the occasional wounded beast. The demons scampered away from the light like vampires. The men ran to the dark, firing above in a nonstop barrage.

Another spotlight snapped on, illuminating the area at the foot of the lighthouse.

A dozen more beasts were gathering, pulling themselves from the jagged shoreline.

The soldiers out there were as good as dead. A few turned their attention from the lighthouse, training their guns on the approaching demons.

"Grenade!" someone to Can Man's left shouted.

An explosion of dirt, men and one of the creatures flew ten feet into the air.

They're killing their own men!

More grenades were lobbed. Can Man had to turn away. So far, no one had noticed him. Crouching, he darted between two jeeps, straightened and ran like hell.

He was no more than ten or so yards away when he felt a presence at his back. He didn't need to turn back to know it was gaining on him.

His foot landed on something hard and his ankle rolled. He fell to the ground, slamming his shoulder. A dark shape flew over him like a man-sized bat.

Can Man looked at his foot. An empty soda can, crushed, wedged itself across the arch of his shoe.

The sound of nails skittering on pavement brought him back to his feet. It chased him back in the direction of the military. The soda can clinked with each step.

For the first time in his life, he prayed his aunt was right.

Take me now, before the demons! I'm all yours, Jesus, if you'll just save me!

CHAPTER 40

The creature bore no resemblance to any of the others he'd seen. A failed experiment in one sense, and yet a grand success if the goal was to create an animal that looked like it was straight from the pits of hell.

Its face was a contorted mass of flesh and bone—one jaundiced eye slumped down into the sagging jowls, a muzzle that looked as if it had been twisted like pulled taffy and pushed into a malformed skull. It was completely hairless, with teal skin, lean, sinewy muscles and paws the size of a man's hand.

It did have teeth, rows and rows of them, a landlocked shark with bat ears.

A strangled growl rumbled in its chest as it swooped down to rip the flesh from Meredith's exposed neck.

"No!"

Dalton jammed the butt of the M16 into the beast's mouth, driving it backward. He kept pushing, wedging the rifle hard into its jaws until there was a loud snap. It pulled away, mouth hanging open, its jaw hinges shattered.

He dropped the infected rifle.

Its head snapped from side to side, its lower jaw flapping like an untethered flag.

Though he'd wounded its mouth, the damn thing's legs worked just fine. It came at him with long, loping strides, back muscles heaving.

He spun to his right just as the creature brushed past, lunging with its corded neck. His shirt ripped as a jagged fang caught the fabric. Dalton stumbled, landed on his knee, and bounced back up.

Frantic, he inspected the rip in his sleeve.

The skin underneath was unbroken. He didn't have time to be grateful because the creature made a sharp turn and was headed back for him. Running, his feet flew from the pavement and onto the hood of the squad car. As he scaled the roof, the car shuddered from the weight of the beast. Dalton's foot caught on the lights and he fell face-first onto the trunk. His top teeth clanged off the unyielding metal, one of them ripping from the root and sailing onto the blacktop.

The pain was like a needle to the center of his brain.

The fall itself was Lady Luck making her presence known. Unable to adjust its trajectory, the beast flew over him, tumbling across the lot.

Before the creature could attack again, he grabbed his Glock, firing four shots into the flayed target that was its mouth. The bullets raced down its gullet, exploding out the rear and sides of the man-made nightmare.

It staggered for a moment, took a step toward him, upper lips curled back, bloody shark teeth hungry for more. Its knees shook, and it collapsed on its side, a pool of blood and bile flowing from its mouth onto the blacktop.

Meredith!

She was rising to her knees, holding her head, blood seeping between her fingers. "What the hell happened?"

"You were almost a Montauk monster meal," he said, checking the gash on her forehead. It didn't look like she'd need stitches. He took off his uniform shirt, wadded it into a ball and pressed it against the wound. "We better get in the car before more of those things show up."

She looked at his bloody mouth and blanched. "You don't look too good yourself."

His mouth throbbed in time with his galloping pulse. "It's just a busted tooth. I'll live."

Helping her into the car, his head swiveled on all points of the compass, looking for the next attack. She leaned her head against the window.

"Be careful what you wish for," she said.

Dalton started the engine. "Huh?"

"All these years, I wanted to get to the bottom of what I saw on the beach that day, to unveil the mystery of these monsters that people have seen. Now I wish I just took the disability after my accident and went back home to Jersey."

Pulling out of the IGA lot, he said, "Yeah, but then you'd have to deal with the Jersey Devil."

She raised an eyebrow at him.

"I'm a hockey fan," he replied.

Meredith fiddled with the radio as they headed out of Montauk. Dispatch was silent. The claustrophobia of dense trees gave way to open views of the ocean on their left. Dalton considered his options when they approached the military checkpoint. Did he stop and try to talk his way through? That would leave them exposed, kill their momentum. He couldn't plow through their trucks. Was there enough room on the sloping shoulder to squeak by? Would the car even stay upright when he tried?

There was always the grenade. He could threaten them with it. No, they'd probably open fire on them. Meredith could toss it, clear a path.

Dammit. That was action-movie crap. He didn't want to kill people.

The radio blared to life.

". . . over on Lake Avenue. Family of four, I can see them on the roof. Three war machines are in the vicinity."

Dalton looked at Meredith, both of them mouthing "war machines?"

"Proceed with caution. If you don't see a safe way to approach, get your men out of there. I need you to report back as soon as you can. We have new directives coming in."

There was a long pause.

"Over."

In his mind's eye, he could see the men running to their jeeps, abandoning the trapped family. All in the name of following orders.

"There are no safe ways to approach those things," Meredith said.

"It's nice to know they now have an official name."

"That also erases any doubts I had about who was behind everything."

Dalton slowed and made a sharp turn.

"Where are we going?"

"The military is going to leave that family there. Lake Avenue isn't far."

She reached over and squeezed his arm. No matter how desperately he wanted to get away from Montauk, he couldn't now. It was good to know Meredith was on the same page.

"When we get to the house, let's not waste any time. You hit them with the flamethrower. I'll use the other M16 we picked up. Take those things by surprise, get the family off the roof and in the car."

"Easy peasy," she said, her eyes fluttering when she touched the tender spot on her head.

Yeah, easy peasy.

* * *

Don Sorely fought against the Winnebago's wheel. Something darted through the headlights. There was another loud crash in the back. He looked in the side-view mirror and his heart fluttered like a spastic hummingbird.

One of the war machines had buried its teeth into the side of the RV. Its front paws, or hooves, if he was seeing right, scrabbled to lift it up to the window.

He took his foot off the brake and goosed the accelerator, turning into the skid and straightening the RV. The doctors and techs in the rear were thrown about like rag dolls.

Driving like a madman down the residential street, he clipped a few parked cars, sending up a shower of sparks. The RV lurched forward as something heavy hit it from behind. He knew it wasn't a car. Those things were determined to get them.

"Everyone hold tight!"

Spotting a large pickup truck parked ahead, he swerved into it, mashing the war machine between the massive vehicles. He watched with grim satisfaction as the wounded beast lost its grip, tumbling into the darkness.

Victory was fleeting.

Dr. Ling shouted, "Two of those things are right behind us. Can you go any faster?"

"Not in this bus."

Damn, the war machines were fast. He had the RV up to fifty and they were still hot on his heels. Speed wasn't the answer. He'd have to use its bulk against them.

"Everyone, brace yourselves," he barked.

He slammed on the brakes. Someone grunted and the floor thudded with falling bodies.

There were also two heavy raps against the rear of the Winnebago.

Weren't expecting that, were you?

He couldn't help the smile from playing across his face.

Getting the RV going again was like chugging through swamp water. Those war machines took a hard hit. That should daze them long enough to put some space between them.

A quick glance in the rearview mirror showed Dr. Greene on the floor, cradling his head. Dr. Ling was trying to help him onto the couch. "Is everyone still in one piece?"

"Barely," Dr. Ling replied.

Her boss moaned before passing out.

"Dr. Greene?" Ling tapped his cheek but got no response. She grabbed his wrist, checking for a pulse.

"Is he dead?" He didn't mean it to come out as callous as it sounded.

"He's alive, no thanks to you. I think he has a concussion."

"Isn't it bad for him to sleep if he has a concussion?"

She glared daggers at him.

He avoided her gaze in the mirror, instead checking on the techs. They were sitting on the floor and conscious. That was a good sign.

Don's cell phone rang. Fumbling to get it out of his pocket, he checked the display. Dammit! It was his boss, Sam Bunker.

"Sir, this isn't the best time to talk," he said, hitting the *speakerphone* button and jamming the phone in a cup holder.

"I don't have time to wait until things are better for you!" Sam Bunker screamed so loud, the tiny speaker crackled with distortion.

Spying the main road ahead, Don gripped the wheel and eased off the accelerator. He didn't want to spill out making the hard right onto the Montauk Highway, their only means of getting out of town on four wheels.

"If you need a status report, it's going to have to wait," Don huffed. At best, his job was over and he'd have to sharpen his skills making fries at a McDonald's somewhere in the sticks under an assumed name. That was a coveted option over the alternative that he sensed coming.

"No need, Sorely. I've gotten sitreps from military command already, which is why I'm calling you. I've spoken to the President and all are in agreement that we need to move to Operation Megiddo." The director fell silent. Don could no longer hear the sounds of the rumbling Winnebago or Dr. Ling's shouted questions. His entire body flushed numb. "I'm sorry, Don. You know as well as I do that we can't take any chances of the war machines or their contagion spreading any further, especially this close to a major metropolitan city. We'll take good care of your family, in honor of your service and sacrifice."

The highway was littered with cars. In the dead of night, it should have been empty. In only a quarter mile, traffic was at a standstill. No one was getting out tonight—or any night.

"Sir, if we just had more time and boots on the ground, I'm sure we could contain this. We were never given a fair chance. Plus we have those DARPA bastards running around, probably making home movies of these things. People are dying out here! But that doesn't mean we abandon them. This thing has been fubar from the jump. If you're going to do this, at least extend me the courtesy of a little honesty."

Bunker sighed heavily into the phone. He cleared his throat and said, "Pandora's Box has already been opened. The military is not about to send more men to die. I just got word that one of the war machines was captured alive by a DARPA-led team and will be en route to a lab in Kansas City."

No! Those fucking lunatics think they can somehow learn from the mistakes made here and use the war machines to their advantage in the future. He'd been around long enough to know that odds were high the war machines would be turned on whatever country had been designated the scapegoat for what happened on Long Island.

"You motherfuckers," Don growled.

There was no sense pleading his case or arguing. Bunker started to say something but Sorely threw the phone on the floor before he could finish.

He turned to see Dr. Ling had crawled into the passenger seat.

"What's Operation Megiddo?"

He jerked the wheel hard, swerving into the empty oncoming lanes. They whizzed past the idling cars, some horns blaring. It was hard to tell whether they were upset at his breaking the rules of the road or just pissed that they didn't think of doing it first. A check of his side-view mirror confirmed that he had started a trend as more headlights gathered behind the barreling RV.

"It's the end of everything," he finally said. "Megiddo is a biblical root for the word *Armageddon*. They're going to burn everything to cinders. The official story will be that terrorists ignited a dirty bomb. The military is going to use their colossal fuckup as a means of strengthening their position. I almost feel sorry for the Middle East bastards that will bear the brunt of this."

Ling punched the dashboard.

"They can't do that! Do they realize how many corporate CEOs are out here in the Hamptons? The economy will go into a tailspin."

"It'll recover. Things will shift from Wall Street to the military. Don't think they haven't considered every option. Operation Megiddo was devised a year after the 9/11 attacks. I'll bet people have been itching to use it ever since."

"So what do we do?"

"I'm going to try to get us past the roadblocks. If we're lucky, I'll catch a buck private I can bluster through."

A mile past Main Street, Dalton and Meredith came upon another roadblock. Two camouflaged Humvees were parked nose to nose, blocking off the westbound lanes. A handful of men bearing rifles stood in front of the all-terrain vehicles, staring down angry motorists.

They had no problem letting them pass on the eastbound side, toward the end of the island, not that Dalton was about to slow down. He didn't even give them a sideways glance as he sped past.

"We're not getting out this way," Meredith said, turning in her seat. She thought she saw a flash of white by the roadblock. The echo of a rifle report filtered through the patrol car's half-open windows. "Jesus, I think they just shot someone!"

Dalton elbowed his window—hard. "What the hell is this, Afghanistan?" Meredith watched the muscles in his forearms ripple as he flexed his grip on the wheel. "Okay, first we have to get to Lake Avenue. I have an idea where we can go after that."

Meredith prayed he did, because turning back was no longer an option. If they were going to make it out of Montauk, it wouldn't be on the roads.

She spotted the road sign for Lake Avenue. "Quick, left up ahead."

The car came to a screeching halt. They were blocked from entering by a barricade of cars. He flashed the lights and hit the siren. No one moved.

Jumping out of the car, Meredith barked at the drivers. "Back up! Back up! We have to get through! Come on, move it, now!"

She tapped a car with the butt of her flashlight for emphasis. It broke the drivers out of their trance and they moved aside.

A flare of pain in her hip almost dropped her when she walked back to the car. "I have no idea where my crutch is," she said, scanning the backseat.

Dalton caressed the side of her face with the back of his fingers. "We must have left it back at IGA. Don't worry. I'll be your crutch from here on." She held his hand and kissed it.

"I'll hold you to that."

Scrambling into the back, she slipped her arms into the flamethrower harness. What a courtship! If they made it out alive, she had resigned herself to happily being called a cougar for the rest of her life.

Judging by the open front and garage doors, most of the residents had hit the road, hoping to get out. There was just no way to get them back. Hunkering down in a secure part of the house had to be better than sitting partially exposed on the road. And now the military was opening fire on them! Meredith's conscience was strained to the max. On the one hand, she wanted to warn everyone and get them back in their homes. But would that be enough? On the other hand, she was going to fight like hell to live. The whole thing had her sick to her soul.

They spotted a family of four straddling the peak of a ranch house. Two of the war machines prowled up and down the front of the house, casting hungry glances at the family. The boys—neither looked older than seven—squealed as their mother pulled them to her chest.

"Ready?" Dalton asked.

"No, but that doesn't matter, does it?"

Honking the horn, he got the attention of one of the creatures. It had a second to glare at them before he mashed it with the front of the car's grille. The beast flipped into the front of the house, hitting the boards with a bone-jarring crack.

Meredith leapt out of the car as best she could, igniting the flamethrower. The second war machine, the first scrawny one she'd seen—it must have been a puppy, or whatever you'd call them—was doused in chemicals and flames before it could lunge for her. Dalton fired into the blaze.

She swiveled to the broken one by the front door and lit it up for good measure. She wasn't going to take any chances.

"You can come down now," Dalton called up to the roof. "Quick, hand the boys down to me."

While the father passed them to Dalton, Meredith watched his back, lighting up the darkness with short bursts. The sobbing boys huddled behind him.

Meredith looked up and managed a strangled cry before the mother and father were tackled by a war machine the size of a Shetland pony. They collapsed onto the slate walkway in a pile, the creature feasting on the woman's face as they fell.

Dalton jumped back, tumbling over the boys. The M16 fired uselessly into the air.

Nerves rattled, Meredith somehow managed to keep her footing. She couldn't get the creature without burning the couple.

The war machine looked up at her, its mouth dripping with the woman's flesh and muscle. One of its massive paws, tipped with long talons, pushed into the man's chest, perforating his lung, followed by a loud hiss of rushing air. Blood gurgled from his lips.

The boys screamed.

The creature locked on to them.

It leapt.

Meredith caught it with a finger of flame in midair. The

beast rolled to the side, setting the lawn on fire as it tried to deaden the flame.

Dalton regained his footing. "Get the boys in the car!"

She reached for both their hands but one slipped free as her leg gave way. The little boy ran to his parents. His father, more dead than alive, reached a quivering arm out to him.

"Dalton!"

The creature was still on fire, but that wasn't enough to bring it down. The flesh had melted from its muzzle. A shelf of bone and teeth snapped at the air. It stalked toward them on sturdy legs, impervious to pain.

She ushered the boy into the car, practically throwing him into the front seat.

Gunfire erupted as Dalton shot at the war machine. The giant beast broke into a run, leaping onto the three members of the family, setting them ablaze.

The boy's tormented screams were beyond words, incomprehensible.

While they burned, the beast tore at their flesh.

Dalton advanced, firing round after round into the creature until it finally collapsed. The boy's smoldering body lay atop his mother. The man was still alive, crying out, his mouth on fire. Dalton fired a round into his head, ending his misery.

It was hard to see everything through her tears. All Meredith wanted to do was fall upon the lawn and curl up into a ball. If she tried hard enough, she could convince herself this night had never happened. If not, she'd gladly wait until someone took her away and loaded her up with enough drugs to forget even her own name.

She snapped out of her paralysis when Dalton grabbed her arm, helping her to her feet.

"Come on, we have to get out of here."

He helped her out of the harness and threw it into the backseat. His sure hands guided her into the car.

The boy sat in the center of the front seat, watching his family burn. She cradled his head, turning him away from the horror.

Be strong for the boy. Be strong for Gray. Don't fall apart now. Not yet.

They turned out of Lake Avenue and had to practically smash through the cars in their way to the Montauk Highway.

Meredith kissed her tears as they melted into the boy's downy hair.

CHAPTER 41

There was no shame when Can Man felt his bladder release. The hideous demon lowered its head and gave a garbled growl. He'd never even imagined that nature could conceive of something so grotesque. It resembled a deformed griffin without the eagle's wings. As a kid, he'd been fascinated by Greek lore and mythology.

His fascination had turned to sheer terror.

Afraid to move, he held his arm across his face. There may have been honor in facing your own demise, but he couldn't look into its cancerous gaze. Better to die with his eyes closed.

He felt a rush of air sweep over his prone form. There was a heavy whump, the shattering of glass, the cracking of bone and another thump.

Shaking all over, Can Man peeked over his forearm.

A forest green vehicle idled by his feet. The creature was twisted within the wheel well, its jaws snapping wildly at the air. A soldier lay sprawled in the front of the car, covered in pebbled glass. Blood trailed from a wound in his head.

Can Man struggled to his feet, pulling the can from his arch. Keeping his eye on the crushed, captive beast, he knelt down to check the soldier's pulse. His fingers came away dripping with blood. He must have severed an artery as well. The poor boy was gone.

He took the man's service revolver from the holster at his hip and walked to the struggling demon. Even though its body had been twisted so badly the front and rear halves would never work in tandem again, it desperately wanted to get him. It tried to bark, an impotent wail of rage.

Standing close to it, Can Man fired into its head.

Only then did he notice the silence.

No one was shooting. There were no more barked commands.

He turned to the lighthouse.

Everyone was dead.

The demons had won.

Dalton got back on the empty eastbound lanes of the Montauk Highway. Meredith had the boy on her lap, the seat belt across them. The boy was in shock. He stared at the dashboard, unresponsive to Meredith's soothing words.

Dalton removed a tear from her cheek with his thumb. If he could get them to the tip of the island, they might have a chance. The Montauk Historical Society, which ran the landmark lighthouse, had a couple of skiffs moored by the beach. They had been taking photographers out around the lighthouse for a series of photo shoots to revamp their webpage and marketing materials. He prayed they were still there and that they had outboard motors. He couldn't remember if they were sailboats. He had no clue how to operate a sailboat.

"You okay?" he said to Meredith.

"Look at all those people," she said, gazing at the terrified faces staring back at them in the bottleneck of cars.

He couldn't. Each face was a reminder that he couldn't save everyone, no matter how hard he tried. He was abandoning the people he'd sworn to protect. Local law enforcement had been usurped by the military and whatever clandestine group had created the creatures in the first place. Their only hope was that the war machines would be contained and they could return to the safety of their homes.

Holding out hope was the only thing keeping him sane at the moment.

"It's like watching one of those disaster movies," she continued, stroking the boy's hair. "Are you sure we're doing the right thing?"

"Getting you both to safety is my only concern, right now. With any luck, we'll be on the water in ten minutes."

"War machines," Meredith whispered, trying to reconcile the mysterious creatures she'd pursued for years with their stark reality.

Dalton looked over at the boy, at the wide brown freckles on his cheeks and nose, his dark, mussed hair. What was going on inside his young mind? How could he even process what he saw?

When his eyes went back to the road, he jerked the wheel to the right, swerving onto the shoulder. The car rode into a dangerous angle, close to tipping over.

A huge RV, followed by a string of cars, plowed ahead, never once veering from their course. If he hadn't pulled over, they would have barreled straight through him.

He slowed down, easing from the runnel that ran alongside the shoulder. Once the last car had passed, he flipped on his lights and got back into the lane. Quite a number of cars had angled themselves so they could take a run at the clear lanes. They held back when they saw him.

Despite everything, there was still a modicum of respect for the law. It made his decision to leave that much heavier.

His heart jackhammered.

"Jesus, that was close," Meredith said, clutching the boy. His expression hadn't changed.

"I can't blame them for trying to find a way out of that jam, but that RV was prepared to kill us in the process. Panic may kill more people than those creatures."

Watching the red taillights fade into the distance, he sped on, hoping to make the lighthouse before complete pandemonium broke out.

A county cop car was pulled across one of the access roads. Meredith gasped and put her hand over the boy's eyes.

"Is that Kanelos?" she said.

Jimmy Kanelos lay in a crumpled, crimson heap a few feet from them. Dying tendrils of smoke wafted from his remains. It looked like the slight man had been turned inside out.

"He must have gotten infected," Dalton said. Poor Kanelos. On a good day, the guy was afraid of his own shadow. But he was a good cop, facing down his fears day after day. He didn't deserve to die like this. No one did.

"Jesus, Jimmy," Meredith said. He could hear the tears in her voice.

"Are you out of your mind, Sorely?" Dr. Ling shouted. Her knees were drawn up and her hands were planted on the dash. "That was a cop you almost creamed."

Don pushed the Winnebago as fast as it could go. "As you can see, law and order has been suspended for the foreseeable future."

"That doesn't give you a right to manslaughter."

He had to remind himself that she was a doctor. Everything for her was about saving lives. She wasn't prepared for a situation like this. Who really was?

"I have to get us to a checkpoint before Megiddo goes into full effect. One second too late and we're toast."

They blew through the plaza, nearly clipping a man on a bicycle weaving in and out of traffic. There were bodies everywhere with no one tending to them.

An orange fireball erupted by the gazebo. Don winced, shielding his eyes.

"Oh my God, no!" Dr. Ling pressed her face against the passenger window.

A line of soldiers, each gripping a flamethrower, marched across the grassy plaza, setting everything ablaze. Both the dead and dying were set alight.

It had begun. Once the cleansing started, it wouldn't stop until there was nothing left.

An eruption of screams rose from the town's center as the soldiers moved from the plaza and turned their deadly flames to the cars hoping to flee the town. Whole families were roasted in their cars. Don never felt so sick in his life.

Bad people, downright evil bastards, were controlling every move from the comfort of their offices far, far from here. With Megiddo in full effect, he assumed the ghosts that were DARPA were long gone. *Mission accomplished, you fucking murderers!* They weren't the only ones to blame. No, the buck didn't stop there. He swore that if he made it out, he would do everything in his power to blow the goddamn lid off. A ton of incriminating evidence was right here, in the Winnebago. All he needed to do was get it and everyone inside to safety.

He laid his hand on the horn, honking like it was midnight on New Year's Eve.

"What are you doing?"

"Hoping people will hear and follow us. They can't stop everyone!"

He waved his hand out the window, urging people to take his lead and fall in line.

Shots rang out, slamming into the side of the RV. The

techs in back dropped to the floor. Don hit the accelerator. Sure enough, more cars joined the caravan behind him.

"You might want to move to the back, and bring Dr. Greene with you."

"Why?"

"Because this big tub is going to be a battering ram. Once I blow a hole through the checkpoint, everyone behind us is free to get the hell out of here."

He saw the flashing lights and wondered if he'd have enough time to jump to safety before the car was on him. Whistling over to the cop several cars down from him, he rolled onto the hood of the Toyota. The woman at the wheel honked her horn as if she could scare him off.

The police car came to a screeching halt, narrowly missing the patrol car parked on the side of the road.

"Crap, that's my car," Mickey Conrad said, sliding off the hood.

He was relieved to see Dalton and Hernandez inside, along with a little boy. At least someone was left.

"You owe me a steak for taking my ride," he said. Dalton sprang from the car, looking like he wanted to hug him.

"I thought you were—"

Mickey shook his head. "Almost. I barely made it out of there. I found a Montauk PD car on a side street and just drove. Dalton, it's a complete disaster. They used local and county cops as bait. I . . . I found Sergeant Campos."

"We saw him, too."

"As far as I can tell, we're the only ones left. Winn and I have been trying to convince people to get to the marinas."

"Winn? Where is he?"

The wounded cop came up to him, leaning against a car. He looked like hell. "I'm not dead yet, no matter how much it hurts not to be." He turned to Mickey. "It's useless. I just spoke to a guy back there. Said his brother and a bunch of other people got on a fishing boat an hour ago. Looks like they were shot down by the Coast Guard. Word's gotten around. No one wants to take a chance on the water." His breathing sounded wet, hampered.

"That's where we're headed," Dalton said. "If those skiffs are still by the lighthouse."

Mickey considered it. "No one is getting out by car," he said. "We overheard on a military walkie that no one from the Hamptons on down is to get out alive. Something about Megiddo."

"They can't trap people here to die!" Dalton shouted.

"They can, and they will," Winn said. "Kid, if what I heard is right, whoever those creatures don't kill, the military will finish the job. Ever since we found out, we've been trying to get people off the roads. They're sitting ducks out here."

"But we haven't convinced a single person," Mickey added.

They looked at the long line of cars.

Something exploded in the distance. The horizon flashed an eerie tangerine.

The big guns had come out. Death was on the march.

Car windows rolled up as if they could hold back the unholy terror that would eventually sweep over the clogged road.

"Where are the skiffs?" Mickey asked.

"Down by the beach. They brought them in special for some photo shoots."

Mickey drew a hand around Winn's waist, helping him to Dalton's car. "I doubt the Coast Guard will be down there. Not enough boats out that way to be worth their time. Let's go."

CHAPTER 42

Dr. Ling stared out the window in wide-eyed horror.

They were too late.

The military checkpoint loomed ahead, drawing nearer at gut-wrenching speed. The gloom lit up with fireflies as soldiers blasted rounds into the cars bunched up at the roadblock.

Working for the CDC, she always feared dying by contamination. No matter how diligent you were, deadly microbes could always find a chink in your armor. In a way, her end would be just as she feared, though it wouldn't be in a hospital bed under quarantine.

She'd secured the still unconscious Dr. Greene in the back with the techs. They all knew that the RV would crumple like an accordion when they hit the military blockade. There was no safe place to be. If they didn't make it, she was glad her mentor wouldn't be awake to feel it. The last six months had been a living hell. Maybe out of everyone, he would be the one to find true peace.

Standing by the galley kitchen, Kathryn saw the soldiers' attention turn toward the Winnebago, a multi-ton rocket on wheels. They opened fire. The windshield was pockmarked with holes and spidery cracks. A bullet whistled past her ear, thunking into a cabinet.

Sorely shouted something, aiming for the soldiers. The RV lurched as the wheels rolled over their bodies.

She dove for the couch a second before he slammed into the Humvee. Her head hit so hard, her spine compressed, bringing a wave of numbness to her extremities.

The RV kept moving, smashing another obstacle. Bullets whined as soldiers behind the checkpoint opened fire.

Suddenly, their world canted ninety degrees. Now on its side, the Winnebago slid, sending up a shower of sparks that lit up the inside of the cabin. She slammed into the side of the RV. The contents of the refrigerator hammered Ling, peppering her with cans and bottles. She screamed, but in the madness, even she couldn't hear her cries.

With a final groan, the RV came to a stop. She heard more shots and men shouting.

Looking to the rear of the Winnebago, she saw a tangle of limbs and equipment. Her ears rang like church bells and she couldn't get her right eye to focus. Staggering to her knees, she crawled to the front of the RV.

Don Sorely's bloody body was still strapped into the chair. His face had been sheared away by glass, his body a pincushion of leaking bullet holes. It was hard to tell through the gore, but she thought he was smiling.

So dizzy she thought she would pass out, she wormed her way through the shattered windshield. Car after car sped by, soldiers chasing after them with barking rifles.

It had worked. She had to hold on to the upturned tire to keep from falling. Dozens of cars sped through the demolished checkpoint. Don was right. The soldiers couldn't get them all.

A small, insane laugh bubbled up. It hurt to let it out. There was no way to stop it as she watched the soldiers try to maintain their hold.

You'll never clean this one up.

Her heart sank when she looked down the road, the path to freedom and salvation. For there was a wall of flame higher than any building on the island. It looked as if they had been firebombed. Everyone who had escaped Montauk was heading straight for the furnace.

Kathryn sank against the RV.

A pair of bright, golden eyes blinked in the darkness.

The war machine, a hideous blue monstrosity, crept toward her, smelling her blood, knowing she was easy prey.

Several more eyes moved about. A shadowy blur dashed across the road. They were surrounding them.

"Come here, boy," she said. She'd rather die by their bite than the infection they carried.

It ran for her, tongue lolling from the side of its bird-like mouth.

The first bite at her throat was painless. Her head spun to the side from the force. She watched another war machine dive into the RV, anxious to get at the men inside.

She wasn't conscious to feel the second bite.

Meredith clamped her hands over the boy's ears when the first helicopter fired a missile into the snarl of traffic behind them. Cars jumped into the air, spewing jets of flame and a mushroom cloud of smoke. Another helicopter hovered alongside the first, launching missile after missile until the night became day.

"Goddamn Nazis," Winn grimaced. "I don't care who you are, you don't follow orders to kill your own innocent civilians."

Dalton's eyes were wild when he looked in the rearview mirror. He pushed the car well over eighty. They passed the end of the traffic. Out here, there were no private residences. They were the only ones headed to the state park.

As they pulled into the lot, they noticed the lighthouse brightly lit by a pair of spotlights. A handful of the war machines clung to the old edifice, scrabbling to get out of the light.

"If they couldn't hold them off, how can we get to the beach?" Meredith said, pointing to the dead soldiers that littered the grounds.

"Look how many of them are out there," Mickey said, pulling the hammer back on his pistol.

The boy was still as a statue in Meredith's lap.

"We need those spotlights," Dalton said. "Those things can't take the light."

"The military had them and look what good it did them," Winn said.

"It looks like they used them to spot the creatures," Dalton said. "We need them to clear a path to the beach, covering our front and backs."

"Leaving our flanks exposed," Mickey said.

"We can't have everything," Dalton answered. "If we turn back, those helicopters will blow us off the road."

The spotlights were mounted on the backs of a pair of Humvees.

Dalton pulled up alongside them, gaining the attention of a dozen war machines. "Meredith, take the wheel. Mickey, come out with me. We'll train the lights on the path leading to the beach. Winn, can you cover us?"

The injured cop held up one of the M16s in the backseat. "I've got you. Go!"

There was no time to waste. Now that they had been spotted, the war machines smelled fresh meat. Meredith slid into the driver's seat, sick with worry. If they so much as slipped, those creatures would be all over them.

They climbed up the Humvees.

"It's locked!" Dalton shouted, yanking the spotlight to no avail.

Mickey fidgeted with a host of knobs and levers on the side of the big light. His palm smacked a bar into an upright position and the spotlight moved off the lighthouse, trailing down the grass embankment.

"Hit that bar!" Mickey commanded Dalton.

The creatures, now freed from the painful light, gathered en masse and began galloping toward their position.

Winn leaned out of the window and opened fire on a beast creeping up from behind Mickey's Humvee. The animal wailed, flipping onto its back.

Dalton freed the spotlight, swinging it down to face the narrow, rocky path that led to the small strip of a beach. Mickey fired off a few rounds at something on the other side of the Humvee. He and Dalton both leapt onto the asphalt.

Meredith watched the war machine numbers grow. She turned the car's spotlight on the driver's side, aiming it at the approaching beasts. It parted them like the Red Sea, but they kept coming.

Winn continued firing, hitting as many as he could. The heavy rounds took their toll, but did little to slow them down. It was as if they had been driven imperviously mad with bloodlust.

The boy had crouched down into a ball in the footwell.

Dalton fell forward as one of the war machines caromed into his upper back. Its cloven hooves thundered over the hood of the car as its momentum carried it forward. He slipped from view. Meredith screamed.

Mickey, turning to help him, was slammed into the side of the car by another creature. His chest crunched into the car's frame. The side of his head thumped off the roof.

Winn tried to shoot it, but the hammer clicked on an empty chamber. An inhuman cry burst from Mickey's lips as a river of blood sprayed across the closed front window.

CHAPTER 43

Dalton's diaphragm hitched painfully when he tried to draw a breath. He had rolled to the front of the car, bathed by the headlights. A pair of war machines paced around the perimeter of the light, anxious to have another chance at him.

He spun in time to see one of the creatures bury its already bloody muzzle into the back of Mickey's neck. He went down in a shower of blood.

Dalton slapped the car's hood, getting Meredith's attention. She jumped when she saw him.

"Drive!" he shouted, pointing to the path.

Her hands shook as she grabbed the gearshift. He rolled onto the hood and clung to the wiper blades, careful not to get close to Mickey's blood.

She steered the car into the harsh shaft of light. The war machines followed, but didn't dare penetrate its radiance. They did, however, gather at the sides of the car, keeping pace with them, a multitude of killing machines. The car bounced and rocked as they descended, and he almost lost his grip.

When they got to the end of the light, Meredith stepped on the brake.

"Winn, throw me the grenades," Dalton yelled.

Searching the backseat, Winn tossed them out the window as he found them. Dalton pulled the pins and chucked them into the darkness. A trio of earth-pounding concussions laid waste to his eardrums. It felt and sounded like someone had stuffed thick swabs of cotton into his ears.

Severed limbs and heads of the assembled creatures bounded into the air, mixing with sand and shattered seashells.

"Everyone out, now!"

Meredith snatched the boy into her arms. Winn came out with the remaining grenades and a pair of pistols. He tossed one to Dalton.

"Run down to the water and turn left," he said to Meredith. "The skiffs should be pulled up onto the beach."

It was hard going for her on the uneven terrain. She limped and lurched as best she could, the boy clinging to her like a second skin.

"I'm going to make a big boom," he said to Winn. "Go follow her."

Winn clutched his ribs with one hand, looking as pale as moonlight. He was in a world of pain. He nodded, trotting after Meredith.

Dalton, standing within the headlights, stared back at the chimeric features gathering around the car. The first grenades didn't get as many as he'd hoped. They were just too fast. And fearless.

Jaundiced eyes narrowed and blinked. He was grateful that he could see little of their malformed faces. But he could feel the heat of their murderous desire.

"A little closer," he said, taking a step back.

True to their form, they advanced a step.

"Just a little more. Look at me, a nice juicy steak, all for you. Come and get it."

His throat was so dry, it was hard to swallow. A pellet of rain splashed over his eyelashes. As much as he wanted to, he didn't dare look back to see how Meredith, the boy and Winn were faring. Taking his eyes off the war machines would be his undoing.

He counted ten of the creatures slinking around the car. "Perfect."

He pulled the pins, tossed the grenades into the car and ran as fast as his legs could carry him, rapidly joining Winn's side.

The car burst into a brilliant halo of fire, igniting the nearby reeds. War machines, those that weren't torn to shreds, dashed around the beach, their flesh engulfed in flame.

Hopefully that buys us enough time to get the boat in the water, he thought. He looped an arm around Winn, helping him along. The man readily leaned into him. He was clearly running out of gas.

They joined Meredith and the boy at the edge of the beach. Her eyes were immense, hopeless.

The skiffs were gone.

"Dammit!"

He had led them to a literal dead end.

Either someone else had gotten the same idea or the historical society had removed them before the shit hit the fan. Now all they had was a bluff filled with war machines on one side, and the roiling Atlantic Ocean on the other.

"Now what?" Meredith said. The boy had wrapped his arms around her neck, burying his face in her shoulder.

Winn dropped to the sand. "Now you get in the water and swim for it while I hold them off."

"We're not leaving you behind," Dalton said.

Winn waved him off. "I'm done. If I got in that water, I'd sink like a stone, dragging anyone with me. I just hope that death by killer animal is covered in my insurance policy. I'd like to leave something for my ex-wife. We were always better apart than together."

"Jake, no. We'll keep you afloat."

"You'll do no such thing."

The sound of scrabbling footsteps drew their attention. They were coming. They were like zombies. No matter what you did, they just kept coming.

Winn was right, but it did little to ease his already troubled conscience.

"Can you swim?" Dalton asked the boy. He didn't reply. "Meredith, I need you to stay close to me, okay?"

She nodded. He pulled her into a kiss weighted with all the potentiality of a final good-bye. Her lips were dry and cracked, but they were still wonderful.

"We're going to get out of this," he said.

"I believe you."

Winn's scream sent jolts down their spines. One of the war machines, a piglike thing with a mix of paws and hooves, clamped its jaws around his arm. He fired his pistol into its eye. It slumped to the sand but didn't release its grip.

"Go! Go!" he implored them.

More war machines converged on him, each taking hold with their deadly jaws as if he was a six-foot chew toy. They tugged at him, whipping their heads. He fired until his gun was empty.

Dalton pushed Meredith toward the water while shooting at the creatures. Winn had gone silent.

Meredith screamed as a war machine sprinted down the shoreline, crashing into her knee. She fell into the receding tide. The boy rolled from her arms.

"Meredith!"

Dalton took aim at the beast and pulled the trigger.

The gun was empty.

He ran, hoping to get the creature's attention so it would go for him instead.

The war machine reared back.

Gunfire sounded behind them. The creature's stomach exploded. Meredith rolled away, avoiding the grisly spray, landing over the boy as a frothing wave washed over them.

Dalton skidded to a stop. He looked back and saw Can Man stepping out from behind a tall stand of sea grass, a military rifle in his hands.

"Can Man! Are you all right?"

The homeless man had a faraway look in his eyes and his clothes were tattered beyond repair. His beard was full of nettles and grass.

"There's a boat out there," he said, pointing. Dalton couldn't see a thing.

"I don't see it."

"Lights are off, but I can hear it."

Dalton saw a war machine heading their way. "Look out!"

Can Man pivoted, aimed, and shot the creature in the neck. It somersaulted, regained its footing and was met with another bullet, this time to its face. Sand piled up in front of it as it plowed on its side to a bloody stop. A wave instantly clawed onto the beach and tried to claim its body as a prize.

"You never forget the lessons Uncle Sam teaches you," Can Man said. "Let's head for that boat."

As impossible as it seemed, Dalton took the boy and helped Meredith to her feet, thanks to a gun-wielding Can Man. The homeless man chucked the rifle into an incoming wave and dove.

They followed him, hoping his ears were right.

Dalton stole a glance at the beach in time to see the war machines head back up the bluff.

* * *

Jason spotted the bobbing heads to their left. So did Grace. "We have to help them," he said.

It sounded like the mother of all Fourth of July parties had erupted on the island. This was no celebration. He was glad as hell that his family was away. There was no telling what would be happening to them right now if they hadn't left.

He angled the boat to intercept the swimmers. "Can you help them up when I get close enough?"

Grace nodded. "I think I can."

It was the most coherent thing she'd said so far. He'd have to hope that the reality star had the strength to pull them out of the water. The waves were getting rougher by the minute. A storm was definitely on its way.

A man was the first to arrive. He held up a little boy. "Please, take him aboard."

Grace hooked her hands under his armpits and lifted the boy to safety. Jason watched the kid scuttle to a corner of the boat, not saying a word.

A woman wearing a cop's uniform was next, followed by none other than Can Man, who then helped another cop aboard. The boat was overcrowded, to say the least, and the motor began to struggle.

"Where are you headed?" the male cop asked.

"Away from here," Jason said.

"Keep away from any other vessels and see if you can make it to the sound. Especially avoid the Coast Guard. Whatever you do, don't turn on any lights. You have enough fuel to make it to the Connecticut coast?"

He looked at the gas gauge. They had three-quarters of a tank. "We should."

The waterlogged trio lay at the bottom of the small boat. Can Man said, "You do what the officer says."

The boat rode up and down the swells. With the added

weight, it was harder to control. Jason white-knuckled the wheel.

"What happened?" he asked. They were cops, they should know exactly what was going on.

The woman cop said with an air of total exhaustion, "The monsters are real, and no one knows how to stop them."

The monsters are real.

He thought of the beach, and Tom, stuck in the quicksand, unable to free himself before those animals—the monsters—got to him.

The wheel jerked out of his hands. He fought desperately to regain his grip. Something smacked into the underside of the boat. It pitched dangerously to the side.

One of the monsters pulled itself up, salt water sluicing from its scarred, cerulean body, leaping into the boat.

The boy shrieked.

Chaos took over. The first war machine was followed by another.

They were trapped.

Dalton looked for anything that could be used as a weapon.

The war machines were hairless, their skin blue-red and raw. They must have been the ones set on fire when he tossed the grenades into the car.

The woman plucked an oar from the hull, ramming it into the open mouth of one of the creatures. Her eyes were wild, boiling with madness. She yowled, pushing the oar as deep as it could go.

The other creature snapped at the kid piloting the boat. He tried to jump high enough to avoid its jaws. A hunk of his calf disappeared down its throat.

Can Man grabbed it behind its ears, pulling it away. It

snatched at him, trying to wriggle its body around and free itself from his grip.

Meredith shielded the boy with her body. Dalton found another oar, jabbing it into the war machine's snout. Something snapped, and shards of teeth bounced off the hull. Can Man pulled so hard, the creature's ears came right off. He tumbled backward and out of the boat, still clutching the ears.

Blood spurted all over the kid at the wheel. He made an unfortunate turn of his head, catching a mouthful. He screamed, "It burns!" His hands jerked from the wheel, leaving the boat at the mercy of the waves.

The war machine skidded over the side of the boat with a tremendous splash.

Meredith had joined the woman, both of them keeping the second creature at bay, wedging the oar until its jaw cracked.

Dalton grabbed the end of the oar with them.

"Toss it over the side," he said.

They heaved as hard as they could, sending the creature sprawling back into the Atlantic.

The kid had stopped piloting the boat. He thrashed around, yowling in agony.

"Dalton, don't let him get near the boy!" Meredith shouted.

"Sit still," he commanded, but the kid's senses were on overload. There was no way he could comprehend what he was saying.

Now, he was more of a danger than the war machines.

"Get away from me!" the woman exclaimed, kicking him to the rear of the boat. Blood leaked from his eyes and bubbled from his mouth.

"Take the wheel," Dalton said to Meredith. The boy scrambled with her.

He pinned the kid's chest with the oar, keeping him in place.

The boat suddenly lurched to the side. Can Man's head popped over the hull, followed by his arm, then legs as he pulled himself back on board. His head swiveled between Dalton and the kid.

"Was he bit?"

"Yes, and he got its blood all over him."

"I saw what that did to those soldiers back there. No man should have to go through that."

"What do you suggest I do? Kill him?" Dalton snapped. They'd lost so many people. He couldn't conceive of losing one more.

With surprising speed and strength, Can Man pulled the oar from his hands and raised it high.

"Can Man, no!" the kid yelled, holding up his hands.

Thwack!

The oar came down on his head, splitting the skull in two. With another quick motion, he used the oar to ease his body over the side.

"Are you crazy?" Dalton screamed.

Can Man shook his head. "Crazy would be keeping him on board when we have ladies and a child. You don't worry. That one's for my conscience to live with, not yours."

Meredith looked back at him, her face ashen.

The woman lay on her rump, staring blankly out at sea.

"Can you get us to Connecticut?" he asked Meredith.

"If no one stops us, yes."

The east end of the island was in flames. Montauk had become a crematorium.

Heavy clouds obscured the moon and stars. The fires of larger vessels dotted the black water. It was if they'd been dropped into a war zone. Thanks to the diminutive size of the boat and the oncoming storm that brought visibility down to zero, they slipped past the patrol ships and out into the open waters.

CHAPTER 44

Just before the light of day, under a steady downpour, they pulled into a deserted marina in Fairfield, Connecticut. This time around, Meredith safely tucked the boat into a vacated slip. Exhausted, they got off the boat, their legs no better than those of a marathoner at the finish line.

Dalton found an old storage shed, climbed through the unlocked window and let everyone inside. It was cluttered with old traps, nets, poles and smelled of grease, but it was safe and dry and would keep them from prying eyes until they figured out their next step.

He lay against one of the clapboard walls, Meredith resting her head on his chest. Can Man and the woman, who in the light of day looked awfully familiar, huddled in the opposite corner. The boy, thumb firmly in his mouth, curled against Meredith. Dalton was the last to close his eyes, and when sleep came, it was mercifully devoid of dreams.

When he woke several hours later, he listened for the sounds of typical morning activity at a marina.

The silence was deafening.

Slipping out from under Meredith, he crept out of the shed.

Gunmetal clouds sat low and heavy in the sky. In the distance, thunder rumbled.

The marina was empty.

His stomach growled. He couldn't remember the last time he'd eaten. He wasn't sure what he wanted more, breakfast or a cigarette. After what he'd been through, he didn't think it greedy to find a way to have both. His wallet was still soggy, but he had forty dollars cash and a credit card. It was a short walk to the small convenience store just outside the marina parking lot. The owner, an older, rail-thin man who wore a jet-black toupee, barely looked his way as he rang him up. An earbud was plugged into his ear, whatever he had on capturing all of his attention.

Dalton left with a bag filled with buttered rolls, snack cakes, beef jerky, coffee, a pack of Marlboro and bottles of orange juice.

He forgot to get a paper.

What will they say happened in Montauk? There's no way they can sweep this under the rug. Who can I get in touch with to tell the world the truth? Who can I even trust beyond my parents and the folks back in the storage shed?

There were so many questions alongside too many painful truths. Ripping off the cellophane, he pinched a cigarette out of the pack, lit it after three matches and inhaled deeply. It burned his lungs but also quieted the noise in his head as effectively as Sister Veronica, his trollish third grade teacher could shush a classroom of rambunctious kids.

He turned back to the store and picked up a *Daily News*, *New York Times* and *New York Post*.

The headlines made his heart stop.

TERROR STRIKES AGAIN
HAMPTONS-MONTAUK WIPED OUT BY DIRTY BOMB

His hands shook too much to leaf through the soft pages. When he returned to the store for the third time, he finally got the owner's full attention. The man eyed his uniform.

"You going out there, son?"

Dalton couldn't get his mouth to work.

"I heard they were evacuating the coast here this afternoon. Storm winds might blow that toxic waste our way."

The man continued to talk while he read the paper.

It's all wrong! They're lying!

"I knew things wouldn't stop at 9/11. We just got deeper and deeper into that mess out there. The only way to stop those fuckers is to kill every one of them." The man's eyes brimmed with tears. "I mean it. We either do it right this time and end it, or we should just give them the keys to the damn country and let them have at it."

It was apparent there was more he wanted to say, but he was too choked up to speak his mind. He pulled the earbud from his ear and went through a door in the back.

Dalton left the store in a daze. He wasn't even sure how he made it back to the storage shed. Everyone was still asleep.

He knelt by Meredith, resting his hand on her knee. She stirred, eyes fluttering open.

"What's wrong?"

"It's all gone . . ." The words trailed off. She reached her hand around his neck, pulling him close. The boy shifted in his sleep between them.

He lost parents, too. He watched them die.

Dalton placed a trembling hand on the boy's shoulder.

"Oh shit!"

Can Man's exclamation made them jump. He scampered to his feet, backing away from the woman. Through the pale light streaming through the window, Dalton saw blood and foam flowing from the woman's mouth, eyes and ears. Her skin looked as if it had been removed, stretched, and draped over her bones like an ill-fitting dress.

Somehow, in the struggle last night, she'd been infected.

Can Man kicked the door open to let more light inside. He checked his hands and clothes.

"Did I get any on me?" he asked, his voice rippling with anxiety.

Dalton saw the mass of bloody foam caked in his hair. A finger of it oozed down the man's cheek.

"Oh no," Meredith huffed.

"You did," Dalton said, pointing at the diseased plasma.

Tears sprang to Can Man's eyes. He winced as the infected blood burned his skin. He wavered in the doorway, gripping the frame with both hands to remain upright.

"I don't want to die like them," he said.

Metal slid against concrete as Dalton reached for one of the gaffing poles. He looked over at Meredith and the boy. He took a deep breath. The boy, who had awoken, saw Can Man and the pile of flesh that was the woman. He instinctively closed his eyes.

"Please, help me." Can Man eyed the pole, closed his eyes and nodded his head.

"I'm sorry," Dalton said.

He thrust the pole into Can Man's chest. Can Man lurched backward, gripping the pole. He took a few stumbling steps before tripping over his own feet. When he landed, blood spewed from his mouth, coating the dock.

Dalton grabbed Meredith's and the boy's hands, leading them out of the shed, careful to avoid the spreading pool of blood flowing from Can Man's still chest. They walked down the deserted dock until he found a boat with an interior galley. Using the butt of his empty Glock, he broke the lock on the door and ushered them inside.

There were cushioned seats long enough to lie down on. “I’ll be back,” he said. Meredith started to protest.

He came back with the bag of food and drinks as well as the paper. No one, despite their gnawing hunger, was up to eating.

“You’ll want to read that,” he said. “Best work of fiction of all time.”

Meredith held a bottle of orange juice to the boy’s lips. He took a small sip, then lay on his side, closing his eyes. “What do we do now?” she said.

“We wait. If none of us are infected, we’ll have to find someone we can trust.”

Meredith asked, “And if we are infected?”

He reached out to hold her hand in his.

“We’ll have to find a way to tell everyone the truth.”

The boat rocked gently, lulling them to a sleep so deep, they didn’t even stir when the evacuation sirens sounded, emptying the entire county.

ACKNOWLEDGMENTS

There are a few people I want to thank for making this possible. First, huge thanks to Gary Goldstein, a fantastic editor and one of the funniest guys I've ever met. Thank you, Carolyn Wolstencroft and Erin Al Mehairi, for making this a far better book than I could have done on my own. Also to top cop Dale Hughes, for his technical expertise, and Woody Woodward, for providing a home away from home to work on the book during a very difficult time—I miss Maine every day. Thank you to my superagent, Louise Fury, and her constant encouragement, and last but not least, to the skunk apes of the Everglades. Without them, this whole thing may never have happened.